Praise for the novels of JoAnn Ross

RIVER ROAD

"Skillful and satisfying. . . . With its emotional depth, Ross's tale will appeal to Nora Roberts fans."

—*Booklist*

"The romance . . . crackles, and their verbal sparring keeps the narrative moving along at an energetic clip. Readers who have read the first book in this trilogy will be heartily entertained; those who haven't will rush out to buy it after savoring this delightful entry."

—*Publishers Weekly*

"Highly entertaining reading—this is major fun!"

—*Romantic Times*, Top Pick

"A delicious read with a vast array of zany characters to keep you glued to the pages."

—*Rendezvous*

BLUE BAYOU

"A woman's attempt to reunite with her father and rebuild her life after the death of her deceitful husband lies at the heart of this atmospheric contemporary romance. Ross is in fine form. . . ."

—*Publishers Weekly*

"As magical as Ireland itself. . . . A masterpiece of writing from the heart. Storytelling at its all-time best."

—*The Belles and Beaux of Romance*

FAR HARBOR

"A profoundly moving story of intense emotional depth, satisfying on every level. You won't want to leave this family."

—CompuServe Romance Reviews

"A wonderful relationship drama in which JoAnn Ross splendidly describes love the second time around."

—Barnesandnoble.com

HOMEPLACE

"This engrossing story of love's healing power will draw you in from the first. . . . A great read."

—*The Old Book Barn Gazette*

Books by JoAnn Ross

Homeplace
Fair Haven
Far Harbor
Legends Lake
Blue Bayou
River Road
Magnolia Moon

Published by POCKET BOOKS

JoAnn Ross

Magnolia Moon

POCKET BOOKS
New York London Toronto Sydney Singapore

This book is a work of fiction. Names, characters, places and incidents are products of the author's imagination or are used fictitiously. Any resemblance to actual events or locales or persons, living or dead, is entirely coincidental.

An *Original* Publication of POCKET BOOKS

 POCKET BOOKS, a division of Simon & Schuster, Inc. 1230 Avenue of the Americas, New York, NY 10020

Copyright © 2003 by The Ross Family Trust

ISBN: 0-7434-5743-9

First Pocket Books printing March 2003

10   9   8   7   6   5   4   3   2   1

POCKET and colophon are registered trademarks of Simon & Schuster, Inc.

For information regarding special discounts for bulk purchases, please contact Simon & Schuster Special Sales at 1-800-456-6798 or business@simonandschuster.com

Cover art by Tom Hallman

Printed in the U.S.A.

To Patty Gardner-Evans,
for all the years. (Sorry about
the gator; maybe next time.)

And, as always, to Jay,
with love.

1

New Orleans, Louisiana

I've always adored a Libra man," the blond purred.

"Have you now?" Nate Callahan grinned and drew her closer. There were few things in life more enjoyable than making love to a beautiful woman.

"Oh, absolutely." Cuddling up against him, she fluttered her lashes in a way only a true southern belle could pull off. "Why, a Libra man can charm the birds out of the trees and flatter a girl right out of her lace panties."

"It wasn't flattery, *chère*." He refilled her crystal champagne flute. "It was the absolute truth."

Nate had always enjoyed females—he liked the way they moved, the way they smelled, their soft skin and slender ladies' hands. From the first time he'd filched one of his older brother Finn's *Playboy* magazines, he'd flat-out liked everything about women. Fortunately, they'd always liked him right back.

He toyed with a blond curl trailing down her neck. It was a little stiff and hadn't deflated much during their session of hot, steamy sex, but Nate was used to that, since most of the women he dated favored big hair. Big hair, big breasts, and, he thought with a pleasant twinge of lust, big appetites for sex.

"Your moon is in the seventh house." She trailed a glossy coral nail down his chest.

"Is that good?" He skimmed his palm down her back; she arched against the caress like a sleek, pampered cat.

Outside her bedroom, a full moon rose in a star-studded sky; inside, flames crackled cozily in the fireplace and gardenia-scented candles glowed.

"It certainly is. You're ruled by Venus, goddess of beauty."

"Seems that'd fit you better than me, sugar." He nuzzled the smooth curve of her shoulder. His accent, always more pronounced when romancing a woman, turned thick as Cajun gumbo. "Bein' how you've gotten more beautiful every year since you won that Miss Louisiana crown."

"I was only first runner-up." She pouted prettily.

"Officially," he allowed. "But everyone in the state knew the judges were obviously blind as swamp bats."

"You are so sweet." Her laugh was rich and pleased.

Nate's mind began to drift as she chattered on about the stars, which, if he were to be perfectly honest, didn't interest him. He'd never thought much about lunar signs until the afternoon he'd shown up to give the blond astrologer a bid on remodeling her bedroom.

Although he'd arrived ten minutes late at her Garden District house, he'd gotten her out of the shower; she'd shown up at the door, breathlessly apologetic for not being ready, prettily flushed, and smelling of jasmine. It was only later, when he'd remembered that her hair hadn't been wet, that Nate realized he'd been set up. Having always appreciated female wiles, he didn't mind.

She'd hung on to his every word as he'd suggested ways to open up the room—including putting a skylight over the bed—declared him brilliant, and hired him on the spot.

"You are," she'd sworn on a drawl as sweet as the sugarcane his granddaddy used to grow, "the first contractor I've interviewed who understands that a bedroom is more than just a place to sleep." She'd coyly looked up at him from beneath her lashes. "It is, after all, the most important room in the house."

When she'd touched a scarlet fingernail to the back of Nate's hand, warm and pleasant desire had ribboned through him.

"You've been so sweet. Would you do me just one teensy little favor?"

"Sure, *chère*. If I can."

Avid green eyes had swept over him in a slow, feminine perusal. "Oh, I think you're just the man for the job."

She'd untied the silk robe, revealing perfumed and powdered flesh. "I do so need to exorcise my horrid ex-husband's memory from this room." The robe dropped to the plush carpeting.

That had been six months ago. Not only had Nate done his best to exorcise her former husband's memory, he'd done a damn fine job on the remodeling, if he did say so himself. Lying on his back amid sex-tangled sheets, Nate looked up at the ghost galleon moon, decided he'd definitely been right about the skylight, and wondered why he'd never thought to put one over his own bed.

"Of course, Venus is also the goddess of love." The *L* word, slipping smoothly from her coral-tinted lips, yanked his wandering mind back to their conversation.

"She is?" he asked with a bit more caution.

"Absolutely. Make love, not war, is a phrase that could have been coined with Libras in mind. You became interested in women at a young age, you make sex a rewarding experience, and will not stop until your lover is satisfied, even if it takes all night."

"I try," he said modestly. She'd certainly seemed well satisfied when she'd been bucking beneath him earlier.

She smiled and touched her lips to his. "Oh, you not only succeed, darling, you set the standard. Libras also rule the house of partnerships."

"Now there's where your stars might be a little off, sugar." He stroked her smooth silk back, cupped her butt, and pulled her closer. " 'Cause I've always enjoyed working alone."

It wasn't that he was antisocial, far from it. But he liked being his own boss, working when he liked, and playing when he wanted.

"You weren't alone a few minutes ago, and you seemed to be enjoying yourself well enough."

"I always enjoy passin' a good time with you, angel."

"If you didn't play well with others, you wouldn't have run for mayor." She rolled over and straddled him.

"Libras are not lone wolves, darling. A Libra male needs a permanent partner."

Nate's breath clogged in his lungs. "Permanent?"

Having grown up in South Louisiana, where water and land were constantly battling, with water winning most of the time, he knew that very few things were permanent. Especially relationships between men and women.

"We've been together six months," she pointed out, which exceeded any previous relationship Nate had ever had. Then again, it helped that she'd spent most of that time away, selling her astrology books at New Age festivals and talking them up on television talk shows around the country.

Doing some rapid calculation, Nate figured they'd probably been together a total of three weeks, and had spent most of that time in bed.

"I've been thinking," she murmured when he didn't respond. Her clever fingers slipped between them, encircling him. "About us."

"Us?"

"It occurred to me yesterday, when my flight was cruising at thirty thousand feet over New Mexico, that we should get married."

Married? Having not seen this coming—she'd certainly never shown one iota of domesticity—Nate didn't immediately answer.

"You don't want to." Danger sparked in her voice, like heat lightning flashing out over the Gulf. She pulled away.

Sighing, Nate hitched himself up beside her and saw any future plans for the night disappearing.

"It's nothing to do with you, *chère*." His cajoling smile encouraged one in return. "But we agreed goin' in that neither of us was the marrying kind."

"That was then." She left the bed and retrieved his shirt from where it had landed earlier. "Things change." The perfumed air swirled with temper. "The moon is also a mother sign."

"It is?" Nate caught the denim shirt she threw at him. Christ, he needed air.

"Yes." Her chin angled up. Her eyes narrowed to green slits. "Which is why Libras often repeat the same childlike behavior over and over again in their relationships."

It was a long way from charming to childish. Boyish, Nate might be willing to accept—in the right context. But he hadn't been a child since that life-altering day when he was twelve and a liquored-up, swamp-dwelling, gun-carrying idiot had blown away his father.

"If I didn't know better, I might take offense at that, darlin'." He bent to pick up his jeans from the loblolly pine floor; one of his boots came sailing toward him. "*Mon Dieu*, Charlene." He ducked the first one and snagged the second out of the air an instant before it connected with his head.

"Do you have any idea how many proposals I get every month?" She marched back across the bedroom and jabbed her finger against his bare chest.

"I'll bet a bunch." Nate reminded himself that he'd never run into a situation he couldn't smooth over.

"You damn well bet a lot!" His chest now bore little crescent gouges from her fingernail. "I've turned down two in the past six weeks—from men who make a hell of a lot more money than you—because I was fool enough to think we had a future."

"You're a wonderful woman, *chèrie*," he tried again, hopping on first one foot, then the other, as he pulled his pants up. "Smart, beautiful—"

"And getting goddamn older by the moment," she shouted.

"You don't look a day over twenty-five." Thanks to a Houston surgeon whose clever touch with a scalpel had carved a good ten years off her face and body.

When she began coming toward him again, Nate backed away and yanked on his shirt. Not pausing to button it, he scooped his keys and wallet from the bedside table and shoved them into his pocket. "Twenty-six, tops." He debated sitting down again to pull on his boots, then decided not to risk it.

"It's not going to work this time, Callahan."

A champagne glass hit the wall, then shattered. She tossed her stiff cloud of honey blond hair. "If I'd taken the time to do your full chart before hiring you, I never would have let you seduce me."

Deciding that discretion was the better part of valor, Nate wisely didn't point out that she'd been the one who'd dropped the damn robe.

"I would have realized that you're suffering from a gigantic Peter Pan complex."

Peter Pan? Nate gritted his teeth. "I'll call you, *chère*," he promised as he dodged the second flute. PMS, he decided. "Later in the month. When you're feeling a little more like yourself."

A banshee could not have screamed louder. Nate escaped the suffocating room, taking the back stairs two at a time. Something thudded against the bedroom wall; he hoped to hell she hadn't damaged the new plaster job.

Feeling blindsided, Nate drove toward his home on the peaceful bank of Blue Bayou, trying to figure out where, exactly, an evening that had begun so promising had gone offtrack.

"Peter Pan," he muttered.

Where the hell had she come up with that one?

The full moon was brighter than he'd ever seen it, surrealistically silhouetting the knobby bayou cypresses in eerie white light. Having just survived Hurricane Charlene, Nate hoped it wasn't some weird portent of yet another storm to come.

2

Los Angeles

*O*h, *God,* doesn't that hunk just jump-start your hormones?"

L.A. homicide detective Regan Hart glanced up at the billboard towering over Sunset Boulevard. "Not really." He was too blond, too good-looking, and even with that ragged hair and scruffy beard, somehow too perfect. Regan preferred men who looked as if they had some mileage on them.

"Any woman who doesn't respond to Brad Pitt needs her head examined," Vanessa Kante, Regan's partner, said on a deep sigh. "Not to mention more vital body parts."

"My head and all my other body parts are working just fine, thank you." At least Regan assumed they were; it had been a while since they'd been subjected to a field test. "And in case you've forgotten, you're married. Aren't you supposed to be directing those leaping hormones toward your husband?"

"I'm married, not dead. Part of the reason our marriage is so strong is that Rhasheed doesn't mind who I lust after, so long as he's the one whose tall, lanky bones I'm jumping when I get home." She shot Regan a knowing look. "Since you've been in a crappy mood all shift, I take it the Santa Monica plastic surgeon wasn't exactly Mr. Right."

Regan heaved out a breath. "He wasn't even Mr. Maybe if a meteor hit Santa Monica and we were the only man and woman left on earth I might just maybe consider having sex with you only to perpetuate the species. Enough said."

"Sorry."

She shrugged. "I don't know why I even let you fix me up with him in the first place."

"Perhaps because it's been too long since you've had sex that didn't involve batteries?"

"It's not that easy. First of all, we're living in the land of gorgeous women, where every waitress is a Cameron Diaz wannabe and any female over a size two is a candidate for liposuction."

"I'm not a size two. And Rhasheed likes me just the way I am."

"What man wouldn't? I've seen stone-cold killers swallow their tongues when you sashay into the squad room." A dead ringer for Tyra Banks, Vanessa even dressed like a supermodel. "And besides, Rhasheed grew up in Nigeria. You keep telling me the brothers like their women with curves."

"That's what he tells me, and if actions back up his

sweet-talking jive, it's true. I think it's one of those Neanderthal things about looking for a woman who'll make a good breeder, even during famine. But Rhasheed says it's mainly so he'll have something to hold onto so he won't fall out of bed."

"Then I'm out of luck with Neanderthals, too. All my adolescent growth hormones went into my height, so I didn't have any left for curves. As Dr. Bill felt obliged to point out when he suggested I consider implant surgery."

"Ouch. I never realized he was such a silver-tongued devil."

"It wouldn't have worked out anyway. If guys aren't intimidated by a woman who wears a pistol to work, they just want to hear gory war stories about dead bodies."

"Which kind was Dr. Bill?"

"The first. We were out on the dance floor for about two minutes when he admitted he couldn't handle getting that close to a woman who was wearing a Beretta beneath her jacket."

Van shot her a disbelieving look. "Tell me you didn't actually wear your sidearm on a date?"

"I got a call while I was in court to testify on the Sanchez case, saying one of the Front Street Crips had some info on that Diamond Street gangbanger who was killed while collecting drug taxes for the Mexican Mafia. Would you go into that neighborhood unarmed?"

"I'll have to give you that one."

"Besides, I looked pretty damn good. I was wearing that suit you talked me into buying last week."

Van had unearthed the designer knockoff at Second Hand Rose, a trendy consignment boutique on Melrose. The label read "Armini," the simple change in vowels keeping the counterfeit police from declaring the suit illegal. It was also several hundred dollars less expensive than the original.

"Couldn't you have left the gun in the trunk of your car?" her partner asked.

"And have it stolen like Malloy's? Boy, wouldn't that be a career booster."

Just last month Devon Malloy, a rookie B&E detective, had left his pistol in the trunk of his car to keep it away from his kids. Unfortunately, his car had been stolen, and the gun ended up being used in an armed robbery that had left a liquor store clerk wounded. By the time IAD eventually got through dragging Malloy over the coals, he might still be a cop, but any chances of advancement were nil; if he stayed on the force, he could look forward to spending all his days on pawnshop detail.

"Actually, it was kind of funny," Regan said. "We were slow-dancing, and every time he'd pull me close and try to cop a feel, his fingers would hit cold steel. After the third time, he suggested we call it a night. Not only was I crushing his libido—apparently it's a little disconcerting to go out with a woman who can shoot your balls off— but the metal in my Beretta was screwing up his *qi*. Whatever that is."

"It's feng shui. In Taoist thought, everything is made up of *qi*—or energy. It's the essence of existence."

"And here I thought that was DNA."

The rain was picking up. Regan turned on the wipers, which dragged across the glass with a rubbery squeal like fingernails on a chalkboard. LAPD never retired their crap cars; they just assigned them to her. The heater hadn't worked for six weeks. By the time it got repaired, the weather would have warmed up, and she wouldn't need it. Which, she thought darkly, was probably exactly the department's reasoning.

"Hey, there are a lot of things in this world we can't understand," Van said. "If it wasn't for feng shui, I wouldn't have gotten pregnant."

Regan shot her a look. "You got pregnant because when you and Rhasheed were off cavorting in the tropics, you had one too many mai tais and forgot to use birth control."

"True. But before we went to Kauai, between the stress of his job and mine, we were having some sex problems—which is why we made the reservations at the Crouching Dragon Inn in the first place."

"Ah yes, the sex palace."

"You make it sound like someplace with mystery stains on the sheets and porno movies playing on a TV bolted to the dresser. The Crouching Dragon Inn was designed on the feng shui principle that we should live *with* nature rather than against it, so it was constructed for all the bed and beach *qi* to flow properly. As soon as we got there, all our problems just flew out the window. Except for going to that luau, we made love all week."

"So you said." From the play-by-play her partner had shared, she was amazed Van had still been able to walk when they got back from Hawaii.

"All that positive loving energy sent out a special frequency that allowed Rhasheed's essential elements to come together with mine and create Denzel's life force."

"It's called a sperm swimming up to fertilize an egg."

With the exception of certain truisms such as full moons make the crazies come out, and you always get a floater the day you're wearing new shoes, Regan didn't believe in feng shui, voodoo, fate, or anything else that she couldn't see with her own eyes or touch with her own hands.

After she'd been set up to be killed by a gang who was tired of her hauling in their dealers, the psychologist the department had forced her to see had blamed her skepticism on all those childhood years waiting for her father to return home from Vietnam. In her child's mind he would walk in, declare her the most beautiful, lovable little girl in the world, get down on one knee just like the prince did in Cinderella, beg her mother to remarry him, and they'd all live happily ever after.

None of which had ever happened. Unfortunately, Lieutenant John Hart, U.S. Marines, had never returned from Vietnam. Her mother, who'd filed for divorce before Regan was born, had returned to her law practice when Regan was a week old, leaving her in the hands of a continuously changing series of nannies and housekeepers who never quite lived up to Karen Hart's standards. When her father never showed up in a suit of shining armor to sweep his daughter onto the back of a prancing white steed and take her away to his palace, Regan had decided fairy tales belonged in the gilt-edged pages of books, not in real life.

In a way, she'd always thought that youthful disappointment had served her well. The very same realism and skepticism the department shrink had advised her to overcome was what made her a good cop.

"Birth's a miracle." Van repeated what she'd been saying since the day the little pink cross had shown up on the test strip. "Rhasheed said he knew I was pregnant that morning when I began glowing from the inside."

"You sure you didn't get confused about what you were putting in your mouth, and swallow your mag light?"

"Very funny. The glow was the red lightwave from baby Denzel's heart." She patted her rounded stomach, which had been showing her pregnancy for the past two months.

Regan shook her head. "Only in L.A. would cops be into New Age."

As happy as she was for Van, Regan wasn't looking forward to losing her as a partner. But Van and her husband had decided a homicide detective's twenty-four/seven lifestyle wasn't exactly family friendly and she'd decided to leave the force in another six weeks.

"Feng shui isn't new. The concept goes back eight thousand years." Van turned in the passenger seat toward Regan. "Maybe you should have a master check out your apartment. You've been under a lot of stress lately."

"I'm a murder cop. Stress comes with the territory."

"Which is why you need to find something that helps."

"What would help would be for the good citizens of Los Angeles to take a forty-eight-hour ceasefire."

"Russell Crowe's going to show up in the squad room in full breastplate and sandals before that happens," Vanessa said dryly. "You know, I took a class last month with the guy who advised Donald Trump to change a set of French doors at Mar-a-Lago to the other wall. If you weren't so hard-minded, you might actually like him."

"I don't need an architectural adviser. I just need to close the Lancaster case. And the fact that Donald Trump wants to pay some so-called building wizard big bucks to tell him to tear out some doors is just proof that some people have more money than sense."

"I hope you didn't tell Dr. Bill all this. He lives by feng shui."

"I know. We had to wait an hour for a dinner table that faced the right direction." An hour she'd spent nursing a glass of wine and eating bar mix. "Give me some credit. I merely told him that the mental vision of scalpels cutting into my breasts had the same negative effect on me that guns seemed to have on him. So, since cold steel seems to be destined to come between us, we might as well give both our *qi*s a break and make it an early night."

"I was really hoping you two would work out. What about the Century City investment banker? Mike something? He was good looking."

"His name was Mark Mitchell." Regan had met him after a real estate developer got shot execution style in a parking garage. Since Mark had discovered the body, Regan had interviewed him, then given him her card in case he thought of anything that might prove useful to the investigation. He'd called that night to ask her out. She'd declined, not wanting to cross the professional/personal line she'd always firmly maintained.

It hadn't taken long to apprehend the shooter, a bumbling first-time hit-for-hire guy. The day the jury found him guilty, she'd received another call from Mark Mitchell. This time she'd made the mistake of taking him up on his offer of a late dinner.

"He kept an iguana named Gordon Gekko in his bedroom." And revealed he'd always viewed the "Greed is good" character Michael Douglas played in *Wall Street* as a role model.

"That is a little weird," Van allowed. "You could always go out with someone on the force."

"I'd rather shoot myself than date a cop." She'd no sooner spoken when she wished she could take the words back. Rhasheed was an L.A. county sheriff's department deputy. "Hell, I'm sorry. Rhasheed's an exception."

"He's special, all right." Van's smile showed she hadn't taken offense. "We were supposed to go out tonight to celebrate the fifth anniversary of when we met."

Then they'd gotten called out on what could well prove a wild-goose chase. It was tough enough to have a normal life when you were a street cop. Homicide detectives might as well forget about relationships, romance, or any type of social life, especially on weekends, when the majority of murders occurred.

On the rare occasion she stopped to think about it, Regan found it ironic that she could have grown up to be so different from her mother, but still end up in a career that discouraged marriage and a family.

She checked out the block-long white limousine gliding past. When she'd worked in Vice, she'd busted a prostitution ring doing a bang-up business using limos as rolling motel rooms. Since this one had a Just Married sign in the back window, she let it pass.

It was turning out to be a quiet night in the City of Angels, almost as if the city had done an aerial spraying of Valium, but neither Regan nor Van commented on it, since another Murphy's Law of police work declared that unspeakable evils would befall anyone who said, "Sure is a quiet night."

The rain streaking down the windshield of the black-and-white patrol car had driven most of the drunks, batterers, and robbers indoors, leaving only the neighborhood's homeless sleeping beneath soaked newspapers and plastic garbage bags. The souvenir shops selling Marilyn Monroe posters, movie clapboards, and maps to stars' homes were closed, their heavy metal shutters drawn down.

There'd been a time, before Regan was born, when the area that made up her precinct had been the glittering home of the motion picture industry. Glamorous movie stars had dined at the Brown Derby, drank champagne from crystal flutes, and attended premieres at Grauman's Chinese Theater in limousines. But T-shirt shops, check-cashing joints, and pornographic bookstores had invaded the once elite neighborhood, and addicts, prostitutes, and homeless men and women were as common a sight as Japanese tourists.

Hollywood was beginning to make a comeback, but Regan knew that even if the area did succeed in becoming Los Angeles' version of New York's Time Square, the dispossessed would simply pack up and drift somewhere else.

"This tip had better pan out," she muttered as they cruised by the Rock & Roll Denny's. "Even the working girls have enough sense to come in out of this lousy weather."

Inside the bright, twenty-four-hour restaurant, forlorn prostitutes seeking relief from the rain hunkered in the booths, drinking pots of coffee, smoking packs of cigarettes, and rubbing feet sore from pounding the pavement in ankle-breaking five-inch platform heels, all the time keeping an eye on the street outside the restaurant window in the unlikely event a silver Lotus might happen to cruise by.

Unfortunately, the average john who frequented these blocks was no Richard Gere, and the *Pretty Woman* Cinderella story about the tycoon falling in love with the heart-of-gold hooker was so far removed from these mean streets it could have been filmed on Mars.

"Word is, Double D's back from Fresno to hit some guy from the Eighth Street Regulars who's been poaching on his territory." Van repeated the phone tip that had gotten Regan to leave the warmth of the station. The seventeen-year-old with the yellow sheet as long as a Russian novel was as elusive as smoke. "He's got a new girlfriend and is laying low at her grandmother's place. The old lady got busted two years ago for running a crack house with her son and grandkids."

"And they say the American family's in decline. How come Granny isn't in prison?"

"Because she looks like she should be baking cookies rather than cooking dope. The DA couldn't get the grand jury to indict."

Regan shook her head in disgust. She'd become a cop because she'd wanted to make a difference, to help make people's lives better. But lately she'd begun to feel like a sand castle at high tide. It seemed that more and more of the idealist she'd been when she'd first put on that blue LAPD uniform was getting washed away each day.

"You're doing it again," Van said.

"What?"

"Humming that damn song."

"Sorry. Sometimes it gets stuck in my head." Some people's minds grasped onto jingles; whenever her mind drifted, it tended to break into "You Are My Sunshine."

She'd stopped noticing it years ago; others, who found it understandably annoying, weren't so fortunate.

A gleaming black Lexus with muddy license plates caught Regan's attention as it passed in the opposite direction.

The passenger was looking straight ahead. The driver turned his face, but not before she caught a glimpse of him. Adrenaline sparked like a hot electrical wire hitting wet pavement. "I'll bet my next pay grade that's our boy."

"Sure looked like him."

Regan made a U-turn, then cursed as a grizzled, bearded man clad in camouflage with an American flag sticking out of his backpack began marching across the street with the determination of the soldier he'd once been.

"Come on, come on." Her fingers tapped an impatient drumbeat on the top of the steering wheel. Having suffered from post-traumatic stress herself, she resisted hitting the siren.

Mad Max was a fixture on the street. Since he claimed to have served in Vietnam, Regan had once, in a rash moment, asked him if he'd ever served with her father. He'd taken a look at the photograph she always carried with her, shook his head, and rattled off a string of gibberish from a mind burned by drugs, alcohol, and God only knew what kind of flashbacks.

It had, admittedly, been a long shot. But Regan could never stop herself from asking.

She took off the second Mad Max cleared the lane. That the vet didn't even glance back when the siren began screeching said a lot about both the neighborhood and his life.

Regan caught up with the Lexus at a red light just past

Hollywood High. Van tapped the car's description, license number, and tag into her computer. The light turned green.

The vehicle started out slowly, testing the waters. Testing Regan.

Every instinct she possessed told Regan this was the murder suspect who'd managed to elude her for the past forty-five days. If she didn't nab the kid in another two weeks, she'd be forced to write up a sixty-day report, the closest thing in the murder business to conceding defeat.

The Lexus picked up speed.

"Come on, dammit." The computer, ancient and as cranky as she herself was feeling, seemed to take forever.

"It's him." Van's voice was edged with excitement. "He and another gangbanger carjacked the vehicle after committing an armed robbery at the Hollywood Stars Motel."

"Guess the son of a bitch ran through the five bucks he stole from that old lady," she muttered.

Last month's beating death of the eighty-five-year-old woman had been the most heinous thing she'd witnessed during her twelve years working Los Angeles' meanest streets: five in a patrol car, a year lost to hospitals and office duty, a year in robbery, another in vice, and the past four in homicide. Regan was thirty-three years old, but there were times lately she felt a hundred. And counting.

She flipped on the lights, unsurprised when the driver rabbited. Regan took off after it, Code 3, blue lights flashing, siren whooping.

3

Blue Bayou, Louisiana

S o," Jack Callahan asked his brother, "how's the search for a new sheriff going?"

"Lousy." Nate frowned as he tackled another stack of evidence bags from the police property room. Since they'd been collecting dust for decades, he figured they should be properly dealt with before he could begin remodeling the office. Opening the bags was like unearthing an ancient city; the deeper he dug, the older the evidence.

"I wasted Monday morning interviewing yet another Dirty Harry wannabe from Shreveport, who opted for early retirement to save himself from being suspended for excess brutality on a prisoner. There's a lawsuit pending on that case, no surprise."

The envelope held a slug that, according to the accompanying papers, had been dug out of a wall.

"Do you remember when Henri Dubois and Julian Breaux fought that duel at Lafitte's Landing?"

"Sure." Jack dug into his brown paper bag and pulled out one of the thick muffulettas he'd brought along for lunch with his brother. "It was Mardi Gras," he said around a mouthful of deli meats and cheese. "They got the fool idea firearms were the best way to settle who'd get the first dance with Christy Marchand." He frowned thoughtfully. "I recall them both being too drunk to hit their targets, but I don't remember what happened next."

Nate skimmed the papers. "Dad arrested them, they pleaded guilty to disorderly conduct, and they were sentenced to give ten percent of their crawfish catch to the parish food bank for the next six months."

"That sounds like something the judge would come up with," Jack agreed.

"Not that there was any excuse for shooting guns off in a crowded dance hall, but I can kind of understand how they might have been moved to passion. I was in love with Christy myself in those days."

The Blue Bayou Mardi Gras queen had gone on to be Miss Louisiana, landed a job as weather girl on KATC in Lafayette, then began working her way up the network ladder through larger and larger markets. She was currently a foreign correspondent for NBC's nightly news, and although her long, dark hair was now a short, perky blond bob, Nate still enjoyed looking at her.

"That's not surprising, since you tended to fall in love with just about every girl in the parish on a regular basis." Jack took a swig from a can of Dr Pepper. "Though I have to admit, Christy was pretty cute. So, got any other hot sheriff prospects?"

"Don't I wish." Since the case had been settled a dozen years ago, Nate tossed the papers and the slug into the circular file.

"How about the guy who was just leaving when I got here? The goofy-looking long-haired guy with the gold stud in his ear."

"Strange criticism from a man who returned to town sportin' an earring himself."

"I'm not applying to be a cop. Besides, Dani likes it. She says it reminds her of a pirate." Jack flashed a rakish grin Nate had to agree was damn piratelike.

Jack had always been the most dashing of the three Callahan brothers. And the wildest, having earned his teenage nickname, Bad Jack, the old-fashioned way: by working overtime to be the baddest-assed juvenile delinquent in the parish.

"The guy was some sprout eater from Oregon who wanted me to know right off the bat that he refused to carry a gun because he was a pacifist. Then asked me if there were any good vegan restaurants in town."

"Not much call for tofu burgers here in hot sauce country."

"That's pretty much what I told him."

"Question is, why he'd want the job in the first place?"

"He's a former soc major." The scent wafting from the bag was mouthwatering. One bite confirmed that the sandwich tasted as good as it smelled. "Seems he's got new liberal ideas 'bout law enforcement that none of the other cities he's interviewed with seem eager to embrace."

"Let me guess. The theory is based on the idea that all those murderers and rapists up there in Angola Prison are merely victims of a harsh, vengeance-driven society."

"From the little I let him tell me, that's pretty much it."

"Hell, that's an old retread idea."

"Well, like I said, it probably isn't real popular in the cop community. Which was why he was willing to come all this way to interview."

"So he thought we were so desperate we'd be willing to end up with him by default?"

"That'd be my guess. I explained that even though the last crime spree was Anton Beloit's kid taking that can of John Deere green paint and spraying his love for Lurleen Woods on the side of every bridge in the parish, I'd prefer the chief law enforcement officer in Blue Bayou to carry a weapon. And know how to use it. He told me he'd have to think about it. I told him not to bother."

"Lucky for you Blue Bayou's a peaceful place."

"Since the town's entire police force consists of Ruby Bernhard, who mostly sits behind her desk and crochets Afghans for her hoard of grandchildren while waitin' for someone to call in a crime so she can play dispatcher; Henri Pitre, who refuses to tell me his age, but has gotta be on the long side of seventy; and Dwayne Johnson, who's eager enough but green as Billy Bob Beloit's damn paint, I sure as hell hope things stay peaceful."

Nate studied the former-DEA-agent-turned-thriller-novelist over the top of the crusty round loaf of French bread. "I don't suppose you're startin' to get bored, being out of law enforcement these past few years?"

"Nope." Jack shook his head. "I figure it's damn near impossible to get bored with a perfect life with the world's sexiest pregnant wife, two terrific good-lookin' kids, a great dog, and getting to tell lies for a living."

The yellow dog in question lifted her huge head, looking for a handout. She swallowed the piece of cheese Jack tossed her in one gulp.

"Nice to hear you put Dani in first place."

"We might have taken a thirteen-year detour, but she's always been first. Always will be." Jack took another hit of the Dr Pepper. "You know, marriage could be the best invention going, right up there with the combustible engine. You might want to give it a try someday."

"No offense, bro, but I'd rather—"

"I know." Jack shook his head. "Go skinny-dippin' with gators. Anyone ever tell you that line's getting a bit old?"

Nate frowned. Three weeks later, and the debacle with Charlene still irked. "Do you think I have a Peter Pan complex?"

"Probably."

This was not the answer Nate had been expecting. Or hoping for.

"That's why it's gonna be so much fun watching when you take the fall, you," Jack said with a pirate's flash of white teeth.

"I wouldn't hold your breath, you. 'Cause it's not going to happen."

"That's pretty much what I said, before Dani came back to town. And I'll bet Finn sure as hell never imagined getting hitched to some Hollywood actress." Jack shrugged. "When it's right, it's right."

"Marriage might be right for you guys, but it's not in the cards for me. Long-term relationships are just too much heavy lifting."

"Never known you to be afraid of hard work."

"It's different in construction. Eventually things come to an end."

"I doubt Beau Soleil will ever be done."

"That's beside the point."

"And that point was?"

"When I'm building something or restoring an old house, eventually I have something to show for the effort, something I can be proud of. The more time you put into a place like Beau Soleil, the better it gets. The more time you put into a relationship with a woman, the more likely it is that you'll fuck it up. Then everyone just ends up angry, with hurt feelings. The trick is to know when to bail, before you get to that pissed-off point."

Granted, he hadn't pulled that off with Charlene, but usually he was able to remain friends with a woman after the sheets had cooled.

"Never met a woman yet who didn't feel the need to change a man," he grumbled.

"Dani's never tried to change me. Guess that's 'cause I'm already perfect."

"Talk about telling lies." Nate looked out the window at the January rain streaming down the glass. "Do you ever just want to take off?"

"I did that thirteen years ago," Jack reminded his brother. "But like the old sayin' goes, there's no place like home."

"Easy for you to say, since you've been just about every place in the world."

"That's true." Jack studied him more closely. "Is there a point to this?"

"I've never been anywhere."

"You went away to college."

"Tulane's in New Orleans, which is not exactly much of a journey. And I came home my freshman year."

"When *Maman* was dying." Jack frowned. "I don't know if I ever thanked you for that—"

"That's what brothers are for. Finn was tied up with that manhunt, and you were off somewhere in the Yucatán Peninsula chasing dope dealers."

Since he'd loved his *maman* dearly, Nate had never regretted his actions. He was happy in Blue Bayou; it was where his friends were, where his life was. Life was good. And if truth be told, there wasn't anywhere else in the world he'd rather live.

But there were still times, on summer Saturday afternoons, when he'd be watching a ball game on TV and wonder whether if he'd stayed in school and not given up the athletic scholarship that had paid his tuition, he might have made it to the pros. After all, the scouts had called him a phenom, possibly the most natural third baseman since Brooks Robinson.

He stifled a sigh. Yesterday's ball scores, as Jake Callahan used to say. He tore open the last evidence envelope.

"Hey, look at this." He fanned the yellowed papers out like a hand of bouree cards.

His brother leaned forward. "Stock certificates?"

"Yeah. For Melancon Petroleum."

Jack whistled. "They've got to be pretty old, since Melancon must've quit givin' out paper certificates at least two decades ago. If they're real, I'll bet they're worth some dough. 'Specially now that the company's rumored to be bought up by Citgo."

"There's also a death certificate for a Linda Dale."

"The name doesn't ring a bell."

"It was thirty-one years ago. Back when Dad first got elected sheriff." Nate frowned. "She died of carbon monoxide poisoning."

"Heating accident?"

"No." His frown deepened. "Suicide." He flipped through a small ringed notebook. "But Dad didn't buy that."

"He thought she was murdered?"

"Yeah," Nate said.

"Blue Bayou's only ever had two murders that I know of. That one back when we were in high school, when Remy Renault got wasted and shot that tin roof salesman he found fuckin' his wife."

"I remember that."

He also remembered the long, hot, frustrating summer when Mrs. Renault hired him to mow her lawn and clean her pool. She'd liked to sunbathe topless. When he got a bit older and realized that she'd been purposefully tormenting him, Nate had been real grateful he hadn't been the one Remy found rolling in the sheets with the woman who'd made the models in Finn's *Playboy* magazines look downright anorexic.

He skimmed some more of the notes, written in a wide, scrawling script not that different from his own. "Seems Dad even went up to Baton Rouge, to try and get the state cops to come in on the case, but while he was gone, Dale's sister showed up and had the body cremated."

"Which would have destroyed any physical evidence he needed to make a case."

"Yeah. But the ashes aren't all the sister took away

with her. There was a toddler in the house. Dad figured she'd been left alone about forty-eight hours. She'd obviously been scrounging for food; he found some empty cookie packages on the kitchen floor and an empty bread wrapper in her room."

"Shit. What about Mr. Dale? Where was he while all this was going on?"

"Appears there wasn't any Mr. Dale."

"Single woman havin' a baby out of wedlock sure wasn't unheard of three decades ago," Jack said. "But it could've created a bit of a stir in a small Catholic town like this one."

"That's what Dad thought." It wasn't that people were more uptight here than other places around the country; people in Blue Bayou certainly knew how to pass a good time. But whatever sexual revolution had taken place during the sixties and seventies had been kept behind closed doors.

"Linda Dale was a lounge singer at Lafitte's Landing. Seems like it would have been hard to save up enough money from whatever salary and tips she was making to buy all this stock."

"How much does it come to?"

Nate checked out the certificates again and did some rapid calculation. "The face value back then was twenty-five thousand dollars."

Jack whistled. "Which means that there's a thirty-three-year-old woman out there somewhere who's due a tidy inheritance. Though if Dale was murdered, it's strange the killer would leave the stock behind."

"The sister was from L.A. When Dad tried to find her, he ran into a dead end."

"That's not surprising. L.A.'s a big place."

"True." Nate picked up a small bound book. "But Linda Dale kept herself a journal, too. If we'd never known *Maman*, but she'd left behind somethin' that would tell us a little about her and then someone stumbled across it, wouldn't you want them to try to find you?"

"*Mais* sure. But finding her's gonna be a long shot. If Dad couldn't find this Linda Dale's sister back then, what makes you think you can after all these years?"

"He didn't have the Internet. Besides, we've got ourselves an ace in the hole. Our special agent big brother."

"Finn quit the Feebs."

"Just 'cause he left the FBI doesn't mean he lost his talent for trackin' people down. And since he's living in L.A., that's gotta make things easier."

Nate picked up the phone and began dialing.

4

Regan called in to Dispatch, requesting all available units in the vicinity to respond. While Van called off the intersections as they sped past them, she floored the gas pedal. The Crown Vic skidded around the corner and flashed through the rain-slick streets, the high-pitched wail of the siren shattering the night.

The police-issue sedan was no match for the Lexus, but the fact that she was a lot better driver was on Regan's side. Working against her was the twinge of fear in the back of her mind at each cross street. It had been seven years since the car chase that had nearly cost her her life, and she still had the scars.

Dammit, homicide detectives didn't do chases. They showed up after the killing and methodically began working a case that would take them from a dead body to a live suspect.

"Shit!"

There was a flash from the Lexus. A slug hit the windshield, shattering it into a spiderweb of cracks.

Regan's already hammering heart was flooded with a burst of adrenaline as the slug buried itself in the backseat. One of the reasons she'd worked so hard to make this division was because any adrenaline rushes were supposed to come from the thrill of putting together all the pieces of a crime so well that when she showed the finished picture of the puzzle to a jury chosen at random, those twelve men and women would find one human being guilty of murdering another. Murder cops weren't supposed to be risking the lives of innocent civilians, not to mention their own, by acting out the raging pursuit myth created by movie and television scriptwriters.

"Shots fired," Van reported.

"Shots fired," Dispatch echoed. "Ten-four."

"That was close," Van said.

"Yeah," Regan agreed grimly, trying not to think about the fact that her Kevlar vest had been supplied by the lowest bidder.

The chase had been picked up by at least five patrol cars. The screaming, flashing light parade, which was now hitting speeds in the sixties, left Sunset to barrel through a quiet residential neighborhood. Regan's murder books—a stack of three-ring binders that contained all the homicide cases she was currently juggling—went sailing onto the floor when she hit a speed bump full-on.

The Lexus took a corner too tight, tilting onto its right two wheels and looking in danger of rolling over; Regan backed off a bit to avoid crashing into it. No sooner had it settled back onto four wheels than it careened over the center line, sideswiping two vehicles

parked on the other side of the street, taking out two
mailboxes and a section of Cyclone fence. Brakes squeal-
ing, it came to a shuddering halt in the front yard of a
tidy 1930s bungalow.

Two males exploded from the car and took off into the
shadows.

"Suspects are on foot." Regan gave Dispatch their
description, as best as she'd been able to tell from the
spreading yellow glow of the porch light.

"Copy. All units, suspects are fleeing on foot. Ten-
twenty. Officer needs assistance," the disembodied voice
announced as Regan sprinted between two houses.

She was within inches of the passenger when he
swerved and ran straight into a darkened swimming pool.
Water splashed into the air and over the deck, drenching
her already rain-wet sweatshirt and jeans.

"One suspect just landed in a pool," she reported into
the radio, pinned to her sweatshirt. "You scoop out Flip-
per," Regan called to Van, who was on her heels. "I'll
stick with Double D."

Having begun running years ago, to get back in shape
after surgery and as rehabilitation, Regan was now nearly
the fastest runner in the precinct. The only guy who
could beat her was a former USC running back who had
a good six inches on her and legs as long as a giraffe's.

Heart pounding painfully against her ribs, Regan
dashed through a hedge. As branches scratched her
hands and face, all her attention was focused on her perp.
The *whop-whop-whop* sound of the police helicopter
reverberating overhead told her the cavalry had arrived.
They beamed a light down on the scene, turning it as
bright as day. "Freeze! Police!" she shouted, just like

they'd taught her at the academy. Twelve years on the job, and she'd never seen it work. It didn't tonight. "Dammit, I said freeze!"

She managed to grab the back of his T-shirt, but since he was as wet as she was, half her age, and outweighed her by at least fifty pounds, he jerked free, scrambled to his feet on the wet grass, and took off again, clearing the fence like an Olympic hurdler.

Regan followed, ripping both her sweatshirt and her arm on the barbed wire along the top of the fence. The shirt bothered her more than her arm; she'd just bought it yesterday. "There's thirty dollars down the damn drain!" she cursed.

They pounded down an alley, splashing through the puddles formed by countless potholes, past huge dogs barking behind fences. Just when Regan was sure her lungs were going to burst, she launched herself into the air and nailed him with a flying tackle that sent them both skidding across what seemed like a football field's length of gravel. They finally came to a stop when they crashed headfirst into a group of galvanized metal trash cans.

"When a police officer says freeze, you're supposed to stop running!"

"How the hell I supposed to know you're a goddamn police officer?" he shouted back. "You ain't wearin' no uniform."

"I suppose you figured all those flashing lights and sirens were just a parade?" Hugely ticked off, she slammed her knee into his back, holding him facedown while a pair of uniforms arriving from the other end of the alley grabbed his arms and legs.

"The guy needs peppering," said one cop, who had to

be a rookie. It was obvious he was having a grand time with all this. Regan was not.

"We don't need it." One absolute truism in police work was that you were always downwind from pepper spray. He'd find that out for himself, but Regan would just as soon not be in the vicinity when it happened. The perp's elbow slammed into her rib cage, nearly knocking the air out of her.

Once they'd finally gotten the suspect subdued, she said, "Congratulations. You win tonight's grand prize by racking up at least a hundred moving violations. That doesn't begin to cover the carjacking and motel robbery. And let's not forget the original murder and rape counts."

Regan snagged one of his wrists. Ignoring the string of epithets, all colorfully graphic, several anatomically impossible, she caught the other wrist, then yanked on the plastic restraints. While she missed the decisive sound of the old metal handcuffs clicking closed, the ratchet sound of the plastic teeth was still damn satisfying.

"What about my rights?" he shouted between curses. "I got rights, bitch."

She scooped wet hair out of her eyes. She was breathing heavily, but felt damn good. "You bet you do. Beginning with the constitutional right to be a boil on the butt of society. But in case you haven't figured it out yet, even most of your homeboys draw the line at killing a little old lady who never did anything but give you a job cleaning up her yard and made you a glass of lemonade."

With the help of the others, she yanked him to his feet and recited the Miranda warning she suspected he'd first heard in grammar school. Then, ignoring the pain in her solar plexus and the burning of the slice on her arm, she walked him down the middle of the street to one of the cruisers angled at the curb.

Tonight's bust, as satisfying as it was, would create a mountain of paperwork. She'd be lucky if she managed a couple hours sleep before having to show up at the courthouse tomorrow.

Six hours later Regan had showered, changed, and was hunched over her laptop keyboard, attacking the stack of report forms, trying to push yet more paperwork through the byzantine legal system.

You never saw television cops doing paperwork. Homicide cops on TV only handled one or two cases at a time, and except for the occasional season-ending cliffhanger, always managed to wrap up the crime in an hour, minus time for commercials. In real life, a detective was forced to juggle dozens of old cases while struggling to stay ahead of the deluge of new ones.

The motto of the LAPD homicide division was "Our day begins when yours ends." What it didn't mention was that it was not uncommon for a homicide detective to work around the clock.

"So," Barnie Williams, who was two months away from retirement and a house on the beach in Mexico, said from the neighboring desk, "this guy calls nine-one-one and says his wife saw a light on out in the garage. He looked out the bedroom window, and sure enough, there are some guys moving around in there, looking like they're loading up stuff.

"Dispatch explains that it's Saturday night, cops are all tied up with more vital shit, there's no one in the vicinity, but stay put and they'll send someone out as soon as possible.

"Guy says okay, and hangs up. A minute later, he calls nine-one-one again and says there's no hurry sending the cops out, because he just shot and killed all the guys in his garage."

He'd succeeded in capturing Regan's reluctant attention. "So, what happened?"

"Well, the shit hits the fan, and it takes less than three minutes for half a dozen cars to pull up on the scene, including Rockford and me, Armed Response Unit, and a producer and cameraman from that TV show *Cops*, who just happened to pick tonight to ride around with a couple patrol officers."

"Jones from Rampart," elaborated Williams's partner, Case Rockford. He was leaning back in his chair, hand-tooled lizard cowboy boots up on the desk. "And that rookie with the Jennifer Lopez ass that even manages to look fine in blues."

"Her headlights aren't bad, either," a detective from across the room volunteered.

"She spends her own bucks to have her uniform privately tailored," offered Dora Jenkins, a female detective. "If she didn't, her ass would look as big as Montana. As for the headlights, they're silicone."

"No way," Williams said.

"Way. She got them back when she was a Hooters waitress. The restaurant loaned her the bucks for the surgery."

"Are you saying those Hooters girls aren't naturally endowed?" another detective asked with mock surprise.

"So what happened with the guy who shot the robbery

suspects?" Regan asked Williams in an attempt to return the typically wandering cop conversation to its original track.

"Oh, turns out they're all alive, and the department's own J.Lo and her partner get to make a bust for the cameras," Rockford replied. "They're happy as white on rice, but Barnie and I were majorly pissed, 'cause we were at the drive-through at Burger King and had just gotten our Whoppers when the call came in."

"I hate cold burgers," Williams muttered.

Rockford picked up the story again. "So Barnie gets in this guy's face and yells, 'I thought you said you killed them!' The man just stands there, puffing away on a cigarette, cool as can be, and says, 'I thought *you* guys said there weren't any cops available.' "

The story drew a mixture of laughs and groans. Wishing caffeine came with an IV option, Regan shook her head and returned to her typing.

"Hey, Hart," called a deep voice roughened by years of cigarettes.

Since another Murphy's Law of police work states that computers only delete reports when they are nearly done, Regan saved her work for the umpteenth time and looked up at the uniformed cop standing in the doorway.

"What's up, Jim?"

"There's a guy here to see you. Says it's personal."

"Obviously he doesn't know anything about cop shops." She glanced around at the bank of desks crowded together, files that no longer fit on desktops piled onto the floor beside them, telephones jangling, computer keys tapping, the cross conversations that kept anything from being personal.

"Should I bring him on back?"

"No need," a drawled voice offered.

The cop spun around, one hand going instinctively to his sidearm; Regan stood up, pulled her .38 from the desk drawer, and quickly skimmed a measuring look over him.

Six-two, one-ninety, blue eyes, brown hair. No scars, tattoos, or identifying marks that she could see. He was wearing jeans that looked faded from use, rather than any trendy stone or acid wash. His unabashedly becoming bomber jacket was unzipped, revealing a blue shirt that whether by accident or design matched his eyes; his leather boots were scuffed and, like his jeans, looked well worn. He was carrying a manila envelope.

He didn't look dangerous. Then again, neither had Ronald Lawson, that Robert Redford lookalike serial killer who'd finally been arrested by the FBI last summer.

"How did you get back here?" It was her street voice, controlled, but sharp enough to cut granite.

"Detective Kante was just coming in and was kind enough to show me the way."

A dimplelike crease flashed at Van, who'd just arrived with coffee from the espresso shop across the street.

"Hey, he came with a letter of recommendation." Van smiled up at the guy with the warmth of an old friend as she handed Regan the brown cardboard cup.

"A recommendation?" Regan lifted her brow, the only one of the three not smiling.

"From the FBI." He took a folded piece of paper from his shirt pocket and held it out. "Well, to be completely accurate, Finn's a former special agent. He said he worked with you on the Valdez murder."

Valdez was one of Lawson's victims, which could only

mean the letter was from Finn Callahan. Regan snatched it from his hand and skimmed the few lines, which were as terse and to the point as the special agent had always been, merely suggesting that she might want to hear Nate Callahan out. It was signed "Just-the-Fucking-Facts-Ma'am-Finn."

Since Finn Callahan wasn't one for chitchat, Regan suspected he hadn't told anyone about the late-night argument they'd had after eighteen hours of canvassing the UCLA area in record-breaking heat, searching for witnesses in the Lawson case. Finn's cut-and-dried method of keeping conversation to the subject certainly allowed for more people to be interviewed, but she'd insisted that by allowing them to chat a bit, you often learned important facts the witnesses might not have realized they'd known. Regan rarely lost her temper, but too little sleep and too much caffeine made her blow up that night. She'd shouted at him, shoved impotently against his chest (the man was huge), and accused him of being Just the Fucking Facts Ma'am Finn Callahan.

He'd surprised her by laughing, and instead of causing things to escalate, her accusation cleared the air. From then on, they'd worked out their own version of good cop/gruff cop.

It had taken Finn another year to bring Lawson down, but the investigation had been a thorough one, with enough evidence gathered that had the killer been tried for the death of the UCLA coed, the DA would have won a conviction.

"I didn't know Finn Callahan had a brother."

"Actually, he's got two," Nate said. "There's another you might have heard of. Jack. He writes books."

That was putting it mildly. Jack Callahan was a former DEA agent turned blockbuster best-selling author. Touted as a new generation's Joseph Wambaugh, he'd soared to the top of the lists with his first novel. Regan had bought all his books for his women characters, who were more richly drawn than those written by most men. Especially former cops turned writers, who, even if they managed to make it past the Madonna/whore stereotype, too often seemed to portray females as victims.

"With both an FBI agent and a DEA agent in your family, you should be aware that wandering around in a police station can get you shot." Why was it the good-looking men were always the stupid ones?

"I realize that, officer."

"Detective." For some reason, Regan felt a need to establish rank in this case.

"Detective," he agreed. His blue eyes warmed; gorgeous white teeth flashed. "Which is why I enlisted Detective Kante's help."

"Want me to throw him out?" the desk cop asked.

Now that she knew the man standing in front of her was Finn's brother, Regan could see the family resemblance. "No, that's okay." His eyes were a deeper blue than Finn's chillier hue, his sun-tipped hair chestnut rather than Finn's black, and his body lankier and more loose-limbed. He was also more casually boyish, but the masculine self-confidence was all too familiar. It had surrounded Finn like an aura, it emanated from the gritty black-and-white author photograph on Jack Callahan's novels, and Nate Callahan, for all his outward, easygoing charm, possessed it in spades.

She reached for the phone.

"If you're calling Finn to find out why I'm here, he won't be able to tell you. Because he doesn't know."

Regan folded her arms across the front of her black silk blouse, angled her head, and narrowed her eyes. "Why not?"

"Because I didn't want to bother him with details."

Details. She already had so many damn details to deal with, she felt as if she was being nibbled to death by killer ducks. "Look, if your car got towed and you need help getting it out of impound, you're out of luck, because we don't do that here. Nor do I fix speeding tickets. If you want me to arrest someone, unless you're talking about a murder, I don't have the time to get involved, but you're free to file a complaint with the desk sergeant."

She picked up a heavy blue binder. The murder book contained everything she'd gathered during the course of her investigation, and she'd spent the few hours between last night's bust and this morning memorizing pertinent facts for today's court testimony.

He tucked his thumbs into the front pockets of his jeans, rocked back on his heels, and appeared to contemplate the matter. Regan had participated in countless interrogations over the years, and had learned from some of the best cops in the business, but she'd never met anyone who could draw a pause out so long.

"My car's back home," he said finally. "I don' know anyone who's been murdered, at least not lately, and except for the street crew that spent last night jackhammering through the pavement outside my hotel room window, I don't really have any complaints."

His slow, easy smile was a contrast to the thoughtful look he skimmed over her face. Even knowing that after all the surgeries she'd undergone, her facial scars were more imagined than real, she was still discomforted by such silent scrutiny. Especially from a man whose own face could have washed off a cathedral ceiling.

"As for why I came, well, it's a long story."

"Then you're really out of luck. Because I have to be in court in thirty"—she glanced down at her watch—"make that twenty-five minutes. And counting."

"That's okay. I'll ride along with you, and we can talk on the way."

"The LAPD police force is not a taxi service. And even if I were willing to allow a civilian to tag along, which I'm not, there wouldn't be any conversation, because I'll be going over the details of my testimony on the way."

"Finn's a stickler for details, too." The nicks and scars on the hand he skimmed over his hair seemed at odds with his pretty face. "We can talk over lunch."

"I wasn't planning to eat lunch." She'd be lucky to score a candy bar from the courthouse vending machine. "So, why don't we just cut to the chase, and you can tell me what you're doing here."

"Like I said, it's a long story. And personal."

"I don't want to offend you, Mr. Callahan, but unless you've committed homicide, I'm not terribly interested in your personal life."

"Not mine, *chère*. Yours."

Regan would have sworn there was no longer anything that could surprise her. She would have been wrong.

"It won't take very long," he coaxed when she didn't immediately respond. "If I wanted to dump it on you without any explanation, I would have used the mail and not bothered flying all this way. So, since my flight back home doesn't leave until this evening, how about I jus' come to the courthouse and we can talk after you wrap up your testimony."

His voice might be as smooth as whiskey sauce over a rich bread pudding, but she refused to be charmed. "They don't have phones in Louisiana?"

"Sure they do. Even in Blue Bayou. That's a nice little town in the south of the state, down by the Gulf," he volunteered. "I'm mayor."

"Good for you." He was certainly the antithesis of the stereotypical sweaty, overweight, south-of-the-Mason-Dixon-line politician wearing a rumpled white suit, seated on a veranda in a rocking chair, sipping from a silver flask of Southern Comfort. "And the reason you didn't just pick up a telephone and call was . . . ?"

"I thought you'd rather talk face-to-face."

She really did have to get going. Judge Otterbein, a stickler for time, ran his courtroom with the precision of a Swiss watch.

Once again he seemed to sense her thoughts. "I promise I won't say a word on the way to the courthouse."

The room had gone unnaturally quiet. Aware they were drawing the attention of every detective in the bull pen, she reached for the gray wool jacket draped over the back of her chair. Moving with surprising speed for someone so seemingly laid-back, he beat her to it.

"I can do that," she muttered, taken off guard as he held it out for her.

"Sure you can," he said agreeably. "But my daddy taught me to help a lady into her coat."

"I'm a detective, not a lady," she reminded him as she slid her arms into the sleeves. "And your father might want to think about joining the twenty-first century."

"Now, that might be a little hard for him to do. Seein' how he's passed on."

"I'm sorry. I didn't know."

He shrugged. "Don't worry about it. I'm not surprised Finn didn't mention it, since my big brother's not real talkative on a good day. Anyway, it was a long time ago."

A less observant woman might have missed the shadow that moved across his lake blue eyes. Regan didn't need her detective skills to spot the No Trespassing sign. Nate Callahan wasn't that old, she mused as they walked out of the station toward the police garage. Maybe thirty, thirty-one tops. So, how long was a long time ago?

Not that she cared.

Since the remote hadn't worked for weeks, she unlocked both car doors with the key. "Since I like and respect your brother, I'm willing to hear you out," she said. "But until court's adjourned, I have more important things to focus on. Say one word, and I'll have to shoot you."

"Works for me," he said agreeably as he climbed in beside her.

"Fasten your seatbelt." She jerked her own shut.

Neither spoke as they cruised into the steady stream of traffic, engine valves rattling. Since the teenage Front Street Crip defendant was the son of a city councilwoman, this was one of her more high-profile murder cases. TV news vans, their satellite uplinks pointed skyward, lined the street outside the courthouse. Wanting to avoid an appearance on the six-o'clock news, Regan pulled into the underground parking garage.

"I know I promised to keep my mouth shut, but you

wouldn't shoot me if I say jus' one little thing, would you?"

"What?"

He turned toward her, putting his hand on the back of her seat. A standard seduction ploy that hadn't worked since she was fourteen and Tom Hardinger had copped a feel while they'd been sitting in the back row of the Village Theater in Westwood, watching *Indiana Jones and the Temple of Doom.*

Apparently undeterred by the gun in its holster on the waistband of her skirt, he leaned toward her, close enough so Regan could smell the coffee and Juicy Fruit on his breath. Close enough to make her muscles tense. Too close for comfort.

"You sure do smell good, *chère.*"

"Detective." She cut the engine and climbed out of the driver's seat. "And I'm not wearing perfume."

His warm blue gaze fastened on hers over the roof of the car. Regan's stomach fluttered. Telling herself that's what she got for skipping breakfast, she ignored it.

"I know." His grin was slow and sexy and had undoubtedly seduced legions of southern belles. "Detective, *chère.*"

Steeling herself against that bone-melting smile, she turned and began walking across the garage with long, determined strides, heels tapping on the concrete floor.

For Finn's sake, she'd listen to whatever Nate Callahan had to say, which she suspected wasn't nearly as personal or intriguing as he'd tried to make it sound. Then, before the sun sank into the Pacific, she'd send the man home and get back to chasing the bad guys.

5

❧❧❧

She was really something. Oh, not his type, of course, Nate had been telling himself from the moment he'd walked into the squad room and spotted her sitting behind her desk, her forehead furrowed in concentration as she typed away at blinding speed. In fact, he wasn't even sure he liked her, which was unusual, since he tended to like most everyone he met. Especially females.

She was tall and willowy, but not at all skinny. Her arms, revealed by the short-sleeved blouse she'd covered up with her jacket, were firm in a way that suggested she worked out regularly. Her hands were slender, her long fingers with their unpolished nails looking far more suited to playing the harp in some southern drawing room than pulling a trigger.

Her lips, which were neither too thin nor kewpie-doll full, but just right, were unpainted. Her hair was styled in a short, thick cut in order, he imagined, to appear more cop than woman. But it wasn't working, because he figured most men—himself included—would be tempted to run their hands through those glossy strands.

The discreet pearl earrings were all wrong. Nate mentally exchanged them for gleaming hoops that would bring out the gold in her whiskey-hued eyes. She'd unbuttoned only the top button on her blouse, and in his mind, Nate unbuttoned another. Then one more.

What was she wearing beneath that unadorned blouse? Something cotton and practical? Or a bit of feminine fluff and lace? The mixing of the tailored charcoal wool suit and silk blouse suggested she was a woman of contrasts.

Her skirt was slim, ending at her knees when she was standing, but revealing an enticing flash of firm, stocking-clad thigh when she crossed her legs.

Like the earrings, the neat and tidy suit was all wrong for her. She was a woman born to wear rich jewel tones. Nate had no trouble imagining the smooth flesh of her breasts framed by emerald silk.

He listened as the defense attorney battered away at her for an hour, the woman's voice rising to stridency as she paced the floor in front of the witness stand, challenging everything about the investigation, attacking the chain of evidence, the veracity of the witness reports, Detective Regan Hart's possible personal prejudice.

"I do have a personal prejudice," Regan agreed.

At the table, the teenage defendant, wearing a suit so new Nate was surprised it didn't still have the price tag hanging from the sleeve, smirked.

"I'm prejudiced against the idea that a human life in some L.A. zip codes is worth less than one in a more affluent neighborhood; and that if several hundred American soldiers were killed in an overseas mission, politicians all over this country would be clamoring for a change in policy, yet when hundreds of citizens die every year in areas of this city that a politician never ventures into without police guard, and then only at election time—"

"Objection, Your Honor." The defense attorney popped up like a jack-in-the-box.

Regan didn't spare her a glance, just kept her gaze directed on the jury as she finished her declaration. "There appears to be a business-as-usual attitude toward murder. And I hope I'll always be prejudiced against the cold-blooded murder of a child."

"Objection," the attorney repeated with more strength.

"Sustained," the judge agreed. "Witness will keep her answers to the questions and refrain from making any speeches."

"I'm sorry, Your Honor." She turned back to the attorney. "Could you repeat the question?"

There was a ripple of laughter among the spectators. The judge frowned, and the bailiff warned everyone to be quiet.

The attorney, who looked angry enough to chew nails and spit out staples, tried again. "Do you have any personal prejudice against my client's race or socioeconomic status?"

Her expression didn't change, but watching her closely as he was, Nate saw the flash of irritation. "No."

The two women's eyes held, and Nate doubted there was a person in the room who couldn't hear the clash of swords.

"So," the attorney began again, "let's walk through what

you did when you arrived on the scene. Step by step."

"If we're going to do that, we're breaking for lunch," the judge decreed. "Court's adjourned until one-thirty."

He slammed down his wooden gavel, signaling the midday recess. While Regan locked herself away with the DA, planning strategy, Nate went next door to a bar and grill, ate an order of wings, and watched a lissome blond on the bar television breathlessly report the latest in the case that seemed to have captured the city's attention. Although the DA had apparently fought it, television cameras had been brought into the courtroom, the better, he thought, for the defense attorney, who appeared prone to dramatics.

"Good-looking broad," the bartender said, watching a replay of Regan's testimony while spritzing seltzer into glasses for the lunch crowd. "For a cop."

Nate agreed.

"She comes in here every once in a while. Doesn't talk much, just orders a Coke, or maybe a glass of white wine at the end of the day. I figure she might be a former waitress, 'cause she tips real good."

Nate took a drink from his pilsner glass of draft. "What's the prevailing opinion on this case?"

"The evidence against the gangbanger is rock solid, but his mother has gotten her kid his own private dream team, so who knows how the jury's going to vote." He shrugged. "Folks seem to respond to star power."

Watching the jury as the questioning resumed after lunch, Nate worried about that. Unlike the defense, Detective Regan Hart's tone remained cool, matter-of-fact, and, like the rest of her, almost too much in control. While he wasn't any expert, he wondered if she might not be better off appealing as much to the jury members' emotions as to their heads. She was beginning to remind Nate more and more of Finn. What would it take, he wondered, to make the woman relax?

As she stepped down from the witness stand, Nate found himself wondering how cool and collected the detective would be when she learned his reason for coming here to L.A.

It was over. Despite some initial discomfort caused by Nate Callahan watching her so intently, Regan had managed to stay calm, cool, and professional. She hadn't let them see her sweat, and by the time she'd finished her testimony, everyone knew that the baby-faced defendant was guilty as sin. Regan knew it, the defense team knew it, the judge knew it, and you didn't have to be a psychic to sense that the majority of the jury members, who'd remained engaged but could no longer look the kid in the eye, had known it, too.

Which was why, of course, the defense attorney had suddenly asked for a recess minutes before the case closed. The deal was swiftly cut by those Great Compromisers, the lawyers on both sides.

Nate Callahan was waiting for her outside the courtroom. "Good job. You sure as hell impressed me."

"Thank you, Mr. Callahan, but impressing you is not high on my list of priorities."

"It's Nate," he said easily, falling into step beside her, adjusting his long-legged stride to hers. "You don't seem real pleased with the outcome."

She stopped in her tracks and looked up at him. "Why should I be pleased?"

"He's goin' to prison."

"For second-degree murder." She shook her head, still fuming. "What the hell does that mean? How can eight-year-old Ramon Consuelo be second-degree dead?" She raked a hand through her hair. "He's one hundred percent dead, dammit." She would have much preferred a slam-dunk win over a lousy, convenient plea bargain.

"You did your best," he said mildly. "Which Mrs. Consuelo seemed to appreciate."

"He was her last living child." Regan wondered how any woman survived the pain. "Her seven-year-old daughter was killed six years ago by a hit-and-run drunk driver who swerved into a group of kids waiting for the school bus. She lost a two-year-old daughter to AIDs back in the nineties. She hadn't even realized her drug abuser husband had passed the virus on to her until the baby was born HIV-positive. She's still alive; the baby isn't. Ramon was her last child and her only son." She blew out a long, slow breath. "And now she doesn't have him, either."

"It must be hard," he said. "Doin' what you do, caring like you do."

"Some days are harder than others." As were the nights when her sleep was haunted by those whose deaths she hadn't managed to avenge. "What time is your flight?"

"It's a while yet. We can talk over supper."

"Do you have a pen?"

"Sure." He reached into an inside jacket pocket and pulled out a ballpoint.

Regan ignored it. "Then write this down. I'm not having dinner with you."

Her hard stare seemed to deflect right off him. "You have to eat to keep your strength up for playing cops and robbers."

"I don't consider my job playing."

"It wasn't meant to be taken literally, detective. Anyone watching you in court today could tell you take your work real seriously."

"It's become almost a cliché," she murmured. "But there's a reason the idea of homicide detectives being the ones who speak for the dead is always showing up in books and movies. Because it's the truth." She slanted him a look. "But I suppose, being Finn's brother, you already know that."

"*Mais* yeah. Finn can be a serious one, he. But he's loosened up some since he got married."

"I heard about that." Regan had been amazed that the most serious man she'd ever met had married one of Hollywood's highest profile actresses. And not just any actress, but the new Bond Girl, for heaven's sake. You couldn't turn on a television these days without seeing some promo for the movie.

"He and Julia didn't hit it off right away, but they're sure happy now."

"That's nice." She meant it. Having had a front-row seat for the horrific things people who'd once been in love could do to one another, Regan had become a conscientious objector in the war between the sexes.

"It'll take a while to tell you my story," he said. "So, how about getting a couple burgers and going out to the beach? I've never been to the Pacific Ocean, but I hear it's real pretty."

That smooth-talking southern steamroller might work

back home in Louisiana, but it wasn't working on Regan. "Look, Mr. Callahan—"

"Nate," he reminded her with a quick smile.

She waved his correction away with an impatient hand. "Why don't you tell me—as succinctly as possible—why you've come here, so I can get back to work, and you can go back to Big Bayou."

"It's Blue Bayou, like the old Orbison song. It was originally named Bayou Bleu, after all the herons that nest there, but over the years it's become Anglicized."

"How interesting." She didn't care about how the damn backwater town had gotten its name. She also wasn't sure this man knew the meaning of succinct. "Now, if we could just get down to business?"

"You know, sometimes it's not a bad idea to take a little break and clear your head." He skimmed a hand over her shoulder, which stiffened at his touch. "You seem a little tense, detective."

"What I am, is losing patience." The roughened tip of his fingers brushed against her neck, causing a spurt of her pulse. "And I don't know how things are done down in the bayou, but touching an armed woman without asking permission could get you shot here in the city."

"You thinking of shooting me?"

"The idea is becoming more appealing by the moment."

Because that lightly stroking touch stimulated hormones she'd thought she'd locked away in cold storage, Regan pulled away just as a detective she'd once worked with walked by. Her week with the man had been spent dodging clumsy passes, and the smile he gave her was close to a smirk, suggesting he believed more was going on here than a frustrating conversation.

"Look." Nate dipped his hands into his front pockets. "We're wasting a lot of that time you said you don't have, standing around this parking garage arguing. So, how about we just stop somewhere, pick up some supper, and drive to the beach, where I'll tell you a little story, then you can drop me off at LAX and I'll be out of your hair."

Regan sighed in frustration. Since he was turning out to be as stubborn as his eldest brother, they'd undoubtedly get things over with a lot faster if she just agreed to dinner.

Nate didn't appear the least bit surprised by her caving in, which only heightened Regan's irritation as she drove the two blocks to the Code Ten, a local cop bar and grill named for the police off-duty lunch code. After another brief argument, which she won, they each paid for their own burgers, then headed toward the coast.

6

This is real nice," Nate said a few minutes later as they sat on a bench on the Santa Monica pier. The air was cool and crisp, and scented with salt and faraway places. "And worth the trip."

"Which *was* about?" She took a waxed wrapped burger from the bag and nearly moaned at the scent of grilled meat and melted cheese. She'd become so used to skipping meals, she'd learned not to notice hunger pangs. Now Regan realized she was starving.

"Like I said, it's a little hard to explain. See, my daddy was sheriff of Blue Bayou when he was killed in the line of duty."

She'd just taken a bite, and had a hard time swallowing. Having attended more funerals than she would have liked, Regan knew how hard the loss of a cop killed in the line of duty could be on a community. She also knew how hard not having a father could be on a child.

"That's rough."

She'd been the only kid she knew whose dad had died. Oh, there'd been lots of divorced dads who only saw their sons and daughters on weekends, some that had taken off to parts unknown, and a couple of kids whose mothers had never married their fathers. But to have a parent, even one your mother had divorced, die? That definitely made you stand out. Different.

"Yeah, it was hard. But like I said, it was a long time ago."

"How long?"

"Nineteen years this May." The way he didn't have to pause and think suggested the memory was still fresh in his mind.

"And you were?"

"Twelve." His expression was uncharacteristically sober. "Anyway, I was emptyin' out a storage room in the sheriff's office before doing some remodeling—I'm a contractor—"

"I thought you were a politician."

"Bein' mayor's a volunteer position. Contracting pays the bills—at least most months. Anyway, I was goin' through some old evidence envelopes when I came across something that belongs to you."

"That's impossible."

She'd been to Louisiana twice in her life. Once was five years ago, when she'd given a workshop about protecting crime scenes at a cop convention in New Orleans; the other was last month, when she'd flown to Shreveport to bring back a robbery/murder suspect.

"Your mother was Karen Hart, right?"

"I suppose you learned that from Finn."

"I did," he said on a smooth, genial tone that probably made him a dandy politician back home. "He was going on the information I gave him from an old police file. It's one of those funny coincidences, seein' as how you two worked together and all."

He'd just piqued her curiosity again. "What police file?"

"The one I got your *maman's* name from."

"Look, Finn Callahan's a crackerjack detective. In fact, he's the best I've ever met. But even he can screw up occasionally. My mother was a partner in a law firm. She was not the type of person to end up in a police file."

"How old are you, detective?"

"I fail to see how my age is relevant to this conversation."

"According to this file, your mother had a sister. One who died and left behind a toddler who'd be thirty-three years old."

Regan took a sip of coffee she had no business drinking this late in the day. The caffeine would mean another sleepless night. "News flash, Callahan, I'm not the only thirty-three-year-old woman in the world. Besides, my mother was an only child."

He pulled a sheaf of papers from the manila envelope he'd been carrying when he came into the station. "Karen Hart's listed as Linda Dale's only living relative. Except for a girl baby named on her birth certificate as Regan Dale."

Regan hated her hesitation in taking the envelope from his hand. Shaking off an uneasy sense of foreboding, she forced her shoulders to relax as she skimmed over what appeared to be a valid police report from Blue

Bayou Parish, Louisiana. Then she looked at the copy of the birth certificate. Linda Dale, whoever she was, had been twenty-five years old when she'd given birth to a seven-pound, three-ounce daughter. The father was listed as unknown.

"I've never heard the name Linda Dale. Or Regan Dale. My name is Hart. It's always been Hart."

"There's a photograph, too." He reached into the envelope again. "Linda Dale was a real pretty lady. You might find her a little familiar."

The photograph had obviously been taken in New Orleans; Regan easily recognized the ornate cast-iron grillwork on the front of the red brick building. The woman was wearing a red, white, and blue Wonder Woman costume, suggesting the picture had been taken either at Halloween or during Mardi Gras. The color had faded over the years, but there was no mistaking the face smiling back at her.

Impossibly, although the hair was a bright, coppery red, not brunette, it was her mother's face. It was also much the same face Regan had seen every morning in her bathroom mirror, until plastic surgeons had dug out the bits of metal that had torn apart her skin and sculpted her features into as close an approximation as possible to what she'd been before that fateful night she'd driven her patrol car into a trap meant to be a literal dead end.

There was another, more important difference between her face and the one in the photograph. Regan didn't think she'd ever experienced the depth of emotion glowing in Linda Dale's light brown eyes. It was obvious that the woman was madly, passionately, in love with whoever was holding the camera.

Regan felt Nate looking at her, waiting for some response that she refused to give him. "Interesting." Not wanting him to think she was afraid to look him in the eye, she lifted her gaze. "But it doesn't prove anything."

"She looks quite a bit like you."

"Somewhat like me," she corrected. "Her nose tilts up more than mine does, and her jawline's softer." Hers was more angular, her manufactured cheekbones sharper. "And her hair's a different color."

"Women have been known to dye their hair. It's still a pretty close resemblance."

"Even if we looked like twins separated at birth, it wouldn't prove anything. They say everyone has a double; in fact, there's a night bartender at the Code Ten who's a dead ringer for Julia Roberts." She did not reveal that this unknown woman could be a dead ringer for Karen Hart, since that would only reinforce his ridiculous argument.

"The evidence folder says she's Linda Dale. Karen Hart's twin sister," he stressed.

"That still doesn't necessarily prove your point. If there weren't all sorts of ways to interpret evidence, court dockets wouldn't be so crowded."

"Good point." He tilted his head and studied her. Quietly. Thoughtfully. "Trust doesn't come real easy to Finn, either."

If he was telling the truth, the woman in the photograph was dead. But Regan felt a familiar, palpable emotional pull. While she was not a fanciful person, Regan knew that it was, indeed, possible for people to speak beyond the grave. She'd experienced it before, when the unseeing eyes of a murder victim seemed to be imploring her to find the killer who'd ended her life.

"Let me put it this way, Mr. Callahan: just weeks ago I sat next to a Christmas tree in the living room of a house that looked like a place the Beav might have grown up in, and listened to a woman insist that the last she'd seen of her four-year-old daughter was when she'd lost her at the mall on a visit to see Santa Claus.

"Two days later, I arrested her drug-dealing boyfriend for being a coconspirator in the mother's plot to kill the little girl for a thousand-dollar insurance policy. A third friend, whom we also indicted, had taken her from the mall and out into the desert, where he'd shot her in the head. She never did get to sit on Santa's lap. And it might have taken us years to get justice for her, if some teenagers hadn't been riding their new ATVs out on those dunes and came across her body.

"I've had to step over the body of a woman whose husband shot her while holding a knife at the throat of their toddler son. When we showed up in response to a neighbor's nine-one-one call, he hadn't even bothered to change his bloody clothes, but still swore he was innocent and insisted on lawyering up.

"I've seen children shot while playing hoops on a public playground, for no other reason than some other kid needed to kill a stranger to make it through some gang initiation. And I worked with your brother for twenty-four hour days during one of the city's worst heat waves, trying to nail a sicko pervert who got his kicks torturing young women. No, Mr. Callahan, I do not trust easily."

He tipped his head again. The California sun, buttery bright even on this winter day, glinted on his short, spiky hair and turned the tips to a gleaming gold that not even the most acclaimed Beverly Hills colorist could have pulled off. Regan found it strange that she, who'd worked years to perfect her intimidating cop look, could be made to feel so uneasy by his silent scrutiny.

"You've definitely got a cop's brain inside your pretty head, Detective *Chère*."

She bit into a salty French fry. "And you've obviously got a chauvinist's brain inside *your* head, Mayor Callahan."

"For noticin' that you're a good-looking woman? It's a man's right to look at pretty things." He slid an appreciative glance over her. The light sparkling in his eyes could have been the lowering sun glancing off the water, but Regan didn't think so. "Doesn't necessarily mean he intends to do anything more without permission."

While she might not be Nicole Kidman, Regan had had men look at her before. Even after her cruiser had been turned into a shooting gallery. But somehow she'd gotten to be thirty-three years old without ever feeling in danger of melting. When his gaze lingered momentarily on her legs, she wished she'd worn her usual pantsuit rather than a skirt to court today. Which in turn made her furious at herself for responding like a giddy high school girl talking with the quarterback.

"A word of advice: don't hold your breath." Emotional need always made her defensive, which led directly to the safer emotion of anger. She crushed the burger bag. "Now if that's all the evidence you have to show me—"

"*Dieu*, are you always in such a hurry? Didn't anyone ever tell you that rushing around is bad on a person's system?" He shook his head as he took some more papers from the envelope. "These stock certificates would make Regan Dale a rich woman."

"They could also make you a rich man, since they appear to be bearer certificates."

"They don't belong to me." He looked affronted that she'd even suggest cashing them in. "I'm pretty sure they're yours."

As he held them toward her, Regan reminded herself that the devil didn't come slithering up to you with horns and a tail and reeking of brimstone; he came courting with engaging manners and a smooth, seductive smile.

"So you say. I still say you're wrong."

"Why don't you take them anyway? Do a little detecting. You might find something that'll make you feel different."

Regan knew otherwise, but there was no way she was going to let him accuse her of having a closed mind. "We'd better get you to the airport before you miss your flight."

His smile was slow, delicious, and in its own charming way, dangerous. "There's still time."

"It's obvious you don't know LAX. It was bad enough before the heightened security measures. Now it's a nightmare." She tossed the bag into a trash barrel.

"You know, the Pacific's even nicer than I've heard," he said as they walked back to the parking lot. "I appreciate you bringin' me here."

"Like you said, I had to eat."

Regan had no idea what those papers he'd shown her meant, but she was certain they didn't have anything to do with her. But still, the cop in her couldn't quite stop mulling over the what-ifs.

Nate Callahan seemed to have an instinct for knowing how far to press his case. He didn't bring the subject up again as she drove to the airport, but instead waxed enthusiastic about his south Louisiana home.

"Well, I can certainly see why you were elected mayor," she allowed as she pulled up to the curb designated for departing passengers. "You're quite an ambassador for the place."

"It's a nice little town." He unfastened his seat belt, reached into the backseat, and retrieved his overnight bag. "Pretty as a picture on a travel poster and real peaceful." He paused before opening the passenger door and gave her another of those slow perusals. Unlike the earlier ones, this didn't seem to have any sexual intent. "We jus' happen to be looking for a new sheriff. If you ever get tired of life in the fast lane, you might want to give us a try."

"Thanks for the offer, but I'm quite happy right where I am." That might not be the whole truth and nothing but the truth, but she saw no reason to share her private feelings with a total stranger she'd never see again.

Once again he surprised her with his speed, reaching out and slipping her shades off her face before she could react. "I'm not one to argue with a *belle femme*." Before she could back away, the roughened pad of his thumb brushed against the skin below her eyes. "But you look like you could use a little bit of R&R, Detective *Chère*."

"Dammit, Callahan—"

"Jus' making a little observation." He ducked away before she could push him out of the car. He was standing on the sidewalk, seemingly oblivious to the driver who was leaning on his horn behind them, urging Regan to move on so he could claim the spot. He reached back into the car, handing her the sunglasses and a white leather book he'd taken from his jacket pocket.

"What's this?"

"Linda Dale's journal. I thought you might like to read it. The details are a little sketchy—she wasn't a real regular writer—but it does mention her baby. And her sister, Karen Hart. I put my phone number on a piece of paper inside the front cover, just in case you want to call and compare notes once you're finished reading." He turned and walked away into the terminal.

The horn behind her sounded again, a long, strident demand. A uniformed cop standing on the curb blew his whistle and began heading toward her.

"All right, dammit." Resisting the urge to ticket the other driver for disturbing the peace—unfortunately, Nate Callahan had already succeeded in doing that—Regan shifted the car into gear and pulled out into traffic.

7

So," Jack asked, "how did it go?"

After arriving in Blue Bayou, Nate had driven out to Beau Soleil, the antebellum home Jack was in the process of restoring. Nate was the contractor, and so far the work had been going on close to two years; he figured it could easily take a lifetime to restore it to its former glory, but fortunately neither Jack nor Dani—whose family had owned the plantation house for generations before Jack had bought it—seemed to mind living in a construction zone. Somehow his brother's wife had created a warm and cozy atmosphere out of what could have easily been chaos.

The kids were upstairs doing homework, and Dani was sitting over in the corner of the former library, knitting. Or, as she'd explained to Nate, attempting to learn to knit, which wasn't nearly as easy as it had appeared in that big yellow *Knitting for Dummies* book she'd brought home from Blue Bayou's library.

"Not as bad as it could have." He bent over the custom-made green-felt-topped pool table, broke the balls, sunk two in a corner pocket, and called for stripes. "Not as good as it might have."

Jack leaned against the wall, paneled in a gleaming burled bird's-eye maple, and chalked his cue. "What's she like?"

"Smart." The ten ball disappeared into a side pocket. "And real pretty, though outwardly tough as nails, which I suppose a cop's gotta be." He banked a red-striped ball against the side and sent it spinning into the far corner. "She reminded me a lot of Finn. Before he fell for Julia."

"That grim, huh?"

"Not grim, exactly." He thought about that as he moved around the table. "She's like our big brother in that she obviously believes in truth, justice, and the American way. And she's definitely not like any of our bayou belles."

Jack laughed at that. "What's the matter, baby brother? Did the old Nate Callahan charm finally fail you?"

"I got her to hear me out." Memories of the unwilling flash of emotion he'd seen in her gaze when he'd touched that shadowed skin beneath her eyes had him, not for the first time, imagining touching her all over. Momentarily distracted, he missed the shot. "She also took the envelope we found in the evidence room."

"What did she have to say about the autopsy report?"

"Nothing, 'cause at the last minute I decided not to give it to her. She'd had a rough day in court, and I was already dumping enough on her, so I figured that could wait until she called."

"She might not be real happy with you, holding back that way."

"Then I'll just have to smooth things over."

"If she's as much like Finn as you say, I'm goin' to enjoy watching that."

Having spent a lot more years of his youth in bars and pool halls than Nate had, Jack went to work, sending three balls in quick succession thumping into holes.

Across the room, Danielle Dupree Callahan cussed as she dropped another stitch. She'd told Nate that the buttery yellow yarn was going to end up a baby sweater. But he sure hadn't been able to picture it from what she'd managed to knit so far.

"Think she'll actually call?" Jack asked. The solid three ball clicked off Nate's fourteen and sent the seven into the far corner pocket

"Yeah." Balls were disappearing from the table like crawfish at an all-you-can-eat buffet. "She's a detective, she. She'll be curious enough to call." He watched as Jack used the ball he'd missed to sink the eight ball. "You know, it gets old, having my hustler brother all the time beating the pants off me."

Jack's smile flashed. "Jus' one of the benefits of a misspent youth." He held out his hand. "You owe me twenty bucks, *cher*."

As he dug into his pocket for the money, Nate glanced up at the wall clock, calculated that it'd be about eight o'clock in Los Angeles, and wondered if Regan had gotten through the journal yet.

She had. As Nate Callahan had said, the journal entries were sporadic, occurring weeks, months, sometimes even years apart. After leaving home at seventeen to become the girl singer in a country band, Linda Dale had bounced from town to town, singing gig to singing gig, man to man, for seven years. She hadn't seemed to mind the nomadic life. Most of the men she'd gotten involved with were musicians, and while she appeared to set limits—bailing on relationships the moment they turned abusive—Regan began to detect a pattern. It appeared the woman was part free spirit, intent on enjoying life to the fullest, and part nurturer, needing to rescue lost souls (even those who might not want to be rescued) and take care of everyone around her.

The entries, Regan noticed as she ate her way through a pint of Ben and Jerry's Chocolate Chip Cookie Dough ice cream, seemed to come at the beginnings and ends of her romances, which gave the impression that when she was actually in a relationship, she was too busy living life to comment on it.

None of the men had been the prince in shining armor Dale professed to dream of; quite a few had been toads. But she'd remained upbeat, positive that somewhere out there in the world her true soul mate was waiting for her.

After a gap of nearly two years, an infant girl she named Regan came into the picture. And then things became really personal. Regan put her head back against her headboard, closed her eyes, and took a long deep breath.

The woman in her sympathized with the single mother trying to balance a singing career and a young daughter. The detective needed more. She turned to the next page and began to read again.

January 1. J surprised me by slipping away from the gala. The champagne he brought with him to toast a new year in my dressing room was ridiculously expensive. It tasted like sunshine, all bright and sparkly, but didn't go to my head nearly as much as his promise: that this year we'd finally be able to live together openly. Our lovemaking, while necessarily quick and silent, was still every bit as thrilling as it had been that first time in New Orleans after he'd walked into the Camellia Club and changed my life.

January 15. I think Regan has picked up on my excitement. Sometimes I wonder if I made the wrong decision, choosing to raise her alone, to risk her growing up without the stabilizing influence of both a father and mother.

Of course Karen, for whom Regan has always been a sore subject, scoffed at me when I suggested that on the phone the other day and said something I couldn't quite understand about women needing men like fish needed a bicycle, which I took to mean that I was foolish to enjoy having a man in my life. In Regan's life. Then again, Karen has always been the most independent person I've ever known. My legal eagle sister makes the Rock of Gibraltar look like a tower of sand by comparison.

It was such a delight watching Regan spin around the room like a small dervish. She's such a sunny child. I like to think she's inherited my talent, but she already has so much more confidence than I did at her age. Sometimes more than I do now, I think. And while I know all mothers think their children beautiful and talented, I truly believe she could be a star someday.

When I told her that soon she'll be dancing at our wedding with her new daddy, she giggled, flung her arms around me, and gave me a huge smack of a kiss. I can't remember being happier.

February 14. Valentine's Day. J and I managed to slip away to be together at lunch. We went out to our secret place and made love, and afterward he surprised me with a stunning heart-shaped ruby pendant. He said I'd had his heart from the day we met. As he's had mine. And always will. He fretted when I wept, but I assured him that they were tears of joy, not sorrow.

February 25. It's the waiting that's so hard. I understand, as I always have, that J's position is not an easy one, and I must remain patient. He came into the lounge with friends tonight, and just seeing him without being able to touch him—and be touched—is so impossibly hard. Soon, he tells me. Soon.

March 4. Regan's second birthday. J showed up this evening with a stuffed elephant. It's a silly, fanciful thing, covered with green, purple, and gold polka dots and wearing a Mardi Gras crown and beads. Regan loves it.

"No." Regan snapped out a quick, harsh denial. She pressed the heels of her hands against her eyes, hard enough to see swirling stars. Emotions she couldn't begin to sort out crashed down on her as the disbelief she'd been trying to hang on to shattered.

Her heart was pounding hard and fast as she forced herself to continue reading, her eyes racing over the page.

He seemed a bit distracted, which isn't surprising, since tomorrow's the day he'll finally tell his wife that he's leaving Blue Bayou. Regan and I will be leaving with him. Anticipation has me as giddy as if I've been drinking champagne from a glass slipper. I won't sleep a wink tonight.

That was the final entry. Regan closed both the journal and her eyes as waves of emotion crested over her. She lifted a hand that felt as heavy as stone and dragged it through her hair.

She'd felt this way twice before: during those weeks she'd spent in the hospital, drugged to the gills, and again three years ago, when her mother had died suddenly and unexpectedly from a brain embolism. Karen Hart, L.A.'s own Wonder Woman, had finally run across something she couldn't control.

The thing to focus on, Regan told herself, was that she'd survived both. She'd surprised all the medical experts with the speed of her recovery, and she'd gone back to work despite the constant need for more surgery, just as she'd overcome the shock and pain of loss to take care of the funeral arrangements for her mother.

She dragged herself out of bed on legs that felt as shaky as they had during her early months of physical therapy, and opened the cedar trunk.

Fighting for breath, she took the elephant, which for some reason she'd named Gabriel, from the trunk. He was tattered and worn, as any child's favorite old toy would be. And while technically in a court of law he might be considered circumstantial evidence, since he couldn't be the only such toy in the world, Regan knew, without a shadow of doubt, that she was holding proof of Nate Callahan's claim.

The gilt crown had long since disappeared, and she remembered breaking the beads during a playground tug-of-war with six-year-old Johnny Jacobs. She'd ended up with the elephant, and he had gone home with a black eye that had caused her to be deprived of television for an entire week after the crybaby had gone home bawling to his mother.

Regan hadn't minded being banished to her bedroom; justice was more important than watching *Starsky and Hutch*. Her father would have understood, she'd insisted at the time.

Her father. The thought struck like a sledgehammer to the head. If Karen Hart wasn't her mother, then John Hart was probably not her father, either. Unless, of course, he was the *J* in the journal?

Could he have been having an affair with his *sister-in-law*? The distance between Louisiana and California would have made it difficult, but then, there was no indication that Linda Dale had been living in Louisiana when she'd gotten pregnant.

And would a woman actually take the child her husband had fathered with another woman into her home, raising her as her own? Especially if that other woman was her own twin sister?

Regan didn't think many women would, but Karen Hart could well have been the exception. She might not have taken the child out of any sense of family or love, but she'd had a steely sense of responsibility. It also might have explained why Regan could not recall a single warm maternal moment spent with the woman she'd always believed to be her mother.

"Damn." A predawn light cast the room in a soft lavender glow. Regan pressed the stuffed toy against her breast, bowing her head against a sudden onslaught of pain. Had her entire life been built on a foundation of lies? And if not, what parts had been true, what parts false?

She picked up the piece of hotel stationery with Nate Callahan's telephone number and stared at it for a long time, trying to decide what to do next. Part of her wanted to call him, to ask the myriad questions bombarding her brain.

She removed the receiver from the cradle, dialed the 985 area code, then slammed it down again. She needed time. Time to absorb the shock. Time to decide her next move.

She had to get out of here. Had to clear her mind, start thinking like a cop, and not a woman who'd just had her world pulled out from under her.

Still numb, she changed into her running clothes, though a cold winter drizzle was falling and fog was blowing in from the beaches. As she began running through the still dark streets, Regan remained oblivious to the weather. The very strong possibility that the woman who'd fed and clothed her, put a roof over her head, and raised her, if not affectionately, at least dutifully, had also created a sham of a life, left Regan with a bitter, metallic taste in her mouth.

And so, beneath the thick gray clouds blowing in from the steely, white-capped Pacific, Regan ran. And ran. And ran.

8

A *breakout of gang wars* kept Regan working nearly around the clock, which, while exhausting, at least occasionally took her mind off her own problem.

She kept her secret to herself for nearly a month, viewing it on some distant level like a cold case she'd get to as soon as the hot ones were solved. Finally, after several marches by residents of the communities that were being torn apart garnered the attention of the press, politicians loosened the purse strings long enough to pay for more cops on the beat, which resulted in a string of high-profile arrests.

Once things seemed to have calmed down, Regan tracked down Finn, whose advice echoed what she'd been telling herself ever since Nate Callahan's visit. There was no way she was even going to begin to get a handle on her past if she didn't visit Blue Bayou—and the scene of Linda Dale's death—herself.

Regan made the travel arrangements. Then, after another long, early morning run on the beach, she called her partner. "Did I wake you?"

"Of course not." Van's groggy tone said otherwise. A male voice said something in the background. Regan could hear her telling Rhasheed who was calling. "So, what's up?"

"I'm going to be taking some leave time."

"Good idea. You've been working killer hours for too long. A break will do you good."

"I hadn't realized there was anything wrong with me." *Terrific. Could you sound any more defensive?*

"You haven't taken any real time for over eighteen months."

Nineteen. But who was counting?

"Where are you going?"

"Louisiana."

"Oh, lucky girl! New Orleans's got great food, great jazz, and lots going on, especially now with Mardi Gras coming up."

"I'm not going to New Orleans. I'm going to Blue Bayou. It's a little town closer to the Gulf," she said, anticipating Van's next question.

"I've never heard of it."

"I doubt if many people have. It's pretty small."

"How did you find out about the place?"

"I did an Internet search." The half lie caused a little pang of guilt. She *had* looked up the town's website, which had revealed what Finn had already confirmed: that Nate Callahan was, indeed, the mayor.

"How long will you be gone?"

"I don't know."

There was a longer pause. Regan could practically hear the gears turning in her partner's head. "This sudden trip wouldn't have anything to do with a man, would it?"

"In a way."

They'd known each other too long for Van not to realize something wasn't quite right. "Would you care to share what you're holding back on your partner and best friend?"

There was no point in trying to pretend everything was all right. "I can't. Not yet."

The curiosity in Van's voice changed to concern. "Anything I can do to help?"

Regan wasn't quite prepared to share details she didn't even know herself. "Thanks anyway, but I'll be fine. It's just some little misunderstanding I have to clear up. In case anything urgent comes up, I'm staying at the Plantation Inn."

"Sounds nice."

"I guess so." It was the only hotel in town. She recited the number she'd called to book her reservation, then, after reassuring Van that she really was fine, Regan began packing.

Fourteen-year-old Josh Duggan had never expected Louisiana to be so frigging cold. It had been snowing when he'd left Tampa, and he'd figured it'd stay warmer if he stuck to the southern states, but he'd been wrong. If someone didn't come along soon, he'd turn into a Popsicle.

He knew it was dangerous to be hitchhiking, but it wasn't like he had a whole lot of choices. After seeing the cop talking to the cook in the restaurant next to the bus station in Jackson, he'd been afraid to get back on the bus and had decided to take his chances with his thumb on the back roads, which was proving not to be the most brilliant idea he'd ever had.

So far only one car had passed on this narrow, lonely stretch of road. When he'd recognized the black-and-white as a trooper's cruiser, he'd dived into a ditch until it had passed. Now his clothes were wet and sticking to his skin, and he could feel the blood from the rock he'd hit his face on oozing down his cheek.

His stomach growled. He'd been promising it something to eat for the last twelve hours. Since he was down to about thirty-five cents, he was going to have to boost dinner. It wouldn't be the first time.

But first he was going to have to get to an effing town.

His spirits perked up just a little when something came looming out of the swirling gray mist. The roar of the diesel engine was unmistakable. But at the speed it was going, would it even see him in time? Josh was desperate enough to consider leaping in front of the cab when the eighteen-wheeler's air brakes squealed.

The semi came to a grinding stop about fifteen feet beyond him. He must have hurt his leg when he'd jumped into the ditch, because it hurt like hell to run on it, but afraid the driver would take off, he ignored the pain and sprinted on a limp past the two trailers to the cab. The big door opened. A man Josh would not want to meet in a dark alley was looking down at him. His eyes were black as midnight; a red scar started high on his cheekbone and slashed through a scrabbly thatch of dark beard. "What the fuck are you doin' out here, kid?"

"Car broke down," Josh lied without a qualm. Everyone

lied. "I was walking into town to try and find a mechanic."

Dark eyes narrowed. "Didn't see no car on the highway."

"I left it on a side road."

"Sure you did. You don't look old enough to drive."

Josh thrust out his jaw and met the openly skeptical gaze head-on. "I'm small for my age."

"That so?" The driver studied him for another long moment that seemed like a lifetime. "It's against regulations to take on passengers." He jabbed a thumb at the sign in the window. "But hell, my old lady would kick my ass six ways to Sunday if she found out I left some skinny kid out in a frog-strangler like this." He shrugged. "Get on in."

Not waiting for a second invitation, Josh scrambled into the passenger seat. The rush of heat from the dashboard, mingling with the mouthwatering aroma that could only be doughnuts, made his head spin. "Thanks. I'd pay you for the ride, but—"

"Hell, I'm not interested in your money, kid. What I'd like is for you to tell me the truth, so I know whether or not I can expect the law to be comin' after you." He glanced up into the rearview mirror as if expecting to see flashing lights behind them.

Blue and red artwork snaked around huge arms the girth of tree trunks. Josh wondered if he'd gotten any of those tattoos in prison, then decided he didn't really want to know.

"I'm not some juvenile delinquent runaway, if that's what you're worried about," he lied.

If the driver picked up that cell phone fastened to the dash and called the cops, he'd be busted. Not that it'd do any good. They could drag his ass back to Florida, but he'd just run again. And again.

The driver didn't answer right away. Every nerve ending in Josh's body jangled as he plucked an empty Coke can from the cup holder on the dash and spat a huge stream of brown tobacco juice into it. "Don't much like the law," he said finally. He reached behind him and pulled a waxed Krispy Kreme bag from the sleeper. "You like doughnuts?"

"Who doesn't?"

The taste of the sugar-glazed fried dough nearly made Josh burst out bawling. Exhausted, he leaned his head against the window and watched the wipers sweeping the rain from the windshield. As the lonely sound of a train whistle wailed somewhere out in the heavy fog, he almost allowed himself to relax.

Nate was up on a ladder, ripping away some water-stained drywall, when she entered the sheriff's office. His built-in female radar detector had never failed him, and it didn't this evening. He glanced back over his shoulder at Regan Hart standing in the doorway of the former storage room.

Raindrops sparkled like diamonds in her sleek hair. She was wearing black jeans, sneakers, and a black Lakers jacket.

"I didn't expect to see you here," she said. No hello, nice to see you again, what a lovely little town you have.

"I was doin' a little work on the place."

"I came to see the sheriff. There wasn't anyone in the outer office." Her tone suggested she didn't approve.

"We're still looking for a sheriff. Mrs. Bernhard, she's

the dispatcher, doesn't work after five. Her husband likes his supper on the table right on the dot, so he can eat it along with WATC's six-o'clock news." As he looked down into thickly fringed whiskey-colored eyes, Nate felt a familiar, enjoyable pull. "I never have figured that out, since it seems watching all that war, politics, and crime'd ruin anyone's appetite, but that's the way Emil likes it. And after fifty years of marriage, Ruby says it's too hard to teach her old man new tricks."

"The town doesn't have a night dispatcher?"

"Nope." She clearly did not approve. Nate shoved the claw hammer back into the loop on his tool belt, wondering how she could remind him so much of his big brother and still have him wanting to nip at that stubborn chin.

"What happens when a crime happens at night?"

"It rings into Henri Petrie's house. He's the senior ranking deputy. Mostly the only after-hours trouble happens at the No Name—that's a bar outside of town—or the Mud Dog, another local watering hole about a mile away from the No Name. Since Henri spends most every evenin' but Sunday at the Mud Dog playing bouree— that's a card game sorta between poker and bridge—he's usually already on the scene if trouble does break out."

He climbed down the ladder and noted her slight step back. Not only was she into control, she liked to be the one setting boundaries. Which wickedly made him want to press hers a little more.

"Though he's been complaining that being on call all the time is cuttin' down on his socializing, being as how he can't get drunk anymore, just in case something does come up."

"He wouldn't be the first cop to drink on duty."

"Probably true. But so long as I'm mayor, I'd just as soon he not." He saw the flash of skepticism in her eyes. "You're surprised."

"I suppose, if I'd given it any thought, I would've expected you to be a bit more laid-back when it came to law-and-order issues."

"Stick around a while, Detective *Chère*, and you'll discover I'm just full of surprises."

He could smell the rain on her hair. Accustomed to women who seemed to bathe in heady perfumes custom-blended in New Orleans, he'd never realized he could find the fragrance of rain and Ivory soap so appealing. Underlying the clean aroma was her own scent, which reminded him of those citrus candles his *maman* used to like, blended with freshly cut spring grass.

"It's real nice if you can have a job you enjoy, but that doesn't mean that everyone should go mixin' work and play. Especially when their job involves guns," he said with a slow smile that more than one woman had told him was irresistible.

Apparently they'd been wrong. Or, more likely, she was just a harder case than the average woman.

"But you do," she guessed with what appeared to be yet more disapproval. "Mix work and play."

Christ, the woman could be a hardass. Though, he thought, remembering how she'd looked marching away from him in that L.A. parking garage, as asses went, it was still a pretty fine one.

"Like I said, it's nice to have a job you enjoy. As for the drinking-on-duty rule, it's hard enough for the parish to make its liability insurance payments now. The last thing we need is a lawsuit from some city slicker who came down here to let off a little steam and got himself thrown into jail on a drunk and disorderly by a cop with whiskey on his breath."

"And you people prefer to handle things yourselves and leave outsiders . . . well, outside."

"That's pretty much the way it's always been down here," he said agreeably. If he didn't suspect that the weeks since he'd dropped his bombshell had been pretty damn tough on her, he might have let her know flat-out that he wasn't real thrilled with the way she seemed to be looking down not just on him, but on Blue Bayou as well. "How much do you know about the Cajuns?"

"I know who Paul Prudhomme is. And that I like Cajun food, and they have a reputation for partying."

"*Laissez le bon temps rouler.* That's the name of a song: 'Let the Good Times Roll.'" If her attitude so far had been any indication, he suspected it'd been one helluva long time since she'd *roulered* any *bon temps*. "It's pretty much a motto down here."

Nate wondered what it would take to get that cool, faintly sarcastic mouth to soften. He'd never kissed a cop before. The closest he'd come had been Jenna Jermain, a reporter who worked the police beat up in Ascension Parish. They'd passed a few good times before she'd landed herself a job on the *Houston Chronicle*.

"I read the journal," she said.

"I was hoping you would." He took another two steps forward; she held her ground. "So, you've come to Blue Bayou to track down some loose ends." Forward.

She didn't budge. The challenge was swirling in the air between them. "That's very perceptive."

"It's what Finn'd do." Forward. He felt a little tinge of victory when she finally retreated half a step.

"It's undoubtedly also what your father would have done, if he'd had the opportunity."

"Yeah." Her long legs, which seemed to go all the way up to her neck, were now pressed against the desk. *Don't like bein' boxed in, do you, sugar?* "He was a good man, my father. And a damn good cop."

"I suppose, never having met him, I'll have to take your word for that."

The little dig managed to get under Nate's skin and remind him that she hadn't come here to give a pleasant boost to his libido. Now that he'd gotten her attention, things could only get complicated, and he'd never liked complications. Which was why he still couldn't quite explain why the hell he'd put himself into the middle of this long-ago story and tracked down Linda Dale's daughter.

"Dad didn't believe the autopsy report," he revealed.

Although her expression didn't change, Nate thought she went a little pale.

"You have the autopsy report?" She sounded more pissed than shaken.

"Yeah." The look she shot him was way too familiar. Finn, who'd taken on the role of man of the house after their father had been blown away, hadn't let either of his brothers get away with much, and Nate had been on the receiving end of it too many times to count.

"And you didn't think that was important enough to share with me?"

"I wasn't even one hundred percent positive that you were the right woman." This time he was the one who took a step back.

"Yet you were sure enough to give me some of the papers."

He swore inwardly. "Not the ones that'd be real rough to read."

"And you felt it your job to protect my so-called delicate female sensibilities why?"

"It wasn' that way." Not exactly. "The autopsy report was an official crime document. The journal was a different matter. Jack and I figured that if our *maman* had died without us ever knowin' about her, and she'd left something like that behind, we'd want to read it."

"Did you?"

"Did I what?"

"Read it?"

"Hell, no. It wasn't any of my business."

Her eyes narrowed, studying him like he was some murder suspect in a lineup. "But you read the autopsy report."

"It was an official document. I'm a city official, so I figured I was entitled. The journal's personal."

"Yet your father obviously kept it for a reason."

"He didn't know where Linda Dale's sister took off to. And knowin' him, he probably wanted to keep it as evidence."

"In the event he reopened the case."

"Yeah. His notes, by the way, say he tried."

"As a rule, small-town police forces aren't equipped to handle a homicide."

"I 'magine that's the case. But Pop wasn't just some

small-town, gut-over-his-shirt hack sheriff. He'd been a homicide cop up in Chicago and had a drawer full of awards."

"Most cops hang them on the wall."

"Dad never believed in skatin' on past accomplishments. He probably wouldn't have even kept the commendations and stuff if they hadn't meant a lot to *maman*. She'd always show them off to any of her relatives who'd badmouth her Yankee husband. After a while, they just shut up."

"Why, if he'd been working for a big force like Chicago, would he want to give it all up and come live in this . . ."

"Backwater hick town?" he supplied.

"It seems it would be a step down. Careerwise."

"Jake Callahan loved bein' a cop. Used to say he was born to the job. But his family was the most important thing in his life. *Maman* was homesick, and he figured Blue Bayou would be a nice safe place to raise his children. But I don' think it could have been easy on him in the beginning. From the stories he used to tell, he'd liked being a big-city cop, and I think the jury stayed out for a long time among the people here as to whether he was really going to try to fit in."

"Did he?"

"*Mais* yeah. He taught us boys that man was put on earth to help out his fellow man and to be part of a community, and that bein' a cop meant taking care of a community, and how organizing a youth baseball league, or taking an elderly widow a hot meal, or changing a tire on a pregnant young mother's car could all be, in their own way, just as helpful as rounding up stone-cold killers."

"Your father sounds like a good man."

"My father was a great man."

Her gaze shifted from his face, out the window to where the cobblestone streets wore a satiny sheen from an earlier rain and the sunset looked like red-and-purple smoke against the western sky. "What was the cause of death cited on the autopsy report?"

"Same as the death certificate," he hedged, even though he knew she was about to find out the answer herself. "Carbon monoxide poisoning."

She returned her gaze to him. "Was it listed as a natural death?"

Nate could tell that she had a lot more invested emotionally into the answer than she was letting on. He supposed cops, especially homicide detectives, grew used to death, but he also knew firsthand that the death of a parent was an entirely different thing. It was more personal. Even, he suspected, if you were talking about a mother or father you'd never known. Maybe Jack had been right; maybe he just should have left well enough alone and tossed the damn file into the trash.

"*Non*. It wasn't natural."

"That leaves either suicide or murder."

Jesus, did the woman have ice water in her veins? The only outward sign that he'd managed to score a direct hit was a quick blink of the eye. A train whistle sounded at the crossing just outside town. "The coroner opted for suicide."

Wishing that either of his brothers were around to handle this, Nate reached into the top desk drawer where he'd stashed the file, suspecting that if nothing else, her cop curiosity would eventually make her want to read it.

"Your father's not alone. Because I don't believe it, either. I'm going to want to see the house where she died."

"Now, there's going to be a little problem with that."

"Oh?"

"It got blown to pieces in a hurricane back in the nineties, and the land where it used to sit is now water."

"It figures." She shook her head and frowned as she read the top page with absolute concentration.

Nate was idly wondering if she'd give the same attention to sex when a sound like a bomb going off shook the building.

9

What the hell?" He jerked his gaze from those tempting, unpainted lips to the window. "That sounded too close to be a rig explosion."

The oil rigs out in the Gulf had always been a hazard; his maternal grandfather had died on one before any of the three Callahan boys had been born. A cloud of smoke billowed over the top of the courthouse.

"Christ. It's coming from the tracks."

He turned back toward Regan. "You remember any first aid from your patrol days?"

"I passed a disaster response test six weeks ago."

"Good. Because we're gonna be needin' all the help we can get." He opened a desk drawer and threw her a badge.

"I don't need that," she said, even as she snagged the shiny sheriff's badge out of the air.

"Stuff like this tends to brings out the lookie-loos and

Good Samaritans. There are going to be a lot of people getting in the way out there. This'll give you the authority to get rid of folks who don't belong or can't be of any real help."

Again proving that he could move damn fast when the occasion called for it, he was out the door like a shot, Regan right on his heels. Without waiting to be invited, she jumped into the passenger seat of the black SUV parked outside and pinned on the badge. It took them less than three minutes to drive to the redbrick fire station where Blue Bayou's fire and rescue department garaged its only pumper truck.

"There's not gonna be room for you in the truck." He was yanking on a pair of tobacco brown fireproof pants that had been folded down with tall rubber boots already inside them, so all he had to do was step into the boots and pull the pants up. "The keys are in the SUV." He grabbed a heavy coat and helmet. "I'll meet you out at the crossing."

Unlike the other narrow towns she'd driven past, which she'd supposed had sprung up in long narrow strips to save valuable waterfront land for crops, Blue Bayou had been laid out in grids. Sweeps of sunshine-bright yellow daffodils brightened squares fenced in fancifully curved wrought-iron fences, and trees lined the clean brick sidewalks. It appeared, as Nate Callahan had described it, a peaceful town.

There was nothing peaceful about the scene at the rail crossing. At least a dozen freight cars left a zigzagging trail along the muddy banks of the bayou. Broken railroad ties were scattered along the track, the metal rails shredded. On the far side of the track, a trailer from an eighteen-wheeler was on its side; farther down the other trailer was crushed and mangled, mute evidence that the semi had been hit trying to cross the track. The cab was upside down, the roof resting inches from the edge of the water; the glass lying on the ground had once been a windshield. It could have been worse. A lot worse.

"Thank God it was a freight," Nate said.

Regan nodded in agreement, not even wanting to think about the number of deaths and injuries there could have been if the railroad cars had been carrying passengers.

"I thought my furnace had blowed up," she heard one onlooker, who appeared to be at least in his eighties, say to another man. "I heard a bunch of grinding and then *boom*," he said. "Ol' Duke jumped clean off the *gallerie* and started barking." He pointed toward an old hound dog who was sniffing the air.

One of the train cars had knocked a utility pole down; its lines were tangled in a tall, moss-draped oak and sagged about ten feet above the top of the truck's cab. Sparks were flying, and as tree limbs burned, the lines drooped lower toward the cab.

"The driver's still in the truck," someone shouted. "There's an arm hangin' out the window."

"Can you tell if he's alive?" a fireman, whose helmet designated him as the fire chief, asked.

"He's not movin'."

"Christ," another fireman said. "There's no way to get the poor sucker out."

"We can't just stand by and let him die," Nate said.

"Can't run onto an accident scene with downed power

lines, either," the chief said. "That's one of the first things they teach you in fire school."

A pair of state troopers arrived, sirens blaring, adding to the din. Walkie-talkies squawked. A crowd began to gather, as if to watch a Hollywood crew film a disaster-of-the-week movie.

"He's gotta have family," Nate argued doggedly, once again reminding Regan of his brother. Finn hadn't been one to back down from an argument, either; not when there was a matter of principal involved. "Mother, maybe. Wife. Kids." He pulled on his gloves. "I'm going in."

"You realize, of course, that truck could catch on fire any time," Regan said. Okay, so it was a pretty impressive gesture; it was also foolhardy as hell.

"One more reason to get the guy out. But I've probably got some time, since diesel fuel isn't as flammable as gasoline."

She knew that, but the knowledge didn't stop her from holding her breath as he cautiously ducked beneath the sagging wires. An odd hush came over the rescue workers as he dropped down on his belly and crawled the last eight feet.

"Hey," a voice called out from inside the cab. "We're trapped in here!"

Regan sucked in a sharp breath at the child's voice. Watching carefully, she actually saw Nate's shoulders tense beneath the heavy jacket.

"It's gonna be all right, *cher*," he said matter-of-factly, as if train-truck collisions were an everyday occurrence in Blue Bayou. Metal screeched as the dented truck cab shifted, tilting precariously closer to the water.

"Shit, we're gonna drown!" the boy shouted.

"Don' you worry," Nate said again, his voice as calm as it'd been when she'd first met him in the station. "We'll be gettin' you out soon enough, you."

He yanked on the door. Nothing. "Shit, it's stuck."

"Can't use the Hurst," the captain pointed out. The Hurst, more commonly known as the Jaws of Life, could chew up metal like taffy. "You try takin' that roof off, you'll hit those wires for sure."

"How about goin' up from the floor?" another asked.

Nate shook his head. "We're sittin' on marsh, here. Even if we set it on blocks, they'd just sink into water. Then there's the little matter of starting up the gas unit while diesel's leaking from the tank."

He yanked again. Cursed again.

Nearby, another tree limb burst into flame as the power surged. The wires drooped even lower, nearing the upturned wheels.

"Anyone got a tow strap?" Nate called.

"I got a cable I use for towing breakdowns in the trunk of the cruiser," a trooper responded.

"That'll do. Go get it and bring it as close as you can." Once again Regan heard him talking in a low, soothing voice to the child inside the truck. "And Henri, why don't you back the ladder truck as near as you can get without hittin' those wires?" Which were currently lighting up the gathering twilight like Fourth of July sparklers. "And can someone toss me—very carefully—a blanket?"

Without giving it a moment's thought, Regan grabbed an army green blanket from a newly arrived ambulance and moved slowly, step by step, toward the cab.

"That's far enough, *chère*," he warned.

"If I throw it to you, it could hit the wires."

"If you get any closer, those wires could turn you into a crispy critter."

"Don't you watch TV? We cops get off on taking risks."

Though her voice was as calm as if she were writing out a speeding ticket, her nerves were jangling with adrenaline.

"That a fact?" Amazingly, his tone was as conversational as hers.

"Absolutely." The overhead wires crackled and sagged. Ignoring his warning, Regan bent lower until she was nearly doubled, and continued inching toward the truck. "Why, a day without danger is like a day without chocolate." Despite the chill, sweat was beating up on her forehead and between her breasts.

"I never heard it put quite that way before."

"Believe me, it's true." She shoved the blanket toward him. "It's in our blood."

"Thanks." He carefully pushed the blanket through the rectangular hole where the windshield used to be. "Hey, kid."

"Yeah?" The boy's tone sounded remarkably defiant, but Regan knew some people responded to fear with aggression.

"Put this over the driver as well as you can, okay? Then hunker down beneath it, because we're gonna have some flying glass in a minute."

Nate waited a moment for the boy to do as instructed. Then he shoved his gloved fingers through a hole in the driver's side window and tore the glass away. By now the trooper had arrived with the cable; the two men wrapped one end of it around the windshield post and the other around the bumper of the fire truck, which began slowly moving forward.

There was an ominous sound of groaning metal, and the cab tilted a bit, as if it might pull right side up. Just when Regan thought for sure they'd land in the water, the door broke off its hinges.

"Hey," Nate said, again to someone in the truck. "Good to have you back with us. Is anything broken?" There was a pause, then a mumbled response in a voice far deeper than the boy's.

"*Bien*. Now, here's what we're gonna do. You take my arm and climb out of here, real careful like, so you don't rock the cab. And I'll grab the kid."

A huge bearded man with the look of a renegade biker appeared in the open door and half jumped, half fell from the cab. Regan flinched inwardly when she heard the crack of a kneecap breaking, but the driver didn't have any time to indulge his pain.

The wires let loose, draping over the cab like Spanish moss just as Nate reached inside, grabbed the boy's denim jacket, and jerked him from the truck. They'd no sooner rolled aside when the cab burst into flames.

A collective cheer went up.

"Thanks, man," the grizzled driver groaned as a paramedic slipped a C-collar around his neck and strapped him onto a rolling half-backboard to protect his spine. "Weren't for you, my old lady'd be puttin' plastic flowers on my grave."

"Jus' doin' my job, *cher*," Nate said agreeably. "Wouldn't want you to get a bad impression of our little town." He put the boy onto his feet. "We'll be taking you into the hospital, too. Just to make sure."

Freckles were standing out like copper coins all over the kid's pale, thin face, but his brown eyes, as he folded his arms, were resolute. "Fuck that. I'm fine."

"Sure you are," Nate said in that mild, deceptively laid-back tone. "Problem is, I've heard of folks saying the same thing at accidents, then passing out without any warning. Wouldn't want to take a chance on you falling into the water and becoming gator bait."

"I'm not scared of any damn gators."

Regan wasn't sure if he was exaggerating or not. But having watched a special on alligators on the Nature Channel, she was uneasy about putting it to the test. Gangbangers she could handle, drug dealers she knew. But there weren't a lot of man-eating reptiles in the normally dry Los Angeles River.

"This your kid?" a paramedic asked the truck driver.

"I just picked him up." He looked decidedly defensive. Regan hoped it was only because he was worried about having violated the No Riders sign. "No law against giving people a ride. 'Specially when it's cold enough to freeze a well digger's ass and getting dark, besides."

"You have to wonder why a grown man was traveling with a child who isn't his own," Regan murmured.

"I was already there." Nate's serious expression revealed he shared her concern. He might not be a cop, and Blue Bayou might look like Louisiana's version of Mayberry, but obviously he'd picked up some sense of the dark side of the world from his brothers' work.

"If I were you, I'd have one of my deputies question him."

"Great minds think alike. Fortunately, I've got an officer capable of doing a bang-up job." He put his hand on her back in a possessive, masculine way that annoyed her. "Since the fog's really startin' to roll in and you don't know the way to the hospital, I'll drive you there."

She shook off the light touch. "Me?"

"You're the most qualified member of the force."

"Force? What force? This isn't my jurisdiction."

"Sure it is. I deputized you."

"Dammit, Callahan, this isn't the Wild West. You can't just put badges on people and make them part of your posse."

"I can, and I did." His expression sobered. "This needs to be done right. There's no way I'm going to put Dwayne on it. As for Henri, he's always tried real hard and done a good enough job, but Blue Bayou doesn't present a lot of opportunities to use real police skills, so even if he ever possessed any, they'd be real rusty about now."

"I didn't come to Louisiana to apply for a job. I already have one back in L.A."

"Where I'll bet you take protectin' kids real seriously." His gaze moved to the young teenager being loaded into the back of the ambulance.

Regan counted to ten. Reminded herself that she'd sworn to protect and to serve. Her professional duty might stop once she went outside her precinct boundaries, but her moral responsibility was an entirely different thing.

"Dammit." She folded her arms even as she felt herself caving. "That's not fair."

"Life's not always fair, detective."

"Tell me something I don't know." She had proof of that every day, even before she hit the streets looking for the bad guys. All she had to do was get out of the shower and stand naked in front of a full-length mirror.

"How about I make you a deal?"

"What kind of deal?"

"You help me out with this one little thing, and I'll do all I can to help you find out the facts about Linda Dale's death."

"A thirty-one-year-old case is about as cold as they get. What makes you think you can find anything out when your father couldn't?"

"He'd probably have had better luck if your aunt hadn't disappeared."

Your aunt. Even after she had read the journal over and over again, those words still rang so false. The ambulance pulled away from the scene, lights flashing, siren wailing.

"Besides, I've lived here all my life, me," he said, his Cajun syntax backing up his words. "I know everyone in the parish, which'll come in handy, since folks around here aren't real eager to answer questions from strangers."

"Small-town paranoia," she muttered.

"There you go, jumpin' to conclusions again. We tend to think of it as mindin' our own business. Now, I can understand why you won't do it for me, or even because, being an independent woman, you don't want any help digging up the truth 'bout your *maman*'s death. But I'm having a real hard time believing that cop who just risked her life for a kid won't want to do whatever she can to find out why that kid isn't sitting at home playing video games like he should be."

It was emotional blackmail, pure and simple. It also worked. "You really are shameless."

"You're not the first person to tell me that, sugar. But that's not the point here. That boy's puttin' on a good enough show, but beneath the surface, he reminds me of a whupped pup. I'd put hard money on the fact that he had a pretty good reason for running away."

"Hell. All right." She blew out a breath. "I'll do it."

"Merci bien."

They drove together through the night, the headlights bouncing back against a dense wall of fog that surrounded the SUV, cutting them off from the outside world. Regan was grateful he was driving; she wasn't sure she could have told road from water.

"I suppose, having grown up here, you know your way around." She certainly hoped he did. She was in no mood for a moonlight swim.

"Mais yeah, though it's always changing." He leaned forward and punched on the radio, which was tuned to a station playing what seemed to be a sad song in French. "What was water yesterday could be land today. And vice versa."

"Then how do you know for certain where you're going?"

"Never gave it any thought." He seemed to now. "Guess it's just instinct. Like a homing pigeon returning to his loft. Once the bayou gets in your blood, I don't think you could ever get it out. Even if you wanted to."

"Which you don't."

"Non. Roots sink deep here. Sometimes I think 'bout taking off and exploring the world, but the truth is, mostly I'm pretty satisfied doing what I'm doin', where I'm doin' it."

Regan wondered how it would feel to be so at ease

with yourself. So comfortable with your world and your place in it. As long as she could remember, she'd always pushed herself harder and harder, trying to please a mother who'd always been incapable of being pleased.

The police shrink she'd gone to, a bearded guy who seemed to be doing his best to look like Freud's twin—which made her wonder about his own identity problems—had suggested that it wasn't the ambush or the resultant injuries and lengthy recovery that had left her feeling constantly edgy and unable to sleep.

She was, he'd diagnosed, suffering from the impossible need to prove her worth not only to her remote, perfectionist mother, but also to the larger-than-life father she'd never known. The man who'd died a hero's death in a jungle halfway around the world.

"Which is, of course," the Freud wannabe had added, "impossible."

Perhaps. On one level, Regan understood that. She had, after all, minored in psychology in college. But on a deeper, more intrinsically personal level, she couldn't stop trying.

"That was a remarkable thing you did," she murmured. "Going in under those high-voltage wires."

"I wasn't alone. You were right there with me."

"Like I said, it's my job. Cops get paid to do stuff like that. I wouldn't think risking your life came under the job description of mayor."

He shrugged. "I wouldn't be able to live with myself if I hadn't tried to get him out of there. I lost my dad when I was twelve. The trucker's kids are going to have theirs. That's all that counts."

"It was still a brave thing to do."

The grin he flashed her was quick and devastating. And dangerous. His eyes, surrounded by soot and dirt, gleamed in the glow from the dashboard like the blue lights atop a police cruiser. "Don' tell me you just found something about me you can approve of?"

"Don't let it go to your head."

"I wouldn't think of it." They'd driven in silence for about five more minutes when he said, "You're probably used to all that."

"Guys with big heads?"

"No. Well, maybe you run into them from time to time, bein' how you live in L.A. But I was talking about wrecks, flashing lights, sirens. Injuries. Death."

"Detectives don't, as a rule, handle car wrecks unless there's evidence of a homicide." She'd thought about death, though. A lot. Her first week on the job, she'd spent hours on the phone after a shift trying to find a shelter and counseling for a woman who'd called 911 for a domestic abuse, then refused, despite two black eyes and a missing tooth, to press charges against her husband. A veteran cop had warned her against becoming too emotionally involved.

"Gotta hold back, Hart," he'd growled around a Reuben sandwich dripping sauerkraut. "The taxpayers of L.A. aren't paying you to hold people's hands and play counselor. If you want to be a social worker, then turn in your sidearm and go for it, because you're not going to be able to keep a cool head and maintain the judgment needed to do this job if you're too damn sensitive."

Easy for him to say. One of the reasons she'd gone into homicide was because she'd figured that if she switched to dealing with bodies, she'd be able to distance herself emotionally from her work. She'd been wrong. The dead often spoke a lot louder than the living. And they didn't stop just because she'd gone to sleep.

"I don't think anyone ever gets used to death." She wouldn't want to.

"Yeah." He pulled up in front of a redbrick building. "I read that in Jack's last book."

"That happens to be a yellow line you're parking by."

"I know." He cut the engine, pocketed the keys, took a placard reading "On Duty" from the center console, and tossed it onto the dash. She'd done it herself numerous times. Still . . .

"And the sign says it's reserved for police vehicles." At least he hadn't parked in the red ambulance zone.

"Then we're in luck, bein' how we're the police," he said reasonably. "At least one half of us is. The other half's fire, so I'd guess we have a right to park just 'bout anywhere we like."

"So how many tickets did you get before you were elected and able to award yourself the privilege of political office?" she asked as she climbed out of the SUV.

"I still get 'em. Blue Bayou runs on too tight a budget to let parking infractions slide." He opened the center console to reveal stacks of yellow slips of paper. "I save 'em up and pay 'em every month or so."

"Wouldn't it be simpler—and cheaper—to just park legally?"

"I suppose it would be. But just think of all the revenue the town'd be missing."

He'd placed his hand on her back again, in that casual way that suggested he was a toucher. Yet another way he was different from his brother; Finn had kept a privacy zone the size of Jupiter around himself. Regan suspected his new bride must really be something to have gotten past that man's emotional barricades.

"Besides, writing out tickets gives Dwayne something constructive to do during the slow times. He's one of our two deputies. Graduated from LSU last summer with a degree in criminal justice, and I think we're coming as a big disappointment. Sometimes I feel like I oughta pay some kids to go out and bash in mailboxes just so he'll have a crime to investigate."

If it were anyone else, Regan might have taken his words as a joke. Since she hadn't yet been able to get a handle on Nate Callahan, she wasn't at all certain he was kidding.

10

The door whooshed open automatically. The smell of disinfectant, blood, and stress sweat was like a fist in the stomach.

Regan hated hospitals. After her accident, when she'd been extricated from the crumbled mass of metal that had once been her police cruiser, she'd spent two weeks in ICU, another month on the surgical recovery floor, and weeks and weeks over the next two years undergoing reconstructive surgery and rehabilitation.

"You okay, *chère?*"

She hadn't realized she'd stopped walking until he'd turned around. "Of course." She had to remain calm. To think like a cop, instead of a victim. "Why wouldn't I be?"

"Now see, that's what I don' know." He laced their fingers together and skimmed his thumb against her palm. "Your hand's like ice."

"Because I'm freezing." She tugged her hand free. "I thought Louisiana was supposed to be warm."

"We have ourselves some cold spells in winter. It's the moisture that makes it seem colder than it really is; it seeps down deep into your bones." He brushed the back of his fingers up her cheek. "That's good."

"What?" She hated to keep backing away from him, but holding her ground would mean staying in too close proximity.

"Your color's comin' back. You were pale as Lafitte's ghost a minute ago."

"I was not," she lied. She'd felt the blood going out of her face as she'd gone light-headed. "I'd really like it if you'd keep your hands to yourself, Callahan."

"That's not gonna be easy, but I'll try my best."

"You do that." She resumed walking. "Who's Lafitte?"

"One of our more colorful citizens. A pirate. I'll tell you about him later, over supper."

"I ate at the airport." She hadn't wanted to waste precious time; the fast food burger she'd eaten in the terminal sat like a rock in her stomach.

"It's a good story. You'll enjoy it."

The little exchange had given her time to adjust to being back in an ER. Her legs were much steadier as she walked toward a counter where a woman sporting an enormous orange beehive was chewing on the end of a pencil.

"Hey, handsome," the receptionist greeted Nate as they approached, "what's an eleven-letter word for "having magnetism'?"

"Callahan," he answered without missing a beat.

She counted on fingers tipped in metallic purple. "Not

that I'm arguing your point, *cher*. But that's only eight letters."

"Charismatic," Regan said.

The woman filled in the crossword puzzle squares. "That's sure enough it. *Bien merci.*"

"I see the ambulance arrived," Nate said.

"It did. Truck driver's down the hall in X-ray. I figured somebody'd be wanting to talk with him, so I told the tech to take her time, so he wouldn't be able to take off for a while. Not that I imagine he'd make it far, with his truck wrecked and his leg broken the way it is. The bone's sticking clear through the skin. Must hurt like the devil."

It did, Regan thought, but did not say. A hideous memory of hearing the snap of bone flashed through her mind. "How about the boy?"

"He's in treatment room A. Lucky thing Tiny Dupree was mopping the floors when the ambulance showed up. He practically had to sit on the kid to keep him from leaving."

"Tiny's the Cajun Days crawfish-eating champion," Nate told Regan. "Probably weighs three-eighty soaking wet. So, the kid's okay?"

"He got himself some bruising across his ribs from the seat belt yanking tight, and a cut on his head, but that's all that showed up when he first came in. That's new, anyway."

"He has old wounds?" Regan asked sharply.

"*Mais oui.* He's got some old white scars that look real suspicious, if you ask me. Dr. Ancelet should be finishing up a more thorough examination any time now."

Regan wasn't surprised by any suspicious scars. Happy,

well-cared-for children did not run away from home.

"We'd like to talk with Eve when she's done checking him over," Nate said.

"Sure 'nough." Her interested gaze settled on the badge Regan was still wearing. "So, *cher*," she said, addressing her words to Nate, "I see you've finally hired us a new sheriff."

"I'm not the new sheriff." Try as she might, it was difficult not to stare at the woman's blinking red crawfish earrings.

"You're wearing a badge."

"That's just temporary, so I could help out at the train wreck."

"Terrible thing, that. If God hadn't had them in his hands . . ." The beehive bobbled a bit as she shook her head. "One thing medicine's taught me is that sometimes you're blessed with a miracle."

"Orèlia's husband was Blue Bayou's doctor just about forever," Nate explained, then introduced them fully.

The woman looked at her more closely through the rose-tinted lenses of the cat-eyed rhinestone-framed glasses. "I seem to recall my husband treating a little girl named Regan. It was a long time ago."

"Was he the only doctor in town?" She wondered if he'd signed Linda Dale's death certificate.

"*Non*. There was a new doctor, came here to work off his medical school bills through some sort of government program. He was a Yankee, from New York City, I think. Mebee Boston. Or Philadelphia. One of those northern cities. He just stayed a couple years." She nodded to herself. "He worked here at the hospital and picked up some extra money working as the parish medical examiner."

Which meant, Regan thought, that he would have been the one who wrote that death certificate.

"My Leon passed on two years ago," the woman continued, "leaving me to rattle around in our big old house where he used to have his office. For a while it wasn't too bad, what with Dani and her son Matt living with me."

"Dani's married to Jack," Nate filled in.

"And about time they finally got together, too," she said. "Well, like I was saying, Dani and Matt lived with me a while when they first came back to town, then when she moved out to live above the library for a time before marryin' Jack, her papa moved in so I could sort of keep an eye on him, bein' as how he has himself a heart condition. But he's back to work three days a week, which left me with too much time on my hands. I was going crazy, me, until Nate saved my life by fixing me up with this volunteer job."

"Orèlia exaggerates," Nate said.

"And the boy's too humble."

Regan couldn't help snorting at that.

"So, what do you do when you're not rescuing children from train wrecks?"

"I'm a detective, in L.A."

"Are you, now? Isn't that interesting?" Her appraising gaze shifted from Regan to a woman wearing dark glasses, who'd just come out of the swinging doors from the treatment rooms. "If this *fille* really isn't going to be the new sheriff, you need to send Dwayne down to the No Name and pick up Mike Chauvet," Orèlia told Nate.

"Does it have something to do with Shannon bein' here?"

"She says she ran into a door." It was Orèlia's turn to

snort. "But this is the second time in the past ten days she's shown up in the ER. The first time she had a cracked rib. Claimed she fell off her horse, and bein' as how she was sticking to the story and the injury matched the excuse, Eve Ancelet couldn't do much for her, 'cepting give her a referral card to the free counseling clinic."

"Do you know if she went?"

"She did. Which didn't go over real well with Mike when he found out she was talking about their so-called private family stuff."

"Shit. Mike always was a goddamn hothead." A temper Regan wouldn't have thought him possible of possessing licked at the edges of Nate's voice.

"And as useless as tits on a bull," Orèlia said. "Lord knows what Shannon was thinkin' when she married him. She can sure do a lot better than that, she."

"Would you mind jus' waiting here a minute?" Nate asked Regan. "While I take care of something?"

"Sure."

Regan watched as he went over to the woman and said something she couldn't hear. He pulled off her sunglasses, the same way he'd done to Regan at the airport, and shook his head at the ugly dark bruise surrounding an eye red-rimmed from crying.

Regan had seen it all too often as a beat cop: a battered wife seeks medical care, maybe goes so far as to kick her abuser out of the house. Occasionally she'd get brave enough to call the cops. But more times than she cared to count, the woman would inevitably end up taking the guy back. And the cycle of pain would begin all over again, inevitably spiraling downward, until in the worst cases, Regan would end up at the house investigating a homicide.

Obviously something Nate said struck a chord. The woman slapped him. Hard. Then, wrapping her arms around herself, she turned away.

"Anybody can talk her into escapin' a dangerous marriage, it's that boy," Orèlia, who was also watching the little drama, said. "Not many people can resist Nate Callahan once he gets an idea into his head."

"I've noticed. They seem close."

"They went together for a while in college. Back when Nate was playin' ball for Tulane. They were Blue Bayou's golden couple: the local boy headed toward a pro baseball career and the pretty, sweet prom queen who'd always wanted to be a first-grade teacher."

"Nate Callahan played professional baseball?" Not that she cared, but it did explain the easy, fluid way he moved. She was not the least bit surprised to learn he'd dated a prom queen. She suspected there were a great many cheerleaders and beauty contestants in the man's past.

"Played all the sports, he, but the big thing was his baseball scholarship. College recruiters were buzzin' around this place like bees to a honeycomb his senior year of high school. Like to drive his *maman* crazy. A lot of people who know a lot more than me about sports said he was a phenom—that's like a natural, but better, so they tell me—but then he ended up havin' to come home his freshman year."

Huh—he'd undoubtedly flunked out after too many frat parties.

Nate took the former prom queen in his arms; she

threw her arms around his neck and clung. He held her tight for a long, silent minute, then curved his hands over her shoulders and put her a little away from him. His expression was warm and caring, but determined.

Shannon Chauvet blinked against the tears that had begun streaming down her face. Bit her lip. Then nodded.

Regan saw not a hint of seduction in his smile as he skimmed a knuckle up one of her badly bruised cheekbones, then dropped a quick kiss on her lips.

"Call Jack," he said to Orèlia when he returned to the counter. "Ask him to come get Shannon so she and Ben can stay at Beau Soleil for a while. Then call the state police and ask for Trooper Benoit. Tell him you're calling for me, explain the situation, and tell him that I'm claiming that favor he owes me."

"Good idea." She reached for the phone.

"Harboring abused wives can be dangerous," Regan said. Violent husbands were often at their most volatile when the women finally got up the nerve to leave. "Shouldn't you have asked your brother if he wanted to take her in?"

"Jack won't mind. He and Shannon had a little bit of a thing back when they were kids, before Jack fell heart over heels for Dani. They stayed friends."

Both brothers had dated her? "Definitely a friendly town you have here," she said dryly.

"I told you it was," he reminded her, ignoring the dash of sarcasm.

"Jack may not mind, but what about his wife? Surely she won't feel comfortable with one of his ex-girlfriends sleeping in her house."

"Dani's got a heart as big as all outdoors," Orèlia offered.

"The important thing is to get her somewhere safe before she gets seriously hurt, or Ben, her fifteen-year-old son, gets hurt trying to protect her. Besides, Jack's thing for Shannon ended long before he and Dani hooked up," Nate said. "Since he gave his heart to Dani, he's become a born-again monogamist. She doesn't have anything to worry about."

"It looks as if you and Shannon stayed real good friends after your *thing*, too."

His eyes filled with humor. "Aren't you supposed to read me my rights about anything I say being used against me before you ask a leading question like that, detective?"

"Skip it." Disgusted with herself for asking, Regan gave him a withering look. "It's not germane to the situation."

"Germane." He chuckled and rocked back on his heels. "Damned if you aren't reminding me more and more of Finn, which tends to get a little distracting, since you sure smell a whole lot better."

He skimmed a finger down her nose.

"I believe we were talking about your brother Jack." That treacherous finger was now trailing around the line of her jaw. She batted at his hand. "And would you *please* stop touching me."

"Sorry. You had a little smudge of dirt on your face." He dipped his hands into the back pockets of his jeans. "And touchin' is jus' one of those natural things I do without thinking. Most women don't seem to mind."

"Maybe they just don't tell you they don't like it."

"Maybe." He considered that possibility. "But I don't think so. Women down here might have a reputation north of the Mason-Dixon line for being too accommodating, and I suppose, on occasion, some might be. But I've never met one yet who won't let a man know when she's not happy. We southern men are very well trained."

"What a sterling testimony to southern womanhood. Scarlett O'Hara would be so pleased."

"You've got a sassy mouth on you, Detective Delectable. Good thing I always preferred Scarlett over Melanie. As for Jack, the trick is going to be keeping him from cleaning Mike's clock for laying hands on Shannon. Which is why I'm having a state cop come make the arrest."

"That sounds like a sensible decision."

"Why, thank you, darlin'. I do have my moments."

The doors to the ER swung open again, and a slender woman wearing a white lab coat came out. She greeted Nate warmly, then drew back and looked at Regan. "I'm Dr. Eve Ancelet. I hear we have you and Nate to thank for saving that little boy's life."

"It's good to meet you. I'm Regan Hart, and I'm just glad I was able to help out."

"As am I." Friendly, intelligent eyes drifted to the badge. "Looks as if Nate's found the perfect person to be our new sheriff."

"I'm not the new sheriff."

"Detective Hart keeps tellin' me that she's going back to L.A. after she gets some personal business taken care of," Nate said. "I'm hoping to change her mind."

"Blue Bayou would be quite a change from Los Angeles." The doctor's gaze turned professional, and Regan knew her expert eye was taking in the faint tracing of scars.

"I suppose it would be," Regan replied equably.

"How's the kid doin'?" Nate asked.

"Fairly well, considering what he's been through. He's a little underweight, but I have no way of knowing whether or not that's a longtime problem, or something that's occurred recently during his time on the road."

"Did he tell you how long that's been?" Nate asked.

"He's claiming he doesn't remember anything prior to the accident, which could be valid, since retrograde amnesia certainly isn't unheard of after a blow to the head or even some traumatic incidents. But it's my guess he's attempting to avoid getting sent back home."

"Did the exam show any sign of abuse?" Regan asked.

"Several, actually."

Every muscle in Regan's body tensed. "What kind?"

"Small white circular scars over his back and chest."

Unfortunately, Regan had seen those before. "Cigarette burns."

The doctor nodded.

"Christ," Nate breathed, "that's out and out torture. What kind of person would do anything like that to a kid?"

"A monster," Regan said grimly. "What else?" she asked the doctor.

"Some longer, narrower scars across his buttocks. I'd say they'd been made with a belt or some sort of strap."

Nate looked as sick as Regan felt. All these years on the job but she'd never get used to the idea of anyone purposefully harming a child.

"What about sexual abuse?"

"There were no physical signs."

"Well, that's good news," Nate said.

"Not all abuse leaves evidence," Regan pointed out. Personally, she didn't have a very optimistic view in this case.

"True," Doctor Ancelet agreed. "And he's so close-mouthed, it's hard to tell what he's running from. But he claimed all the truck driver did was give him a ride. I spoke with the driver, who didn't appear to fit any profile."

"Do you have experience with abuse profiling?"

"Actually, I do. Before I went into family practice, I was in a residency program specializing in the treatment of both abused children and their abusers, who, with the exception of sexual abuse, are often merely people who never learned parenting skills."

"Even if the driver's not a pedophile, he's still guilty of breaking regulations against taking on passengers," Regan insisted. "He could also possibly be charged with criminal recklessness at the crossing."

"The troopers are handling that, since the accident was on a state highway," Nate said. "The state cops will probably also question him about the kid. But meanwhile, we don't even know the accident was his fault. It was awfully foggy."

"I heard the whistle from your office. He should have heard it from the tracks."

"Maybe he made a major mistake. But you've got to give the guy credit for being a Good Samaritan by picking up the kid. What was he supposed to do, leave the boy alone out there and freezing?"

"He had to know he was a runaway," Regan argued

doggedly. "He should have called the cops." She turned back to Eve. "I don't suppose the kid told you where he's from, either."

"No." The doctor shook her head. "I'm afraid his so-called amnesia struck again. I have a call in to the Department of Social Services. Hopefully once they get him temporarily settled somewhere, he might begin to open up."

When they entered the treatment room, the teen was sitting atop the metal examining table, clad in thread-bare jeans and an Ozzie Osbourne T-shirt. A huge man wearing navy blue coveralls and a custodian's name tag stood at the doorway, arms like tree trunks folded across his mighty chest. His speckled face, which appeared per-petually sunburned, was set in a forbidding scowl. Regan doubted many people would want to test him.

"How are you doing?" Regan asked the teenager after Nate had introduced her to the misnamed Tiny Dupree.

"Fine. Or I will be when I get the hell out of here."

"Hospitals aren't the most fun places," she agreed. "Just tell us where you're from, and we'll call and have some-one come get you. You can be back home by morning."

His face and eyes hardened. "I already told the doc I don't remember."

"Well, I'm sure we'll be able to help you with that," she reassured him in her best Good Cop voice. "Have you ever heard of NOMEC?"

Those hard young eyes narrowed suspiciously. "No."

"It stands for the National Center for Missing and Exploited Children. It lists every child reported missing in America. I'm sure it won't take any time at all to find out who you are."

He met her mild look with a level one of his own. She'd seen that expression on the faces of kids who'd grown up in dangerous, violent homes. He wasn't the least bit afraid of the badge she'd pinned to her shirt. In fact, he seemed to be daring her to do her best.

"Cool. 'Cause it's a real bitch not knowing who I am."

"Well now," Nate entered the conversation. "I've got myself an idea. How 'bout you and me go get a bite of supper? I haven't eaten since noon, and after all that happened out at the crash site, I've got a powerful hunger."

"May I speak with you out in the hall, mayor?" Regan asked on a frosty tone.

"Sure." He squeezed the kid's too-thin shoulder. "We'll be right back."

"Like I care."

Regan turned on Nate the moment they left the room. "You dragged me into this, Callahan. So would you care to explain why you felt the need to interrupt my questioning?"

"I thought he might find it easier to talk to me."

"Because you're a man? I'm not surprised you'd take a chauvinistic view of the problem."

"I wasn't thinking about the man/woman thing." When his finger skimmed over the badge she'd yet to take off, Regan could have sworn the metal heated. "Given his situation, he might not feel all that comfortable with a police officer."

They were wasting time. As relieved as she was that they'd been able to get the driver and kid out of the truck, she hadn't come here to take part in any rescue operation. She certainly hadn't wanted to get involved with an uncooperative runaway. What she wanted, dammit, was to find out some facts about the woman who could very well be her birth mother.

Unfortunately, until this situation was taken care of, she wasn't going to have Nate Callahan's help. Only a few hours ago she wouldn't have thought she'd needed it, but having watched him in action, she realized that he could be an asset. Not only did he seem to know everyone in town, he also possessed some sort of aura, as if he was sending out brain-altering vibes that made everyone do exactly what he wanted.

No wonder he'd been elected mayor. Regan was just grateful he'd chosen to use that personality trait for politics, because if he'd decided to be a con man, he probably would have been a crackerjack one.

"Well?" Nate asked.

"You've got a point," she allowed. "But if he starts saying anything that could implicate anyone in a crime—"

"I promise I'll shut my mouth and save any further questioning for you so I don't mess up a court case."

It wasn't a bad solution. And right now it was the best they had. "Okay. Then let's get this show on the road."

She still didn't quite trust Nate Callahan, but didn't see that she had much choice. The thought of Dwayne the parking-ticket-writer tackling such sensitive questioning wasn't at all appealing.

11

The cafeteria was small and designed to cater more to staff than to family members of patients. Since it was past visiting hours, most of the Formica tables were empty. Someone was making French fries. The smell made Josh's mouth water.

The guy who'd dragged him out of the truck handed him a tray, then picked one up for himself. "You ever have crawfish étouffée?"

"Hell, no. Crawfish look like bugs. Who'd want to eat a bug?"

"They may not be real pretty. And you're right about them looking kinda buglike, which I guess is how they got the name mud bugs. But they sure taste good."

"I'd rather have a burger." His stomach growled at the thought of a huge hunk of ground beef dripping with mayo.

"One burger, coming up," the woman wearing a hair

net and white apron standing behind the open pans of food said. "What you want on that, *cher?*"

"Everything."

"You know," Nate said, "I think I'll have a burger, too. But hold the onions." He shot Josh a grin. "Never know when you might have the chance to kiss a pretty girl."

"Like that cop?"

"Detective Hart?"

"Yeah. You got something going with the bitch? Like are you shacked up together or something?"

"Contrary to what you may hear on the radio these days, life's not a rap song," Nate said mildly. "Why don't you try calling her a lady?"

"What kinda lady packs heat?"

"An interesting one. And we're not shacked up together or anything. What gave you the idea that we were?"

"Don't know." He shrugged, wishing he hadn't brought it up. "She's kind of okay looking. For a cop."

"She's real pretty, cop or not. And she smells good, too."

She did. But not like she'd bathed in some too-sweet stink oil, like Josh's mother's old hooker pals. He looked around. This place wasn't exactly Mickey D's, but it was sure a lot better than some of the places he'd been eating in lately. Hell, back home if you turned your back on a bologna sandwich long enough to get a can of Dr Pepper out of the refrigerator, the roaches would carry it away.

"That sure was some wreck," Nate said conversationally. "Lucky thing nobody got hurt too bad."

"Yeah." Although he couldn't admit it, he was grateful to the guy for having saved him. Not that he was sure he deserved saving.

When he'd been younger and a lot smaller, his mother had gotten arrested for drug dealing and he'd been sent to live with his grandmother, who had never let alcoholism get in the way of her old-time fire-and-brimstone religion. She used to beat him with a leather strap, trying to knock the devil out of him, and although Josh didn't really believe in God or the devil or heaven and hell, deep down inside, he wondered if maybe the reason no one had ever wanted him was because he'd been born bad.

He tried to think of one person he knew who'd risk his life for strangers and was coming up with a big fat zero when the woman slapped a white plate onto the tray. The burger had been piled high with lettuce, tomato slices, and onion.

"Fixin's are on the table," she said. "You want fries with that, *cher?*"

"Sure he does," Nate answered for him. "And dessert."

"We got rice custard or molasses pecan pie."

"Got any vanilla ice cream for the pie?" Nate asked.

Her gaze flicked over Josh in a measuring way he'd come to recognize. "I suppose I can round some up. You gonna want whipped cream on the custard?"

"Darlin', you read my mind. We'll take both for the *jeune homme*, here, and I'll take the custard and some coffee."

"I don't want any of that rice crap," Josh said.

"Is that any way for a risk taker to talk?" Nate asked. "Joe, the cook, isn't quite up to my *maman*'s standard—she made a *riz au lait* that could make the angels sing—but his comes pretty damn close. Antoine's, up in N'Awlins, tried to hire him away last year, but his wife is a nurse up in ICU and neither of them was all that eager to leave Blue Bayou, after havin' lived their whole lives here, so we were lucky to keep him."

"They've always lived in one place?"

"Sure. Mos' folks around here were born on the bayou."

Josh figured that counting the foster homes and two residential treatment homes, he'd probably moved twenty times in his fourteen years. Everytime those envelopes with the flourescent red Overdue stickers would start coming in, his mother would pack up their stuff and they'd take off in the middle of the night. The last time his backpack had gotten left behind, along with class records from three previous schools, which always made it tough to enroll in a new one.

Not that his mother had cared if he showed up in class, but he did. Not only was school an escape, so long as he could survive the inevitable challenges from the bullies; the classroom was the only place he'd ever felt safe. And in charge of his own life.

"Okay," he said when he realized they were both looking at him, waiting for an answer. "What the fuck. I'll try it."

"Good choice," the woman said with a nod. "Maybe I should get you some soap, too. So you can wash out that potty mouth."

"She's got a point," Nate said as she retrieved their desserts.

"Excuse me, your Heinass."

"Cute." They carried their trays to a round table in the far corner of the room. The better, Josh figured, to conduct the interrogation.

Nate picked up a small bottle of red sauce and doused his fries and burger. "Want some peppers?"

"On French fries?" Josh reached for the catsup.

"Pepper juice goes on jus' about anything. You haven't tasted fried eggs till you've had them with Tabasco. We grow the peppers right outside Blue Bayou. Most kids grow up eating it as soon as they graduate off their *maman*'s milk. Guess you're not used to that."

"No."

"So that'd mean you're not from around here."

The burger was halfway to his mouth. Although it was one of the hardest things he'd ever done, nearly as hard as spending the past month on the run, Josh lowered it to the plate. "Did you bring me down here to feed me? Or pump me for that effing cop?"

"A little of both. But since you're on to me, how about we skip the questions till after supper?"

They ate in silence, the boy wolfing the food down as if he'd been starving for days. Which, Nate figured, could well be the case.

"You know," he suggested after a while, "Detective Hart is only trying to help."

"She's a cop."

"So?"

"So all she cares about is making busts and taking bribes."

"That's quite a negative viewpoint you've got goin' there. Did you pick it up on the streets? Or from someone you know? Like, maybe, your dad?"

"I never had a dad."

His face grew hard, once again reminding Nate of his brother. Jack had prided himself on being the hellion of Blue Bayou. The truth was, he'd just been hurting so bad, he hadn't known any other way to deal with his anger.

Nate had been mad, too, but at twelve he'd been a lot more afraid of Finn than Jack was.

Besides, although no one would have ever said it out loud, as the baby of the family, Nate had been their *maman*'s favorite. Which was why it'd fallen to him to try to ease her hurt after that terrible day that was scorched into his memory.

"That must be tough. I lost my dad when I was twelve. About your age."

"He take off?"

The kid didn't agree about the age thing, nor did he correct him. So much for that ploy. "No. He passed on. But at least I got to know him for a little while."

"Yeah, some guys get all the luck." Ignoring the big red-and-white No Smoking sign just a few feet away, the teen reached into a pocket and took out a book of matches. "You got a cigarette?"

"No. Besides, this is a nonsmoking building, and you're too young to smoke."

"Am not. I'm just small for my age."

"Won't get a whole lot bigger if you smoke," Nate said. "And die of lung cancer by the time you're in your forties."

"Everyone's going to die of something."

"True enough. But me, I'd rather drop dead after makin' love to a *jolie fille* rather than going bald from chemo and hacking my lungs out."

"Is that how your dad died?"

"No. He was shot and killed by some crazy, mad-as-a-hornet swamp dweller tryin' to murder a judge." Nate sighed at the memory. "He was as big and strong as ever at breakfast, when he lit into me for getting caught up in a ball game and forgettin' to mow the lawn the day before. By lunch he was lying on the courthouse floor, bleeding to death."

"That sucks."

"Yeah."

A silence settled over them.

"Did it make you mad?"

"*Mais* yeah. I used to lie in bed at night and imagine going down to the jail with his service revolver—he was sheriff of Blue Bayou—and blowing the guy away. But my *maman* was real torn up about losing him, so I didn't want to make things worse for her by getting myself sent away to prison. 'Sides, like we say in bouree, you gotta play the cards you're dealt."

"What if you're playing against a stacked deck?"

Nate suspected the kid had been born with the cards stacked against him. "I don't know," he said honestly.

"You damn bet you don't. Like I said, some guys get all the luck." This time the silence lengthened. Grew deeper. "I don't even know who my dad was."

"That's gotta be tough."

"Nah." He drew in on a paper straw, making a loud sucking sound in the bottom of the milkshake cup. "I figured if she didn't know, I didn't want to. I never would have wanted any of those scumbags she brought home to be my dad, anyway."

"Brought? As in the past?"

"She died." She'd died of a drug overdose, but that wasn't any of this guy's business.

"I'm sorry, *cher.*"

"Well, that makes one of us." The chair legs scraped on the vinyl tile as he pushed away from the table. As they returned upstairs, Nate figured it was a good thing he hadn't followed Big Jake Callahan into law enforcement, because he couldn't even get a confession out of a half-starved kid.

After leaving the teenager in the more than capable hands of Tiny Dupree, Regan and Nate went to Eve Ancelet's office, where Judi Welch of the parish Department of Social Services was waiting.

"Hey, Judi," Nate greeted her with a hug. "Aren't you lookin' as pretty as a speckled pup?"

"Flatterer." She punched him lightly on the shoulder. "But actually, you're close. I've been sick as a dog all week with morning sickness. Which, in my case, is inaccurately named, since it pretty much lasts all day."

"Sorry to hear that, *chère*. But Matt must be real happy about the news."

"He is. Especially since he got a promotion last week," she said proudly. "He's now assistant bank manager. It pays enough to add another bedroom onto the house."

"Good for him." Given the choice between being thrown into a pool of piranhas in a feeding frenzy or spending his days wearing a suit and tie and sitting behind a desk counting other people's money, he'd go with the man-eating fish any old day. "How're the girls?"

She had three. When the third one, Angelique, had been born and he'd shown up at the hospital with flowers, Matt had jokingly said that he'd always wanted his own basketball team, but had gotten a harem instead. Since Judi had always been Blue Bayou's most outspoken, card-carrying feminist, Nate had been stunned when, instead of lighting into her husband, she'd laughed as if Matt had been doin' standup on *Letterman*.

Love, he'd figured, obviously scrambles your brain.

Which was why he'd decided a long time ago to stay clear of it.

Regan watched their easy banter, noticing how the social worker didn't even back away when he brushed a curl off her temple. She'd bet *her* last pay raise they'd slept together. Reminding herself that it was none of her business if Nate Callahan had affairs with all his constituents, Regan yanked her mind back to business.

"Mrs. Welch is here to interview the boy," she told Nate.

"I figured as much. Not going to be easy," he said. "The kid's wearing pretty tough armor. I did manage to find out that his mom's dead. And he doesn't know who his father is."

"If he's telling the truth," Regan said.

"Well, since we've no idea who he is, DSS is going to have to take charge of him and find temporary placement," Judi said.

"He can come home with me," Nate said.

"You?" Judi appeared as surprised by the offer as Regan was.

"What's wrong with me?"

"You're not married," Judi pointed out.

"So? You never heard of single fathers?"

"Sure. I just never thought of you as being one." She tapped the tip of her ballpoint pen on her clipboard. "Are you actually volunteering to become a foster parent? Or to adopt the boy if it turns out he's available?"

"You said you needed a *temporary* home. I've got an extra room. And I think we understand each other well enough that we could get through the next few days without him burning down my house."

"Don't be so sure of that," Regan said. "He's at a ripe age for pyromania."

Nate thought of those matches the kid had taken out of his pocket. "We'll be okay." He hoped.

Judi frowned. "You haven't been prequalified."

"Got anyone else in town who is?"

"No. Well, there are the Duprees over on Heron, but they've already got three kids staying at their house along with their own two. And since the Camerons are currently between kids, they decided to take that vacation in California they've always dreamed of. The McDaniels just took a newborn last week, so she's pretty swamped."

"See," he said as if the matter had already been settled, "I'm the logical solution."

"That's very sweet of you to offer, Nate, but you're not in the system. I don't have the authority to just let you take him home like he's some stray puppy you picked up off the street."

"We've kinda bonded." Okay, so it was a stretch.

"He belongs in an official juvenile care facility."

"You mean a kid jail." Regan was surprised by the way his jaw tightened and his eyes turned hard. "Dammit, Judi, you know what happened to Jack when he landed in one of those."

"From what I've heard, it was difficult. But he survived and became a better person for it."

"He survived because he was a lot tougher than this kid, and because he'd come from a family who cared about him with a mother who never failed to show up on visiting day the entire year he was there."

"That was a boot camp for repeat offenders. I'm talking about a residential care center."

"Center, boot camp, they're still no place for a messed-up kid." He folded his arms, which, while not nearly the size of the gargantuan custodian's, were admittedly impressive. Regan suspected those rock-hard biceps and well-defined muscles came from swinging a hammer, not reps on some spa weight machine. "I may not be the perfect solution, but I'm a helluva lot better than one of those places."

"You'd have to get judicial approval."

"No sweat. Since Judge Dupree got himself reappointed to the bench, he can vouch for me."

Judi rubbed her forehead with her fingers. Sighed. Then gave him a warning look. "You know, this isn't going to be a walk in the park."

"I realize we're not talking about the Beav here. The kid might try to come off like Eminem, but deep down he's just a kid." He winked at Regan. "And if he gives me any real trouble, I'll have the detective shoot him."

Judi shook her head. "Lucky thing I know you well enough to know that you're joking. Some DSS workers might just find that statement worrisome."

"See? Who better to vouch for me than the lady in charge of placement, who knows me so well?" he said with one of those devastating smiles.

She studied him again. "Peter Pan and the lost boy," she murmured.

Peter Pan again? Obviously she'd been talking to Charlene. Nate had forgotten the two women had been on the high school prom court together. Terrific.

"All right. We'll give it a try," she said finally. "But I can't cut corners just because it's you, Nate. Since jurisdiction crosses parish and perhaps even state lines, depending on where the kid ran from, I'm going to have to make sure all the *i*'s are dotted and the *t*'s crossed."

"The judge is staying with Orèlia during the week to save himself the drive into town from Beau Soleil, so we can stop on the way to checkin' Detective Hart into the inn."

Regan held up a hand. "I don't need—"

"Of course you don't need me to drive you, *chère*," he cut her off. "But I figured you'd want to get down to working on that project of yours, which I promised to help with," he reminded her. "You can come along with me, and I'll have Dwayne drive your car over to the inn first thing in the morning."

"I'm not here for a vacation. I want to get an early start."

"The car'll be there before you get up," he promised. "Besides, you'll get a lot better break on the rate if I'm with you when you check in."

"Oh?" She arched a brow. "I suppose the night clerk is an old *friend?*"

The sarcasm slid right off him. "Well now, you know, she is. But that's not the reason I can get you a discount rate. The reason is that I'm part owner."

"You own a hotel?"

"Only about a third." He glanced at his watch. "But it's gettin' late, and I hate botherin' the judge at home, since it wasn't that long ago he had heart surgery. How about we just save the explanation for after we check you in?"

12

Nate called the judge to let him know they were coming. Ten minutes later, they were stopping in front of a white two-story house on the corner of a tree-flanked cobblestone street.

"I'll wait in the car," the kid said.

"Sorry, *cher*," Nate said. "But you're coming in with us."

"I didn't hear anyone reading me my rights," he grumbled.

"And I didn't hear anyone putting you under arrest," Regan said mildly. "So why don't you make it easier on all of us and come along? Unless you'd rather the mayor call for a trooper to take you to the nearest residential facility."

Apparently deciding he was outnumbered and better off with them than in some juvenile detention center, he gave in.

"You didn't lock the door," Regan reminded Nate as they began walking up the front sidewalk.

"No need. This is—"

"A peaceful town."

"Got it on the first try."

"This house would cost a small fortune in L.A.," Regan said as they climbed the steps to the front door. "The porch is nearly as wide as my apartment living room."

"It was designed for sleeping outside during the summer," Nate said. "Back before air conditioning." He rang a doorbell that played the opening bars of "Dixie." "It's also good for sitting out, watching your neighbors, and chatting with folks that walk by."

"People still actually do that?"

"Not as much as they used to," he allowed. "But probably more than in the city."

"Sounds boring," the kid said.

Sounds nice, Regan thought. Unfortunately, if the citizens of her precinct were to try it, they could be hit by a stray bullet.

The judge might be old enough to be her grandfather and a bit frail looking, but his voice had the deep, sonorous tones made for projecting throughout a courtroom.

"Heard you're a detective," he said after Nate had introduced them.

"Yes, sir. I work homicide in L.A."

"So what brings you to town?"

"I was overdue for some R&R, and I've always enjoyed Louisiana." It wasn't exactly the truth, the whole truth, and nothing but the truth, but this wasn't a courtroom, and she hadn't sworn an oath.

"Most people go to New Orleans."

"I'm not most people, Your Honor."

He gave her a razor-sharp look she suspected he used to keep order in his courtroom. Then he turned to Nate. "So you need a temporary custody order."

"Yessir."

"You have any idea what you're getting into?"

"No, sir. Not exactly. But it just seems like the thing to do."

The judge shrugged. "You always were the soft one in the family. Just like your *maman*." His stern expression softened for the first time since he'd opened the front door. "She was a good woman."

"The best," Nate agreed. "*Maman* was the judge's housekeeper," he told Regan. "After my father was killed."

"I would have liked her to be more than a housekeeper. But Jake turned out to be too tough an act to follow."

Regan noticed Nate looked surprised by that revelation. "My parents had something special."

"That's what she said when she rejected me."

"I hadn't known you proposed."

"No need for you boys to know, since she turned my proposal down. Of course, she was real nice about it. No one in the parish sweeter than your mother." Appearing embarrassed by the glimpse into his personal life, the judge squared his shoulders, cleared his throat, signed the temporary custody papers with a flourish, then handed them back to Nate.

"This is just temporary," he warned the teenager. "You give Mr. Callahan any trouble, and I'll rescind the order so fast your head will spin." He snapped his fingers to underscore the warning.

"Well, that scares the shit out of me," the boy muttered beneath his breath.

"What did you say?" The judge's voice cracked like a whip.

"I said, okay."

Eyes locked, and challenge swirled between the youngest and oldest males in the book-lined room. Regan let out a breath when the judge decided not to wield his authority to just ship the kid off right now.

"You've definitely got your hands full," he warned Nate.

"We'll get along fine."

"If he doesn't steal you blind," the judge muttered, as if the teenager wasn't standing right there in the room. "Always were too good-natured for your own good. Just like your mother."

"I'm proud to be compared to *maman*."

"Blue Bayou might be a small town," Regan said as they drove away from the house, "but the judge could hold his own on any bench in L.A." The teen was in the backseat, nodding along with whatever was blasting out of his Walkman earphones.

"You should have seen him in the old days. He's softened a lot the past few months."

"Seems he had at least one soft spot for a long time. You didn't know about his feelings for your mother, did you?"

"No fooling a cop," he said with a casualness she suspected he wasn't quite feeling. "That was a surprise. Though I suppose it does explain a lot of things. Like why he was always bailing Jack out of trouble and trying to straighten him out, like he was his own son. Looking back on it, I guess you could say he was giving him tough love. At least he didn't ignore him, the way he did Danielle."

"Jack's wife?"

"Yeah. I guess I didn't mention that part. She's the judge's daughter."

"Is everyone in this town connected?"

"Pretty much so, I guess. It's a small place, and people tend not to move away, or move in. So while there are some distinct circles, they all pretty much overlap."

"Which means that most of the people, of a certain age, anyway, would have known Linda Dale."

"Yeah. I'd suspect so." He glanced up at the rearview mirror, then over at her. "Which should make your cold case not as cold as it might be in the big city."

"True. It also suggests that if she didn't commit suicide, whoever murdered her may still be living in Blue Bayou, which makes it personal." For both of them, if Dale did turn out to be her mother.

"Yeah."

Having come to the conclusion that things really were different in the South, Regan didn't bother to argue when Nate insisted on seeing her up to her room. Which meant, of course, that they had to take the teenager with them so they wouldn't risk him rabbiting the minute he was alone.

"Shit, you two are paranoid," he muttered as he slumped across a lobby boasting huge bouquets of hothouse flowers, lots of rich wood, exquisite antique furniture, and leafy plants.

"Not really." Nate stuck the coded card in the slot and pressed the button for the third floor. "You just remind me of someone I used to know, so I just think about what he would have done in a similar circumstance."

The elevator doors opened onto a luxurious suite that would not have been out of place in the Beverly Wilshire.

"I need some time alone with the detective," Nate told the kid. "We need to talk."

"Yeah, right. That's what everyone does in a hotel room."

Nate heaved an exaggerated sigh. "You know, you really can be one pain in the ass." He opened the mini-bar and pulled out a Coke, a can of peanuts, and a Snickers bar. "This doesn't concern you, so why don't you go into one of the bedrooms and play some video games on the TV?"

Mumbling beneath his breath, he snatched the snack food out of Nate's hands, disappeared into the adjoining room, and shut the door behind him.

"He's going to have junk-food overload," she warned.

"Probably won't be the worst thing that happened to him."

She couldn't argue with that. She skimmed a finger over the glossy top of a Queen Anne desk. "You didn't have to upgrade my room to this suite."

"It wasn't any big deal." Nate was bent down, perusing the contents of the mini-bar. "It was jus' sitting here vacant."

"So, how did you end up owning a third of a hotel?"

"The hotel was built in the 1800s but burned down last year. When the owners rebuilt, they figured they'd get

more tourist business if it was redone to look more like
Tara, so they hired me to do the job, but they couldn't
afford what it was going to cost to do it right. So I took
some draws to cover the subcontractor and material bills,
then agreed to take a piece of the place as my cut."

"Blue Bayou doesn't exactly seem like a tourist mecca.
Won't it take an awfully long time to get your money
back?"

"Probably. But I've always had this perverse feeling
that it was more important to be happy than rich."

She could identify with that. "And restoring this hotel
made you happy."

"As a crawfish in mud."

"You did a very good job." She studied the crown
molding, surprised that such an outwardly easygoing man
would pay such strict attention to detail.

"Thanks."

"Though, to be perfectly honest, it reminds me more
of Twelve Oaks than Tara."

"Sounds like you've got a nodding acquaintance with
a certain movie."

"I've seen it a few times." She didn't feel any need to
mention that a few translated to a dozen. Her mother
once accused her of having hidden southern blood, to be
so taken by a mere movie. Regan sighed. She'd never
realized at the time how true that might be.

"How about a little Bailey's nightcap?"

"At mini-bar prices?" The TV came on in the other
room, the low bass sound of the video game thrumming
through the wall. "Who's buying?"

"It's on the house. Besides, even if it wasn't, you're a
rich lady now. You can afford to indulge yourself."

"We still don't know, for sure, that I am actually Linda Dale's daughter."

"You wouldn't have come all this way if you didn't think there was a damn good chance." He took down two glasses from the overhead rack, poured the Irish Cream, and handed her one.

"Thanks." She took a sip and felt the liquid warmth begin to flow through her veins. "And no, I wouldn't have come here if I hadn't thought there was a possibility."

Regan wasn't yet prepared to share the story of the Mardi Gras elephant. She sank down on the couch, tilted her head back, and looked out at the flickering gas lights of the town's main street. The Irish Cream was going straight to her head, conspiring with a lack of sleep last night and the long flight, followed by the adrenaline rush of the rescue wearing off.

"I really hate to admit this, but I think I'm afraid to discover the truth."

"You're a detective," he reminded her. "Digging out the truth is your job."

"Yeah, it seems I've done a bang-up job of that." Her head had begun to feel light, but she took another sip anyway. "If the woman who died in that garage is my mother, I've been lied to my entire life and never had a clue."

If there was one thing Nate had always had a handle on, it was knowing precisely what to say in the getting-to-know-you stage of an affair. He let out a deep breath and wondered why he couldn't think of a single word to make this right.

"She probably had a good reason for not telling you the truth."

"Sure she did. Being honest would have brought up a lot of questions she probably didn't want to answer." Regan's strangled laugh held not a hint of humor. "I don't know why I should be surprised. Everyone lies."

She'd told him that the first day. She'd also told him to get lost, but there'd already been too much passed between them to walk away now.

"You'll figure it out, *chère.*" He sat down next to her. "Put all the pieces together."

"Yeah." She jerked a shoulder. "You're damn right I will." Nate found the renewed spark of pride encouraging. It was good that she was beginning to convince herself. "There was this detective I worked with when I first got promoted into homicide, who'd drive everyone crazy because he was so slow and methodical." She ran her finger around the edge of the glass. Nate was finding it disconcerting to imagine those smooth lady hands holding a gun, those long slender fingers tipped with their tidy, unlacquered nails pulling a trigger. Especially when he was experiencing this low, thrumming need to have them on him.

"Watching him work a crime scene was like watching a glacier flow," she continued, unaware of the hot, uncensored direction of his thoughts. "Whenever anyone'd rag him about it, or a new partner would complain, he'd just shrug and say that he'd solve no crime before its time."

"It's been thirty-one years. Seems about time, to me."

"Cold cases are the hardest."

"Which is why you should be gettin' some rest." As he'd done at the airport, he skimmed a finger beneath her eyes. "I'll get the kid, take him home and get him settled, and be back in the morning."

"Don't you have to work?" Video game explosions were coming from the bedroom; his outwardly casual touch had ignited other ones inside her.

"Nothin' that can't be put off."

"What about the boy?"

"That's the nice thing about having family. I'll drop him off at Jack's."

"What makes you think your brother can handle a delinquent, runaway teenager?"

"After our dad was killed, Jack became a wannabe delinquent. This kid reminds me a lot of him back then. He's angry and a whole lot lost. 'Sides, I figure any guy who can hold his own with Colombian drug lords should be able to take care of one teenage kid for a few hours."

He went over to the table, where a ballpoint pen inscribed with the inn's name and a notepad were sitting, scrawled some lines onto the paper, and handed it to her. His handwriting was as illegible as hers was neat.

"Is there a codebook that goes with this?" she asked

Regan knew she was in trouble when his deep laugh pulled sexual chords. What she'd told Van was true: all her parts definitely were in working order.

"It's how to get to the library. Not that you wouldn't have found it yourself—this town's pretty easy to get around, bein' that it's all laid out in squares like Savannah, but this might save you some time. The local paper's the *Cajun Chronicle*. Dani—she's Blue Bayou's librarian—can help you dig into the archives."

"How did you know I was going to go digging in the archives?" She'd already tried to do that online, but the thirty-year-old newspaper issues she'd needed hadn't been uploaded to the Internet.

"That's what Jack or Finn'd do."

He had her there. "I'm also going to pay a call on Mrs. Melancon."

"The old one, or the young?"

"Old. Since she was running the company back then, she might know something about how Linda Dale got those stock certificates."

"I doubt that visiting the old lady will do much good, bein' how she's turned pretty reclusive and rumors have her mind going south, but . . . Jesus," he said on an exasperated breath when she shot him a sharp, suspicious look. "You really don't trust anyone, do you?"

"Would you, if you were in my situation?"

"I don't know. Maybe. Maybe not."

His smile turned a little distant as he gave her a considering look.

"What?" she asked, growing uneasy when he didn't look away for a very long time.

He slowly shook his head. "Damned if I know," he said, more to himself than to her. Vivid blue eyes, fringed by lashes most women would kill for, blinked slowly. The air between them grew thick and far too steamy.

Just when Regan's nerves were feeling stretched to the breaking point, he broke the silence. "Guess I'd better interrupt the intergalactic wars."

He retrieved the teenager, who, not surprisingly, wasn't all that wild about leaving the video game. "Two more levels, and I would've been emperor of the universe," he complained.

"Next time," Nate said easily. He paused in the open doorway and skimmed a finger down Regan's nose. "See you tomorrow, *chère*."

After they left the suite, she listened to the footfalls on the hallway carpeting, the *ding* of the elevator, the *whoosh* as it opened, then closed.

Regan leaned back against the door, closed her eyes, and let out a long breath. "*Detective chère* to you, Callahan."

The two-year-old girl lay in her trundle bed, huddled beneath her sheets, hiding from the full moon that her baby-sitter, Enola, had told her would make her eyes go crossed. She heard her mother's high heels tapping on the wood floor. The voices grew harsher. Louder. Angrier. A sound like a glass breaking had her peeking out from beneath the sheet; the moonlight streaming in through the window cast a silver light over the bedroom, but the corners were draped in deep shadows.

Regan shivered, fearful that the loud voices would wake the cauchemar. *Whenever her mama went out and Enola stayed with her, the sitter would sprinkle holy water from a little bottle over Regan's pillow to protect her from the witch who crept around in the dark, looking for little girls to eat.*

They were shouting now. Regan had never heard her mother shout and wondered if she was fighting with the cauchemar *just on the other side of the door. She tried to climb out of bed, but her legs wouldn't move. She tried to call for her mama, but the witch had wrapped its bony crawfish claws around her throat, so no sound came from her lips. Huddling beneath the sheets at the bottom of the bed, she hid from those shining red eyes Enola had told her could set children on fire.*

She heard a scream; then a crash, then silence.

* * *

Regan jerked awake, bathed in sweat, her mouth open in a silent scream she'd never been able to make heard, her heart beating triphammer hard, triphammer fast.

"It was just a dream," she told herself with a mental shake as she retrieved the pillow that had fallen onto the floor. The nightmare was an old one, going back as far as she could remember.

She took a deep breath, looked over at the clock radio, and saw it was not even three A.M. yet. Groaning, she climbed out of bed and retrieved the journal from her carry-on bag. There'd be no more sleep tonight.

13

The kid had slept like the dead, revealing that it had been a long time since he'd had any real rest. He also had the appetite of a horse. A Clydesdale. He was single-handedly burning through breakfast as if he hadn't eaten for weeks. Which, Nate considered, just might be the case, seeing as how he was mostly skin and bones.

"What's this stuff?" he asked, poking at the milk-drenched hot cereal Nate had gone to the trouble of fixing.

"*Couche-couche.*"

"That doesn't tell me a frigging thing."

"It's cornmeal, salt, baking powder, milk, and oil." A lot of oil. "My *maman* used to make it just about every morning for my brothers and me when we were kids. But she used to serve it with *sucre brule*, which is kind of a syrup." Thinking back on the ultrasweet, golden brown syrup made by cooking water and sugar together,

Nate was surprised any of them had any teeth left.

Food had always been an intrinsic part of the Acadian culture; his mother had turned it into a celebration.

"It's not bad." The kid pushed aside the empty bowl. "But I like these better," he said, biting into a sugar-powdered Cajun doughnut.

"They're beignets." Nate wasn't that good a cook—never had to learn since, on the occasions when there wasn't a woman willing to feed him, there was always takeout from Cajun Cal's Country Café. But any idiot could fry up a bunch of dough in a skillet of hot oil. "I don't suppose that, having slept on it, you remember where home is?"

"Nope." He used his third piece of raisin toast to wipe up some yolk from the fried eggs.

"You do realize that DSS will probably end up putting you in some sort of facility if they don't get an answer soon."

His faced closed up. "I thought I was staying here with you."

"Temporarily. Talking Ms. Welch into letting you come home with me for a couple days was one thing, since we're old friends from our school days. But I don't exactly fit a foster family profile. 'Sides, they don't have any way of knowing that you're not a regular Jesse James, running from robbin' a bank or something."

"I didn't rob any bank. And the damn social services assholes can put me anywhere they want, but that doesn't mean I'm gonna stay there."

Nate sighed. The kid reminded him a bit of Turnip, the raggedy old stray yellow dog that had shown up at Beau Soleil last spring. The difference was that the dog had deftly insinuated herself into Jack's life with her unrelentingly cheerful personality. But thinking about Turnip gave him an idea.

"You like dogs?"

"They're okay, I guess. I had me a puppy when I was a kid."

"What kind?"

"I don't know. Some kinda black-and-brown mutt. Someone dumped it in a field by our house. I brought it home and kept it hidden in my room, but the guy my mother was livin' with drowned it."

"Damn." This picture the boy was painting was getting worse and worse. "He still around?" he asked casually.

"I guess." He shrugged and wiped the white powdered sugar off his mouth with the back of his hand. "He'd moved into the apartment, anyway."

"Which is why you're not there?"

"I guess you could say that."

"You realize, don't you, that if you'd be a little bit more open and come clean about your situation, there's a very good chance I might be able to help."

The kid rolled his eyes.

"I guess that's a no." Nate stood up. "Come on."

"Where?"

The unrelenting suspicion was beginning to drive him nuts. "My brother's house."

"Why?"

"Because it's a cool place. With a dog who's always happy to meet new folks who'll throw her a Frisbee to catch."

"You gonna stick around?"

"Well, now, that's the thing. I promised the detective—"

"Yeah, yeah. I get it. Why spend time with a kid when you can be doin' a hot chick?"

"Okay, dammit, that's it." Nate turned on him, the flare of temper catching them both off guard. "I've been trying my best to give you the benefit of the doubt, since you look like you've been rope-drug from the tailgate of a pickup down a long patch of bad road. And if you're not lyin' about that drowned puppy—"

"I'm not."

"—then I've gotta figure that whatever you're running from has got to be a helluva lot worse than what you've gone through on the road, which sure doesn't look like it's been a picnic."

"It hasn't," he mumbled.

"Shut the hell up." It worked. The kid dropped his eyes to the heart-of-pine floor. "Like I said, I'm willing to cut you some slack, but if you don't stop talking such trash—"

"Yeah, yeah, you'll dump me back with the cops."

Nate saw the fear beneath the tough veneer and, though it wasn't easy, held firm. "If you'd quit finishing my sentences when you don't know what the hell you're talking about, you'd discover that you're not the only one with problems."

"Cops don't have problems. They make problems."

"Like when the detective crawled under that electrical wire to save your life?"

"I don't remember asking her to do that."

Damn, what he wouldn't give to have Jack or Finn here right now. Or both of them. They could double-team the kid, who probably wouldn't hold up two minutes when being played by experts.

Nate dragged a hand down his face, wondering what the hell he'd done in a previous life to deserve all this crap dumped on him at one time. Peter Pan was sounding real good about now. Flying off to the island of lost boys had to be a lot more fun than dealing with this runaway kid. If that wasn't bad enough, thanks to him, Detective Delectable's entire life, as she'd known it for thirty-three years, had just come crumbling down around her. How the hell was he supposed to make up for that?

"Like I said, the detective's got some private, personal problems. And I promised to help her solve them."

"What are you, a priest or something?"

Nate laughed at that and put his arm around the kid's shoulder. When he felt the sudden rigidity he lightened up a bit, but did not take his arm away. "Son, I am about as far away from a priest as you can get."

They were on their way to Beau Soleil, the Porchdogs singing "Hello Josephine" on the SUV's CD player, when Nate turned toward his passenger.

"You know, it'd be a helluva lot easier to carry on a conversation if I at least knew your first name. 'Hey, kid' is a little limiting."

He could see the wheels turning behind those pale blue eyes, then the kid blew out a long breath of surrender. "Josh."

It wasn't much. But it was a start.

Regan had to say this about Nate Callahan. He was true to his word. The rental car was waiting for her at the front of the inn when she returned from her early morning run. It had even been washed, she noticed immediately. Since according to Nate's scrawled directions the library was only two blocks away, Regan decided to walk.

The rain had moved on; the day had dawned bright and sunny and as warm as she'd been expecting when she'd left L.A. The library was located on Magnolia Avenue, next door to the Acadian Butcher Shop, which boasted displays of plump chickens and sausages beneath green-and-white-striped awnings, and across the street from a small park ablaze with naturalized daffodils. The interior of the building was brightly lit, and dust covers of upcoming releases were displayed on a wall covered in green, purple, and gold burlap (which she'd read in the hotel's visitor guide were Mardi Gras colors). The windows sparkled like crystal, and old-fashioned oak catalog cases gleamed with lemon oil, which added a fresh scent to the air.

"Good morning." The blond woman's smile, which was echoed in her eyes, was as warm and welcoming as her library. "You must be Regan." She held out a hand. "I'm Dani Callahan, Jack's wife. Nate called this morning and told me you'd be coming."

"It's good to meet you." Regan was momentarily put off by Dani's outgoing attitude; cops weren't accustomed to people being happy to see them.

"Oh, it's wonderful to meet you." Moss green eyes moved from Regan's face to her wrists. "Though I am a bit disappointed you're not wearing your bracelets."

"Bracelets?"

"Wonder Woman's magic bracelets. You and Nate ended up on the front page of the paper." She held up a copy of the *Cajun Chronicle*. In color, above the fold, was a photo of her ducking beneath the wires to hand Nate the blanket. There was another of Nate pulling the boy from the truck.

"That was a brave thing he did, for a civilian." Or idiotic.

"I doubt if, in his mind, he had much of a choice," Dani said. "Though the fact that there was a child in the truck undoubtedly added to the urgency. Nate's terrific with kids."

"Probably because his emotional growth stopped about twelve himself," Regan murmured.

"You may have a point, since that's how old he was when his father was killed. He told me that he'd told you about that," she said. "It's not something he talks about often, so it's interesting that he chose to share it with you."

"It was just part of the general conversation. He insisted on helping me into my coat because, as he put it, his daddy taught him to, and I suggested his father might want to join the twenty-first century." She still felt a twinge of guilt about that. "He seems all right with it."

"Yes, he does, doesn't he?" Dani braced her elbows onto the glossy surface of her desk, linked her fingers together, and rested her chin atop her hands. "You know, that was a dreadful time, but looking back and seeing all three Callahans from an adult perspective, I think it ended up being hardest on Nate."

"Why?"

"Jack and Finn were older, so they latched onto their roles right away. Finn became the man of the family, something he did very well."

"I'm not surprised."

"No, I expect you're not, having worked with him."

"Seems Nate's been talking about me."

"He's like my brother. We share everything." Her eyes momentarily sparkled. "Well, almost everything. Anyway, Finn just got more adult and serious, and Jack became Blue Bayou's James Dean. He calls it his rebel-without-a-clue period.

"Nate was closest of the three to his mother, which I suppose isn't surprising for the youngest child in a family. They lived out at Beau Soleil, the house I grew up in, so I had a front-row seat after the tragedy. I don't think he left her side from the time she got the terrible news to days after the funeral. Wherever she was, he was, holding her hand, talking her into eating something, telling her jokes."

A small, reminiscent smile teased at the corners of her mouth. "I remember him making her laugh at some silly story the night of the viewing. Mrs. Cassidy, from the market, was scandalized a woman could laugh when her husband was lying in a casket in the same room. I was the same age, and watched him all during that time and wished, just a little, that I could fall in love with him."

"You don't seem to be alone, there."

"Women like Nate," Dani agreed mildly.

"I figured that out for myself."

"You don't have to be a detective to see it." Dani's expression turned a little serious. "He's certainly sexy enough, and charming, but what attracts women is that he's one of those special men who genuinely admires all aspects of us. Which is why most of us like him right back."

"I'll admit he's difficult to dislike." Regan wasn't quite ready to make the leap into Nate Callahan's female fan club.

"I can't think of anyone who's ever had a reason to. As I said, there were a lot of times when I thought how much easier it would be if I'd just fall in love with Nate. Or Finn."

"But you didn't."

"No." She twisted a gold ring as her eyes warmed with private thoughts. "My heart's always belonged to Jack."

Regan wanted to get on with her reason for coming to the library, but there was one thought that had been running through her mind since she'd been jerked from a restless sleep by that nightmare. "I met this woman volunteer at the hospital—"

"Orèlia." Dani nodded. "She's definitely one-of-a-kind, isn't she? My father lives with her during the week."

"So Nate said. He seems like a nice man. Your father, that is."

"He's a good man." Regan, who was used to listening for what people *didn't* say, caught the qualification in that statement. "It's no secret that we've had some rough patches, but fortunately we had a chance to straighten them out before we lost the opportunity." She shut her eyes briefly as she realized what she'd said. "I'm sorry. I didn't mean—"

"I know." Regan sighed. "I guess Nate told you everything."

"He filled me in on what he knows of your situation. If it's any consolation, he was unusually reticent. Except for a brief synopsis of your possible family situation, all he'd tell us was that you reminded him of Finn, were very pretty, and smelled good."

Regan wasn't at all pleased to hear he'd compared her to Finn. Okay, maybe they were both cops, but surely she didn't come off as remote, cool, and rigid as the eldest Callahan. She shook off the momentary pique.

"It's not easy to have to consider that the woman I always thought of as my mother may be my aunt," she allowed. "Orèlia mentioned something about Nate's mother dying, as well." She was not trying to pump Danielle Callahan, but she couldn't help but be curious.

"Oh, that was a terribly sad time. She was diagnosed with breast cancer when Nate was a freshman at Tulane. She tried to keep him in school—he was planning to become an architect—"

"I thought he was going to be a baseball player."

"Oh, I think he could have been a very good one. All the Callahan men are naturally athletic, but Nate enjoyed the game-playing aspect of sports more than the other two. But he was smart enough to realize that even if he did make it to the majors, he wouldn't be playing all his life, so he decided it'd be good to have a backup occupation."

"That's more planning than I would have expected."

Dani smiled at that. "Every once in a while, just when you think you've got Nate figured out, he surprises you. I think he probably has more layers than either of his brothers."

"Finn certainly always seemed straightforward."

"With Finn, what you see is pretty much what you get," Dani agreed. "Though I have to admit that it was fun watching Julia Summers pull the rug out from beneath his tidy, orderly world."

Regan definitely could identify with that feeling.

"Nate's always loved construction. When they were kids playing cowboys and Indians, while Jack and Finn were practicing their fast draws, Nate was dragging home boards he'd find in the swamp to build the jail."

Regan laughed at the idea of Finn Callahan in a cowboy hat, having cap pistol shootouts. "So Nate's an architect?" Her admittedly sketchy investigation of him hadn't revealed that.

"No. He dropped out of school the day he heard the news of his mother's cancer and came home to be with her. I've always thought that he was somehow convinced he could single-handedly save her with love and determination. I firmly believe he's the reason she lived two years longer than the doctors predicted. It was a difficult three years, but he was always there for her.

"Jack was working for the DEA somewhere in Central America when she died, but Finn and Nate were with her at the end. Finn said she died smiling at a joke Nate had told her."

"That's nice." Regan didn't run into all that many people who died smiling in her line of work.

"There was a time when I don't know what I would have done without him to talk to. He was the only person during some hard times who could make me forget my troubles for a little while. And if part of him is still twelve years old, well, perhaps that's what makes him able to slough off his own problems while taking on everyone else's."

Regan didn't want to consider that possibility. It was easier to believe that Nate Callahan was just some immature, hormone-driven southern charmer.

"That's all very interesting," she said, her smile a bit forced. "Could you tell me where you keep your newspaper archives?"

"The newer ones have been scanned into the computer. The ones you're looking for are still on microfiche. I've pulled up the reels for you." She gestured toward a chair and a reader across the room. "If there's anything else you need—"

"No, thanks. That'll do it."

"Great. Do you know how long you'll be staying?"

"I suppose it all depends on what I find and how soon I find it."

"Hopefully you'll be here for the Fat Tuesday party out at Beau Soleil."

Regan hadn't come to Blue Bayou to party. "That's very nice of you, but—"

"Please come, Regan. How else can we live up to our reputation for southern hospitality? Nate and Jack have done wonders with Beau Soleil, and I do so love to show it off. Have you ever visited a plantation house?"

"No."

"Beau Soleil was the model for Tara," Dani said, sweetening the pot. "Margaret Mitchell was a visitor before she wrote the book."

"That's quite an endorsement."

"It's really worth the trip to see what Nate's done with the house. He's more than just a contractor, he's a master craftsman. His millwork is phenomenal. There was a time when I felt sorry for him, dropping out of school and all, but it's obvious that he never belonged building skyscrapers; he's really found his niche."

"That's important."

Regan had once been certain she'd found hers. She was no longer quite so sure. It's not burnout, she assured herself. You just need a break. Like a month in Tahiti. Or maybe in bed. Sleeping.

"If I'm in town, I'll try to come by."

"I'm so pleased. Jack will be, too." Dani's smile suggested she hadn't expected any other outcome, making Regan wonder if all southerners had velvet-bulldozer personalities. Had Linda Dale? "Jack lived in Los Angeles for several years, so you'll be able to share stories."

Regan liked Dani Callahan. If Dani lived in Los Angeles, the two of them might have been friends. Other than Van, whose life these days revolved around Rhasheed and her unborn son, Regan didn't have many women friends. Her job didn't allow time for socializing. If she did take time from work, she was likely to be found sharing a pitcher of beer with a group of cops at the Code Ten.

She realized Dani had asked her a question. "I'm sorry. What did you say?"

"Nate told me he'd asked you to take the sheriff's job?" Her voice went up a little on the end of the sentence, turning it into a question.

"He did. And I turned him down."

"Having met you, I'm doubly sorry you didn't accept." Her slight frown turned into a smile. "Well, perhaps you'll change your mind. My brother-in-law can be very persuasive."

That was an understatement. But Regan had no interest in leaving L.A. for such a small, isolated town. Pigs would be spouting gossamer wings and flying over Blue Bayou before she pinned on that badge again.

As if to prove how different the town was from Los Angeles, the story of Linda Dale's death, which would have been buried in the back pages of the local section in the *Los Angeles Times*, had captured nearly the entire front page. There was also a picture of Dale captioned "In Happier Days"—the New Orleans Mardi Gras photograph. Inside were more photographs, including the red car in which her body had been discovered by her employer. Another picture showed a woman carrying a toddler out of a tidy, narrow white frame house. Regan recognized her as the woman she'd always thought was her mother, and a chill skimmed up her spine as she realized she was, indeed, that toddler.

Josh was trying his best not to be impressed, which was frigging hard when the house Nate pulled up in front of reminded him a lot of the White House.

"Your brother lives here?"

"Yeah. Jack."

"He must be rich."

"I think he probably does okay for himself. He writes books."

"Yeah?" Josh liked to read; books had often proven an escape from his life. But he'd never actually given any thought to people writing them. "What kind of books?"

"Thrillers, I guess they're called."

The name clicked. "Your brother is Jack Callahan?"

"Yeah, I guess you heard of him."

"Heard of him? Shit, I just finished reading *The Death Dealer*! It's in my backpack." He'd swiped it from a CVS in Tallahassee, along with a can of Vienna sausages and a Milky Way bar. "He rocks."

"He sure does. And I'd say that even if he wasn't my brother. But there's a lot of sex, drugs, and violence in those stories."

"Like there's not a lot of sex, drugs, and violence in life."

"Not in everyone's life." A cold, lethal anger uncurled in Nate's gut. It wasn't often he understood the passion that drove people to do murder. This was one of those rare times. "Look, let's get something straight, right now, okay?"

"What?"

"The folks at DSS are eventually going to find out who you are. But when that happens, you're not going back."

"You're damn right I'm not."

"That's not what I mean. You've got to promise me you won't take off again."

"What kind of chump do you think I am?" Josh sneered.

"I don't think you're a chump. I think you're a kid who got dealt a lousy hand. But you're not going back to an abusive home."

"Says you."

"Yeah." Nate tamped his rare but formidable temper. He was murderously furious at anyone who'd hurt a child.

"What are you going to do to stop them?"

Murder, while surprisingly appealing, wasn't the answer. "I don't know." Nate figured after all he'd been through, Josh deserved the truth. "But I will. Scout's honor."

"It figures," Josh muttered.

"What?"

"That you'd be a friggin' Boy Scout."

Nate threw back his head and laughed at that. Even Josh's lips quirked into a hint of a smile.

"Come on, *cher*," he said as a huge yellow ball of fur

the size of a compact car came barreling out the front door of Beau Soleil. "You can meet the family, and Jack can autograph your book for you."

The dog, which Jack claimed to be a Great Dane–yellow Lab–Buick mix, leaped up, put her huge paws on Josh's shoulders, and began licking his scrunched-up face in long, welcoming slurps. When the kid fell to the ground and began wrestling with Turnip, he looked like any normal teenage boy. Which, Nate figured, somewhere, deep down inside, past all that hurt and teenage bravado, he was.

"Uncle Nate!" The nine-year-old wearing a Baltimore Orioles cap and a shirt declaring him to be a member of the Blue Bayou Panthers, sponsored by Callahan Construction, tore out of the house behind the dog. "Guess what?"

Nate pulled off the cap and ruffled his nephew's hair. "You just got called up for the Orioles' spring training camp."

"I'm too young to play in the majors," he said with a third-grader's literalness.

"Well, I already know you're gonna have a baby brother or sister. And I can't think of anything else, so I guess you're just gonna have to tell me."

"Mrs. Chauvet and Ben moved into the guest house last night."

"Yeah, seems to me I heard about you havin' company." He reached down, grasped Josh's arm, and pulled the teenager to his feet. "Josh, this is my favorite nephew, Matt—"

"I'm your only nephew," the boy reminded him. "At least for now."

"Well, there is that. Matt, this is Josh. He's visiting me for a while."

"Cool." The grin was quick and revealed a missing tooth. "Want to see my Hot Wheels collection?"

Josh shrugged in that uncaring way Nate was getting used to. "Hot Wheels are for little kids."

"They're for collectors, too. My uncle Finn found me a deep purple Nomad with Real Rider tires in California. It's really cool." Matt turned and raced back toward the house, Josh with him and Turnip happily nipping at their heels, just as Jack came ambling out.

"Does that kid walk anywhere?" Nate asked.

"Not if he can help it. So, Dani says that she invited your new lady friend to the Fat Tuesday party, and while she didn't exactly agree to show up, she didn't out-and-out refuse, either."

"Terrific." Nate smiled. As much as he'd always liked having brothers, there was something handy and decidedly cool about gaining a sister. "You realize, don't you, that marrying that woman was the smartest thing you ever did."

"Won't get any argument from me on that one," Jack agreed cheerfully.

Nate caught up with Regan as she left the library. She glanced past him toward the SUV he'd parked across the street. "Where's the boy?"

"I took him out to Beau Soleil so Jack could keep an eye on him. And his name, by the way, is Josh."

"Josh what?"

"He wasn't willing to share that yet."

"Well, at least it's a start." As she crossed the street

with him, Regan could almost imagine the sound of horses' hooves on the rounded gray cobblestones. "So did you take along a whip and a chair to your brother's?"

"Hey, Jack used to hunt down international drug dealers." He opened the passenger door, put his hand on her elbow, and gave her a little boost up into the front seat. "I figured he could take care of one runaway for a few hours," he said after he'd come around the front of the SUV and joined her. "Besides, he's got himself this big friendly mutt I thought might loosen Josh up a bit."

"Animals have a way of making a connection when people can't. The canine corps is one of the more popular groups in the police department, and using a mounted patrol at concerts is effective because most people like the horses . . . And why are you looking at me that way?"

"I was just wondering about something."

"What?"

"If you taste as good as you look."

"In case you've forgotten, this is a public place."

"The windows are tinted. 'Sides, I don't see anyone watching."

He could tell she was tempted. Having wanted her the first time he saw her in that prim no-nonsense gray suit that showcased a magnificent pair of legs, he opted for giving in to temptation.

"Dammit, Callahan."

"It's Nate," he said absently, not about to apologize for the desire he knew she was reading in his gaze. "I'd say we've worked our way up to first names, wouldn't you, Regan?"

"We've only known each other two days."

"True. But you've got to admit that a helluva lot has happened in those two days."

"Granted. But I definitely don't want to get involved with you."

"I know," he said.

There was a part of him that didn't, either. With the exception of the two women his brothers had married, Nate wasn't used to complex women. Didn't want to get used to them. He preferred easygoing belles who understood that shared desire was a game, a game both parties, if they kept things simple, could win. He doubted there was a single simple thing about this woman.

"Then my suggestion would be to stop before things get out of hand."

"I don't think I can do that, *chère*." He ran his thumb along the tightly set seam of her lips. What was a man to do but take a taste when her lips were so close? So tempting?

"Tell me to take my hands off you," he said, "and I will."

She drew in a breath.

When her golden brown eyes softened, giving him his answer, he lowered his mouth to hers.

14

Oh, he was good! He didn't ravish, which would have made it too easy to push him away. He beguiled. He took his time, gently, so unbelievably gently, his mouth brushing against hers in a touch as delicate as a dream.

No one had ever kissed her like this. Not ever. How could such a slow, gentle kiss rock her to the bone?

Regan was unaware she was holding her breath until it shuddered out when her lips parted. Rather than invading with his tongue, as so many other men would have automatically done, he surprised her yet again by scattering light kisses at the corners of her mouth, up her cheek.

Her cheek. She tensed, wishing she were perfect. Or, at least not so imperfect.

"Nate—" It was the first time she'd said his name. But the voice couldn't be hers. It was too low. Too ragged. Too needy.

She felt his smile at her temple. "Shhh," he whispered. "Just a little bit more."

Her brain was shutting down. He was muddling her thoughts, stirring up unruly needs she'd always managed to keep tightly reined in.

His lips returned to hers, once, twice, a third time until they finally—thank you, God!—lingered. Even then he was patient. So amazingly, achingly patient.

He drank slowly, savoring her as he might a fine wine. He drank deeply, stealing her breath, along with whatever ragged bits were left of her resolve. One of them trembled. Because she feared it was her, Regan drew away now, while she still could.

Not that he let her completely escape. He pressed his forehead against hers, even as his fingers continued to stroke the back of her neck in a way that was far from comforting. "Kissing you could become a habit, Detective *Chère*."

"A bad habit."

His grin was slow and carelessly charming. "Sometimes those are the most fun."

"You're not my type."

"Well, now, I sure wouldn't want you to take this the wrong way, but you're not exactly mine, either." His eyes lit with easy humor. "But sometimes that doesn't have a damn thing to do with chemistry."

"I suppose you'd know more about that than I would." Hell, she sounded petulant. Pouty.

"Since we don't know each other real well, I couldn't be the judge of that. But if you'd like, I can kiss you again. See if maybe it was a fluke."

"It was. My life's gotten dicey since you charged into

it. I suppose I shouldn't be all that surprised that I respond inappropriately to events."

"Inappropriately," he said mildly, as if trying out the word on his tongue. "Now, see, darlin', that's where we're going to have to agree to disagree. Because it seems to me that when a man and a woman have electricity together, it only makes sense to enjoy the sparks." He bent his head again and nipped lightly at her bottom lip. "I've been wanting to behave inappropriately with you since I watched you testify."

"Sure you have." She could feel whatever little control she'd managed to hang onto slipping away. Regan didn't like losing control. She didn't know how to function without it.

"It's God's own truth." He lifted his right hand like a man swearing an oath. "When you first got up on that stand, I started wondering what you were wearing beneath that prim, tidy little suit, then that thought led to another, and another, and pretty soon I was imagining getting you out of it and making passionate love to you in that big black leather chair the judge kept swiveling back and forth in."

"That behavior would have gotten you thrown in a cell for public indecency."

"But I'll bet we would have had ourselves one helluva ride. And I know it would have been worth it."

His easy arrogance irked her. All right, so he was the most gorgeous man she'd ever seen who wasn't up on some movie screen. So he moved with a natural, lazy grace that suggested he was immensely comfortable in his skin. So he was really, really built. That didn't mean he had any right to act as if he were God's gift to women.

"I should have just shot you back in L.A."

"And I should have gotten that kiss over with in L.A. Then we'd have already moved to the next step."

"And that would be?"

He rubbed his jaw. Studied her silently. Then, just when her nerves had begun to screech like the brakes on her crappy cop car, he shook his head. "I think I'll just let you figure that out for yourself when we get there."

She was *not* going to let him get to her. She was a cop, dammit. And not just any cop, she was the cream of the cream, the best of the best. She ate gangbangers for breakfast and sent bad guys up the river for life plus ten, without parole. She could handle Nate Callahan.

"We have this little thing in law enforcement," she said. "Perhaps you've heard of it."

"What's that, *chérie?*"

Her smile was sweet and false. "Excessive force."

"Well, now, I've never been one who got off on rough play, but if you want to drag out some handcuffs, I'm willing to give it the old college try.

"There's this stripper down on Bourbon Street in N'Awlins. Calls herself Officer Lola Law. She starts out wearing police blues, then eventually works her way down to a G-string, some pasties that look like badges, and some shiny black vinyl boots with ice-pick heels that go up to mid-thigh. I don't suppose you'd have an outfit like that?"

She wasn't about to dignify that with a response. "Don't you take anything seriously?"

"I try not to. Life's too short for getting bogged down in details."

"You make details sound like a bad thing."

"Didn't someone once say the devil was in the details?"

"It's a bit hard to solve a crime without details. And while I've never restored a building before, I'd suspect it's probably a good idea to measure before you cut a piece of wood."

"Got me," he said easily. "But since there's no way of knowing when you get up in the morning if you're going to be around by nightfall, it only makes sense to enjoy the moment. Drift with the currents."

"Drifting with the currents can land you into the doldrums. If everyone shared that philosophy, we'd all still be living in caves, hunting woolly mammoths and cooking our meals over a fire."

"Doesn't sound that bad to me." When he tugged on a strand of hair, his knuckles brushed the nape of her neck again and made her skin sizzle. "I like the idea of ravishing you in the firelight."

"How do you like the idea of getting whacked in the groin by your woolly mammoth hunting club?"

"Ouch." He winced. "Some people might think you were a difficult woman, *chère*."

"I work at it. And some other people might think you were a Neanderthal southern male."

"Now, see, that's where we're different. 'Cause I don't work at it at all."

It was hard not to be charmed by his smile. "Look, Callahan, this partnership, or whatever you want to call it, isn't working. Unless you can get me into Mrs. Melancon's house." Regan had called this morning and had been brusquely told that Mrs. Melancon was not entertaining visitors. Not today, nor tomorrow, nor anytime in the near future.

"As it happens, I've been doin' some pondering on that, and have a couple ideas. But since I haven't quite worked them out yet, I figured you might like to take a little drive out into the country."

She arched an exaggerated brow and looked around. "This isn't the country?"

"Cute. Who would have guessed the cop had a sense of humor?"

"I have my moments. And where did you have in mind?"

"The actual destination wouldn't mean anything to you anyway, you not being all that familiar with Blue Bayou," he pointed out. "I just thought you might like to have a little chat with the man who owned Lafitte's Landing thirty years ago."

She remembered something from the newspaper report. "The man who found her body?"

"That's him. He just also happens to be the guy who hired Linda Dale. As well as the guy rumored to be having an affair with her."

"How do you know that?"

"I stopped by Orèlia's on the way here. Between her and the judge, there aren't any bodies buried in town they don't know about." He inwardly flinched when he realized what he'd said. "I'm sorry. I didn't mean that literally."

"I know." She sighed.

"Anyway, the judge proved a regular font of information. Seems Boyce's wife was suing Dale for alienation of affection, then for some reason changed her mind."

"He was married?" It had started to sprinkle, the drops of rain dimpling the dark water on either side of the road.

"Yeah."

"She mentioned my father was married," Regan murmured. "In the journal." She was looking at him again in that hard, deep way that made him feel as if he were undergoing an interrogation. "That's his name? Boyce?"

"It's his family name. His first name's Jarrett."

He wondered if she even realized that she'd reached out and grabbed his arm.

"She called the man she was in love with 'J.' What happened with the lawsuit?"

"Marybeth Boyce dropped her case."

"Maybe he killed her to keep from losing his business in a divorce division of property."

"I suppose that's always a possibility," Nate acknowledged.

"There are probably more cold-blooded murders done over money than passion. Or perhaps his wife dropped the lawsuit because she decided to save the legal fees and take care of the problem herself."

"By dragging Dale out to the garage, stuffing her in her car, and turning on the engine?"

"People can do a lot of things when they're angry that they wouldn't be able to do otherwise. Women have been known to lift cars off their children under the force of an adrenaline rush," Regan said.

"I always wondered if that's true. I've spent most of my life carrying 'round lumber, and I'm not real sure I could lift up a car, even if I had buckets of adrenaline pumping through my veins. Personally, I think all those stories about women lifting cars may be urban legend."

"Do you do that on purpose?"

"What's that, chère?"

"Take a conversation all the way around the block before you get back to the topic."

"Oh, that." He considered it for a long moment that had her grinding her teeth. "No," he finally decided.

"No, what?"

"No, I don't do it on purpose." He smiled at her. "I guess it's like my charm—it just comes naturally. And since you want to get back to the topic, murder by carbon monoxide poisoning seems an awfully iffy way to kill someone. Why wouldn't Dale have just gotten out of the car and opened the garage door to let in some fresh air?"

"Maybe she'd been tied up," Regan considered.

"Dad would have put that in his report. And even if whoever'd killed her had stuck around to untie her after she was dead, she would have been left with rope burns. The medical examiner back then might not have been the sharpest tack in the box, but I think even he would have spotted them."

"The wife could have knocked her out. That would explain the contusion on her skull."

"I'm no expert, but could a woman actually slug a person hard enough to raise a knot?"

"That depends upon the woman. I could."

He slanted her a look. "I'll keep that in mind."

Regan tapped her fingers on her knee. "She could have used a weapon."

"Sure. She could have gone in with a baseball bat and started swinging. She could have hit her with a lamp. Or a telephone. Anything's possible."

"But you don't think so."

"Doesn't matter much what I think. You're the detective."

"True. But I never in a million years could have imagined I'd be investigating a murder in my own family." The idea was still incomprehensible. Even more than the fact that her life had been a sham. Which brought up another thought. "When your dad died, did people make fun of you?"

He thought about that a minute. "No," he decided. "But they did treat me a lot like some folks treat Homer Fouchet when they first meet him. He's this guy who takes the classified ads down at the paper. He lost both his legs in 'Nam and came home with really bad burns on his face and hands. He doesn't have any facial hair or eyebrows or lashes, and although he's a nice enough guy, there are still people who have trouble looking at him, because he makes them uncomfortable, you know?"

"There but for the grace of God go I," she murmured, having experienced the same behavior from some of the well-meaning cops who'd visited her at the hospital after her near-fatal accident.

"I think that's probably it," he agreed. "Anyway, that's how they treated me. Nobody at school knew what to say, and that made them uncomfortable, so they mostly stayed their distance. And couldn't look me in the eye."

"At least you had your brothers."

"Yeah. Life was pretty rocky then for all of us, but it would have been a helluva lot harder without Jack and Finn."

"Kids can be so mean."

"You won't get any argument there." He thought some more. "There was this girl in school, Luanne Jackson, who had an alcoholic mother and a no-good father. Jack found out later that her father had been raping her and nearly killed the guy, but none of the kids even knew about stuff like that back in grade school, and if any adults knew, they sure as hell didn't tell Dad.

"Anyway, her mama used to spend a lot of time down at the No Name whenever her husband was out shrimpin', which was most of the time, and she'd leave with men she'd pick up there. Kids would hear their parents talking about her at home and rag Luanne somethin' awful. She got suspended a lot for fighting." He smiled at a memory. "If we were anywhere in the vicinity, Jack and I tended to get into it with her. Which usually ended up with us gettin' grounded."

"But you stood up for her."

"*Mais* yeah." He made it sound as if there'd been no other choice. Which, she was beginning to suspect, there hadn't been.

"Sounds like you were close friends."

"We were. Not as close as Jack, though."

"Let me guess. Luanne and Jack had a 'thing.' "

"Now, I wouldn't be one to spread tales, but they were close for a while. But that was before Dani."

"Sounds as if your brother's life is divided into two periods. Before Dani and after."

"I guess it pretty much is. I never would have thought it possible, but she's got him downright domesticated."

"You make it sound as if he's been neutered."

Nate laughed at that. "When you meet Jack, you'll realize that there's not a woman on earth who could do that. But he's pretty much settled down these days and seems real satisfied with his life."

She guessed, from his slightly incredulous tone, that he wouldn't be satisfied to settle into domestic bliss. Which she honestly doubted she would be, either. Having had no role model of husband-and-wife behavior to observe while growing up, she wouldn't have the faintest idea how to be a wife.

"Other than the accusation that Linda Dale was having an affair with Jarrett Boyce, did the judge have any other information about them?"

"Not much. Like I said, the case was dropped. Shortly after that, Dale was found dead, so I guess they just sort of faded back into a normal life that kept them out of courtrooms."

They fell silent for a time. Clouds rolled across the sky as they drove past flooded stands of leafless trees the color of elephant hide. Under ordinary circumstances, Regan would have enjoyed the drive. But these were far from ordinary circumstances.

The house was small and narrow with a deep front porch. The white paint had faded, but an explosion of orange honeysuckle covered a white trellis at one side of the porch. A red-and-white Caddy with fins harkening back to Detroit's 1960s glory days was parked on a white crushed-shell driveway. A brown-and-black hound dozed in a sunbeam on the porch amid a green array of houseplants.

"It looks cozy," Regan murmured, wondering if this was her father's house. And if so, how her life would have been different if she'd grown up here in Blue Bayou, rather than L.A.

"It's a shotgun house," Nate said. "There are literally thousands of them scattered all over south Louisiana. Freed blacks brought the style here from Haiti. They're called shotgun because all the rooms are lined up behind one another, so if you fired a gun from the front door, it'd go right out the back door."

"Not a shotgun, unless you were shooting a slug. When a shotgun's fired using a multiple-pellet shotshell, the pellets spread out into a pattern that increases in diameter as the distance increases between the pellets and the barrel. Depending on the size of the shot, the mass starts to break up somewhere between five and ten feet."

"Anyone ever tell you that you're damn sexy when you're talking like a cop?"

"No." She shot him a warning look that would have had most men cowering in their boots. The problem was, Nate Callahan wasn't most men.

"What's the matter with the men in L.A., anyway? They all must be either blind or gay."

"Perhaps they know enough not to hit on a police officer."

"Maybe someone who met you while you're armed and investigating a murder might want to be a bit cautious about bein' too forward," he allowed. "But you can't spend all your time chasing down bad guys."

"There's where you're wrong. Being a cop isn't just what I do. It's what I am. My life pretty much *is* my work, and the only men in it tend to fit into three categories." She held up a finger. "Suspects." A second finger. "Cops." A third. "And lawyers."

"Maybe you need to expand your circle of acquaintances." He brushed his thumb along her jaw.

She shoved his hand away. "What I need," she said as she unfastened her seat belt, "is for you to back off and give me some space."

He climbed out of the SUV and caught up with her on the way to the porch. The rain had lightened to mist. "Okay."

"Okay, what?"

"Okay, I'll give you all the space you need."

That stopped her. "Why don't I believe you?"

"Maybe 'cause you're a skeptic all the way to the bone. But that's okay. It's sort of an interesting change for me. I can just see you, a sober-eyed, serious four-year-old, sitting on St. Nick's knee in some glitzy L.A. department store, giving him the third degree."

He made her sound grim and humorless. Worse yet was the realization that she actually cared what he thought.

"I never sat on Santa's knee." She started walking toward the house again. "My mother never encouraged me to buy into the myth." Or the tooth fairy or Easter bunny, for that matter.

"Now that's about the most pitiful thing I've ever heard."

"Then you've been blissfully sheltered." Despite the car parked outside, no one seemed to be home. The dog obviously hadn't been bought for his watchdog skills, since he was snoring, blithely unaware of their presence. "Let's check around back."

They found Boyce in a small cemetery surrounded by a low cast-iron fence. Some of the standing stones were so old the carving had been worn down, making it impossible to know who'd been buried there. He was planting roses into a raised bed beside a small stone angel.

When Nate called his name, he turned, then dropped

the shovel. "Hey, Nate. I figured you'd be showin' up sooner or later." His rugged face, with its lines and furrows, suggested years of hard living. His age could have been anywhere from fifty-five to seventy.

He pulled off a pair of canvas gardening gloves as he studied Regan's face. "The judge was right," he said, revealing that Judge Dupree had called ahead. "You do take after Linda some, around the eyes." He skimmed a look over her. "I predicted her little girl was going to be a heartbreaker when she grew up, and it looks like I was right."

He glanced toward Nate, who'd leaned down and was scratching the hound, who'd belatedly awakened and ambled over, behind his ear. "It's also going 'round that you hired this little lady to take on the job of sheriff."

"That's a misunderstanding," Regan said, one she was getting weary of correcting. "The mayor only gave me the badge so I could help out at an accident scene."

"Heard about that, too. Sounds like you two did a bang-up job. Maybe you might want to stay on."

"I'm afraid that's not possible. I already have a job in Los Angeles."

"Too bad. The town really needs a sheriff. Last one we had was purely pitiful and a crook besides." He cocked his head and gave her another long look. "Damned if you don't remind me of Linda when you talk."

"She didn't have a local accent?"

"No, which wasn't real surprising, since she wasn't a local girl."

"Do you know where she was from?"

"She didn't talk much about her past. I got the feeling that she wasn't really happy growing up, but it seems she was from someplace in California." He rubbed a stubbled chin. "Modesto, maybe Fresno, somethin' like that. Not the places you usually think of, like Los Angeles or San Francisco."

"Could it have been Bakersfield?" The woman she'd always believed to be her mother had been born in the San Joaquin Valley city.

His eyes brightened as if she'd just given him the answer to the million-dollar question. "That was it. I remember because she said the Mandrell sisters were from there, and she'd always wanted to grow up to be rich and famous like them." The light faded from his gaze. "She could have made it, too, if things had worked out differently. Your mama was a real pretty woman. Talented, too."

"I haven't yet determined that Linda Dale was my mother." Her tone was cool and professional and gave nothing away.

"Regan here's a detective," Nate volunteered. "She likes to get all the evidence in before she makes a decision."

"A detective." His tone was gravelly from years of smoking too many of those cigarettes she could see in his plaid shirt pocket. "Don't that beat all. Never met a lady detective before."

A little silence fell over them.

"Roses are lookin' real nice, Jarrett," Nate said.

The man swept the raised beds with a satisfied look. "They're comin' along. I got some antique bushes from a plantation down in Houma that's crumbling away. The new owner's razing the place to build some weekend getaway, and when I went over there with the idea of buying them off him, he just told me to take the lot."

"That sure is a lot, all right," Nate said, looking at all the burlap-wrapped bushes. Bees were buzzing from flower to flower.

"Marybeth has always liked her roses," he said. "This autumn damask is her new favorite. She's been hankerin' for one 'cause it's supposed to be real good for making oil. Me, I'm sorta partial to the color of this General Jack. You don't get many old garden roses that are such a dark red."

"Your garden's lovely." Having found herself in a discussion about flowers when she just wanted to solve the mystery of her birth, Regan was beginning to understand Finn's impatience with detours. "Marybeth's your wife?"

"Yes, ma'am. We'll have been hitched forty years this March."

"That's a long time." And obviously not all of it had been married bliss, according to Judge Dupree. Regan decided to take a different tack. "How did you meet her? Linda Dale, not Marybeth."

He narrowed his eyes. "You're here about that alienation-of-affection suit Marybeth filed against her," he guessed.

"I am interested in the circumstances behind that, yes."

He let out a long, slow breath.

"Thought I'd put that foolishness behind me a long time ago." He stretched, took a red-checked handkerchief from the pocket of his overalls, and wiped his brow. "Digging holes is thirsty business. Marybeth made a pitcher of sweet tea this morning. Let's go sit on the porch, and I'll fetch you some."

15

❧❧❧

We're not going to get out of here anytime soon, are we?" Regan asked Nate as they sat on the porch in rocking chairs, while Jarrett Boyce went inside to get the tea.

"Nope. But the truth, whatever it is, has been waiting this long to come out. Won't hurt to sip a little sweet tea, chat a bit about some roses. You'll find out what you need to know."

"Eventually."

"Things move a little slower down here," he said, telling her nothing she didn't already know. "You gotta learn to go with the flow."

She'd never gone with the flow in her life. As she watched a hummingbird dipping its long beak into the red bloom of a potted plant by the porch steps, Regan wasn't sure she knew how.

"Here you go." The screen door opened, and Boyce came out carrying three canning jars filled with a dark liquid.

Nate took a long drink. "That just hits the spot, Jarrett," he said with a flash of that smile that seemed to disarm everyone. She watched Boyce's shoulders relax ever so slightly, and decided that she'd love to have Nate Callahan in an interrogation room playing good cop.

She murmured her thanks and studied the opaque liquid, which didn't look like any iced tea she'd ever seen. It was as dark and murky as the brown bayou water, and there were little black specks floating around in it that she dearly hoped were tea leaves. A green sprig of mint floated on top.

She took a tentative sip. Surprise nearly had her spitting it back out. "It's certainly sweet," she managed as she felt her tooth enamel being eaten away.

"Lots of folks don't take the time to do it right, these days. Marybeth boils the five cups of sugar right into the water she brews the tea into."

"Five cups," she murmured. She could feel Nate looking at her with amusement and refused to look back. "That much." She imagined dentists must have a thriving practice here in the South.

"That's why they call it sweet tea." He leaned back in the rocker, crossed his legs, and said, "It wasn't true. Those stories about me and Linda."

"Your wife seemed to think so," Regan said carefully.

"Marybeth wasn't quite right in the head back then." He frowned and stared down into the canning jar as if he were viewing the past in the murky brown depths. "On account of what happened to Little J."

"Your son?"

"Yeah." He reached into his pocket, pulled out the pack of cigarettes, shook one loose, and lighted it with a kitchen match he scraped on the bottom of his boot. "He was two when we lost him." It still hurt—Regan could see it in his eyes, hear it in the roughened tone of his voice. "He drowned."

"I'm sorry." She'd seen it more times than she cared to think about when she'd been a patrol cop.

"So were we." He sighed, and suddenly looked a hundred years old. "Marybeth was hanging laundry, right over there." He pointed to a clothesline about ten yards away. "Little J was playing with his toy trucks right here on the porch. She heard the phone and went into the house to answer it. It was her mama, checking on some detail for the church supper."

He paused. The silence lengthened.

"Mr. Boyce?" she prompted quietly.

He shook off the thought that had seemed to fixate him. "Sorry. I jus' realized that I never knew exactly what the detail was that was so damned important it couldn't wait for some other time." She sensed the obviously repressed anger was directed more toward whatever fate had caused his mother-in-law to call at exactly that moment than at either of the two women. "Carla, that's Marybeth's mama, can talk the ears off a deaf man. Marybeth used to be the same way." The pain in his gaze was, even after three decades, almost too terrible to bear. "She never would talk on the phone again after that day. In fact, she made me rip out the line the day of the funeral."

A funeral for a toddler. Could there be anything more tragic? "You don't have to talk about it," she said.

"You wanted to know what was goin' on between me and your mama, you got to know the circumstances behind it." He squared his shoulders, blinked away the moisture that had begun to sheen his gaze. "We had a puppy back then. A blue-tick hound name of Elvis. I'd bought it the month before, 'cause every kid needs a dog, right?"

"Right," she agreed. She'd never had one; whenever she'd asked, her mother had said they'd shed and bring fleas and ticks into the house.

"The sheriff—your daddy"—he said to Nate, who nodded—"figured that Little J must've gotten bored with playing cars and decided to play fetch with Elvis. 'Course he couldn't toss real good, and this old tennis ball was floating on the water, so it seems that's what happened." He squeezed his eyes shut, as if to block off the memory. Then he swallowed the tea in long gulps, looking like a man who wished it was something stronger.

"Marybeth just fell all to pieces. She got the deep blues and couldn't do much but just lie in bed all day. Talking to her was like talking to one of them stumps." Ashes fell off the burning end of the cigarette as he gestured toward the cypress stumps out in the still, dark water. "She wouldn't eat, wouldn't let me touch her. Never did cry. Not even when they were lowering Little J's tiny blue casket into the grave.

"Everyone else—her ma, my ma, all the aunts, cousins—was sobbing. Even my dad teared up some, and her daddy looked to be about to have a heart attack. I'm not ashamed to admit that I had tears pourin' down my face, too. But folks who say it's good to get things out must not have ever lost themselves a baby, because crying sure didn't help me none that day."

He exhaled another long, slow breath, then drew in on the cigarette. "Marybeth's eyes stayed as dry as that little stone guardian angel I'd got to mark his grave."

The small angel in the cemetery. Nate reached over and laced his fingers with hers; Regan didn't pull her hand away.

"Marybeth didn't want the angel. I found out later that she'd thought it was too damn late for Little J to have himself a guardian angel, but since he'd always been afraid of the dark, the idea of him having an angel nearby comforted me some. So I might have stood up to her about that, if she'd even said anything at the time, which she didn't."

Like during the conversation about roses, Regan was wishing he'd cut to the bottom line. She hadn't realized it fully until now, but she'd just about reached her capacity for human tragedy. Understanding that he had to tell his story his way, though, she held her tongue and looked for signs of herself in the lined face that appeared to be a road map of his life.

"After a while, Doc Vallois decided that she wasn't going to get better here, so he sent her up to this sanitarium in Baton Rouge, where they knew how to treat people who were suffering depression by sending electricity through their brains."

"Electroshock treatment." Regan exchanged a brief look with Nate.

"That's what they called it. She was there six months."

Another silence settled over them like a wet gray blanket.

"Leaving you to grieve all alone," Nate prompted quietly.

Boyce gave him a grateful glance. "Yeah." He took one last long drag on the cigarette, dropped it onto the porch, and crushed it beneath his boot heel. Then he looked back at Regan. "Your mama wasn't stuck-up like some good-looking women are. She was a lot of fun to be around. Had a heart big as all outdoors, and when she smiled at you, it was like the sun came out from behind a cloud. Everybody round these parts loved her."

"That doesn't sound like a woman who'd commit suicide."

"No, it don't," he said thoughtfully. "Didn't know anyone who wasn't real surprised by that. I sure as hell was." He shook his head. "But I guess you never really do know a person, deep down inside."

"I suppose not." She certainly hadn't known the woman she'd grown up believing to be her mother.

"Before she came to Blue Bayou, she was workin' in N'Awlins. Even tried to break into country-and-western music in Nashville, but the way she told it, she was playing in this little club way off Music Row one night when this guy came in and offered her a job singing in some place he owned in the Vieux Carré. That's the French Quarter."

"I know. What made her leave New Orleans?"

"Well, now, she never did say, but I was sure glad when she showed up at the Lounge lookin' for a job. Lord, that girl could sing like a warbler. First week she was there, I brought home an extra ten percent. After six months the profits doubled, and the place was packed every Friday and Saturday night."

"As nice as Blue Bayou appears to be, it seems she could have had more chance to land a record deal if she'd stayed in New Orleans."

"That thought crossed my mind, too. A lot, but I

never asked, and like I said, she never did tell me. I always figured it had something to do with a man. Mebee your daddy."

Regan felt every nerve in her body tense. "Did you know him?"

"Nope. She never did talk about him, neither. But I guess that's 'cause she didn't have real happy memories, and besides, whenever we were alone, she was too busy trying to cheer me up. I was pretty much of a mess in those days." Pale gray eyes narrowed as he studied her. "I guess little girls grow up to be like their mamas even if they don't live under the same roof. She was a fixer, too."

"A fixer?"

"One of those people who always want to help other people out. Cheer them up, get rid of their problems for them. That's what Linda was. Isn't it what a police officer does, too?"

"I suppose." How strange to think she might take after her mother, rather than her father. "It sounds as if you had a close relationship with Linda."

"Not as close as some of the old gossips around these parts seemed to think. I never went to bed with her. Never even kissed her. Not that I didn't think about how it'd be, from time to time," he admitted.

"Day a man stops thinking about kissing a pretty woman is the day he's just lost any reason to keep on livin'," Nate said.

Boyce surprised her by laughing at that. A rich, bold laugh that gave a hint of the man who appeared to have been close friends with her mother. Unfortunately, not close enough to know what Regan had come out here to learn.

"Did she have any other men friends?"

"Just about every man in town. Like I said, she was real popular." The smile Nate had tugged out of him lightened the dark conversation. "Even with most of the women who'd show up at the Lounge. Most nights she'd bring you along, and I never met a woman yet who didn't like playing with a pretty baby."

"She took a baby to a nightclub?"

"Wasn't like the nightclubs you're probably used to in California," Nate explained. "Lafitte's Landing was a family sort of place, where everyone in town got together on the weekends to pass a good time. The supper crowd would range from great-grandmère, who didn't speak a word of English, to mamas with their newborns, to teenagers showing up to flirt with one another."

" 'Sides, it was a good deal for Linda," Boyce said. "She didn't have to pay for a sitter. And since I knew she could be earnin' a lot more in the city, but couldn't afford to give her a raise, I'd toss in dinner on the house. She even worked a little duet into the routine."

"A duet?" Regan asked. Once again he'd surprised her.

"Yeah. You couldn't string a whole sentence together, but you sure knew all the words to 'You Are My Sunshine.' "

Regan drew in a quick, sharp breath of shock.

"It's a favorite 'round here, since it's the state song and was written by Jimmie Davis, a sharecropper from up north in Jackson Parish who grew up to be governor. It was a real cute act, especially since even when you were in diapers, 'cepting for the color of your hair, you took after Linda. It was kind of like looking at the little girl and seeing the woman she'd grow up to be, both at the same time."

"You said the other men in town liked her." It was her cop voice; controlled and impassive, revealing none of the emotions churning inside her. She felt Nate looking at her again and wouldn't—couldn't—look at him.

"Yes, ma'am, they sure did."

"So she dated a lot, did she?"

"Now, I didn't say that. I said she had a lot of men friends. She was a friendly girl, but she wasn't fast. Whenever she went out, she was always in a crowd of folks. Didn't seem like she had any one fella she was sweet on. She used to read you fairy tales all the time, and I guess she sort of bought into the stories, because she told me her prince was going to show up on a big white horse to take you away from Blue Bayou, and the three of you were going to live happily ever after." He shook his head. "Guess it didn't work out that way."

"No. Apparently not."

Perhaps that's why Karen Hart hadn't encouraged Regan to believe in myths or fairy tales. Perhaps that's why she'd stressed duty and discipline. Perhaps, believing that her sister's freewheeling temperament had led to Linda's death, she'd been trying to save her niece from a similar fate.

"I'd just gotten the Fleetwood then, and started picking her up at her little house and driving her to the club," he said. "Bein' how her own junker was so undependable."

Regan glanced over at the red-and-white Cadillac. "You don't see cars like that on the road much anymore."

"More's the pity," he said. "I'd bought her off a helicopter pilot over in Port Fourchon. She'd been in an accident, and the hood looked like an accordion. The interior was shot to hell, and the paint was primer, but I could see the possibilities. Linda used to help me sand the primer down on Sunday afternoons."

"It sounds as if you were very good friends."

"We both had a lot in common, bein' alone, but not being free to be with anyone else. Oh, we never talked about her man, and I only told her about Marybeth once, on a really dark day when I got drunk and broke down and bawled like a baby, but it was always there between us, and created a bond. But it was always an innocent friendship. Despite, like I said, what some busybodies liked to say."

"People talked."

"Sure. It's a small town," he said with a resigned shrug of his shoulders. "There's not a lot to do, so talking about your neighbor is sorta the local recreation."

Although Regan suspected living in such an environment could prove stifling, there might be advantages to being a cop here—unlike L.A., where you could arrive at a club that had broken fire regulations by packing people in like sardines, have someone get shot in the head at point-blank range, and not a single person in the place would have seen a damn thing. Of course, she doubted there were all that many homicides in Blue Bayou, which made it a moot point.

"Marybeth was a lot better when she got back from the sanatorium, but she was still about as fragile as glass. I used to walk around on tiptoe, not knowing what might set her off."

"Did you keep driving Linda to the club after your wife returned home?"

"Oh, no, ma'am. Not because anything had been going on," he stressed again. "But because I didn't want to be responsible for sending Marybeth back to that place. Her being away was hard on both of us, though it did seem to help with her blues, so I still think it was probably a good thing."

"But someone shared the gossip with her."

"Oh, there were a few women who were jealous of Linda and real eager to let Marybeth know what her husband had been doin' while she'd been gettin' electricity shot through her head." If the sparks glittering in his eyes were any indication, it still made him angry as hell. "Meddling old biddies who, since they don't have any real lives of their own, spend their time sticking their pointy noses into other people's business."

"That's when MaryBeth filed the alienation-of-affection complaint."

"Yeah." He took off his billed cap and dragged his hand through his still-thick white hair. "She didn't mean nothin' by it, though. She was just hurt and went on a tear. By the time I got over to the judge's house, he'd pretty much talked her out of the idea.

"She and I spent all that night talking, and the next day she withdrew the complaint. I thought everything was going to be okay. Then, when Linda didn't show up for work, I went to check on her, and found her in the garage."

Dead. While a two-year-old child was left to fend for herself. Regan had witnessed similar things, and while she'd always felt terrible for the children, never had their loss and the confusion they must have been feeling hit home as it did now.

"You said you and your wife talked all night," she said, carefully wading into deeper conversational waters. "Was that a figure of speech? Or were you literally with her all night long?"

His eyes narrowed as he read the underlying meaning in the question. "We were together all night. So, if you're here on police business, I guess you could say I'm her alibi. And she's mine."

"I wasn't—" Hell, Regan thought, there was no point in lying. "I didn't mean to imply that either you or your wife had anything to do with her death, Mr. Boyce." It wasn't an out-and-out lie. "I'm just trying to get at the truth. If you were as close friends as you say—"

"I don't lie, ma'am." His tone had turned from gravel to flint.

"Yessir. I understand that. And for what it's worth, I believe you. But surely you, as a friend, would want to know what happened to her."

"Killed herself. It said so right on the front page of the *Chronicle*."

"Sometimes newspapers get it wrong, Jarrett," Nate said.

"I read about there bein' an autopsy."

"Sometimes medical examiners get it wrong, too," Regan said. Even knowing that it might tell Nate more about herself than she would have wished, she took the old photograph of her father from her billfold and held it out to Boyce. "Have you ever seen this man before?"

He gnawed on his lower lip as he studied it for a long, silent time. "His face doesn't ring a bell," he said finally.

"Perhaps you never met him," she suggested, not quite willing to give up. "Could you have perhaps seen this photo at Linda's house?"

"No, ma'am." This time his answer was quick, decisive. "The only pictures Linda had around were ones she'd taken of you." He began thoughtfully turning his cap around and around in his hands. "You were the cutest little thing. There were times when I used to hold you on my lap and wonder if things might have been different if I hadn't met Marybeth first, and Linda wasn't hung up over some guy who sure wasn't actin' much like a prince, if you want my opinion. I would've liked bein' your daddy. I told your mama once that if I ever had a daughter, I would've liked her to be like you."

He put the hat back on his head and stood up, declaring the conversation closed. "I still would."

Regan was deeply, honestly moved. "Thank you, Mr. Boyce. That's a lovely compliment."

"It's the truth," he said gruffly. The sound of a car engine a ways down the road captured his attention, and he cursed softly under his breath. "That'd be Marybeth, coming home from the market."

Regan wondered if his wife had entirely recovered. There were certainly drugs available to treat depression these days, but did a mother ever truly get over the death of a child?

Not wanting to inflict another wound on the possibly still fragile Marybeth when there was no hard evidence pointing at any guilt, she turned to Nate. "We'd better be going."

"Thank you, ma'am." The older man's relief was obvious. They were nearly to the SUV when he called out to her.

"Yes?" Regan asked.

"If someone did kill Linda, I sure hope you find him. Lynchin's too good for any sumbitch who'd snuff out such a special life."

16

They backed out of the driveway just as a late-model Honda pulled in. "That was a nice thing to do," Nate said.

"I didn't want to waste time. After all, we got what we needed. There was no point in questioning his wife."

"And you believed him? About not sleeping with her?"

"I got the impression he was being truthful. Didn't you?"

"Sure. But I'm the civilian here."

She glanced back, watching as Boyce took the groceries out of the car. He literally towered over his wife, who appeared to be about four-eleven and probably wouldn't weigh a hundred pounds soaking wet. "You could have told me Marybeth is so small."

"Seems to me I mentioned my doubts about her dragging Linda out to the car, and you mentioning adrenaline. Since I knew you'd want to check out all the loose ends, it made more sense to let you talk to Jarrett and make your own decision about the involvement of either one."

"Of course, there's always the chance that he was lying to me about their relationship," Regan mused. "Which could give him a motive for killing Dale himself. It certainly wouldn't be the first time the person who reported finding a body turned out to be the one responsible. It's obvious he loves his wife, or they wouldn't have survived the loss of a child and her depression and still be together thirty years later. If he'd wanted to protect his marriage, he'd have a motive for wanting to stop her from telling Marybeth the truth about an affair."

"Thus risking the chance of sending her back into a depression, which in turn would have her returning to the hospital," Nate said. "Do you believe that's a possibility?"

"Anything's possible. But no, I don't believe that's what happened."

"Then I guess we keep looking."

We. Strange, how having Nate Callahan as a partner in this investigation didn't seem quite as impossible as it did yesterday.

"Do me a favor?" she asked.

"Sure." She didn't know anyone who'd agree without first finding out what she was asking. "What do you need?"

"Pull over. I need to get out of this car."

He shot a concerned look. "You feelin' sick, *chère?*"

"No." She took a deep breath. "Frustrated. And when I'm frustrated, I need to walk."

"Makes sense to me."

He pulled the SUV over to the side of the road. Regan jumped out before he could open her door and headed off down the road with no goal but to try to clear her head and sort things through.

The energy was radiating from her like sparks from a fire as she marched along the bank of the bayou. Leaving her to her thoughts, Nate kept quiet and just fit his stride to hers.

"I just keep going over and over it," she ground out after they'd gone about two hundred yards. "And I still can't figure out why she never told me the truth."

"Maybe to protect your feelings?"

"Lies always come out."

Sister Augustine had always said the same thing. The nun had warned her often unruly second graders, who'd technically reached what the church considered the age of reason, that lies of omission were no different from those spoken out loud, which meant the transgressor was required to confess to the priest on those long Saturday-afternoon penance sessions Nate had spent on his knees, reciting Our Fathers and Hail Marys when he'd rather be outside playing ball.

"Maybe she kept putting it off until she thought you were older and could handle the news better."

She spun toward him. "I was an adult when she died. How long was she planning to wait?"

"I guess that's something you'll never know."

"I wonder what else she didn't intend me to know." She shook her head and began walking again, then stopped again and looked out over the bayou. "Damn. I sound so damn pathetic."

She didn't look anything like the woman he'd first seen as an island of calm in the midst of a chaotic police station. Nor that intelligent, capable detective who'd testified so calmly and succinctly at that gangbanger's murder trial, sticking to the facts no matter how often the defense attorney had tried to draw her off-track by attacking not just the L.A. police force in general, but her own investigation.

She looked small. Feminine. And strangely vulnerable.

"You don't sound pathetic at all, you." Unable to watch any woman in such distress, he smoothed her too tense shoulders with his palms. "You jus' sound like a woman who's had her world turned upside down. Suddenly the sky's green." He ran his hands down her arms, linked their fingers together. "The grass is blue. The sun's spinning in that green sky, and you're figuring how to handle this new way of seein' things." He drew her closer; not to seduce, but to soothe.

She slapped a hand against the front of his shirt. "I realize this will come as a terrible shock, but not every woman on the planet is panting to fall into bed with you."

"Well, now, that suits me just fine, since I'm not interested in falling into bed with every woman on the planet."

"Dammit, Callahan, if you don't quit hitting on me—"

"*Non, chère.*" He caught hold of the hand pushing against his chest, lifted it, touched his lips to the soft, warm skin of her palm, then folded her fingers again, holding the kiss in. "This isn't hitting."

"People must use a different dictionary in Louisiana. What would you call it?"

"Fixing." He moved a little closer, so they were touching, thigh to thigh, chest to chest, her slender curves to his angles. They fit well. He'd thought they would, back when she'd been on the witness stand and he'd been fantasizing taking her to bed.

"Fixing?"

"That's what I do." He pressed a kiss against her hair and drew in the scent of herbal shampoo. "I'll never make as much money as Jack. Or be as driven as Finn. But I've always been pretty good at fixin' things."

Having accepted early on that a person couldn't change nature, Nate had been happy in his role as a handyman of sorts, fixing houses, people, lives. But until now, until Detective Regan Hart, the only time he'd tried to fix a broken heart had been that horrific day that his *maman* had been widowed.

"I think you and I just might have that in common, Detective *Chère*." He felt the stiffness easing out of her as she slipped her arms around his waist. "So why don't you let me fix you? Just a little?"

"I suppose your method of fixing up will involve getting naked?"

"No. Well, not right this minute," he amended, wondering if Sister Augustine was looking down from some fluffy cloud and admiring the deft way he'd avoided committing a sin of omission. "Maybe later, when you get to know me a little bit better and are more comfortable with the idea."

He was rewarded by something that sounded a bit like a smothered laugh, then felt the moisture when she pressed her face into his neck.

"I am not crying."

"Of course you're not." He slid a hand through her hair, sifting the silky strands like sand between his fingers.

"I never cry." Her voice was muffled. "Not even when my mother died."

He felt her stiffen again as she realized the woman she'd always thought of as her mother probably wasn't.

"Don't think about that right now." He cupped her face between his hands. Her eyes, underscored by shadows revealing too many sleepless nights, were dark with pain.

"That's easy for you to say."

"You know what you need?"

"What?"

"Somethin' to take your mind of all your problems. Jus' for a little while."

Unlike that earlier kiss, when he'd slowly, tantalizingly led her into the mists, this time he dragged her, head spinning, heart hammering, into a storm. Thunder rumbled inside her, lightning sparked every raw nerve ending, and she could have sworn the ground beneath her feet quaked.

It shook Regan to the core. She'd never realized she could feel so much. Never imagined she could want so much more.

Too soon, he drew his head back. "I want you."

"Now there's a surprise." The surprise was that she could actually speak when she was so close to begging. "Have you ever met a woman you didn't want?"

"From time to time." He smiled a bit at that, but his eyes were thoughtful. "This isn't one of those times."

"Then you're going to be disappointed. Because I'm not into casual sex."

"I'd be disappointed if you were."

She arched a brow. "Ah, the double standard lifts its ugly head. Why is it okay for a man to be a player, but if a woman enjoys variety, she's a slut?"

"I have no idea, never having subscribed to that belief, myself." He slipped a hand beneath the hem of her white T-shirt; roughened fingers skimmed over the unreasonably sensitive skin of her abdomen. "I'm going to touch you, Detective Darlin'. All over." The sound of those callus-tipped fingers rasping against the lace of her bra was one of the sexiest things she'd ever heard. "Then I'm going to taste you." He dipped his head again and touched his lips to the nape of her neck. "Every last inch of your delectable female body."

Who could have suspected there was a direct link from that surprisingly sensitive spot behind her ear to her legs, which were turning to water?

"And then, just to prove I'm no chauvinist, I'm going to let you do the same thing to me. But not yet."

His quiet declaration took the wind right out of her sails.

"What?"

"Although I'm surprising the hell out of myself, I'm thinking we should step back a little. Take our time. Slow things down. Get to know one another better. It'll be all the more satisfying in the end."

"You make it sound like a foregone conclusion."

"Isn't it? You say you don't go in for casual sex, which fits, since from what I've seen, you don't take anything lightly. Including that kiss we just shared."

"It was only a kiss. No different from any other."

"You just keep tellin' yourself that, *chère*. I promise

not to rub it in too badly when you realize how wrong you were."

She blew out a frustrated breath. "I'm amazed, given your supposed way with the opposite sex, that it's never sunk in that you can be annoyingly, insufferably arrogant."

"You know, if you keep talking like that, you're going to have me falling head over heart in love with you." His smile warmed and widened. "I've always been a sucker for flattery."

They returned to the car, and after a brief drive Nate pulled up in front of a building.

"What are we doing?"

"I thought we'd pick up some lunch to eat while we plan our next move," he said. "You haven't eaten till you've tasted one of Cajun Cal's po' boys."

Two seconds after they walked into the café, conversation dropped off like a stone falling into a well.

"Small towns," Nate murmured.

"Doesn't it get old?" she asked, pretending not to notice that everyone was staring at her. Since at least half the people in the place were too young to have even known Linda Dale's name, Regan could only assume that the news of her arrival in town had preceded her. "Not being at all anonymous?"

He thought about that for a minute. "Not anymore. I guess you get used to it. It was hard when I was in my teens and was trying to get away with anything. One time Jack and I were cruisin' home from school in his GTO, and by the time we arrived at Beau Soleil, at least a dozen folks had already called *maman* to tell her we'd been speeding."

Regan couldn't help smiling at that idea.

He smiled back, then sobered. "I think it was also worse because we were just about the only kids in school whose daddy had died."

"The dead dad's club," she murmured.

"Yeah. Guess you and I are both charter members."

"I guess we are."

The restaurant seemed to be made up of a connecting series of small rooms, each of which had an inordinate number of tables crowded into it. The tables were covered in newspaper, the chairs were a jumble of different styles and colors, and the front counter was red Formica. Daily specials had been printed in white chalk on a standing blackboard beside the counter. The walls, which she supposed had once been white but had become smoke-darkened over the decades, were covered with huge stuffed fish, photographs that, from the outlandish costumes, she assumed had been taken during many Mardi Gras over the decades, and old metal signs advertising various beers—Jax seemed the most popular—soft drinks, and White Lily flour.

The smells emanating from the kitchen made Regan's mouth water.

Cajun Cal was the oldest man Regan had ever seen who was still alive. Nearly black eyes, as bright as a parrot's, looked out at her from a face as dark and wrinkled as a raisin.

"So, you're Linda Dale's little girl all grown up."

She forced a smile, as much for the audience as for the man behind the counter. It was clearly going to be impossible to keep the purpose of her trip from becoming common knowledge. "That's what I'm in Blue Bayou to find out."

"Yeah. That's what I heard." The unlit cigarette in his mouth bobbed up and down as he spooned dark coffee grounds from a bright red bag of Community Coffee into a huge urn. "Your face isn't exactly the same, and your hair isn't the same, but lookin' at your eyes, it'd be my guess you are." He studied her some more. "I also heard you're a big-city cop."

"I'm a detective, yes."

"Detective, cop, G-man, they're all the same thing. I got my start in this business when I was still a kid and my uncle hired me to deliver jugs of white lightnin' around the parish during Prohibition. Best customers we had were the cops." If there was a challenge there, and Regan suspected from his tone that there was, she refused to rise to it.

"That's the trouble with passing a law the majority of the people in the country don't agree with," she said mildly.

"Sure as hell is. Nobody down here paid much attention to Prohibition. Hell, my uncle didn't even bother to hide the stuff. Kept it right behind the counter, servin' it up by the glass to whoever wanted a snort. He brewed the best hootch in south Louisiana."

"Well, good for him." She smiled. "But if it's all the same to you, I'll just have a glass of iced tea. No," she corrected, having already tasted what appeared to pass for tea down here, "on second thought, water will be fine."

"Why don't you make that two lemonades," Nate suggested. "Regan got to sample sweet tea out at Jarrett's place."

The old man cackled. "Marybeth's sweet tea does take

some gettin' used to, even if you're not a Yankee. You sing, *chère?*"

Regan didn't so much as blink at the question that had come from left field. She could also feel everyone in the restaurant who was over fifty years old waiting for her answer.

"Not really." She decided belting out Aretha Franklin in the shower didn't count.

"Now, that's a crying shame. Linda had a real pretty voice. As pure a soprano as you'd ever want to hear. But I guess genes are an iffy thing. Lord knows, I'm the best cook in the South, and my daughter Lilah can't even boil water without burning the bottom out of the pot. As for my son, well, I've been pulling dinner from the Gulf since God was a pup, but he's a piss-poor fisherman."

"Maybe there's something your wife never got around to tellin' you, Cal," offered a man the color of coal, wearing a stained white apron and shelling shrimp. "I hear the mailman y'all had fifty years ago couldn't fish worth beans, either."

"Hardy har har," the old man scoffed, then turned piercing dark eyes back to Regan. "I also heard tell you're gonna be our new sheriff."

"I'm afraid the grapevine has it wrong."

"Wouldn't be the first time," he said equably. "We sure could use ourselves one."

"I'm sure Mayor Callahan's doing everything in his power to find the perfect candidate."

"Seems to me any cop who'll crawl under hot wires to save a kid is real close to perfect herself." He lifted a basket of golden fried fish from a deep fryer and dumped it onto a platter.

"We'll have two po' boys," Nate ordered, saving Regan from having to respond. "You want shrimp, fried fish, or roast beef, sugar?"

Not only was there something unnerving about eating fish with all those glass eyes looking down at her, the roast beef in the display case was so heavily marbled she could feel her arteries clogging just looking at it.

"I guess the shrimp."

"Good choice," Nate said. "I'll have the same as the lady, dress 'em both, and throw in a couple cartons of slaw and some hush puppies."

"Why is it called a po' boy?" Regan asked.

" 'Cause it used to only cost a nickel, so poor boys could afford it."

She watched the sandwich being made and decided that a family of six could probably eat quite well on it for a week. She also wondered if she should just call ahead and make an appointment at the hospital for bypass surgery rather than wait for the heart attack.

"Do you eat here often?" she asked Nate quietly.

"Jus' about every day. Why?"

"I was wondering why you don't weigh a thousand pounds."

"I work it off." He paused a wicked beat. "Want to know how?"

"No." Her smile was as sweet as Marybeth Boyce's tea. "I don't."

Nate had been teasing, mostly. Enjoying a little flirtation. Then he made the mistake of looking at her mouth and remembered, with vivid clarity, the taste of those full, inviting lips. The blood suddenly rushed from his head to other, more vital regions, making him feel as dizzy as he had that day Jack had swiped a case of Dixie out of a beer truck delivering out back, and the two of them had taken the pirogue out to their daddy's old camp and gotten drunk by the light of a summer bayou moon.

Easy, boy, he warned himself as he felt an almost over-whelming urge to kiss her, right here in Cajun Cal's Country Café, in front of just about everyone in town. He wanted to taste that delectable mouth again, wanted to feel it roaming all over his hot, naked body.

His hunger must have shown in his expression, because her eyes suddenly widened, and he was caught in that gleaming amber, frozen in it, which didn't make much sense, since the air between them had turned about as sizzling hot as a steamy dog-day August after-noon. Yet he couldn't have moved if someone shouted out a hurricane was blowing in from the Gulf and they were standing right atop the levee.

17

Leave this be, the angel perched on Nate's shoulder warned. *She isn't like Charlene, or Suzanne.* Or any other of the women he'd tumbled happily, easily into bed with over the years since that memorable day when he'd lost his virginity in the backseat of Jack's borrowed GTO with Misty Montgomery.

Don't listen to him, the devil on the other shoulder said. *She's a grown woman.* Nate had already determined that for himself, but what he hadn't noticed, until now, was how tight those low-slung jeans were. He wondered if she'd had to lie on the bed at the inn to zip them.

That idea led to another, of knocking all those salt and pepper shakers, metal napkin holders, and bottles of hot sauce off the chipped red counter, lifting her up onto it, unzipping those jeans, and dragging them down those smooth thighs he'd wanted to bite when she'd been up on that witness stand back in L.A.

He imagined her wearing a pair of skimpy red panties that barely covered the essentials, and although she'd beg him, "Please, Nate, rip them off, please, please, darling," he'd torture them both by taking his time, enjoying the way her eyes glazed with lust when he slipped his fingers beneath the silk, jangling her senses, causing every nerve ending in her body to sizzle.

And when he'd tormented them both to the point of no return, when he had her exactly where he wanted her, hot, needy, ravenous, he'd peel those panties down her long legs, inch by erotic inch, and as she cried out his name, he'd—

"Hey, Nate." The voice was deep, way too deep to be hers.

Nate slowly, painfully, dragged his mind back from the sensual fantasy, crashing headfirst into reality when he viewed the fifty-something man standing beside her.

"Hey, Charles," he answered on a voice roughened with lingering lust. "How's it goin'?" Like he cared.

"Fine, just fine." Charles Melancon turned his smile from Nate to Regan, who also appeared to be shell-shocked as she returned from wherever the hell they'd both been. "Hello. You must be the new sheriff I've been hearing all about."

"She ain't the sheriff," Cal said around his unlit cigarette as he wrapped the enormous sandwiches in waxed white paper. "Was just filling in during the accident out at the crossing 'tween that freight and the eighteen-wheeler."

"What a terrible, terrible thing." Melancon shook his silver head. "It was a miracle no one was seriously hurt."

"It sure could've been a lot worse," Nate agreed. His

head was beginning to clear, and he was no longer in immediate danger of bustin' the zipper out of his jeans. "Detective, this is Charles Melancon. Charles, Detective Regan Hart, from Los Angeles."

"It's a pleasure meeting you, detective." He shook her hand with the robust action of a small-town politician, which he was. Along with being CEO of Melancon Petroleum, Charles Melancon was head of several redevelopment committees, president of the Blue Bayou Rotary Club, and past president of the Chamber of Commerce. "I was very impressed by your bravery. Did the mayor happen to mention we're in the market for a new sheriff?" he asked.

"As a matter of fact, he did. But I already have a job. I'm an LAPD homicide detective."

"Are you now?" His silver brows shot up. "That must be exciting work."

"Actually, homicide's pretty much society's clean-up crew. We're like the guys with the wheelbarrows who follow the elephants in the parade and shovel up the shit."

Behind the counter, Cal gave a bark of a laugh.

"Still, it must be interesting," Melancon said. "The closest thing to excitement here in Blue Bayou is watching paint dry."

"Oh, I wouldn't think running an international oil company could possibly be dull."

Interest turned to surprise. "You know about Melancon Oil?"

"It would be hard not to, since I see the blue sign every time I fill up my car. Though I never realized the home offices were located in southern Louisiana."

That was, Nate knew, a lie. He suspected that after

having learned about the stock certificates, she could probably quote the company's latest balance sheet.

"We're not the biggest fish in the pond, but we make a right nice splash." Charles Melancon might not be the type of guy Nate would swap stories and go fishing with, but he'd always seemed fairly down-to-earth for someone whose father had probably owned half of southern Louisiana at one time. "What brings you to Blue Bayou, detective?"

"Oh, this and that." Despite seeming half the town knowing what she was up to, and the other half undoubtedly finding out by Mardi Gras, she wasn't one to give anything away. Her smile turned as vague as her tone. "Partly I'm here for a little R&R."

"Most folks go to N'Awlins for that."

"I've been there and done all the touristy, French Quarter things. This trip I decided to see the real Louisiana."

"Well, you've certainly come to the right place."

"I don't suppose you conduct tours of your facilities?" she asked.

He frowned. "Not as a rule. Refineries can be dangerous to those not familiar with the work, and our insurance company likes us to keep our liability risk down."

"Well, it never hurts to ask." She sighed heavily in a very undetective-like way. "I suppose I'll just sign up for the alligator swamp tour instead."

"You'd pretty much be wastin' your money," Nate volunteered. "Seein' as how the gators are hibernating right now."

"Oh." Her mouth turned down in a little moue that was far more woman than cop. "Well, I'm sure I can find something to occupy my time. I seem to recall reading that

Exxon Mobile has a refinery in Baton Rouge. Perhaps—"

"I suppose," Melancon interrupted her, "it would be all right to show you around, just this once." His eyes swept over her in what Nate decided was an unnecessarily intimate way for a guy who had a wife at home. "After all, what Louisiana Liability and Trust doesn't know won't hurt them."

"It'll be our secret." Her smile would have done a Miss Cajun Days queen proud. "Why don't I drop by Monday morning?"

"I'm afraid I'm going to be out of town on Monday. A meeting in Houston."

"Oh. Well, Tuesday will be fine."

"That's Fat Tuesday," Cal volunteered.

"He's right," Charles Melancon said with what appeared to be a bit of honest reluctance. "Which means that while a skeleton crew will be working, I'm afraid the offices won't be open."

"How about Wednesday?" she pressed on. "Say, about eight o'clock?"

"I'm afraid the office isn't open quite that early."

"Especially on Ash Wednesday, when everyone in the parish is going to be hung over," Cal said.

"Not everyone," Melancon corrected. "Why don't we have lunch together in the company dining room at one on Wednesday?"

Her smile could have lit up Blue Bayou for a month. "That sounds fab."

Fab? Nate stared down at the surprising metamorphosis from cop to belle.

"I'm staying at the Plantation Inn, in case something opens up before then," she said.

"Good choice," he said.

Only choice, Nate thought.

"The inn's a famous historical landmark," Melancon continued.

"So Mr. Callahan tells me. I'll be waiting for your call." She held out her hand like a princess to some duke she was considering marrying. "It was lovely meeting you, Mr. Melancon."

"The pleasure was all mine, Ms. Hart." He flashed his Chamber of Commerce meet-and-greet grin and returned to his table across the room.

"Isn't he a charming man?" Regan said.

"An absolute gem," Nate agreed dryly.

"Order's up," Cal announced.

Nate took the brown bags. "It's on me," he said when Regan began to take some money from her billfold. She looked inclined to argue, then merely shrugged.

"What the hell was that all about?" Nate asked Regan when they were back in the SUV.

"What was what all about?"

"That Scarlett O'Hara act you pulled with Charles Melancon."

"I've no idea what you mean."

"You're not the type of woman who normally goes around batting your eyelashes."

"Too bad you missed my days in vice, when I did undercover prostitution stings." She pulled her seat belt across and clicked it. "I'll have you know, some men found me very appealing."

"Of course you're appealing, dammit. But not in that way."

"And what way is that?"

"You know." Feeling as if he'd somehow landed in verbal quicksand, he skimmed a hand over his hair. "That over-the-top come-and-get-me-big-boy way. You were sending off signals that you were open for a lot more than a damn oil refinery tour."

"That's quite a comment from the man who's claimed he wants to take me to bed, and was undressing me with his eyes when Melancon interrupted."

"I didn't hear you complaining." He jerked his own seat belt closed.

"We were in a public place. I didn't feel the need to embarrass you by telling you to knock it off."

"What a bunch of bullshit." He twisted the key in the ignition with more strength than necessary and pulled away from the curb with an angry squeal of tires.

The heat that had sizzled between them in the restaurant shifted into a low, seething anger. Regan was tempted to tell him to take her back to the inn; she didn't need his help. After all, if she couldn't handle one cold case committed in a town where everyone knew everyone else, which meant someone had to hold the key to solving the murder, she might as well turn in her shield and go sell Avon products door to door.

The problem was, if she stomped back to the inn, she'd risk letting him know how affected she'd been by that suspended moment in the restaurant, when she'd been fantasizing about Nate dragging her down to the black-and-white-checked floor and making mad, passionate love to her.

"I wasn't flirting with him," she said into the heavy silence. "I need to talk to him about the stock certificates. Since I don't have any police powers down here to force the issue, and since he's undoubtedly used to calling the shots, I figured he might be more amenable to charm."

"You couldn't just come right out and ask?"

"With everyone in the place watching us and listening to every word?"

"Yeah, I can see how you'd rather them think you were coming on to a married guy twice your age than have them overhearing you ask a basic business question."

"It's not basic when a woman got killed over it."

He shot her a surprised look. "You think Linda Dale was murdered for her Melancon Petroleum stock?"

"She wouldn't have been the first person to be killed over money."

"And wouldn't be the last," he allowed. "But if that was the motive, then why were the stocks left behind?"

"Maybe the murderer got interrupted and had to leave before he could retrieve them. Maybe she had them hidden." Regan shrugged. "There could be any number of answers. Which is why I want privacy when I talk with Melancon. Not that he sounded real eager for a meeting." She frowned. "I wonder why that was?"

"Are you suspicious of everyone? Never mind," he said before she could answer the rhetorical question; "I know the answer to that. But just because he's CEO of the company doesn't mean he'll be able to tell you anything. His mother was running the place thirty years ago."

"From what you said about Mrs. Melancon, the chances are she wouldn't recall details. But not only would he have access to the records, this is a small town. It seems implausible that anyone living here—especially a nightclub singer—would own that much stock without the family being aware of it."

"Good point."

"Thank you. That's why L.A. pays me the big bucks." Which barely covered the rent on her closet-sized apartment in Westwood and insurance on a five-year-old tomato red Neon. "I wonder if he knew her?"

"Like you said, it's a small town, and it sounds like she was a local celebrity."

"I got that impression from the newspaper even before we talked with Jarrett Boyce." She chewed thoughtfully on a buffed fingernail. "Do you suppose they could have been lovers?"

"That's unlikely."

"Why?"

" 'Cause I already checked it out. Charles got married two years before Linda Dale's death."

"That doesn't mean anything. They could have been having an affair."

"That's also unlikely. Not only does the guy consider himself a pillar of morality, the conventional wisdom around these parts says that he married into money to keep his family in the style to which they'd become accustomed back when oil was king."

"You'd think being CEO of a family petroleum company would pay very well."

"Not well enough. There was a time when his daddy probably had more power than the governor. He'd had more than one governor and several congressmen in his pocket. Regulation slowed the money flow, then the bust tightened things even more. The family's richer than most around these parts, but if it wasn't for Charles's wife's money, they'd probably have to give up the plane, the yacht, the ski chalet in Aspen, and the villa in Tuscany."

"I didn't find any villa when I did my search."

"The title's in his mother-in-law's name. But she lives in one of those retirement communities in Baton Rouge and hasn't been out of the country in a decade."

"I suppose you got that from Finn."

"He did a little digging."

"I don't even want to know," Regan muttered. "I'm beginning to feel as if I'm dealing with the Hardy boys. Maybe Melancon gave Linda Dale the stock to pay her off."

"To get rid of her once he tired of the affair?"

"That's always possible."

"Sure it is. But if that was the case, then why would he kill her?"

"Maybe she refused the offer."

"She had the certificates."

"Okay, maybe she changed her mind. Maybe she took them, then threatened to go to his wife."

"Because she wanted more money?"

"Or because she was in love and decided that she couldn't live without him."

"So he killed her to shut her up."

"That's one scenario."

"You realize, of course, that if you're right, Melancon could be your father?"

"We can't all have heroes for fathers." It was looking more and more likely that she probably didn't. "But the name's wrong. Dale referred to the man she was going to run off with as J," she reminded him. Then paused.

"There's something I haven't wanted to bring up. But I don't think we can overlook it."

"What?"

"You do realize that there's someone else who could have been involved with Dale."

"More than one someone. There are a helluva lot of names in this parish that begin with *J.*"

"Like Jake."

She'd expected him to swear. Maybe even rage. At least snap back a denial. He did none of that. He threw back his sun-gilded head and roared with laughter.

"It's not that funny."

"If you'd known my dad, you'd think it was. There's no way he would have looked at another woman. He and *maman* used to embarrass the hell out of us kids, the way they used to neck like teenagers. They renewed their vows on their twentieth wedding anniversary, right here at Holy Assumption.

"The very next weekend, on the night before he was killed, they were partying at his fortieth birthday party. I remember groaning with Jack when they were dancing to this slow Cajun song about love goin' wrong and they kissed, right there, in front of God and everyone in Blue Bayou. And not just a friendly little husband-and-wife public peck on the cheek. They were really gettin' into it." His expression turned reminiscent and understandably sad. "Everyone in the parish knew Jake Callahan flat-out adored my mother. And she adored him back."

"I believe that." It wouldn't be that hard to fall in love with a Callahan man, if a woman was looking to fall in love. Which she definitely was not. "But nobody's perfect. People make mistakes. Get themselves in messy situations they never could have imagined."

"Even if he had slipped, and I'm not saying he did, since I don' believe it for a damn minute, if he'd gotten a woman pregnant, he would have done right by her."

"*Done right*. Does that mean marry?"

"Hell, I don't know." He was no longer laughing. In fact, he was as sober as she'd ever seen him. Even more serious than when he was crawling beneath those electrical wires to rescue the trucker and a runaway teenager.

He blew out a long ragged breath. "Maybe. Maybe not. I told you, he took his marriage vows seriously, so I can't see him signing up for a lifetime sentence if he wasn't in love."

"Sentence. Well, that certainly reveals how you think about marriage."

"Actually, I try *not* to think about it. I'm also not real wild about the way you're analyzing every damn word I use, like this is some kind of interrogation. However, as I was about to point out, even if Dad were to go plantin' his seed somewhere, he would have insisted on contributing to his child's support.

"I watched him chase down men who didn't pay their child support and toss them in jail until they decided it'd be better to write the checks, long before it got politically popular to crack down on deadbeat dads. Dad was big on birthdays and holidays, and just taking us boys out to the camp for a lazy summer day of fishing, or even tossin' a ball around the backyard before supper. He'd never desert his own flesh and blood." His hand had curled into an unconscious fist. "He wouldn't have let your mother live in the same town and never acknowledged you."

"I understand why you'd want to stand up for him. I also understand why you'd find it hard to believe that he might possibly commit adultery, since it's obvious you respect him—"

"There's not a man, woman, or child who knew Jake Callahan who didn't respect him."

"I'm also willing to accept that. But we can't ever really know our parents, Nate, because they try their best never to let us see their flaws. I'm proof that an otherwise honest parent might think it's in everyone's best interest to keep a secret from their children."

"Not my dad, dammit. Look, you've met Finn."

"Of course."

"Let me put it this way: our father would make Finn look downright flexible."

"You're joking." She'd never met a more rigid, black-and-white person than Finn Callahan. And living in the world of cops, that was really saying something.

"This is not exactly a joking matter. It's also a moot point, because Dad was working in Chicago when your mother got pregnant."

"He was sheriff of Blue Bayou when she lived here."

"When she died," Nate corrected. "But you're the same age as Jack, and he and Finn were both born in Chicago. We moved here when I was six weeks old."

"Oh. Well, I guess that does take him out of the picture, since there's no indication Dale ever lived in Illinois."

"Not unless you want to concoct some theory about them meeting on some plane trip and becoming members of the mile-high club over Kansas, then going their separate ways after it landed."

The uncharacteristic sarcasm in his tone was sharp enough to cut crystal. "I suppose I deserved that."

"No." He sighed and shook his head. "You didn't. I understand this is tough on you, and you're only doin' what comes naturally. Detecting."

"I'm sure as hell not doing very well at it so far," she muttered.

"Like you said, it's a cold case. You've only been in town two days."

"I know. I just get impatient."

"That's not good for you. Raises your blood pressure and all sorts of bad stuff. Move here, and you're bound to slow down. Live longer."

"Maybe it just seems longer."

He chuckled at that.

"Do you know Melancon's wife?"

"Sure. She's on just about every charitable committee in town. As mayor, I have a lot of dealings with her. She tends to keep busy, and her fingers are in most of the pies around town. She does a lot of charity work, but it's seldom the hands-on kind of stuff. She's more likely to donate a wing to the hospital than drive around in her Jag delivering Meals on Wheels.

"She can be so condescending your teeth hurt from being clenched, and she's a snob, along with being Blue Bayou's self-appointed morality czarina. But I can't see her killing anyone, if that's where you were going. Especially if it'd involve anything that might involve chipping a fingernail."

"There's one thing I learned early on in homicide."

"What's that?"

"Everyone's a suspect."

"You're a hard woman, Detective *Chère.*"

"I'm a realist." She had to be. "I'm going to want to meet her."

"Mrs. Melancon?"

"Yeah. The way I see it, I can do it three ways. I can find out her daily activity pattern and just happen to run into her by chance and get to chatting, but that's iffy, and if she's in a hurry, it doesn't give me a real good opportunity to talk with her.

"Or I can just go to her house, knock on the door, tell her that her husband may be a suspect in a thirty-year-old murder case, and could we have a little chat about whether or not he used to sleep around on her back when she was a young bride.

"Or," she said as he pulled up to a four-way stop, "I can have you arrange things."

He braked and briefly shut his eyes. "Why did I know you were going to say that?"

"Because you've spent all your life surrounded by cops. Some of it's got to have rubbed off onto you."

"I use that soap with pumice in it so it doesn't stick."

"You might not want to admit it, Callahan, but on occasions, you, too, can think like a cop."

He frowned. "I don't know if I've been complimented or insulted."

She laughed for the first time, and Nate was struck by how much he enjoyed the rich, full sound. She reached over and patted his cheek. "Why don't you think on it."

18

They stopped for a while in a peaceful spot next to the bayou for lunch. The sandwich was the richest she'd ever tasted. She'd only been able to finish half of it and still didn't think she'd be able to eat again for a week. They'd parked beside a metal marker memorializing the victory of a battle against the Union Army.

"Isn't that the pirate you were going to tell me about?" She remembered him mentioning that when they'd first entered the ER.

"That's him. Jean Lafitte. Actually, there were three of them—Alexander, Pierre, and Jean—but Jean was the most infamous. Alexander, who, I guess you could say was most respectable, was Napoleon's artillery officer. Jean and Pierre were privateers who earned their living attacking the trading ships comin' and goin' between the Gulf and the river cities."

"I imagine there was a fairly good profit in piracy."

"*Mais* yeah. Jean and Pierre had thirty-two armed warships under their command, they, which was more than the entire American navy at the start of the War of 1812. Both the British and the Americans recruited them, but Andrew Jackson was the one who promised them amnesty if they'd fight in the Battle of New Orleans."

"Which they did," she guessed.

"They did. After they won the battle and sent the Redcoats packing, they went right back to raiding. Tales about his final restin' place flow as freely as Voodoo beer at Mardi Gras, but folks here in Blue Bayou prefer the one where he was buried in an unmarked grave after bein' on the losing end of a duel with one of his lover's husbands. His ghost is real popular, showin' up all over the bayou, sometimes at the wheel of his warship."

"Have you ever seen him?"

"Now, I can't say that I have. But I think I did hear him one night in Holy Assumption's cemetery, back when I was in high school."

"What were you doing in a cemetery at night? Never mind," she said an instant later as the answer came to her.

"I don't expect you'd believe I was studying the stars?"

"Only if you happened to be studying them with a girl."

He rubbed his chin. "Studying was always more fun when you had someone to do it with. I have to admit, the sound of those chains rattlin' nearly scared the pants off me."

"I have the feeling they wouldn't have stayed on long anyway."

He put a hand against his chest. "You wound me, Detective *Chère*."

"I strongly doubt that's possible," she said lightly, enjoying sparring with him. As she'd sat in the SUV and drank in the absolute silence surrounding them, Regan had found herself beginning to relax. It had been an odd sensation; she had actually taken a few moments to recognize the feeling.

Unfortunately, they couldn't suspend time forever. After driving another ten minutes, Nate turned off the main road again and headed through a cane break.

"Where are we going, now?" she asked.

"Beau Soleil."

"Jack and Dani's plantation house?"

"Yeah. I've got some work to do there, and it'll let me check up on the kid."

"Construction work?"

"Sorta. Blue Bayou usually has the Mardi Gras party in the park, but this year Dani decided it'd be fun to host it at Beau Soleil, like back in the old days when her daddy pretty much ran the town. The party's free, of course, but for an extra five bucks you get a tour of the house and some autographed books Jack's donating. Between the home's history and my brother's fame, the tickets have been sellin' like popcorn shrimp. The money goes into the parish's community chest."

"That's nice."

"It's more of a necessity. The parish still hasn't fully recovered from the oil bust, when a lot of folks had to leave land that had been in their families for generations and move into the cities. Those who stayed behind have to work harder to keep things together."

"You really do fit here, don't you?"

He didn't have to think about that for a moment. "Yeah. I do."

"There are a lot of things I like about L.A. The beach, my friends, my work. The fact that I may be making a difference. But I've never actually felt as if it was home."

"Must be hard for roots to settle in concrete and asphalt."

Part of Nate had decided long ago that perhaps not reaching his youthful dream of playing third base for the Yankees hadn't been such a bad thing, after all. He'd have hated to get to New York and discover that the fantasy hadn't been anywhere near the reality. He wasn't, after all, a hustle-bustle kind of guy.

"Maybe you never felt like you belonged in California because Blue Bayou's your true home," he suggested.

"Even if I do turn out to be Regan Dale, I didn't live here long enough to have a connection. I certainly haven't recognized anything, or had any feeling of déjà vu."

"Maybe you're tryin' too hard. Sometimes the answer comes when you're not looking for it."

"Is that something else you've read in one of Jack's books?"

"Nope. That's mine. From when I'll be wrestling a set of blueprints all night, trying to make something work, and later, while I'm having morning beignets and coffee at Cal's and arguing sports scores, the solution will just come right out of the blue."

She'd experienced the same thing, when she'd been working a case that seemed a dead end, and suddenly the answer would occur to her.

"Stay around a while, and Blue Bayou will start to grow on you," he suggested. "Maybe I will, too." He skimmed a hand over her hair.

"Like that Spanish moss hanging from all these trees."

He chuckled, unwounded.

Nate turned onto another unmarked road, which took them down a narrow lane lined with oaks that appeared centuries old. When he turned a corner and the white Greek Revival antebellum plantation house suddenly appeared, gleaming like alabaster in the sunshine, she drew in a sharp breath.

"It really is Tara."

"Pretty damn close," he agreed. "There are those around here who swear Margaret Mitchell used Beau Soleil for the model in her book."

"That's what Dani said, but I'm not sure I took her seriously. Wow. It's stunning. It's also hard to believe that anyone—any normal person, that is—actually lives here."

"Dani and Jack are as normal as you get, basically. Her family first got the deed to the place in the mid-1800s. Her ancestor, André Dupree, won it in a bouree game on a riverboat. Her daddy, the judge, nearly lost it to taxes a while back when he had himself some personal problems, but Jack came to the rescue and bailed him out."

"That was certainly a grand gesture."

"He said at the time he liked the idea of bein' a man of property, and wanted to stop this New Orleans mob family from turning it into a casino, but personally, I think he bought it for Dani's sake, since he still had strong feelings for her. When they got married, it landed back in the Dupree family again."

"Well, that's certainly convenient."

"Neither one of them married for the house. When you see 'em together, you'll realize they could be just as happy living in a one-bedroom trailer."

"This is certainly not a trailer." Her gaze swept over the white-pillared facade. "I'd feel as if I were living in some Civil War tourist attraction. Did you say you grew up here?"

"Not in the big house. We moved into one of the smaller ones after Dad was killed." He pointed toward a small white house on the outskirts of the compound. "After *maman* died, it sat vacant for a lot of years. Dani's turned it into a guest house. It's real cozy, even bein' haunted like it is."

"Of course. What would an old antebellum home be without a ghost?"

"There you go, bein' skeptical again," he said easily. "He's a Confederate officer who got lost here in the bayou after the Battle of New Orleans. Since the Union Army had taken over Beau Soleil, one of Dani's ancestors hid him in the little house. According to the story, she sent her own personal maid to take care of him during the day, then every night, she'd be real liberal when it came to pouring the port. After all the Yankees would pass out, she'd sneak out of the house and take the night shift trying to nurse that poor Confederate boy back to health, which was a pretty gutsy thing to do, since harboring the enemy was a hangin' offense. Even for a woman."

"That couldn't have been an easy decision." Easier, perhaps, if the southern soldier had resembled the man sitting beside her. She could see a woman taking foolish risks for Nate Callahan. "I take it she failed?"

"Yeah. The poor guy's leg had been blown off, and he ended up dying, probably of sepsis. When we were growing up we heard stories about the lady, who lived to a ripe old age, tellin' folks that he used to come visit her at night, but people figured she'd just gotten a little touched in the head."

"But you believe the stories," Regan guessed.

"I like the idea of them findin' happiness together. I've never seen him, though Jack claims to have heard music in the ballroom, where they're supposed to dance."

"I'll bet Finn never saw the ghost, either."

He rubbed his jaw. "Now, see, that's what you get for stereotyping. Finn's the only one of the three of us who actually has seen him."

"I don't believe that." Finn Callahan was the last person, other than herself, she'd expect to believe in such fantasy.

"My hand to God." He lifted his right hand. "Though I suppose, in the interest of full disclosure, I oughta add that he was feverish with flu at the time, and once he got better he tried to back away from his story about seeing the two of them waltzing."

"It seems as if it'd be hard to waltz with one leg."

"Oh, I don't know," Nate argued. "People can do a lot of things when they're in love that they might not do otherwise. Or so I hear."

She wasn't surprised he referred to hearsay. Nate Callahan did not strike her as a man who'd fall in love. Lust, sure. But the forever-after kind of love? No way. Another thing they had in common

The front door opened, and a huge yellow ball of fur came barreling toward them. "Brace yourself," Nate warned as she tensed. Every cop who'd ever worked the rough parts of town, and a lot who were assigned the cozier suburbs, had learned the hard way that it was best to be wary of strange dogs. "She's not dangerous, 'less you consider gettin' licked to death a problem."

What appeared to be a mix between a yellow lab and a school bus came skidding to a halt in front of them. Her tail was wagging like an out-of-control metronome. "Hey, Turnip." Nate took a Milk-Bone from his jeans pocket and tossed it to her. The treat disappeared in a single gulp.

The dog turned to Regan, who did usually carry dog treats with her, partly because she liked dogs and partly to make friends with the territorial ones. "Sorry, doggie. I'm all out." Wishing she'd saved the other half of the sandwich from lunch, she rubbed the huge head thrust toward her. "Her name's Turnip?"

"Yeah." He grinned as the enormous pink tongue slurped the back of Regan's hand. " 'Cause she just turned up one day." He glanced up as Josh appeared on the front *gallerie*. "She was a stray. Just like some kid I know."

"You just missed her," Josh announced as they approached.

"Missed who?" Nate asked.

"That social worker. Isn't that what you're doing out here?"

"Actually, I came to do some carpentry work. Didn't even know Judi was coming out today. So, I don't suppose your memory happened to make a comeback?"

"Nope."

Nate shook his head. "Terrible thing, amnesia. Who knows, you might turn out to be a spy, just like that Matt

Damon character in *The Bourne Identity*. Sure would hate for Blue Bayou to be overrun with international assassins."

"Like that's goin' to happen." He smirked.

"Never know," Nate said mildly. "You have any talents you don't remember learning? Like maybe some martial arts or driving a getaway car?"

"No, but if I did have any, I wouldn't have time to notice, since the famous fuckin' author's been making me sand woodwork ever since you dumped me here."

"Well, then, we'll just have to keep thinkin' on it and keep alert for any clues. Meanwhile, sanding is an important job. Can't stain without getting the wood all smooth first."

"It's boring."

"I suppose it can be if you do too much of it for too long. So, how'd you like to switch to something a little larger?"

"Like what?"

"I've got to build a stage for the band and could always use an extra hand."

"Shit, this is turning out to be like prison."

"The detective here might know better than me about jailhouse fashion, but I've driven past prisoners workin' the fields up at Angola, and can't recall ever seein' anyone wearing an Ozzie Osbourne shirt. They all seem to favor stripes. So, what do you say?"

"What's in it for me?"

"I'm not real sure. But it's always good to learn a new skill, just in case it turns out you're not a secret agent. Plus, it could just look good on your juvie report in case you've got some police problem that's slipped your mind."

Nate glanced over as another teenager appeared in the doorway. This one was a girl, tall and willowy, with pale hair down to her waist and thickly fringed green eyes. Looking at her, Regan had a very good idea what Dani had looked like at thirteen.

"Hi, Uncle Nate." When she went up on her toes and gave him a peck on the cheek, Regan noticed a flash of something that looked like old-fashioned envy in Josh's eyes. "Guess what? Ben and his mom moved into the guest house last night."

"Good for them, Holly.

"Ben's Misty's boy," Nate explained to Regan. "He's a sophomore."

He glanced over at Josh, who was staring at the girl as if she were a gilt angel atop a Christmas tree. "Guess you and Ben'd be about the same age."

The only answer was a shrug.

"They both play ball, too." Holly Callahan's revelation drew a sharp warning look from Josh, but she appeared unaware that she'd just given away something he hadn't wanted them to know.

"Is that so?" Nate said casually. "I played a bit in my day."

"I told him that you played third base for the Buccaneers and went to Tulane. Josh plays shortstop."

"Must have some fast moves."

"I get by," Josh mumbled. Regan was amused when he began rubbing the worn toe of his sneaker in the dirt like a shy six-year-old.

"We usually end up playing a softball game while the Mardi Gras supper's cooking. I don' suppose I could talk you into bein' on my team," Nate said.

Josh was tempted. Regan could see it. But once again trust didn't come easily, and she knew he was looking for the catch.

"You gonna be the cheerleader?" he asked Holly.

"No." Her eyes flashed in a way that suggested a bit of steel beneath that cotton-candy blond exterior. "I play first base. When I'm not pitching, that is." Her smile was sweet and utterly false. "If you don't want to be on Uncle Nate's team, we could always use a mascot. Maybe you could dress up like a pirate. Or a chicken."

The gauntlet had been thrown down.

Josh narrowed his eyes. His cheeks flushed with anger, embarrassment, or both. "I'll play," he told Nate with all the enthusiasm of a death-row inmate on the way to the electric chair.

"Great." Nate threw an arm around both Josh and Holly's shoulders in that easy way he had. Regan saw the boy stiffen again, but Nate ignored it. "Let's keep the fact that you played back home our little secret," he suggested. "No point in helping the other team with the point spread."

"You fixin' softball games again, *cher?*" a deep voice rumbled from inside the house.

Jack Callahan emerged from the shadows, looking even more rakish than he appeared on the back of his books. With his dark hair tied with a leather thong at the nape of his darkly tanned neck and that gold earring, Regan thought he could easily be a buccaneer in the flesh.

"Wouldn't be any challenge if there wasn't money on the line," Nate said.

"With that attitude, it's a good thing you didn' make the pros, since last I heard, gamblin' on games was illegal." Jack turned toward Regan. "Hi. You must be the lady I've been hearing about. Regan Hart."

"Yes." She smiled, truly appreciative he'd used the name she'd always known. "At least that's always been my name."

"We've got ourselves a little family experience with long-lost kids comin' to Blue Bayou to find their roots," he said, flashing a grin at Holly. The way she beamed back told Regan there was another story there. "Even if you find out some stuff about your past you didn't know, it doesn't negate all those other years."

He glanced up as a tall, lanky, dark-haired boy came around the corner from the direction of the guest house. "Looks like the lunch break's over," he said. "I'll drive you and Ben back to school," he told Holly. "If you're going to be here for a while," he said to Nate.

"Yeah. Josh's gonna help with the stage."

"Good idea." He bestowed another warm smile on Regan and walked toward the classic cherry red GTO parked beside the house. Regan watched Josh watching the trio get in the car.

"You just want to make sure I don't run away," Josh said.

"You thinkin' of running, *cher?*"

"None of your business if I am."

"Well, now, you know that's not 'xactly true, since I signed a paper taking responsibility for you."

"I can take care of myself."

"Maybe on a good day. But I get the impression there haven't been many of those lately."

Josh's only answer was to spit into the dirt. Then his gaze drifted to the departing car. He looked like a starving child staring into a bakery window.

"Holly sure is a pretty *fille*," Nate observed.

He didn't respond.

"Smart, too. Gets straight As."

Again no answer.

"She and Ben are really close friends, having as much in common as they do."

"Big freakin' deal."

Bull's-eye. "Having a friend is sure enough a big deal. And, not that you asked, because you're probably not real interested in pretty blond girls who smell like gardens, but they're not boyfriend and girlfriend.

"Ben's goin' with Kendra Longworth, whose *maman* teaches third grade at Holy Assumption school. Holly was seein' Trey Gaffney for a time when she first got to town last spring, but they broke up after Christmas, so she's pretty much available. Not that I'd be all that fond of the idea of my favorite niece spendin' Mardi Gras with an amnesiac secret agent," he said.

"I'm not any damn spy."

"That's good to hear. Seems she might jus' have somethin' in common with a ballplayer. Bein' how she's on the girls' varsity team."

"Big deal. It's still just a girls' team."

"You keep that in mind when she strikes you out with her slider," Nate said. "Now, why don't you go get my toolbox out of the back of my truck and we'll get to work."

"I'm not sure your brother would be real happy with you playing matchmaker with his daughter and a runaway juvenile delinquent," Regan said as they watched Josh make his way in unenthusiastic slow motion toward the SUV.

"I wasn't matchmaking; jus' suggesting a couple kids play ball together. After all, there's nothing more American than baseball. Besides, like I said, Jack spent some time in juvie himself. He's not one to pass judgment."

"And Dani?"

He laughed at that. "If there's anyone who knows both the appeal and the downside of bad boys, it's Dani. I figure she can give her little girl the appropriate motherly advice. Besides, it's not like they're going to be alone. The entire town'll be here chaperoning them. Meanwhile, it gives the kid a reason to stick around at least one more day, so maybe we can find out who he is. And what he's running away from."

Seeing how they all seemed to watch out for each other somehow made small-town life not quite so suffocating to Regan.

The outside of Beau Soleil was gorgeous. The inside quite literally took her breath away. She stared up at the mural that covered the wall of the two-story entry hall, rose to the plaster ceiling medallions, then swept up the wide curving stairway she recognized from more than one movie.

"It's stunning. Is it original to the house?" she asked.

"No, but it's real old. André Dupree had the mural painted in memory of the Grand Dérangement, when the English kicked his people out of eastern Canada, where they'd ended up after fleeing for religious freedom even before the Pilgrims landed at Plymouth Rock."

He was telling the story as if it'd happened yesterday. Which, in some people's minds, probably wasn't that far off.

"The Acadians, which is what we Cajuns were officially called, were pretty much left alone to do their own thing for the next hundred years, but after the French and Indian War, the British weren't really happy about these French-speaking people livin' halfway between New England and New France. They demanded the Acadians renounce their Catholic religion and pledge allegiance to England. Well, now, they were a pretty stubborn people—"

"Were?" She arched a brow.

He grinned. "Things don't change much down here in the bayou. Anyway, when they refused, they were rounded up and deported. Some were sold as indentured servants to the American colonies, others were sent back to France, some ended up in concentration camps in England, and a few managed to evade deportation by hiding out in Nova Scotia.

"Things were looking pretty bleak for them when the Spaniards entered into the situation. Since the Acadians were staunch enemies of the British by now and Catholic to boot, the Spanish decided they'd be dandy people to populate their Louisiana settlements. The Acadians, happy for a chance to reunite their families—families have always been real important in the Cajun culture— liked the beauty of the land, not to mention all the bountiful fresh foods, which tasted pretty good after their years in exile. So they dug into the swamp like crawfish."

"Sounds like a happy ending." She wondered what it would be like to grow up in a place where everyone seemed to be related, if not by blood then by common experience.

"I guess it pretty much is. There's about a quarter million descendants of those original Acadians living around here, though the economy's taken a hit from time to time and caused a lot to move to the cities. But wherever a Cajun goes, he always takes a bit of this place away with him. And his heart always stays here in the swamp."

"Is that why you stay?"

"I don' know." He shrugged. "When I was a kid, I had big dreams and left for a while, but I ended up coming back and stayed for family reasons."

"Dani told me about your mother. I'm sorry."

Another shrug. "It was a bad time I wouldn't want to relive. But there's not much a person can do but keep on keeping on, is there?"

"No." Regan sighed, thinking about her own mother's death. Karen Hart's death, she amended.

"Gotta be hard, losing *two* mothers."

"It's not easy." She no longer doubted that Linda Dale had been her birth mother. "Which is why I'm going to find out the truth of what happened, and make certain that whoever was to blame for her death pays."

"Why if the autopsy report turns out to be true?"

"Those entries in her journal weren't written by a woman about to commit suicide."

"Something could have happened. Maybe your father didn't show up. Or maybe he did, and told her that he wasn't going to leave his wife."

"Eliminating maybes is what I do. I need to know about her life."

"So you'll have a better handle on your own."

Regan wasn't as surprised as she might have been even

yesterday at his understanding so well how his news had packed an emotional punch.

"Yeah."

He led her to the huge ballroom, with high ceilings that had been painted a pale lemon yellow and lots of tall windows designed to bring the outdoor gardens inside. It took no imagination at all to envision beautiful women dressed in formal satin, hoop skirts skimming along the polished floor as they danced in the arms of their handsome, formally clad partners. The sconces circling the room were electric, but she could easily picture the warm glow of candlelight.

"It just keeps getting better and better," she said on a deep, appreciative sigh, surprised to discover a romantic lurking inside her.

"You should have seen it back around Thanksgiving. Since it's the biggest room in the house, we've been using it as an indoor workshop for winter and rainy days. You couldn't go more than a couple feet without bumping into a sawhorse. Plaster and sawdust were all over everything, and the floor was covered with paint cans. After Dani decided to hold the Mardis Gras festivities here, about every carpenter, painter, and electrician in the parish has been pulling overtime."

"Well, they definitely earned it." She ran her fingers over a chair rail that had been sanded as smooth as an infant's bottom. "I wouldn't have expected to find such craftsmanship in such a small, out-of-the-way place."

"Actually, towns like Blue Bayou probably hold the last remaining old-time craftsmen. Since we're not in a real dire need for more parking spaces, we tend to hang onto our old buildings. Which means that people who know how to do restoration will probably always be able to find work, even if the annual income probably isn't what they could make in the city."

"The city's more expensive to live in, though." She looked up at the glorious ceiling fresco someone had painstakingly restored. "And I'd imagine this sort of work is more artistically satisfying."

"I've always thought so." He smiled easily, then opened his arms. "*Viens ici*, sugar."

"I thought we'd agreed you were taking a moratorium on trying to seduce me."

"I am. We just finished the floor last week and I figured we should try it out. See if it's smooth enough for dancing, in case it rains tomorrow and we have to bring the party indoors."

Dammit, she was tempted. Too tempted. "There isn't any music."

"No problem." When she didn't go to him, he closed the small distance between them. "We'll make our own."

"Good try, but I think I'll pass."

He tucked her hair behind her ear. "Afraid?"

"Of you?" Her laugh was quick. "No, Callahan, I am definitely not afraid of you."

His fingers curved around the nape of her neck. As she watched his eyes turn from calm to stormy, she felt another one of those inner pulls that both intrigued her and ticked her off. "Maybe you should be." He slowly lowered his head. "Maybe we should both be."

It would be an easy thing to back away, but just as she was about to do so, he shifted gears and dropped a quick kiss on her forehead.

"We'd best go see what's holdin' up the kid, before he

steals all my hand tools and heads off to the nearest pawnshop."

Feeling shaky, Regan followed him outside. "You're a strange man, Callahan. I can't get a handle on you."

"Me?" His laugh woke up Turnip, who'd been dozing happily in the shade of a weeping willow. Brown eyes turned limpid, as if hoping for another Milk-Bone. "I'm an open book."

"And I'm the queen of the Mardi Gras. That good-old-boy routine may work with your hometown belles, but I'm not buying it."

He grinned. "Maybe I'm one of a kind, me."

As irritated as she was with him for being so damn appealing, and herself for being attracted, Regan could not dispute that.

19

While Nate and Josh worked on the stage, Regan took her laptop into the book-lined library and began writing up her notes before the details began to slip her mind. She'd finished with the Boyce interview and her impression of Marybeth when she made the mistake of looking out the window, and her mind went as clear as glass.

The sun had burned off all the morning fog, warming the day. She watched Nate wipe his brow with the back of his hand. He said something to Josh, who shook his head in characteristically negative response. Nate shrugged, then pulled the black T-shirt over his head, revealing a rock-hard chest that looked gilded in the golden afternoon light. A light sheen of sweat glistened on tanned flesh, drawing her attention to the arrowing of gilt hair that disappeared below the waist of his faded jeans.

He took a long drink from a canteen; when some of

the water ran down his body, he casually wiped it off his belly, then returned to work, the long muscles in his back flexing and releasing, again and again, as he pounded the nails with that large, wooden-handled hammer.

Determined to avoid the sensual pull of that hard mahogany body, Regan sighed and returned to work.

After turning down dinner invitations from both Dani and Nate—after so many sexual jolts to her system today, she didn't want to risk being alone with him—Regan spent the evening alone in her suite, trying to create a time-flow chart of Linda Dale's life in Louisiana.

Outside the French doors leading out onto a cast-iron-railed balcony, the citizens of Blue Bayou began to get an early start on Fat Tuesday celebrations. Music poured from the bar downstairs, people were literally dancing in the street, and the sound of firecrackers being set off all over town—sounding like random gunshots—made her edgy. Edgy enough that she jumped when the phone rang.

She picked up the receiver.

"There's nothing for you here in Blue Bayou." The voice was muffled, and so low she couldn't tell the gender. "You should go back to California where you belong. Before you ruin good people's lives."

"Who is this?" Regan reached for the phone pad, but the dial tone revealed that her caller had hung up.

"Damn." She went over to the window and stared down onto the street and the park beyond. Looking for . . . what? Who?

The phone rang again. This time, when she grabbed it, she didn't immediately speak, hoping her caller would say something that would allow her to recognize his voice.

"*Chère?*"

"It's you." She let out a deep breath she'd been unaware of holding. "What do you want?"

"It'll wait." Nate's voice was rich and deep and concerned. It was also not the voice of whoever had called her earlier. "What's wrong?"

Her laugh held no humor. "How about what's right?" She dragged a hand through her hair. "Someone just called me and warned me off the Dale case."

"You were threatened?" The sharp tone could have been Finn's.

"Not in so many words."

"Give me thirty minutes to drop Josh with Jack, and I'll be there."

"That's not necessary." That was also so Finn, determined to take control of a situation. "Besides, the boy's not a puppy. You can't just keep dumping him on your family."

"That's what family's for. Not for dumping, but for taking care of one another."

She thought about pointing out that Josh no-last-name wasn't family, then didn't. "Well, I'm capable of taking care of myself. Besides, I'm exhausted, and I'm going to bed. I'll be asleep by the time you'd get here." Actually, she was so revved up from the call, she wasn't sure she'd get any sleep tonight.

"I'll call the state cops." The fact that he didn't suggest spending the night in bed with her showed how seriously he was taking the anonymous phone call.

"You will not. The only way anyone can get up here is with a coded key, which probably makes this suite the safest place in the state, other than the governor's mansion. I'll be fine. Besides, I have a gun, remember?"

"It's hard to forget when a woman threatens to shoot you." The edge to his tone was softening. "Maybe we should call Finn. Get a tap on the phone."

"You've been watching too much television. Even if Finn was still FBI, getting a judge to sign off on a wiretap isn't that easy."

"I wasn't thinking about going through a judge."

"That's illegal."

"And your point is? I don't want anything happening to you, *chère*."

"That's very sweet, but—"

"There's nothin' sweet about it. You and I have some unfinished business, detective. I want to make sure you stay alive long enough to experience my world-class, mind-blowing, bone-melting lovemaking."

She snorted a laugh, her tension finally loosening. "You really are shameless."

"You just wait and see," he promised on a low, sexy rumble. "Dwayne's on duty tonight, to make sure people don't start gettin' a jump on passing too good a time. I'll have him keep an eye on the inn. Meanwhile, have yourself a nice sleep, and I'll see you in the morning."

"What's happening in the morning?"

"There's a final meeting of the Mardi Gras dance committee at the courthouse at eleven-thirty. I thought you might want to attend."

"Why would I want to do that?" She'd planned to use the time to track down the doctor who'd signed Linda Dale's death certificate.

"Maybe 'cause the head of that committee is Toni Melancon?"

"Charles Melancon's wife?"

"Got it in one. She and Charles live with the old lady up at the Melancon plantation. I figured if anything just happened to go wrong with her Jag—"

"You're going to screw up her engine?"

"I wouldn't even know how to do such a thing, me."

"But you're not above having someone else do it," she guessed.

"I think I'm going to have to take the Fifth on that one, detective. But let's just say that maybe something *was* to go wrong with that tricky, hand-built British engine, it'd only be gentlemanly for me to offer her a ride home. Havin' been brought up to be a southern lady with manners, she's bound to feel obliged to invite me in for a refreshing beverage after that long drive, and bein' how you just happen to be with me—"

"She'd have to invite me in, too."

His low whistle caused her lips to curl and something in her stomach to tug. "Hot damn, you are a clever woman. I'll wonder if that L.A. mayor knows how lucky he is to have you fighting crime in his city."

"He hasn't mentioned it lately."

"Well, now, there's another reason for you to think about comin' to work here. As mayor, it'd be my civic duty to make sure you felt duly appreciated."

"Dammit, Callahan, I really am beginning to like you."

"That's the idea," he said easily. "So, here's the plan. I've got to enroll Josh in school tomorrow morning—"

"I don't envy you that."

"Strangely, he didn't seem down on the idea. If I didn't know better, I'd say he was actually looking forward to it."

"He's probably scamming you. Pretending to go along with the idea, then tomorrow morning you'll wake up to find him and all your silver gone."

"Lucky for me I've only got stainless steel. Though there was this woman, a while back, who tried to get me interested in flatware. Which would you pick out if you were gettin' married? Chrysanthemum or Buttercup?"

"It's a moot point, since I'm not getting married. And I don't even know what you're talking about. I assume these are sterling patterns and not flowers?"

"Yeah."

"Gee, Callahan, is this a proposal?"

There was nearly a full minute of dead air on the phone line. "I'm sorry, *chère*, if I gave you that impression." His earlier light tone was regretful. "I thought we were just talking, fooling around to lighten the situation up a bit."

"That's exactly what I thought. And it was going along pretty well until you decided to get domestic."

He chuckled at that. "There are those who'd tell you that my name doesn't belong in the same sentence as anything resembling domesticity."

"I've not a single doubt they're right. So why bring up that question in the first place?"

"It just sorta popped into my head. Suzanne—that was her name—always said you could tell the kind of person a woman was by her flatware pattern."

"You're kidding."

"That's pretty much what I said, thinking that she was just bein' a little precious, but no, she had this book that had it all laid out, sorta like horoscopes. Apparently Buttercup girls are always cheerful and upbeat, and Chrysanthemum girls are more flamboyant. She liked to think of herself as being cheerfully flamboyant."

"Apparently there was a limit to her cheerfulness. Since you're not married, one of you obviously broke the engagement."

"Oh, we weren't engaged. She sort of got it into her mind that we were engaged to be engaged, but I never made her any promises about a ring, or anything."

"Or brought up registering for silver."

"Not a word."

Regan had begun to relax again. She twined the telephone cord around her fingers. "So does this story have a happy ending, other than you escaping the institution of marriage? Should I feel sorry for poor Suzanne, living alone with felt-lined drawers full of flatware she never gets to use?"

"Oh, she got hitched to an old boyfriend she met at an Ole Miss reunion, so it worked out well for everyone. She finally decided on Chantilly, which hadn't even been in the early running." When she had no response to that, he added, "I went and looked the book up in Dani's library after I heard. Seems Chantilly girls can be a bit prissy. And though they may seem real sweet, they were often fast in high school. Not that I'm sayin' that about Suzanne."

"Of course not. Being a gentleman and all." She was starting to get a handle on how this southern thing worked. A man might roll in the hay with every female in town, but reputations stayed more or less intact, since a southern gentleman didn't roll and tell. "I realize the only reason you're telling me about all this is to calm me down so I can sleep. But since you brought it up, want to know what kind of girl I am?"

"I already know."

"Oh?"

"You're a mismatched stainless-steel person, just like me, when you're not using the plastic fork and knife from the takeout package."

Nailed that one, she admitted.

"But if you did ever decide to go all out, you'd be an Acorn."

"I'm almost afraid to ask why. Is Acorn for belles who swear and pack heat?"

"No, but you're close. Brides who choose Acorn have a rebellious streak. They've been known to drink beer straight from the bottle, venture north of the Mason-Dixon line to college, and some of them even marry Yankees."

"Horrors." Regan smiled. "They sound downright dangerous."

"That's part of their appeal. My *maman* had Acorn. And the only other person I've ever met who's as out-and-out spunky as her is you, Detective *Chère*, which is how I know you'd be an Acorn."

"Well." What do you say when a man just compares you to his mother, whom he obviously adored, during a conversation where he's reminding you that he's not interested in any serious relationship? "Thank you."

"*C'est rien.* Now it's your turn."

"My turn?"

"To pay me a compliment."

Fair was fair. "All right. You may be frustrating and annoying at times, but you're also very sweet."

"Sweet?" She heard the wince in his voice. "And here I was hoping for something more along the lines of the sexiest man you've ever met, who can turn you into a puddle of hot need with just a single dark and dangerous look."

"Your brother Jack got dark and dangerous. You got cute and sweet."

"Hell. Well, we're jus' going to have to work on that." He paused. "If I asked you to do something for me, would you?"

"I suppose that would depend on what it is."

"Tell me what you're wearing. Right now."

"Is this going to be one of those dirty phone calls, Callahan?"

"One can hope. What are you wearing, Regan?"

"Why?"

"Because I'd really like to be there, but since I can't, I'm trying to picture you."

"Well, you're going to be disappointed if you're looking for sexy, because I'm wearing a navy blue T-shirt that says 'Property of the LAPD Athletic Department.' " She looked down at the oversize cotton shirt that covered her from shoulders to thighs. "I suppose you would have preferred me to lie and say I was barely wearing some skimpy lace number from Victoria's Secret."

"Lace is nice. Skimpy's even better, most of the time. Sometimes, though, contrast can be real intriguing. How long is it? To your knees?"

"Not that long. And you're just going to have to use your imagination from there, because I'm not having phone sex with you."

"Too bad, because if you want to moan lots of sweet nothings in my ear, I sure wouldn't object. But since I'm enjoying just talking with you, how about I tell you a little Cajun bedtime story?"

"Could I stop you?"

"Sure. Anytime you want, you can just hang up."

"I will."

"*Bien*. Now, there was this Cajun who called himself Antoine Robicheaux, and he had himself this camp, which you'd call a cabin, way back in the bayou, miles from civilization. He was a handsome devil, he. Tall, real strong from swinging a hammer all day—"

"He was in construction?"

"General contractor." A vision of Nate as he'd looked this afternoon—shirtless, tool belt slung low on his hips like a gunfighter—flashed through her mind, bringing with it a hot, reckless, sexual need.

"Same as you."

"Now that you mention it, I guess we both do have that in common."

"Life's full of coincidences," Regan said dryly.

"Isn't that the truth? Well now, one night he was coming back from checkin' his traps when he came across this *jolie blon*. She was on her knees on the bank of the bayou, tears flowing down her cheeks, mingling with the falling rain, leaves and moss tangled in her hair. And for a moment, seeing her in the moonlight, he thought he might have stumbled across a wood nymph.

"But then he looked a little closer, he, and saw she was really just a pretty *fille* in trouble. He didn't recognize her, and she didn't seem able to speak, which made it harder for him to figure out how he was going to find out where she belonged. But having been raised up by his *maman* to be a gentleman, he decided she could spend the night at his place, then he'd decide what to do with her in the morning."

"And they say chivalry is dead."

"Like I said, he was a gentleman. Though he did have a bit of misgiving, since he'd heard tales of a witch living out in the swamp. But since she sure didn't like your stereotypical wicked witch, like the one he'd seen when he was a kid in *The Wizard of Oz*, he helped her into his pirogue and took her back to his camp.

"Dark clouds drifted over the moon. As the boat wound through the darkness, lit only by the lantern at the bow, Antoine felt as if they were being watched. Occasionally, he'd see gleaming points of yellow amid the moss-draped trees, but he reminded himself that these waters were filled with animals and he was being overfanciful. Bein' with a beautiful woman tended to do that to him, 'specially after he'd been working away from civilization for a while.

"Even though the night was warm, the earlier rain had drenched the woman, and her cotton dress was still clinging to her like a second skin when he got her into the little camp. Now, he was a big man, and knew that his clothes would swim on her, but he gave her one of his shirts, pointed her to the bathroom, and went to put on some coffee, since she still seemed a bit in shock.

"After some time, when she still hadn't come out, he began to worry, so he knocked on the door. Since she hadn't latched it, there she stood, still standing there in that same wet dress, staring out the window into the darkness. She was trembling badly, and he was afraid she might be chilled from the rain."

Regan could see where he was going with this. Still, she plumped up the goosedown pillows, leaned back, and prepared to enjoy the journey. "So, Antoine, being a gentleman, decided to help her out of her wet clothes."

"That's 'xactly what he did. But he could tell she was a real nice girl, and shy, and he didn't want to give her the wrong idea about his intentions—"

"Which were only honorable."

"*Mais* yeah. He decided the best thing to do, so he wouldn't scare her, would be to take things real slow."

"Sort of like this story."

"Want me to fast-forward to the good parts?"

"No. It's your story; go ahead and tell it your own way."

"Like I said, she was a real nice girl, and even though it was a hot and steamy evening, she'd fastened that dress all the way up to her pretty throat. So, he began talking to her, real quietly, like you might if you wanted to get close to a skittish fawn. When he flicked the first button open, his knuckles brushed against that little hollow where her pulse took a jump. But not nearly as big a jump as his own."

His voice was deep and vibrantly masculine, without any overt sexuality. But that didn't stop her from lifting her own hand to the base of her throat, where it seemed her own blood had begun to beat a little faster. It had gotten warm in the room, so she threw off the comforter. Then the sheet.

"He moved down, button by button," Nate continued, "opening up that flowered cotton as if he was unwrapping a precious present."

Regan's fingers unconsciously stroked her warming flesh along a similar path.

"Her bra was a teensy bit of lace that looked real pretty against the curve of her breasts, which were rosy pink, like the inside of a summer rose, because she was blushing a little bit, due to the fact, he figured, that she wasn't used to getting undressed in front of a total stranger."

"Even if he was a gentleman." Regan could hardly recognize her voice. It was deep, throaty, undeniably aroused.

"Even if," he agreed, his own voice sounding more rough itself, as if her reaction might be turning him on.

"Of course the bra had to go, too, but since he knew his way around women's underwear, he didn't have any trouble unfastening the front hook. 'Mon Dieu,' he breathed as her lovely breasts spilled into his hands, 'you are the most beautiful woman I've ever seen.' He wasn't lying and found the way she blushed even deeper unbearably appealing. And erotic.

"He asked if he could kiss her breasts. Her white teeth worried her full bottom lip as she considered the request, but he could see the answer in her eyes before she managed a shy little nod. Her skin was the color of pink marble, and just as smooth. But a lot softer. And warmer. As he took one of those little ruby nipples into his mouth and drank in the warm womanly scent of her, Antoine knew that one taste would never be enough."

Regan slid a hand down the front of the T-shirt and began touching herself as Antoine was caressing the mystery woman: shoulders, chest, then breasts. She rolled a taut nipple between her thumb and her index finger and felt a corresponding tug between her legs. The soft moan escaped from between her parted lips before she could stop it.

"Tell me what you're thinking. Right now," he demanded softly.

"About how Antoine's hands felt on her." Regan licked her lips, which had gone unbearably dry. *And how your hands would feel on me.* She braced the receiver against one shoulder. Both of her hands moved beneath the shirt, caressing, squeezing, stroking breasts sensitized by that deep seductive voice and her own erotic imagination. "What are *you* thinking?"

His answering laugh was quick and rough. "That I'm going to have to get bigger briefs."

"Maybe you should take them off." Had she really said that?

"I will, if you will."

She had never been a woman to play sexual games. In bed, as in all other parts of her life, she was straightforward and to the point. But there was something about being alone in the dark, with just that deep voice touching her all over, that allowed her to imagine she was the naked wood nymph in his story. "I'm already one step ahead of you."

There was a pause. Then a groan. "Wait just a sec, sugar." A longer pause, during which time her hands stilled, waiting for him to make the next move. And then he was back. "I wanted to make sure the door was locked."

"You're not used to talking about sex on the phone with a teenager in the house."

"No. But if Josh wasn't here, I wouldn't be talking to you on the phone right now. I'd be in the truck on my way over there, so we could be doing this in person. In the flesh, so to speak."

His flesh against hers was an arousing prospect. It also wasn't going to happen tonight. "You were telling me about Antoine."

"Yeah, wouldn't want to leave the poor guy hanging out there," he said. "Well, as luscious as her breasts were, Antoine reminded himself that the goal was to get her undressed so he could get her into a hot shower. So he forced his mind back to the task and finished unbuttoning the dress, then let it drop to the floor. She was wearing little bikini panties that matched the bra, and he hooked his thumbs in the elastic and pulled them down. Over the swell of her hips, past the lush blond curls between her thighs, down each long, tanned leg to her ankles.

"She stepped out of them without being asked. Crouched on the floor, looking up at her, he saw tiny beads of moisture glistening like dewdrops in those soft blond curls, and it took all the restraint Antoine possessed not to lick them off."

Moisture was flowing from her; Regan lifted the T-shirt above her waist and let her legs fall open a little bit more, to allow the breeze from the air conditioning to cool her heated flesh.

"Antoine, he stood up, put his hands on her shoulders, turned her around, and walked her into the little tin shower, which barely had room for one person, and turned on the water. Then he stripped off his own clothes.

"Her eyes widened a little at the amazing size of his erection, whether from fear or anticipation, Antoine could not tell. Wanting to reassure her that he'd never do anythin' to hurt her, he touched his mouth against hers in their very first kiss and felt her sigh against his lips.

"He drew her into the shower and lathered the soap

between his palms, and as the water pelted down on them and the stall filled with fragrant steam, he smoothed the lather all over her, his slippery hands sliding over her body from her shoulders to her feet, and everywhere in between. When he began washing his way down one smooth firm thigh and up the other, she closed her eyes and leaned back against the wall, her fingers linked together.

"She was shivering, but not from the cold; it was as hot as a sauna in the shower. But not as hot as the thoughts scorching their way through his brain. Seems he wasn't the only one aroused by their situation. '*S'il vous plaît*,' she said on a soft little moan, which is French for please. So she *could* talk, Antoine thought. 'I want . . . I need . . . Touch me . . . There.'

"Antoine smiled. *Mais* yeah, he smiled at this request, since it was just what he'd been wanting to do himself, but had been afraid of pushing her."

"Being a gentleman and all," Regan said as her own wandering hands fluttered down her rib cage and over her bare stomach. Then lower still.

" 'Xactly. So he carefully, with his softest touch, parted those slick folds. Now, you have to understand that Antoine considered himself a bit of a connoisseur of women, and there was nothing he found more beautiful than the female sex. It brought to mind a flower, with soft pink petals on the outside, and a deep rosy color inside. The little nub hidden in there was as hard and gleaming as a perfect pink pearl. She jumped a little when he brushed his thumb over it."

Regan did the same, imagining Nate's clever, callused fingertip.

"He stroked it again, then again, changing the pressure, sometimes hard, sometimes light, fast, then slow. Her back was against the stall, but her hips were thrust out at him, offering, begging for more."

The muscles in her legs contracted. Regan was breathing quickly now, and no longer cared if he could hear her. The world narrowed to his voice, the story of Antoine and his mystery woman, her tingling, burning clitoris.

"He knelt at her feet like a man worshiping a goddess, which to him, she was, and put his mouth on her. She climaxed instantly, cried out, and tried to jerk away, but the stall was so small there wasn' any room to move. And besides, his hands were on the backs of her legs, and he wasn't quite finished with her yet.

"He feasted on her like she was the sweetest, ripest fruit, loving the way he could make her come again and again, and when he felt her body going limp, he stood up again and lifted her onto him."

Oh, God! Regan bit her lip to keep from crying out herself as the orgasm ripped through her.

"Well, when Antoine felt her hot body tighten around him, it was like nothin' he'd ever felt before, like Mardi Gras fireworks goin' off inside him. Her lips pressed against his throat while the water streamed over them, and that's when he found out he'd been right about her not bein' a witch.

"His blood turned hot and thick as her sharp white teeth sank into him, and his own explosion, as he came into her, was like nothing he'd ever felt before. As they sank to the floor, arms and legs entwined, Antoine found himself looking forward to the idea of spending eternity with this sexy vampire."

"I should have seen that one coming," Regan managed to say. "Seeing how we're not that far from Anne Rice country."

She also belatedly realized that he'd never broken stride in the narration. "Did you . . . ?" Regan, who never blushed, felt the blood flow into her face, making her doubly glad he couldn't see her right now. "Never mind."

"The story was for you, *chère*," he said simply, gently. "A bedtime tale to help you get to sleep."

Amazingly, it had worked, she realized. The sexual release had left her more relaxed than she'd been in ages. Certainly since Nate Callahan had arrived in Los Angeles and turned her life upside down.

"It seems I keep having to thank you."

His deep chuckle rumbled in her ear. "Believe me, sugar, it was my pleasure. Sweet dreams."

She hung up the phone, pulled the crisp sheet back over her body, and instantly fell into a deep, nightmare-free sleep.

"I don't see why we're bothering to do this," Josh grumbled the next morning as they drove from Nate's West Indies–style home into town.

"It's not that complicated. You're a kid. The state of Louisiana, in one of its rare acts of wisdom, decreed kids need to go to school. Ergo, you're going to school."

"My name isn't Ergo. Besides, what's the point of enrolling in school if I'm just going to be gone in a few days?"

"You still planning on leaving?"

"I may be."

"Well, I'd just as soon you didn't go taking off without any word."

"Yeah, your life dream has always been to have a delinquent kid around to screw up your sex life."

"Did I say you're screwing up anything?"

"No." He'd give him that. "But you probably would have been with that cop last night if you hadn't had to stay home and play prison guard to me."

"Should I be offended that you called my home, which I built with my own two hands, a prison?" Nate asked mildly. "And yeah, I might have driven over to the inn to be with Regan last night. But not for the reason you think."

"You saying you don't want to fuck her?"

"There are a great many things I'd love to do with Detective Delectable. But when you get older and have some experience, you'll discover that there's a huge difference between fucking someone and making love."

"So you're in love with her?"

"I'm not saying that. I'm jus' stating that there's more to being with a woman than what fits where. That's just plumbing. What two people do together should be more special than that."

"Sex is sex," Josh said stubbornly. Hell, he'd probably listened to more sex in his life than this guy, as cool as he seemed to be, had ever experienced.

"We'll have to continue this discussion later, when we have more time," Nate said as they pulled up in front of a redbrick building.

Students were headed up the wide front steps in groups, talking, laughing, seeming to have a high old time. Josh felt the familiar new-school clench in his gut and, although he'd chain cement around his ankles and throw himself in the bayou before admitting it, he was glad he'd allowed himself to be convinced to take off his Dead Rap Stars T-shirt and change into a plain old black one Nate had pulled from his own closet. Apparently the guy wasn't lying when he said there was a no-message-shirts dress code.

Not that he cared about fitting in. Since he wasn't going to be staying in Blue Bayou all that long.

20

*T*hings *were definitely going downhill.* Not only hadn't she been able to find a California marriage license for Karen Dale, or a divorce decree for a Karen Hart, the death certificate was proving yet another dead end. Regan had been working her way through neighboring state licensing files and had found several doctors with the same name, but calls placed to their offices turned up a big fat zero.

The stocks were obviously the way to go. Surely either the mother or the son knew something. Twenty-five thousand dollars might not be a lot of money to a family who owned an oil company. But it wasn't chicken feed, either.

She *was* going to solve this crime. Linda Dale deserved to have her murder solved and the perpetrator put behind bars. Then Regan would donate the stocks to a local charity, return to Los Angeles, and get on with her life.

She had just gone off-line when the phone rang. She

paused for a moment, wondering if it was Nate, calling to tell her he was on his way. Or perhaps it was last night's first caller, wanting to make certain she'd gotten the message. The lady or the tiger. Wishing hotel phones had caller ID, Regan picked up the receiver.

"Hey, partner," Van said, "I was thinking about you last night. Rhasheed and I rented *The Big Easy*, and I was wondering if you'd met up with one of those sexy Cajun men."

"There are a lot of Cajun men down here. Some, I suppose, are sexy."

"I hope you're passing yourself a helluva good time."

"Of course." Regan forced a smile she hoped would be echoed in her voice. She told Van about Cajun Cal and Beau Soleil, and meeting Jack Callahan, whose books Van enjoyed as well. She did not mention Nate or her real reason for being in Blue Bayou.

"I'd better run," Van said after about twenty minutes. "My sister's throwing me this baby shower. Can you picture me sitting in a room decorated with paper storks, nibbling on cookies with blue frosting and crustless sandwiches?"

"Just keep focused on all the loot you're going to get." Regan's contribution, which she'd sent to Van's sister before leaving L.A., was a music-box mobile from the registry list at Babies R Us.

"Easy for you to say," Van grumbled. "You're not the one playing name-the-baby games."

"Seems a small price to pay for a feng shui miracle."

Van laughed. "I'll keep that in mind when I'm huffing and puffing through delivery."

"That's what you get for being one with nature. If I

ever find myself about to give birth, I'm calling for heavy drugs at the first contraction."

They joked a bit longer, sharing cop stories about babies born in patrol cars, on the beach, in jail. After Van had hung up, as happy as she was for her partner, Regan felt a little tug of regret at how much she was going to miss their daily bantering. The problem with life, she thought as she went downstairs to wait for Nate, was that it just kept moving on, taking you right along with it.

Regan was vastly grateful when Nate didn't mention last night's phone conversation, other than to ask if she'd received any other threats. In the bright light of morning, she was uncomfortable with her behavior. She would have been even more embarrassed if he'd had any idea of the dream she had of him just before dawn. A dream that had involved a steamy shower and a bar of soap.

Blue Bayou might not make much of a mark on the map, but Regan certainly couldn't fault its architecture. The mayor's office was housed in a majestic Italianate building with wide stone steps, gracefully arched windows, and lacy pilasters. A red, white, and blue Acadian flag hung on a towering brass pole below the U.S. and Louisiana flags. There was a life-size statue of a soldier astride a prancing horse. The carving at the base of the bronze statue identified the soldier as Captain Jackson Callahan.

"Is he an ancestor?" she asked.

"A bunch of great-grandfathers."

"I thought your father moved here from Chicago."

"He did. But his grandfather was originally from the area. Great-grandpère Callahan moved north looking for work during the Depression, found it, and stayed. When *Maman* met Dad at a fraternity party, they started talking and it turned into one of those 'small world' kind of things. Dad always said that they were destined to find each other, and though he didn't buy into a lot of the voodoo stuff that coexists with Catholicism down here, he also believed that he and *Maman* had shared previous lives and kept finding each other over and over again."

"That's sweet."

"I always kind of thought so. Even though I'm not so sure I buy into the concept, myself."

"Now, why doesn't that surprise me?"

He laughed at that, then sobered a bit. "I think, along with wanting a safer place to raise his kids and knowing *Maman* was homesick, he wanted to get back to his roots.

"Old Captain Jack was one of our local success stories. He'd been orphaned on the boat coming to America from Ireland, and had pretty much grown up wild and barefoot here in the swamp. When they started recruiting for people to fight against the Yankees in the War between the States, he figured this might be his chance to make something of himself. Being Irish, he could identify with the little guy fighting against an oppressive government, so he signed up with the Irish Sixth Volunteer Infantry, which got the nickname the Confederate Tigers."

"Because they fought so hard?"

"Like tigers," he agreed. "Jack, he entered the army as a private and ended up fighting in every eastern-front battle, beginning with the Shenandoah Valley campaign in 1862 under Stonewall Jackson. Since those battle-grounds were pretty much killing fields, the men who managed to survive to fight another day won a lot of battlefield promotions. When Jackson returned home as a captain, folks around here considered it pretty much of a miracle. A lot of people still believe that touching his horse's nose brings good luck."

Regan was not as surprised as she might have been only days ago at the way he spoke about hundred-year-old events as if they'd just happened yesterday. And even though it made her feel a little as if she'd just landed in Brigadoon, a very strong part of her admired his connection with the past.

Antoinette Melancon had strawberry blond hair, a pink Chanel suit, very good pearls, and an attitude.

"I understand the concept of Mardi Gras," she said for the umpteenth time. "After all, my husband is not only a member of the Knights of Columbus but a deacon at Holy Assumption, and the women in my family have belonged to the Altar Guild for decades. I understand that is an opportunity to party before we begin preparing during Lent for Easter. I merely do not understand why Blue Bayou can't set the standard as a community who celebrates with grace and style."

"It's Fat Tuesday," Emile Mercier, owner of the Acadian Butcher Shop, pointed out. "Not Lean Tuesday. People are supposed to have a good time."

"It's unseemly." Her pink lips, color-matched to her suit, turned down in a disapproving frown. Regan suspected the Puritans had probably passed a better time at their Sabbath meetings than Charles Melancon's wife did on Fat Tuesday. "However, I suppose I should not expect anything different from a man who makes a very good living supplying sausage for the cookout."

He folded massive arms across his chest and glared at her from beneath beetled gray brows. "Maybe in my next life I can come back as an oil king," he shot back. "And make a fortune dumping poison into the bayous and rivers."

She lifted a chin Regan suspected had been sculpted a bit. "I take offense at that remark."

"Well, some of us take offense at ending up with bags of three-legged, three-eyed bullfrogs when we go out gigging," a bearded man in the back of the room growled.

"Melancon does not pollute."

"Tell that to the EPA," a woman who Regan remembered was an assistant DA for the parish shot back.

"That complaint is in error. My husband is working with the government to correct the misunderstanding."

"Meaning he's lining some congressman's pockets," Cal, who'd winked a welcome to Regan when she'd first arrived, suggested.

Nate was leaning against a wall map of the parish, legs crossed at the ankles, watching the meeting with patient resignation. Now he pushed away from the wall and entered into the fray.

"We're here to discuss the band situation," he reminded everyone in the same easygoing tone he might use to order a po' boy from Cal's. "Now, the Dixie Darlings pulling out at the last minute put us in a bit of a bind, but I played ball with Steve Broussard at Tulane, and since I read he and his group have given up touring for six months to work on their new CD, I thought, What the hell, tracked him down in Houma, and invited him to come play for us."

"Like Broussard and his Swamp Dogs are going to play for us," the attorney scoffed. "Their last CD went platinum after they did the sound track for that movie."

"Said he'd be glad to," Nate said calmly. "And the best part is that the band agreed to donate their fee to the boys' and girls' club."

"Awright," Cal said as nearly everyone in the room broke out in spontaneous applause. Even the ADA looked impressed. Toni Melancon did not, but Regan had already gotten the feeling there was little about this parish that she would find to her liking.

That the woman was a snob was obvious. That she was probably as cold-blooded as those hibernating alligators was also apparent. All of which had Regan wondering, yet again, if her husband might been sleeping with Linda Dale. Although she certainly didn't condone adultery, she could imagine why a man married to such a woman might stray. And now that she'd gotten an opportunity to see Toni Melancon in action, it didn't take a huge mental leap to imagine her killing a rival. Not for love; Regan suspected she didn't have a romantic or passionate bone in her body. But money was always a prime motive. Granted, the name was still all wrong, but there was still an outside chance that the murder didn't have anything to do with the mysterious J.

Which didn't, she mused, explain why, if Linda's lover hadn't killed her, he seemingly hadn't said a word to anyone when she'd died.

The meeting drew to an end. Toni Melancon was the first to leave, Nate and Regan the last. As they walked from the steps to the sidewalk, Nate reached out and touched the horse's nose.

"Are we going to need luck?" Regan asked.

"A little luck never hurt, sugar."

Of course, sometimes luck just needed a little help.

Toni Melancon was standing beside her racing-green Jaguar, the toe of her Bruno Magli pump tapping furiously on the sidewalk.

"Got a problem?" Nate asked.

"This stupid car won't run." She looked as if she was considering kicking the tire. "I told Gerald we should buy German. But no, he wanted this piece of British trash."

"It's a classic," Nate said. "When it came out back in '68, it was called the most beautiful car in the world."

"It's classic trash." So much for grace and style. Her petulant behavior reminded Regan of Josh, who probably had an excuse for his bad attitude.

"Why don't I take a look at the engine, see if I can spot anything?"

"All right." She sighed heavily, seeming more put out than grateful for his assistance.

Regan watched as he opened the hood and began fiddling with wires as if he knew what he was doing.

"Well, the good news is that it doesn't look like it's going to be a real big problem to fix."

"What's the bad news?"

"I'm not going to be able to get it running."

"Why not?" she said, seeming to take it personally.

"See this red-and-white wire?"

She sighed again and humored him by glancing in the direction of the engine, but she clearly wasn't willing to risk dirtying her suit by getting too close. "What about it?"

"It leads to the solenoid on the starter motor. It's loose, which we could fix, but if you look here"—he pointed to a spot about three inches from the dangling end of the wire—"it's also stripped. It'll have to be replaced."

"I knew we should have bought that BMW," she huffed.

Regan wondered who he'd gotten to take a pocketknife to that wire.

"No problem. I'll just call Earl on my cell phone, have him pick it up and tow it over to Dix Automotive, and I'll drive you out to the house."

His quick, boyish grin appeared to charm even this gorgon. "I suppose that's the best solution."

"It'll be my pleasure," he assured her. "You don't mind if Ms. Hart comes along, do you? I've been showin' her around the parish."

The older woman looked at Regan as if noticing her for the first time. "You must be the new sheriff I've been hearing about."

"People are mistaken. I'm just visiting."

"Well, that's too bad, because we could certainly use one. I still don't know what you were thinking of, hiring Dwayne," she complained to Nate.

"He's a little green. But he's catching on real fast."

"But he's—" Her lips curved downward in what appeared to be her usual expression. "You know."

"A college graduate?" Nate asked blandly.

"Don't be cute with me, Nathaniel Callahan. You know very well what I mean."

"I believe I do, ma'am, and the way I saw it, not only is Dwayne qualified, having earned a degree in criminal justice, he's overly so. We were lucky he even considered coming to work for the force. Along with his qualifications, he's local, so he's got a real proprietary feeling about the parish, a bonus in someone hired to keep the peace. Then there's the little fact that we haven't had an African-American officer since Dad hired Dwayne's uncle back in the seventies. It seemed about time. Past time."

"I realize Jake Callahan has been raised to hero status in Blue Bayou, and I'm truly sorry about the tragic way he died, but as I told him back then, change for change's sake is not always a good thing. Since the subject's come up, I feel the need to say that it's important that Blue Bayou maintain the traditions that have kept it above the decline of so much of the rest of our state."

"Maybe some traditions deserve to die," he said evenly as he opened the passenger door of his SUV, which was parked behind the disabled sedan. "Like slavery. Or were you referring to lynchings?"

"That's precisely what your father said. I made allowances, since he was, after all, a Yankee. But I would have hoped your mother would have taught you more about your heritage."

"Oh, *Maman* sure enough did do that."

Seeming not to notice the way his jaw had gone rigid and the steely cast to his eyes, Toni Melancon allowed him to help her up with a hand to the elbow, and settled into the seat like Queen Elizabeth settling into her gilt coach for a ride from Buckingham Palace to Westminster. It had to be obvious to anyone less egocentric than Gerald Melancon's wife that she'd pushed his patience and charm to the limits.

Regan knew Nate had only held his tongue for her sake, and when his eyes caught hers in the rearview mirror, she mouthed a silent thank-you.

21

❧❧❧

The private driveway to the Melancon house was at least three miles long, flanked by an oak alley created to build anticipation in visitors approaching the plantation. Small one-room buildings Regan suspected were former slave cabins were scattered across abandoned fields, crumbling relics of another time. Untidy formal gardens that at one time must have been magnificent were now in need of a guiding hand.

The house was large as Beau Soleil, but lacked its grace. Unlike the soaring white pillars at Jack and Dani's house, four massive Doric columns squatted thickly on the thick slabs of granite making up the four front steps. Green mold tinged red brick that had faded to a dull rose over the centuries. Although Regan had never been fanciful, St. Elmo's Plantation—named, Nate told her, for the phosphorous green swamp gas that glowed at night—and its surroundings seemed to give off a desolate aura, as if it was inhabited by the Adams family's southern cousins.

Nate pulled up beneath the crumbling portico. "Well, thank you, Nate," Toni said, as if realizing such manners were required, if not honestly felt.

"Anytime," he said as he helped her down from the high seat.

There was a lengthy pause.

"Well, good day," she said. So much for inviting them in for a cool drink.

"You know," he said, "it's been a long time since I've visited with Miz Bethany. I think I'll just pop in and say *bonjour*. Wouldn't want her to hear the SUV and fret that I've come all this way out here without payin' my respects."

Regan watched as his trademark slow, easy smile appeared to do its magic.

"All right." Toni breathed out another of those deep sighs suggesting she found the world so very tiresome. "But don't expect her to recognize you. The old woman's gone absolutely batty."

"Now, that's a real shame," he said as they walked up to the huge front door, carved with what Regan suspected was the Melancon family crest, surrounded by an unwelcoming quartet of gargoyle faces. "Maybe we'll get lucky, and she'll be having a good day."

They were met in the great hall by a nearly six-foot-tall woman who could have been anywhere from sixty to a hundred. Her black dress was relieved only by a heavy chain loaded down with various charms. "Mrs. Melancon is not receiving visitors," she informed them in a deep voice that rumbled like thunder.

"Now, Miz Caledonia, you know I'm not just any ole visitor, me," Nate said, turning up the wattage on his natural charm. "I come bearing gifts." He held out two small gilt boxes he'd retrieved from the glove compartment of the SUV. "Brought you and Miss Bethany some of those candies you like so well from Pauline's Pralines."

She shook her head and clucked her tongue but took the boxes. "You shameless, Nate Callahan."

"Now, you know, Miz Caledonia," he said with a quick wink Regan's way, "you're not the first person to tell me that."

" 'Xpect not," she huffed, then caved. "You can only stay jus' a minute. It's time for Miz Bethany's nap."

"I'll be in and out in a flash," he promised, making an X across the front of his denim shirt.

She shook her head again, then turned and began walking away.

"You probably never read *Rebecca*, did you?" Regan murmured as they walked down a long hallway lined with busts of what she suspected were former Melancons.

"No. But that *fille* I told you about, the Chantilly flatware one, liked to watch the Romance Channel, so I saw the movie."

"Caledonia makes Mrs. Danvers look like Mary Poppins."

"She's a tough old bird," he allowed. "But she's devoted to Mrs. Melancon. Apparently she was her nurse, then just sort of graduated through the household ranks over the years, until she pretty much runs the place."

"Toni didn't appear to like her overly much." The woman had walked past the housekeeper without so much as a word.

"It's my guess she's afraid of her, since rumor has it that when she first married Charles, she wanted to move the old lady out of the house so she could be queen of the manor. Caledonia threatened her with a voodoo curse, and that was pretty much the end of that discussion."

They were led into a parlor filled with plants. Framed photographs of yet more Melancon ancestors frowned down from water-stained, red-silk-covered walls. The atmosphere in the room was so steamy Regan was moderately surprised that the oriental carpet hadn't sprouted mushrooms. The scent of all those flowers hit the minute she entered the room, giving her an instant headache.

Almost hidden by a towering philodendron, an elderly woman, as fragile appearing as a small bird, was swallowed up by a wheelchair. Despite the sweltering heat, she was draped in a trio of colorful shawls.

"*Bonjour*, Miz Bethany," Nate greeted her. "Aren't you looking as lovely as a spring garden today?"

Her gaze remained directed out the floor-to-ceiling windows, where a trio of stone nymphs danced around a green algae-clogged fountain.

"Mr. Nate brought you some of those pralines you like so much." Caledonia's stern voice had turned surprisingly gentle. She opened one of the boxes, selected a pecan candy, and held it in front of the old woman's face.

A beringed, age-spotted hand, laden down with diamonds, snatched it from the outstretched hand like a greedy toddler, and it disappeared between lips painted a garish crimson. She thrust out the hand again, palm up.

"After your nap," Caledonia said, putting the box high up on an ornately carved black teak shelf. She could have been talking to a child.

A heated string of what appeared to be French babbling, interspersed with curses Regan was surprised any southern lady of Mrs. Melancon's generation ever would have allowed herself to think, let alone say, turned the air blue.

"You know you can't sleep when you've had too much sugar," Caledonia said matter-of-factly. "The box will still be here when you get up." She adjusted the shawls. "You gonna say good afternoon to Mr. Nate and his friend?" She put dark fingers beneath the sagging chin and lifted the woman's gaze.

"Miz Bethany." Nate tried again, but he'd finally found a female impervious to that winning smile. She was looking straight through them, her pale brown eyes unfocused. They might as well have been ghosts. Regan's heart sank a little as she realized that her long shot wasn't going to pay off.

"It's time for her nap," the other woman said, announcing that the brief visit had come to an end.

"Thank you, Miz Caledonia." If Nate was disappointed, he didn't show it. "I appreciate your hospitality."

They'd made their way down the hallway, past the busts, across the slate floor of the great hall, and had just left the house when Caledonia caught up with them.

"I've got something for the *fille*," she said. Reaching into a skirt pocket, she pulled out a dime that had been drilled through and strung on a narrow black cord.

Regan exchanged a glance with Nate, then took the necklace. "Thank you."

"You make sure you wear it." Vivid turquoise eyes burned in her burnished copper complexion. "You've stirred up the spirits, you. This gris-gris will protect you."

The ancient woman's intensity, coupled with their brief meeting with the old woman who could have been Norman Bates's mother, sent a chill up Regan's spine.

"We appreciate that a bunch, Miz Caledonia," Nate said, jumping in to rescue her. He took the cord from Regan's nerveless fingers and slipped it over her head. It had to be her imagination, but she could have sworn the coin warmed her skin as it settled at the base of her throat. He bestowed his most reassuring smile on Regan. "No one in the bayou makes better gris-gris than Miz Caledonia. She's a descendant of the Marie Laveaus," he said.

"He speaks the truth, he," the woman said, taking on a queenly bearing as she rose to her full height.

"Isn't that interesting." Regan forced a smile. "*Merci.*" It was one of the few French words she knew.

The woman didn't answer, just shut the tall heavy door in their faces.

"Well." Regan let out a long breath. "That was certainly an experience."

"Caledonia is a little colorful even for southern Louisiana," he said. "I'm sorry about Mrs. Melancon bein' so out of it."

"You said she would be."

"I said I'd heard talk. I didn't realize she'd gone so far downhill since the last time I'd seen her, about a month ago."

"Is it Alzheimer's?"

"That'd be my guess, since the old girl used to be sharp as a tack. She inherited the chairman's chair at Melancon after her husband died making love to the mistress he kept in New Orleans's Faubourg Marigny historical district."

"Why does that not surprise me?" Regan said dryly as she climbed into the SUV.

"It was a pretty good scandal, even for down here. Turns out that the woman and Charles senior had three kids together. The fight for inheritance rights took three very litigious years."

"Obviously the family won."

"Mostly, but the mistress and the kids did end up getting to keep the house and the stock he'd put in each of their names before he died."

"There seems to be a lot of Melancon stock floating around down here."

"That's not so unusual, since they're the biggest employer. It'd be like living in Atlanta and ownin' Coca-Cola stock."

"Who are the Marie Laveaus?"

"Oh, now they were an interestin' pair. The first Maria was a hairdresser to wealthy New Orleans Creoles back in the 1820s. Technically she was a practicing Catholic, but she was also the spiritual adviser to slaves and their masters. And, of course, the master's wives, whose hair she fixed. She earned a reputation as a voodoo queen, but she must've had a good heart, since she was also the first to go out and tend to sick folks whenever the fever epidemics swept through the city.

"She still has her cult of believers who mark her tomb with red X's and leave coins to pay for spells. Her daughter, Marie II, took the fame thing one step further and put on elaborately staged voodoo rites that became real popular among New Orleans society. It's been said that she grew so influential, even some of the priests and bishops would go to her for advice."

"And Caledonia's descended from them?"

"So they say."

"Voodoo's just a myth." Regan touched the dime at her throat and wondered which of them she was trying to convince. "She couldn't really know anything about me possibly being in danger."

"Of course not." He shot her a smile designed to lift any lingering dark mood. " 'Less you're talkin' about falling under the spell of my expert lovemaking."

She laughed and began to relax. But there was still the niggling problem of the stock certificates. "I'm really going to have to talk with Melancon."

"Won't have much of a chance to do that till after Fat Tuesday," he said. "So you may as well just plan on enjoying Mardi Gras."

"I suppose you're right."

"Don' worry, Detective *Chère*." He skimmed his right hand over her shoulder and down her arm, took hold of her hand, and lifted it to his lips, brushing a light kiss against her knuckles. "I'll be makin' sure you enjoy yourself, you."

As much as he regretted the unproductiveness of the visit to the Melancon house, Nate couldn't deny that he was grateful for anything that kept Regan in Blue Bayou a little longer. It was strange, the way time was beginning to blur. They'd only known each other a handful of days, but he was beginning to forget how his life had been before she'd come into it.

It was lucky that with the exception of the ongoing work at Beau Soleil and finishing up the sheriff's office remodel, he didn't have any jobs demanding his attention at the moment. He wasn't sure he could have paid enough attention to do them justice. It was as if he'd begun looking at life through the wrong end of a telescope: nearly his entire focus—except what the hell he was going to do about Josh—had narrowed down to Regan Hart.

He thought about her too much and too often. Hell, all of the time. He pictured her intelligent golden brown eyes when he was brushing his teeth in the morning, and visions of her long, lean body were the last thing to pass through his mind before he'd finally fall asleep.

She'd pop into his mind during the day when he'd be fiddling with a set of blueprints, and suddenly, instead of looking at a bearing wall, he'd picture her as she'd looked out on the Santa Monica pier, her smooth sleek hair ruffled by the sea breeze, her fresh clean scent more enticing than the gardens of Xanadu.

During the time he'd been waiting for her to show up in Blue Bayou, she'd filled his mind. So much so that he hadn't even noticed that he was painting the wainscoting in Beau Soleil's dining room French Vanilla, instead of the Swiss Coffee Dani had picked out, until she'd pointed it out to him. Hell, he hadn't made a mistake like that since those summers during high school, when he'd begun learning the construction trade.

It had been bad enough before she'd arrived with big eyes, wrap-around legs, and problems any sensible man would stay clear of. And he'd always considered himself an eminently sensible man when it came to women. But now, it was as if she'd put a voodoo love spell on him, fevering his mind and tormenting his body.

Which was, of course, the problem, Nate told himself

as he turned onto Bienville Boulevard, two blocks away from the inn. While his reputation for romancing the Blue Bayou belles might be a bit exaggerated, he couldn't remember ever being this sexually frustrated. Not since he'd made the grand discovery that women liked sex as much as men did. Once he got the delectable detective into his bed and satiated his lust, while giving her a damn good time, too, of course, he'd be free of what was rapidly becoming an obsession.

"Oh, my God."

"What?" The mental image of kissing his way down her slender torso popped like a soap bubble. She grabbed his arm so hard they nearly ran off the road.

"You need to stop."

The stress in her voice made him immediately pull over and cut the engine. "What's wrong?" She looked as pale as Beau Soleil's Confederate ghost.

"It's that house." Her hand trembled in a very un-Reganlike way as she pointed toward a bright cottage, built Creole-style against the front sidewalk. The stucco-covered brick had been painted in historically correct shades of putty and Egyptian blue, and a For Sale sign was tacked to the French red door.

"What about it?"

"It's Linda Dale's."

Obviously the unsuccessful meeting with the old lady and Caledonia's spooky voodoo shit had taken its toll on her.

"Linda Dale's house got wiped out by a hurricane, *chère*," he soothed. His palms stroked shoulders as stiff as the Melancons' granite steps. "Remember? I already checked the real estate records before you came to town."

"They've got to be wrong. Dammit, that's the house." Her eyes were huge and earnest.

"I know the realtor," he said, deciding no good would come from arguing. Best she discover she'd gotten confused on her own. "Let me give her a call and we'll get her out here to let us in."

He knew how serious this was when Regan didn't even make a crack about him knowing a woman named Scarlett O'Hara.

"The key's under the mat," he said after he ended his cell phone call to the real estate office. "She leaves it there in case people want to take a look for themselves without a salesperson hovering over them."

"The living room is to the left when you walk in," she murmured as he retrieved the key from beneath the green mat. "The dining room to the right."

"That's pretty much the way Creole cottages are laid out," he said carefully, not wanting to upset her anymore than she already was. "Four rooms, two back to back on either side of the door."

"How would I know that? I tell you, this is the house." She walked into a back bedroom that had been painted black. Nate figured Josh would feel right at home here. "This was my bedroom. It was yellow with a pale blue sky. The sky had white clouds painted on it."

"That's a nice memory," he allowed, still certain she was confused.

She didn't respond. "She was killed in the living room. My bed was there, against that wall." He was losing her; she was looking at things he couldn't see. "It was covered with stuffed toys, but my favorite was a purple, yellow, and green elephant I got for my birthday."

"Mardi Gras colors."

"Yes. I still have him," she surprised him by revealing. "Back in L.A. His name is Gabriel." Regan's brow furrowed. "I have no idea why I named him that."

"It'd be my guess your *maman* helped you name him after Longfellow's poem about the lovers separated during the Grand Dérangement."

"I've never read it."

"It's one of those typically tragic love stories. We had to memorize it practically every year in school. Evangeline Bellefontaine is an Acadian maiden who's torn from her beloved, Gabriel Lajeunesse, on their wedding day. They're separated, and she finds her way here to Louisiana with a group of exiles, only to discover that he's already been here but has moved on. So, she keeps searching and years later, when they're both old and gray, runs across him dying in an almshouse in Philadelphia. They embrace, he dies in her arms, she dies of a broken heart, and they're buried together."

"That is tragic." She sighed heavily. Wearily. "So many love stories seem to be."

"And a lot aren't. One of these days, I'll tell you about Jack and Dani. *Dieu*, they had a hard time, in some ways harder than Evangeline and Gabriel, but look how great things worked out for them."

"That's nice," she said a little absently. "That it worked out." She was looking back at the door to the bedroom. "She died in the living room. I heard shouting and hid under my sheets because I was afraid the *cauchemar* had come to eat me."

"That's an old Cajun folktale people used to tell kids

to get them to behave. Be good, or the *cauchemar* will get you."

"It had crawfish claws for hands." She shook her head. "Do you know, as many times as I had that nightmare, it never seemed odd to me that I'd know anything about a witch like that." It had merely been part of her subconscious, a part of her. "There was a terrible crash."

She'd faded away again, into the past, leaving Nate feeling helpless. "I was too afraid to come out of my room. After a while I did, but Mama was gone. I went from room to room. I was so hungry."

He followed her out of the bedroom to the cheery leaf-green kitchen. "I climbed up on a chair and got some cookies out of the cupboard. And some bread." She ran her fingertips over the door of one of the pine cupboards. "I think I slept. I must have."

She went out the back door, stood on the loggia beneath the gabled roof, and looked out at the small cottage that was now the garage. "I don't know how long I waited for her to come back, but I just kept thinking what Mama had told me about never going outside onto the street by myself, or I'd get run over by a car. So I just stayed. For what seemed like forever."

He no longer doubted she'd lived here. Watching her face, he suspected she was reliving every moment. Not caring whether or not she came up with any clues, but understanding that she probably needed to get the memories out, Nate looped his arms around her waist as she continued to stare toward the garage. She leaned back against him, in what he took as an encouraging sign that she'd come to trust him.

"A nice doctor gave me a lollipop. It was cherry, my

favorite. And then another nice man with dark hair and kind eyes picked me up and took me home with him."

"That'd be my dad." He learned that from his father's notebook, but hadn't wanted to tell her earlier; hadn't wanted her to think he was trying to somehow take advantage of an act of kindness that would have been second nature for Jake Callahan.

"I'm not at all surprised by that." She turned within his loose embrace and looked up at him, her moist eyes shining. "Finn's not the only Callahan brother who takes after his father."

When she lifted a hand to his face, Nate was lost.

"I don't want you to take this the wrong way, Regan." He covered her hand with his own, turned his head, and pressed his lips against her palm. "And I'm honestly not trying to take advantage of your emotional situation here, and I've been tryin' to do the gentlemanly thing and give you time—but I don't know how much longer I can wait." He skimmed his hand over her hair, down her neck, her spine, settling at the small of her back. Then he drew her to him, letting her feel his need. "I want you to come home with me."

Her remarkable eyes gave him her answer first. Then her sweet-as-sugarcane lips curved, just a little. "Yes."

22

Regan had accepted the idea that Linda Dale had been her mother. She'd even begun to suspect that the terrifying events that had haunted her sleep for years were more memory than nightmare. But being in the house had triggered images long buried.

"It was pink," she said as they drove down the two-lane road along the bayou. "The house," she explained when he glanced over at her. "It was painted pink. Mama said it was a house just right for two girls to live in." She pressed her fingertips against her forehead, where a killer headache threatened. "At least I think it was pink. I can't separate real life from the nightmares."

"Seems in your case, they'd be pretty much the same thing, *chère*. It could have been pink. Creoles tended to like their colors, and a lot of people replicate the original look."

"If I can remember the color of the house, and the

clouds on the ceiling, you'd think I could picture who my mother was having an affair with."

"The trick is probably not to push it."

"I suppose not." Her laugh was short and humorless. "Boy, Callahan, what is it with you and amnesiacs?"

He was wearing sunglasses to block out the bright midday sun, but she could sense the smile in his eyes as he glanced over at her again. "I guess I'm just lucky."

He returned to his driving, and a strangely soothing silence settled over them. He was a man comfortable with silence, which she suspected was partly due to having grown up in a land as hushed as a cathedral. They passed a cemetery, built aboveground as she remembered them in New Orleans, to prevent the bodies from floating to the surface during floods. Sunlight glinted off a broken angel's wing.

"This is like another world," she said as a pair of giant herons took flight from the bayou in a flurry of blue-gray wings.

"I'll bet, before you came to Blue Bayou, if anyone had mentioned the word *swamp*, you'd think of snakes, mosquitoes, and gators."

"You'd be right."

"Tourists come down here from New Orleans and go out on the commercial boats—which I'm not knockin', since everyone's gotta make a living, and it's better than not seeing the swamp at all—but they watch the guide toss some chicken to a gator from a fishing line, down some boiled crawfish and oysters with hot sauce, hear a little canned zydeco, and think they've been to the bayou.

"But they've got it all wrong. You can't roar down here

from the Quarter, snap a few pictures, then go racing off on a plantation tour. It's a wandering kind of place. It takes time to soak in."

They came around a bend onto what seemed to be a small, secret lake. On the bank of the lake, perched on stilts, was a single-story house with a low, overhanging roof and a wide porch that appeared to go all the way around it.

"It looks as if it just sprang naturally to life from the bayou."

"It's a West Indies–style planter's house. It's designed for hot climates. The roof line and the porch allow air to flow from open windows through all the rooms." He flashed a grin. "I can also fish from bed, which is a plus."

She smiled at that, as he'd intended.

"Did you build it yourself? Or refurbish it?"

"From scratch. I was hoping to keep the original, but carpenter ants and termites had been using it for a smorgasbord, so it'd been condemned. I mostly kept to the original footprint and tried to replicate it as close as possible, including pegging the timbers instead of nailing them."

"I'm impressed." But not surprised, having seen the work he'd done at Beau Soleil.

He shrugged. "I told you, bein' mayor is pretty much a part-time thing. Building's what pays the bills."

"You didn't choose to restore old houses for the money," she said, remembering his saying he'd rather be happy than rich. Though he could probably make a fortune if he moved to a wealthier area. "It's important to you. And this house was undoubtedly a labor of love."

"There are still a lot of things I want to do to it. It's

taken me the last five years, workin' on it part-time between other jobs, but I figure if there's one thing I've got plenty of, it's time."

"Now I *really* envy you." She sighed as she thought of her never-ending stack of murder books, then decided that she wasn't going to dwell on them. Not here. Not now.

The inside of the house was rustic, but warm and inviting and surprisingly neat. The wood furniture was sturdy enough for generations of children to climb on, the upholstered pieces oversize and overstuffed, obviously chosen more for comfort than style. The floor was wide planks, and the open ceiling beams appeared hand-hewn.

Another of those little silences settled over them, this one not nearly as comfortable as the last.

Regan had always thought of herself as a courageous woman. Now that the moment they'd been leading up to since Nate Callahan had appeared in her squad room had arrived, she was beginning to lose her nerve.

Nate was backlit by the sun, making him appear to be cast in gleaming bronze. She remembered how he'd looked with his shirt off, his muscled arm swinging that hammer. He'd been as close to physical perfection as she'd ever seen. She was not.

"You're going to hate me."

"Impossible."

She dragged a hand through her hair, appalled at the way it was trembling. She had the steadiest hands of anyone she knew; she always made the top score in marksmanship. "This is impossible."

His lips curved slightly at that. "Nothing's impossible, *chère*."

"It can't go anywhere."

"It already has."

He didn't exactly sound any more thrilled about that idea than she was. "You don't understand."

"Then tell me."

"I have these scars."

"No one can get through life without a few scars, *chère*. Jack has 'em, so does Finn, and even me, as perfect as I am," he said with a slight smile that turned what could have been arrogance into humor, "have picked up a few over the years."

"No." She pulled away. Turned away. Unreasonably nervous, she went over to a window looking out over the water and wrapped her arms around herself. "I mean real ones." She closed her eyes to shut off the image of the flawed body she'd taught herself not to study in the mirror. "Physical ones."

Nate knew that if he was going to stop this from becoming emotionally heavy, the time to move away had come. If he wanted to prevent himself from falling into a relationship he hadn't asked for, hadn't wanted, all he had to do was to back off. Now.

A very strong part of him wanted to do exactly that, to prove to himself, and to her, that he still could. He hadn't wanted the responsibility of a woman whose life was turning out to be more complicated than even she could have imagined. But he wanted Regan.

Whatever was happening to him—to his mind, his body, and his heart—was beyond his power to stop. Which was why, instead of retreating to safer emotional ground, he crossed the room. "Where?"

"All over."

He took hold of her shoulders and turned her around to face him. "Here?" He skimmed his fingertips over the crest of her breasts. They fit so perfectly into his hands, Nate could almost imagine she'd been created solely for him and him alone.

With her eyes on his, she nodded.

Every other woman he'd ever been with had approached this moment with a casual air of experience, expectancy. Regan, who was proving to be the strongest of them all, trembled when his thumbs brushed her nipples, which hardened beneath the light touch.

Need hammered at him, along with a previously unfelt fear that he wouldn't be—couldn't be—gentle enough. His body urged him to ravish; his mind counseled restraint. His heart, which was expanding in his chest, opted for a middle ground.

"How about here?" His caressing hand moved downward, fingers splayed over her torso.

"Yes." As if not wanting to see what he might be thinking, she closed her eyes. Her usually clear voice was barely a whisper.

Her stomach. "How about here?"

"Yes. Dammit, Nate . . ."

"And here?" Down her thigh.

"Everywhere. And they're ugly."

"Now, I wouldn't want to be accusing you of stretching the truth, sugar, but my *maman* used to have this saying, about pretty is as pretty does."

"I've heard it."

"I 'magine you have. So I'm having a hard time believing that there's anything about you that isn't downright, drop-dead gorgeous." She didn't resist as he drew her closer. When she sighed and rested her head against his shoulder, he brushed a kiss atop her shiny cap of hair.

They remained that way for a long silent time. Outside the house, clouds gathering for an afternoon rain shower moved across the sun, casting the room in deep shadows. As he felt her trembling cease, Nate thought how good she felt in his arms. How perfect.

"I'm afraid," she admitted.

He drew back his head. "Of me?"

"I could never be afraid of you." She trailed a fingernail along the top of his lips. "I'm afraid of what we're getting into."

"Don't feel like the Lone Ranger. Since this seems to be a day for surprises and sharing secrets, want to know what I'm most afraid of?"

"What?"

"That I'm not going to be able to make love to you as well as a woman like you should be made love to."

She surprised—and pleased—him by laughing a little at that. "Now, that may be the only thing in my life I'm *not* worried about." She went up on her toes. Her lips brushed tantalizingly against his, then clung. "Take me to bed, Nate," she said, her words thrumming against his mouth.

He didn't need a second invitation. He swept her into his arms, feeling a lot like Rhett carrying Scarlett up that staircase, but wanting to pleasure more than ravish. Ravishment, he thought with a flare of hot anticipation, could come later.

"Oh, it's like sinking into a cloud," she murmured as he laid her with care atop the mattress of the roomy bed he'd made with leftover pieces of cypress from the house. "I smell flowers."

He lay down beside her. She turned toward him, her eyes shining like a pair of the pirate Lafitte's gold doubloons. "It's stuffed with Spanish moss and herbs."

Her rich, throaty laugh started a thousand pulses humming beneath his skin. "I'm never buying an innerspring mattress again."

Nate knew he was in big trouble when he almost suggested she stay here with him. In Blue Bayou. In his house. His bed. He wasn't prepared to share those thoughts with her yet, not when he hadn't figured them out for himself, but there was one thing he wanted, needed, to get straight before they moved on.

He framed her face between his palms. "You're different from any other woman I've ever known." He could hear a sense of the wonder he'd tried to ignore in his tone, and suspected she could hear it, too. "*This* is different."

"I know." When her gorgeous eyes grew suspiciously bright, Nate felt something inside him move that had nothing to do with sympathy, or lust. "It's the same for me."

Because he'd been raised to be a gentleman, Nate felt obliged to give her one last chance. "We can still stop this. Before things get out of hand."

"Is that what you want?"

"Hell, no."

"Me, neither."

What was the matter with him? Taking a woman to bed had never been this complicated. This important. Frustrated with the situation, even more frustrated with himself for giving in to these sudden self-doubts, Nate decided if he was going to be this lost, he damn well wasn't about to take the long fatal fall alone, and took her lips.

She tensed again when he pulled the T-shirt over her head, and instinctively covered her breast with her hand.

"It's okay." He kissed her again, his tongue dipping in to seduce hers into a slow, sensual dance. "I want to see you, *chérie*." He caught her lower lip between his teeth. "All of you."

Her body softened in a silent, submissive way he knew was deceptive as he undressed her slowly, deliberately, taking time to kiss each bit of uncovered flesh, just as Antoine had done in the erotic story he'd told her on the phone. He smiled when he got down to her panties, which were practical cotton woven into a barely there red bikini, just like the one he'd imagined in his fantasy at Cal's. Contrasts, he thought, as he drew them slowly down long legs, firm and sleek as a Thoroughbred's from daily running.

"I told you," she said, as he cupped the weight of her breast in his hand and pressed his mouth against a long jagged line snaking from her dusky pink nipple to the wall of her chest. What in the hell had happened to her?

"The plastic surgeon was the best in L.A. You can't go to a movie or watch television without seeing his work. He couldn't exactly make me look the way I had before the accident, but he used tiny stitches on my face, and special dressings, and hid the stitches beneath my hair as much as possible. But with all the surgeries to put me back together again, I just got tired of operations, so my body—"

"Is beautiful." He kissed her wounded breast, then proceeded to move his hands, his lips, over her in a sure, leisurely way, feeling the pleasure seep through her.

"You don't have to lie."

"I'm not. Perfection is boring." His tongue glided lower, over her stomach, then lower still. She sucked in a quick, sharp breath when he scraped his teeth along the pink ridge at the inside of her thigh, then laved the flesh with his tongue. He was telling the absolute truth. He found her wonderful. "Whatever marks you might have are merely points of interest on a fascinating tour, *mon ange*."

Nate felt her going lax with pleasure, and even as he enjoyed the absolute control he knew she did not surrender easily, he reined in his own rampant need, keeping his caresses slow and gentle as he moved over every graceful curve and sensual hollow. He touched her everywhere, watching her face. Where his hands played, she burned; where his mouth warmed, she trembled and arched in utter abandonment.

And still, even as the deep, painfully sexual ache went all the way to the bone, he waited.

His fingers sketched slow, tantalizing circles in the dark curls between her legs, then tugged lightly, drawing forth a moan. He did it again, this time covering her parted lips with his, so he could feel the ragged sound as well as hear it.

"*Mon Dieu*, I love you like this." Hot. Hungry. His. He trailed his hand down the soft, silky, smooth flesh of one inner thigh, then back up another. "Open for me, *chère*," he coaxed. "Let me see all of you."

She couldn't believe what was happening to her.

She'd known Nate Callahan would be a good lover, skilled in knowing how to please a woman. But what he was doing to her went far beyond pleasure. Although his caresses were achingly slow, his clever hands were everywhere as he discovered erogenous zones she'd never known existed.

Regan had never—ever—ceded control to any man. She'd always preferred being on top, physically and emotionally. But that was before Nate. Lying naked on his moss-filled mattress while he was still fully dressed was strangely erotic, and for the first time in her life she understood that absolute surrender to the right man, a man you could trust absolutely, could be glorious. There was nothing, she thought with a stunning sense of wonder, that he could ask for that she would not give. When he pressed his palms against the inside of her trembling thighs, she opened her legs, offering the most feminine part of herself to his view. Despite the rain, there was enough daylight for him to see her imperfections. But it didn't matter. He still wanted her. Still found her desirable. Even beautiful.

She smiled, unable to remember when any man had called her anything beyond pretty.

"Lovely," he murmured. She moaned as those wickedly clever fingers skimmed over flesh heated from the blood rushing from her heart. She was as exposed, as helpless as she'd ever been, but felt no embarrassment as he parted the tingling flesh.

"Like petals, smooth and soft and glistening with early morning dew."

Her senses swam. Her mind was shutting down. She reached for him, needing to touch him as he was touching her. She wanted to yank down that zipper on his jeans and take him into her mouth, deeper than she'd ever taken a man; she wanted to burrow her face into the crisp male hair around his penis, she wanted to torment him as he was tormenting her.

"Please, Nate." Another thing that was so, so different. She'd never begged any man for anything, least of all sex. "I want you." *Need* you.

"Soon, *chère*." He braceleted both her wrists in his hands. "There's no hurry."

"Easy for you to say," she complained as he lifted her imprisoned hands above her head. Never in her life had she been so helpless. Helpless to resist Nate. Helpless to resist her own escalating desire.

"Easier to say than to do," he agreed in a deep, rumbling voice roughened with sex. "But like I said, down here in the South, we take things a little slower than in the rest of the world."

Just when she thought for certain that she'd die from the wanting, the waiting, his free hand cupped the source of heat and sent her soaring. She peaked instantly, sharply, and as she did, he pressed his mouth between her legs.

He was feasting on her, as a man might devour ripe passion fruit. Drowning in emotions, Regan writhed beneath his ruthless tongue and hungry mouth, the line between pain and pleasure blurring as he drove her up again. Even as this second climax shuddered through her, all Regan could think was *More*.

As if possessing the ability to read her thoughts, he left her only long enough to rip off his clothes. When he took the extra time to protect her, something that had somehow recklessly escaped her sex-fogged mind, she felt something powerful move inside her heart.

His long fingers splayed on her hips, lifting her to him as he slid into her with silky ease. Had anything ever felt so glorious? So right?

As he began to move with a deep, age-old stroke, slowly at first, then faster, harder, deeper, driving them both into the fragrant mattress, she scissored her legs around him and met him thrust for thrust, matching his pace. They came together, catapulting them both into oblivion. And into a relationship neither had planned, or been prepared to accept.

23

❧❧❧

*N*ate *had collapsed on her*, loath to move, not sure if he could even if he'd wanted to. He could feel her heart beating against his chest, synchronized with the rhythm of his own as they both slowly returned to normal. He listened to the rain tapping on the roof and knew he'd never hear the sound again without thinking of Regan. He could cheerfully spend the rest of his life in this bed, he decided. So long as he could keep his delectable detective right here with him.

"Incredible." He threaded his hands through her dampened hair, brushing it back from her face, which was flushed from her orgasms. Her eyes were closed, her long, thick lashes looking like dark silk against her cheeks. "Absolutely incredible."

"Mmmm." She ran a limp hand down his sweat-slick back. "I honestly never experienced anything like that."

"Neither did I."

That had her opening her eyes.

"It's the truth." Realizing that he was probably crushing her, he rolled over onto his side, taking her with him. Her lips were deep rose and swollen from kisses. Unable to resist, he nipped at them lightly, savoring her taste. "This changes things."

What had just happened between them was no ordinary event. They'd connected in a way that would have scared the hell out of him if he hadn't been feeling so satisfied.

"It doesn't have to." He felt a pang of loss as she put a bit of distance between them. "We're both adults. It was amazing, hot, mind-blowing sex. But there's no irate father waiting in the wings with a shotgun."

"Well now, I'll have to admit, that comes as a relief," he drawled. "Seeing as how the idea of gettin' peppered with buckshot doesn't sound all that appealing." Speaking of appealing . . . Unable to resist the lure of her silken flesh, even after what they'd just shared, he skimmed a slow caress down her throat and over a pert breast.

"I told you," he said, when she stiffened again, ever so slightly, "they don't matter."

"I don't want to talk about it."

"I want to know, *chère*."

"You do realize that you can't always get everything you want."

"Believe me, I'm well aware of that," he said, thinking about the murder of his father, the agonizingly slow death of his *maman*.

As if sensing his thoughts, she sighed and hitched up a little in the bed as the postsex languor disintegrated. "It's no big secret. Finn could easily have found the story. Probably even Dani, since I learned later that it not only made all the local papers but got picked up nationally. I was even asked to sit next to the First Lady at the State of the Union address, but I turned the offer down."

"Why?" He knew a lot of women who'd sell their collection of tiaras for such an opportunity to be in the national spotlight.

"Partly because I'm not a real fan of politicians. But mostly because I don't think stupidity deserves a reward."

"You couldn't be stupid if you tried."

"Thank you. That's a very nice thing to say. But unfortunately, it's not accurate." She breathed a resigned sigh. "It was several years ago, back when I was still a patrol cop. I wasn't real popular in the 'hood, because I'd been working with a community policing group and the narcotics guys, doing a lot of drug busts. I was working the graveyard shift and went to pull this vehicle over for expired tags, when it took off. I took off after it."

Her lips curved in an oddly regretful smile Nate suspected was directed inward. "I'd never taken part in a high-speed chase before, and I have to admit, I was enjoying the hell out of it. The adrenaline was jangling in my veins, and everything was intensified—the sound of the siren, the squeal of the tires, and the smell of burning rubber as we kept tearing around the corners."

He thought he could see this coming.

He was wrong.

"I must have been going eighty when we went into the projects." Her voice, her eyes, turned flat and distant. "The car headed down this alley, with me right on its bumper. The minute it got back onto the street, a moving van blocked the exit. I slammed the patrol car into the side of it."

"Christ." His blood went cold as the mental image seared itself into his mind.

"That would have been bad enough, of course," she continued with what he thought was amazing matter-of-factness. "But an accident's chancy, what with airbags and seat belts, and such. The dealers I'd been screwing up came up with a plan to shift the odds in their favor.

"Right after I wrecked the cruiser, they pulled out the automatic weapons and began firing away. I don't remember anything after the windshield shattered, but I saw the pictures afterward, and the car looked like one of those tin cans people use for target practice. There were more holes than metal left. A lot of that metal and glass ended up in me." She sighed and unconsciously touched her hand to her breast. "End of story."

Rage came instantly, steamrolling over sympathy. He'd always thought what had happened to his father had been tragic. But the horrific thing she'd been through was nothing short of evil. "And you went back to those streets?"

Even Jack, after being ambushed by drug dealers down in South America, had resigned his DEA job, cashed in his pension, and returned to Blue Bayou, where he'd spent several months trying to drink himself into oblivion.

"Not right away. There was a lot of recovery time and rehab." Her slender shoulders lifted and dropped on a long, exhaled breath. "But I'm a cop. There was no way I was going to let those gangsters scare me away from doing what I'd always wanted to do."

"Always?"

"Dani told me how you used to drag wood in from the swamp while Jack and Finn were practicing their quick draws."

"Someone had to build the jail."

She attempted a faint smile she couldn't quite pull off. "Well, when I was a little girl, I used to have Police Officer Barbie arrest Ken."

For the first time in his life, Nate understand how someone could do cold-blooded murder. A very strong part of him wanted to get on a plane, fly to Los Angeles, find those lowlifes who'd done this to her, and kill them with his own hands. Slowly. Painfully. Thoroughly.

"You've no idea," he said, "how much I admire you."

"Why?"

"For surviving such a horrific thing. For being who you are. What you are." Words usually came trippingly off his tongue. But Nate couldn't think of any that even began to express the emotions battering at him. "I can't even begin to tell you."

"Well, then." The light had returned to her remarkable eyes, and her lips curved in a slow, seductive smile. "Why don't you show me?"

Outside, the rain continued to fall.

Inside, with slow hands and warm lips, they lost themselves in a shimmering, misty world of their own making.

Afterward Regan lay snuggled in his arms, listening to the sound of the rain on the roof, and knew that from this day forward, every time it rained, she'd think of Nate.

"What are you thinking?" he asked, skimming down her side with those fingertips that had stimulated every inch of her with a touch like the finest-grade sandpaper.

"How much I used to hate the rain." She caught his hand as it slid ever lower and lifted it to her lips. "And how I'm never going to be able to think of it the same way again."

"Great minds." He pulled her tight against his body. His kiss was slow, deep, and possessive. "I was thinking earlier how nice it'd be if I could just spend the rest of my life right here in bed with you."

That sounded wonderful. Too wonderful. If she wasn't in such a blissful mood, she might have been unnerved by how perfect a scenario he'd just painted.

"Unfortunately," he continued on a long deep sigh, "we're going to have company."

"Company?" She touched her mouth to a small scar on his knuckles.

He glanced over at the watch he'd taken off and put on the bedside table. "I figure we've got about ten minutes before Josh gets home from school."

"Oh, my God, how could I have forgotten about him?" Regan leaped up and raced around the room, gathering up discarded clothing where it had landed on the wide plank floor and furniture. Making love with Nate had wiped her mind as clear as glass. She shot him a frustrated look. "Would you please get out of bed?"

"You don't have to be in such a tizzy, *chère*." He unfolded himself from tangled sheets that had slid mostly to the floor. "There's still plenty of time."

"Don't you have any other speed but slow?" Where the hell were her panties?

"You weren't complaining a little bit ago."

"Actually, I was." There they were. How on earth had

they gotten on top of that floor lamp across the room?

"Next time we'll try for a slam-bam-thank-you-ma'am session," he said obligingly.

Regan suspected he'd turned her into a sex addict, since even that sounded appealing.

"What are you doing now?"

"Opening the windows." Thank God for the over-hanging roof and wide porch that allowed her to do so while the rain poured down. "It smells like sex in here."

"Well, I'd say we'd probably have had a pretty disappointing time if it didn't. He won't have any reason to come in here, Regan."

"You never know. I don't want him to know that we were having hot, wild sex in the middle of the day." She couldn't remember the last time she'd had afternoon sex. Years, perhaps. She'd always been careful to arrange for dark rooms brightened only, if her partner insisted on light, by the soft glow of a single flickering candle.

"I think he knows men and women have sex. Sometimes even in the daytime."

"It appears he knows a great many things he shouldn't. I don't want to set a bad example for him." She turned to see how much progress he was making and discovered he was still as naked as the day he was born, leaning against an old bureau, with the strangest smile on his face. "What?"

"I don't want to scare you, *chère*. But I think there's something you should know."

"What?" she repeated impatiently.

"Now, you've got to understand, I may be wrong. I'm not real familiar with the feeling, having never experienced it before—"

"Nate, you're a wonderful man—kind, caring, talented, and a marvelous lovemaker—but time is running out here. Could you please, this one time, just cut to the chase?"

"I think I could, just maybe, fall in love with you."

The bra she'd retrieved from the bedpost dropped to the floor from nerveless fingers. Stunned speechless, she could only stare at him. A yellow school bus lumbered to a stop outside the house. Jesus, did she need any more complications in her life? *"Don't."*

She scooped up her bra and disappeared into the bathroom, slamming the door behind her.

"Well." Nate pulled on his briefs and, since he had no idea where his shirt had landed, pulled another from the cypress chest. "She certainly took that well."

24

After a long, hot shower intended not only to wash off the scent of their lovemaking but to clear her mind so she could deal with this latest problem, Regan took the time to blow-dry her hair so she wouldn't look like a drowned spaniel.

Before getting dressed again, she unwrapped the fluffy white towel from her body and studied herself in the bathroom mirror, running her fingertips over the curved raised lines that truly hadn't seemed to distract him from his goal of making sure that she'd never be able to enjoy sex with any other man ever again.

When she finally came out of the bedroom, she found Josh standing at the old soapstone sink, husking corn. He glanced up. "Hi," he said almost cheerfully. "Nate's outside. He's said you're invited to dinner, and he'll be right back in."

She wasn't at all eager to stay after Nate's out-of-the-blue declaration, and Josh's matter-of-fact attitude about her being there made her feel even more uncomfortable. And what had Nate done with the foul-mouthed delinquent when he'd replaced him with this Stepford teen? "How was school?"

"Okay." He shrugged shoulders clad in a normal denim shirt. "I thought I might be behind, but all except for geometry, I'm pretty much ahead of a lot of the class. The counselor's thinking of putting me in the accelerated program. If I'm going to be staying around, that is."

"That's terrific." Her heart tugged as she realized that the chances of that were slim unless Judi Welch could find a family for him to stay with here in Blue Bayou. "I always had trouble with geometry. The teacher said if you just memorized the theorems you'd be able to solve any of the problems. But even though I could recite them all, it never helped me know what to do with them."

"Yeah." He pulled some pale silk off a fat yellow ear of corn and rinsed the corn beneath the tap. "Same with me. I hate those effing sines and cosines. I mean, why the hell do I have to learn that stuff anyway?"

She was almost relieved to see a flash of the Josh of two days ago. "I suppose it comes in handy for something." She glanced up at the intricate placement of the pegged wooden beams. "I'd think Nate would need to know it, to build houses like this."

"Yeah, that's what he said. He also said he'd help me figure it out." His gaze scanned the homey, if decidedly masculine room that, as wonderful as it was, could use a bit of a woman's touch. "This is a cool place, isn't it?"

"It certainly is."

"It'd be way radical to live here."

"Yes," she heard herself saying. "It would."

The door opened, and Nate came in, carrying a handful of the purple-and-yellow irises she'd seen growing wild around the house when they'd first driven up. "I figured," he said, "since Josh and I are having a lady to dinner, I ought to get some flowers for the table."

"They're lovely." And definitely a woman's touch. Now he was reading her mind even before she had the thoughts. Fortunately, there was nothing in his casual manner to suggest that a mere thirty minutes ago, he'd dropped a bombshell on her.

"Trouble is, while I'm a man of many talents, I'm not real good at flower arranging."

"I'll do it." Their fingers brushed as she took the irises from his hand, creating a spark that shot right down to her toes. She looked up into his face to see if he'd felt it as well, but his expression remained absolutely smooth.

Perhaps, she thought, as she arranged the flowers in a hammered pewter pitcher, he'd only been speaking off the top of his head. Perhaps he'd been carried away by great sex and mistaken it for the start of something deeper. Or perhaps he was going to do exactly what she'd told him to do. Not fall in love with her.

As she set the pitcher in the center of the old pine farm table, Regan told herself she should be vastly relieved.

He might not be the cook his brothers were, but Nate thought the dinner of spicy grilled shrimp, dirty rice, and salad turned out pretty damn good for a guy more used to having females cook for him. The conversation flowed surprisingly easily, considering all the undercurrents. Josh was amazingly well behaved, watching his language for the most part. He seemed to respond to Regan, who appeared honestly interested in his desire about maybe being a writer when he grew up, which led to a discussion about Jack's books, which in turn led to a discussion of drugs, which the kid swore he'd never done and never had any intention of doing.

"Drugs are for chumps," he'd muttered as he'd polished off his third plate of dirty rice.

Then, as if to prove that miracles did, indeed, exist, he offered to wash the dishes while Nate took Regan back to the inn.

They were almost down the steps when he called out to Nate, who returned to the porch. "Thanks, man."

"For dinner? Hey, I may not be Emeril, but any idiot can stick some shrimp on the grill."

"No. Well, that was okay, too. I liked the rice stuff."

"Yeah, I could tell."

"I was talking about today. About letting me come home on the bus instead of making it look like I was living with my probation officer."

"You're not," Nate said mildly. "If you decide to take off, there's not much I can do about it." He squeezed Josh's shoulder. "Why don't you get started on that homework after you finish the dishes? I'll be back in a while, and we'll tackle the geometry."

"That's okay." He glanced over at the SUV, where Regan was sitting in the passenger seat in the dark. "I know you've got better things to do."

"I said I was going to help you, and I will." Nate was proud of the firm, paternal tone that sounded a little bit like Jake Callahan's had when he'd been dealing with his sons.

As he drove away from the house, he could see Josh standing in the open doorway, watching the taillights until they'd turned the corner.

"I don't know what you're putting in his RC," Regan murmured, "but I'd never know that was the same kid who was mouthing off at everyone at the hospital the other night."

"He's a good kid. He just needs a little encouragement. Besides, right now he's on his extra good behavior, trying to find himself a home."

"I noticed that. It's a little sad. He reminded me of a stray dog trying to infiltrate itself into whatever family feeds him."

"Yeah. Turnip was the same way. But she's settled in with Jack and Dani and the kids like she's been there since she was a pup."

"There are a lot more people in the world willing to take on a stray dog than a teenage kid with issues."

"You're probably right about that," he agreed, thinking of how hungry the kid looked when he'd been driving away. And not for food.

"About earlier," she said tentatively, obviously feeling her way. "What you said."

"Don' worry about it. It was jus' something that came off the top of my head."

She combed her hand through her silky dark hair. "I wasn't very nice about it."

"A lot happened today. I didn't mean to make you feel pressured or anything."

"It's just that my life is so confusing right now."

"I know, sugar." He reached out and laced their fingers together and rested them on his thigh. "Like I said, it was just a random thought." He squeezed her hand. "You were right about that mind-blowing sex. It was probably leftover hormones speaking."

"Now *that* I can identify with," she said in what sounded like relief.

When they arrived at the inn he accompanied her up to her suite but forced himself not to coax her into inviting him in, which, he suspected from the renewed desire he felt swirling between them in the closed confines of the elevator, wouldn't take that much effort. He kissed her good night, a brief flare of heat that ended too soon for both of them, then walked back to the SUV, absently whistling "You Are My Sunshine."

She was being ridiculous, Regan told herself the next morning. It wasn't like they were going steady. She'd gotten along for thirty-three years of her life just fine without Nate Callahan. Certainly she could survive one morning alone without him around to stir up her hormones and tangle her mind.

He was only out at his cabin with his brothers for a day of fishing that she suspected was mostly a rite of male bonding, which would involve a lot of swearing, spitting, and belching. She wondered what Nate was telling Jack and Finn, who'd come home for Mardi Gras, about her, if anything. Wondered what they were telling him back.

She'd decided to spend the morning at the courthouse, searching through old parish real estate records for the names of people who'd been in the neighborhood when Linda Dale had been living here. So far she'd found ten names, made ten phone calls, and come up with nine dead ends and a man who seemed to erroneously remember Linda as a go-go dancer at the Mud Dog.

"Here's another one," Shannon Chauvet said, bringing a third thick green leather-bound book from a back room.

Regan had immediately recognized the woman as the one Nate had comforted at the hospital the night of the train wreck. The scrape on her cheek was healing, and her black eye had faded to a sickly yellow-green hue that couldn't quite be concealed by makeup. Her surprised expression when Regan walked into the courthouse suggested she'd recognized her as well, and while their conversation had revolved around the records, Regan decided that before she left the office, she was somehow going to bring up the subject of Shannon's abusive husband and assure her that she was doing the right thing by staying away from him.

"Hey, Regan." She glanced up and saw Josh standing in front of the table. She'd been so absorbed in her thoughts, she hadn't even heard him enter the courthouse.

"Shouldn't you be in school?"

"The sewer line broke, and since tomorrow's Fat Tuesday, the principal decided she might as well let us out of school early."

She'd had a hard time believing Nate could have turned the kid around so quickly. If he was determined to become a juvenile delinquent, he was going to have to become a better liar.

"Well, that's a lucky thing for you. If you need a ride to Nate's, I can drive you out there."

"Nah. It's not that far. I could've walked, or hitched—"

"Hitching isn't safe."

"Life isn't all that safe. But I'm not hitching," he pointed out.

She began moving her pen from one hand to the other. "So what are you doing? Other than ditching school and risking being thrown back to Social Services?"

A red stain filled his cheeks. "Jesus H. Christ, a guy can't get away with anything around here."

"You might keep that in mind next time you try. And don't cuss."

"Like you don't?"

"I'm a cop. It occasionally comes with the territory."

He looked as skeptical as a fourteen-year-old-boy could look. "Shit, that's a real good excuse."

"Seems to me you're the one who needs an excuse. What *are* you doing here?"

"Okay. I saw your car parked outside when the bus went by, and thought maybe you could use a little help finding out about your mother."

She lifted a brow. "You know what I'm doing?"

"Sure." He shrugged. "Just about everyone at school knows. Except a few Columbine wannabes and some nerds who haven't looked up from a computer screen since they got their first Game Boy."

"You have a group of Trenchcoat Mafia kids at the school?" Blue Bayou looked like a place where the Brady bunch would be out playing the Partridge family on the softball diamond in the park.

"Nah. They just try to act that way to be cool. The school board voted in a dress code that got rid of their stupid coats, like that's going to turn them into human beings. It's also why I'm stuck wearing these geek clothes of Nate's."

"I think you look very nice. Besides, white T-shirts are classic. James Dean wore them."

"Who's James Dean?"

She sighed. Somehow, when she hadn't been looking, she'd landed on the wrong side of a generation gap. "Just an actor who died tragically young. Well, since you're here, why don't you sit down?" The way he was shifting from foot to foot reminded her of a bail jumper about to split town. "You can help me go through a few more pages, then we'll head over to Cajun Cal's for lunch."

"Okay." He dumped the books he was carrying onto the table and sat down.

Suspecting she hadn't heard the real reason for him showing up here, Regan handed him one of the ledger pages and waited for the other shoe to drop.

She did not have to wait long.

He watched Shannon Chauvet filing some papers. "She's a nice lady," he said.

"She's certainly been very helpful."

"She invited me to spend the night at the guest cottage with Ben and her. If Nate says yes."

"I guess you'll have to ask him for permission." No way was she going to start interfering in disciplinary matters.

"Yeah. . . . Her husband hit her."

"So I heard."

"He hit Ben, too."

"I didn't know that." But she wasn't surprised.

"Yeah, he tried to get in between them last summer, and the son of a bitch broke his arm."

"Domestic violence sucks."

"Now who's cussing?"

"That isn't cussing. But you're right, I could have chosen a better word."

"Nicer one, maybe. But not better. If I ever have a kid, I'm never going to hit him."

"I'm glad to hear that." Warning sirens were blaring in her mind. She turned the pen around and around, treading softly. "Did someone hit you, Josh?"

He couldn't quite meet her eyes. "It's no big deal. It's what adults do."

"Not all adults."

"Cops can't go around arrestin' everyone who spanks a kid."

"Flat-handed spankings are allowed in every jurisdiction I know of." Though just because it was legal, that didn't make it right.

"How 'bout fists?"

"I suppose again, you're talking jurisdictional differences. But that would be unacceptable to me, and I certainly wouldn't let it slide."

"How 'bout pimping?"

The question had been asked so matter-of-factly, and she'd been so distracted by the way he seemed to be picking up Nate's Cajun patois, that it didn't immediately sink in. "What did you say?"

He still wasn't looking at her. "I figure you wouldn't let a guy pimp a kid, either."

"Shit." She dragged a hand through her hair when he arched a sardonic brow. "Okay, you caught me. That's definitely cussing." Out of the corner of her eye, she saw Shannon headed toward them with another thick record book. "Come on." She pushed back from the desk and stood up.

"Where are we going?"

"For a drive."

"You're not going to call the cops, are you?"

"Of course I am."

"You can't."

"Dammit, Josh—is that even your name?"

"Yeah."

"Well, you've done a real good job of stonewalling so far, but you're not going to be able to get away with it forever. Mrs. Welch is going to find out who you are and where you're from, and she's going to try to send you back." She put one of his icy hands between both of hers and held his tortured gaze with a solemn, determined one of her own. "I'm not going to let that happen. He's never going to hurt you again." Regan would not allow this to turn out any other way.

"He can't."

"That's what I said."

"No." Josh shook his head. Bit his lip. Tears were swimming in his eyes. "You don't get it. He can't hurt me because I killed him."

When she heard the heavy book crash to the floor, Regan thought Shannon must have heard Josh's heated declaration and dropped it in her shock.

"Oh, shit," Josh muttered.

Regan followed his bleak gaze to the doorway and felt exactly like a deer in the crosshairs. The man standing there had a fully loaded ammo belt strapped across his chest, and a Remington 7mm deer hunter rifle pointed directly at them.

25

It had been planned as a guy's day out, a chance to get together out at the camp that had been in their family for generations, shoot the bull, drink some beers, catch some fish, and talk about women, which admittedly wasn't as raunchy a topic since his brothers had gotten themselves married. Nevertheless, Nate had been looking forward to this day. He had not planned to get ragged to death.

"You actually came right out and told her you loved her?" Finn asked in disbelief.

"I said I thought I might, just maybe, be able to fall in love with her," Nate responded as he dug through his tackle box and came up with a silver and copper spinner that had worked real well for him last week.

"That's pretty much the same thing," Jack said. "Once you start thinking the *L* word, you're pretty much hooked."

"Not like you to be so stupid." Finn was looking at him the same way he had back when he was fourteen and had filched a pack of cigarettes from the market. "You're supposed to be the Callahan who knows his way around women. Even I would have known better than to just blurt out something that important."

Nate cast from the porch, landing the lure precisely where he'd wanted it. Of the three brothers, he was the only one who actually used this camp a lot for its original purpose.

"You're a fine one to criticize, you," he drawled. "I seem to recall, not that many months ago, you screwin' things up so bad you went on a bender, leaving Jack and me to sober you up and send you off to Kathmandu to grovel. After you broke my nose."

"I was going to go to Nepal, dammit," Finn grumbled. "I was just giving Julia time to adjust to the idea of us being together."

"You're lucky she didn't use some of that time to fall for another guy," Jack said.

"Wouldn't have happened." Nate gave Finn grudging credit for that. "I was there at the beginning. From the time our big brother met her plane in N'Awlins, she never looked at another man. And God knows, I tried to get her to notice me," he said with a wicked grin.

He'd taken to Julia Summers the first time he'd met her at the reception the parish council had held for the visiting TV cast of that prime-time soap, *River Road.* Unsurprisingly, ratings had taken a nosedive after she'd left the show to go to Kathmandu for her role as Bond girl Carmen Sutra, and there were rumors the show was about to be canceled.

"It was only two weeks," Finn shot back, ignoring Nate's fraternal dig to reply to Jack's accusation. "You took thirteen years to get back with Danielle."

"Most of which she happened to be married," Jack pointed out.

"She only married that politician creep because you didn't stay around to make an honest woman of her. You're just lucky that piano dropped on the guy's cheatin' head, or you still might be hanging around here mooning after her like a lovesick pup."

"Goddammit." Jack shot to his feet, ready to rumble. "How was I supposed to know she was pregnant when the judge ran me out of town? If anyone had bothered to tell me—" He shot a blistering accusatory look Nate's way.

"That's bygones," Nate said quickly, hoping to defuse things before they got out of hand and he got his nose broken again. He reeled in the line, cast once more. "Water under the bridge."

"Yesterday's ball score," Finn quoted their father.

"Yeah." Jack blew out a long, calming breath, sat down, leaned back in the rocker, and put his booted feet up on the railing again. "You're right. So," he asked Nate, "what are your plans regarding the lady?"

"If you're talking about my intentions, I don't know."

"What a screwup," Finn muttered. "You take her to bed, have some hot sex—"

"World-class sex," Nate clarified.

"You have sex," Finn forged on in that doggedly determined way that had made him such a good serial killer hunter, "blurt out you love her—"

"Maybe. Possibly. Down the road." He wasn't about to

admit it, but Nate was beginning to agree with them. He had screwed up by letting his mouth run away with his brain.

"Same thing," Finn echoed Jack's assertion. "And you bring the subject up when there's no time to talk about it, because a teenage runaway kid has just arrived home from school. You ever think of coming up with a plan beforehand?"

"If I'd had a damn plan, I wouldn't have said anything. I've always been up-front with women; it seemed like the thing to do at the time." He wasn't about to admit the woman had scrambled his brains. "Not all of us live our lives in rigid, controlled, planned-out A to Z fashion. Some of us like to go with the flow."

"Meaning," Jack suggested as he popped the tops on two bottles of Voodoo beer and handed one to Nate, "you don't have any fuckin' idea what you're going to do next, you."

Nate threw back his head and took a long swallow. "Not a clue."

"It's going to be okay," Regan quietly assured Josh as they faced the gunman.

"Oh, dear Lord, he's going to kill us," Shannon, who was standing beside them, whispered back.

"No, he's not." Regan certainly hoped she could stop that from happening. "I've been in this situation before." Her psychology degree had made her a natural for being called out during similar situations over the years.

"You moved out on me, bitch!" the man shouted at Shannon. His throat, his face, even the tips of his ears, were a brilliant, furious scarlet.

Shannon's hand lifted unconsciously to her face. "I didn't have any choice. You hit me."

"Because you wouldn't shut the fuck up!"

Regan thought she heard more pain than anger in his harsh voice. Which could be a good thing, so long as he didn't start feeling so sorry for himself that he became suicidal, and decided to take his wife with him.

"I was only suggesting that maybe we move to town. Just for a little while." Shannon Chauvet's voice was little more than a whisper.

"I'd suffocate in the city. I'd rather die right here. Right now."

Oh, shit.

"It's not exactly the city, Mike." Regan suspected he'd heard those coaxing words before. "Breaux Bridge only has about seven thousand people."

"That's ten times the number who live here. How the hell am I supposed to trap there?"

It sounded like they'd had this argument many times before. Regan decided it was time to inject herself into the conversation. "What do you trap?"

He looked toward her as if noticing her for the first time, then moved massive shoulders that would not have looked out of place on a pro linebacker. "Nutria. Gators. Crawfish."

"This must be a good place for that line of work."

"Not this year. Hell, if the crawfish get any scarcer, I'll have to start trapping for cockroaches."

"That's why I thought you could work for my uncle," Shannon said.

"I already told you, goddammit," he said through gritted teeth. "I'd rather shoot myself atop the Huey P. Long Bridge than sell used cars."

"He happens to make a very good living."

"Selling junkers on the weekly pay plan, then repossessing them every Monday, ain't living. It's dyin'. Jus' slower than most ways."

He'd begun cradling the rifle like a security blanket, his fingers absently stroking the barrel. If they slid downward to the trigger, they were in real trouble.

Regan had learned in her negotiation training that all hostage takers had a reason for going off that went beyond just holding some innocent person at gunpoint. It was up to the negotiator to figure out what that reason was.

Mike Chauvet's, she suspected, was about regaining control.

She vowed to make sure he didn't.

They'd had a good time. Hadn't caught any fish, but then again, Nate thought as he drove back to Beau Soleil, the morning hadn't been about fishing. They were about five miles from the house when his cell phone rang.

He viewed the caller screen and flipped it open. "Hey, Dwayne. What's up?" The deputy was talking so fast, Nate could only catch about one word out of four. "Slow down. Take a deep breath. And start again, okay?"

There was a deep gulping breath on the other end of the line as Dwayne did as instructed.

"It's that lady, Ms. Hart."

Nate felt his blood turn to ice when he learned that Regan was locked inside the library with Shannon, Josh, and a drunk, angry, and armed Mike Chauvet.

Telling himself that there'd be time to be terrified later, once she was safe, Nate punched the gas.

* * *

Regan heard the squeal of brakes outside.

"Don't move," Mike warned them. "Or you're toast." Still aiming the lethal rifle at them, he went over to the window. "Shit. It's the state cops."

Regan had been wondering if anyone knew they were in there; someone must have seen Chauvet coming into the courthouse with a rifle. So much for Blue Bayou being a peaceful little town. She'd been in town less than a week and had already unearthed one murder and landed in a hostage situation.

Since domestic situations could be particularly volatile, Regan wasn't wild about having a team she didn't know out there working the standoff—the last thing they needed was a SWAT team arriving on the scene like a bunch of road warriors.

"We haven't been formally introduced," she said. "I'm Regan Hart."

"Yeah. I heard about you. You're the cop from California who's going to be the new sheriff."

"I'm a detective. And that's a mistaken rumor goin' around, about me becomin' sheriff." Strange, now she was dropping her own g's. Nerves, Regan told herself.

"What kinda detective?"

There was no way she was going to give him any ideas he might not have already thought of himself by telling him she worked homicide. "I've handled all sorts of cases over the years. Sometimes I've helped out guys who have found themselves in your situation."

"I don't need any friggin' help from a woman."

"Well, now, Mike—that is your name, right? Mike?"

"Yeah. So what?"

"I was just asking. That's one of my favorite names."

"Yeah. Sure." His response dripped with acid sarcasm. "I know what you're doing. You're playing me, trying to get on my good side."

"No fooling you, Mike," Regan said easily. "That's pretty much what I'm trying to do, but you know, I really am on your side."

His response was brief and vulgar.

"The thing is," she continued on an even tone meant to calm him, "we've got ourselves a little situation here. Right now, it's not too bad. Everyone gets frustrated from time to time, and we all need to let off a little steam. I can understand that. But the one thing we don't want is for things to get out of hand."

His laugh held no humor. "Just my luck there'd be a cop in here today. Cop killing's probably a one-way ticket to death row. Do not pass Go; do not collect your fucking two hundred dollars." His eyes crawled over her in an asexual way that nevertheless made her flesh crawl. "You carrying?"

"No." She certainly hadn't expected to need her pistol when she'd left the inn this morning.

"Lift up your arms, turn around, and put your hands on the wall so I can frisk you and make sure."

At the moment, Regan had a wide wooden table between them. There was no way she was going to give that up. And while he might put down the rifle to frisk her, she wasn't prepared to take the chance.

"It's got to be difficult, frisking someone with one hand. I don't think I could do it."

"Good try, but I'm not putting this down. I got another idea. Take off your top."

"What?"

"Are you deaf, lady? Take off the shirt!"

She opened her mouth to try to shift his thoughts to something else when there was an earsplitting squawk from outside.

"Mike Chauvet," the voice shouted. "Throw out your weapon and come out with your hands up."

Terrific. That's all she needed, some guy on an electronic bullhorn entering the picture. Hostage negotiation was all about personalizing the situation. There was nothing personal about a bullhorn.

"Take it off." He shifted the gun a few inches. "Or the kid's gonna be one knee short."

"Go ahead, sucker," Josh sneered. "Make my day."

Damn! That's all she needed, for Josh to recover his stupid teen attitude.

"You don't have to do that, Mike." She'd been taught to speak calmly and empathetically to hostage takers. Unfortunately, the guy standing behind the white cruiser continued to shout out orders.

Some cops, she thought darkly, watched way too much television.

Nate slammed on the brakes when he came around the corner and saw the phalanx of state cops and cars. Tires squealed but didn't skid on the damp cobblestones. Jack and Finn were out of the SUV before he'd fully stopped; he caught up with them seconds later, frustrated when some giant cop wouldn't let him pass.

"Hey, Nate." A trooper ambled up to him as if it was just another rainy afternoon.

He looked familiar, and reading the name tag pinned to his uniform shirt, Nate recognized him: Steve Tandau had played third base for the South Terrebonne Gators the year the Blue Bayou Buccaneers had won the state 4-A finals. He'd been a long ball hitter, and a helluva defensive player who'd gone on to play for LSU, spending two years in the Atlanta farm system before a bad knee from Little League days had caught up with him.

"What the hell's going on?" Nate demanded.

"We've got a domestic situation going on. Remember Mike Chauvet?"

"Sure. He was arrested for domestic abuse the other day."

"Well, he's out now."

"Shannon withdrew the charges?" He'd been so sure he'd gotten through to her. If either Regan or Josh were hurt because he'd been arrogant enough to think he could talk her into doing what her therapist couldn't, he'd never forgive himself.

"Naw. The way I heard it, he's out on bail."

"Shit." He listened to the cop yelling on the electronic bullhorn. Though he didn't have any police experience, he didn't believe that shouting out orders like some marine drill sergeant was a good idea.

"Have you tried just calling him?"

"Yep. Phones aren't working. It's my guess he either tore them out of the wall or cut the wire."

"How about tear gas?"

"That's too dangerous." Finn, who knew about such things firsthand, entered the conversation. "Tear gas doesn't work all that well on drunks, and it'd be my guess the guy's been drinking."

"Bobby, down at the Mud Dog, said Mike's been

drinking Dixie and Johnny Walker boilermakers all morning," Dwayne Johnson said. The deputy's expression managed to be both serious and excited all at the same time. It was obvious this was a helluva lot more adventure than he'd been expecting when he'd joined the force. Personally, Nate would rather have him dealing with mailbox bashing.

"Besides," Jack said, "the stronger stuff is pyrotechnic. You don't want to risk setting the place on fire with Regan and Josh in there."

If Mike did one thing to harm one hair on either Regan's or Josh's head, he'd damn well better kill himself, or Nate would do it for him. "So, what do we do now?"

"He's not going anywhere," the former third baseman said. "So, what we do is wait. Try to get him to listen to us. Hope that cop inside can convince him to surrender."

If anyone could, it'd be Regan. But Nate wasn't in a waiting mood. "And if he doesn't?"

"Then we'll just have to hope he wanders into the kill range."

Nate followed his gaze to the roof of the building next door and felt his heart stop when he saw the sniper rifle.

"Most often they come out, though," Tandau assured him.

"How long do you wait?"

"As long as it takes."

Well, that told him a helluva lot. Nate glanced at Finn.

"It all depends," Finn said with a reluctant shrug. "I've seen guys cave after thirty minutes."

"We're already past that. What's the longest you've ever seen?"

There was a significant pause. "Ever hear of Ruby Ridge? Waco?"

"Screw that." Before either of his brothers or the cops could stop him, Nate started walking toward the courthouse. He paused to touch Jackson Callahan's horse's nose, then headed up the steps.

26

Regan believed she was getting to him. Chauvet may not have put the gun down yet, but he was no longer pointing it directly at them.

She was about to suggest again that he allow his wife to leave, when the courthouse door opened. Mike spun around, pinning the newcomer in his sights.

"What the hell are you doing here? And how did you get in? I locked that sumbitch door."

"I'm the mayor. This is the courthouse, where the mayor's official office is. I may not show up in it all that often, but I do have a key. As for what I'm doing here—"

Nate held out his arms, revealing he had nothing up his short sleeves. "I come offering a trade. Let the women and kid go, Mike. I'll stay. We'll talk."

"I got nothin' to say to you."

"Well, that's too bad, because I've got something to say to you, and you better damn well listen. I like you,

Mike." Okay, so it was a lie. "I want to help you out here, but you've got to understand that there are a lot of guys with guns outside, who won't be real eager to cut you any slack while you've got these hostages in here."

Mike shot a nervous look out the window. Hopefully he couldn't see the sniper, but there was no way he could have missed all those State Police cars.

"Let 'em go, Mike. If nothing else, it'll be easier on you, not having to worry about keeping an eye on three people. You'll only have me to focus on."

"Why should I listen to anything you have to say?"

"Because Brittany Callais is the presiding family court judge."

"So?"

"So, she and I went steady back in high school, and I dated her some when I first got back from Tulane. Now, I wouldn't want to brag, but when we were working on the food committee for tomorrow's Fat Tuesday festivities, I got the impression she's still sweet on me."

Mike's wide brow furrowed. He reminded Nate of a slow-witted mastodon as he tried to process this piece of information. "You saying you can get her to cut a deal?"

Nate didn't dare look at Regan. "That's exactly what I'm saying."

There was more slow, rusty grinding of mental gears. "Okay," Mike said finally. "The cop and the kid can go." He pressed the barrel of the rifle against Nate's chest. "But you and Shannon are stayin' put."

Nate saw Regan sit down on the table and cross those long legs he'd spent a great deal of time fantasizing about. "I'm not going anywhere."

Josh, damn the crazy kid, stood next to her and crossed his arms. "Me neither."

Terrific. Just goddamn terrific.

Nate was trying to come up with an alternative game plan when the door behind him opened.

"Shit," Mike groaned when Jack and Finn came in, deflating like a balloon with a slow leak. "One Callahan is bad enough. No way I need three in my life." He held the rifle out, the wooden stock toward Regan. "I effin' give up."

"I still can't believe you did that," Regan complained later that afternoon. They'd all gathered in the kitchen at Beau Soleil, where Jack, who was the cook in the Callahan family, had fixed platters of baked stuffed oysters and smothered chicken over rice.

Dani had broken out the coconut pralines she'd baked for tomorrow's festivities. Matt, Dani and Jack's eight-year-old, was upstairs watching *The Lord of the Rings* for what Dani swore was the hundredth time; and Holly, Ben, and Josh, who seemed to be no worse off for his threatening experience, were engaged in a noisy game of horse on the basketball court Jack had built out back. "You had no business just walking into the courthouse like that."

"I'm mayor. What happens in Blue Bayou is my business."

"You could have been killed, you idiot."

He grinned and leaned over and gave her a quick kiss. "Would you have missed me, *chère?*"

"It was irresponsible," she repeated for the umpteenth time.

"It worked," Nate repeated, as he had every time she'd brought it up. "Besides, I had backup."

Jack and Finn returned his satisfied grin, as if what had happened earlier was no more serious than the shootouts they used to have when they were kids.

"At least now the mystery of where Josh came from and why he left is solved." Considering all he'd been through, she was not overly surprised that he appeared to have survived today's excitement with no ill effects.

"Helluva thing, what his mother's boyfriend did," Jack said. "Snatching the kid on his way home from school."

Between their conversation with Josh, and calls to the Florida State Police and the Department of Children and Families, they'd determined that the teen had been placed in a foster home after his mother had died of an overdose. Her boyfriend, angry at having lost the income she'd made hooking, had decided if he didn't have the mother, he might as well make some bucks off her kid.

"He must have been terrified all this time," Dani murmured, shaking her head. "Believing that he could be arrested for having killed that monster."

"I can't say I'm not relieved, for Josh's sake, that the guy ended up with only a concussion from being knocked out," Nate said. "But I sure wouldn't mind if he ended up being some burly lifer's girlfriend for the next fifty years."

"I still can't understand why no one was looking for him," Julia said. Finn and his new wife had returned home for Mardi Gras, and when she'd first met the actress this afternoon, Regan had been a little intimidated by her beauty and lush, natural sensuality. But Julia had turned out to be warm and caring, and had lightened the conversation over dinner by entertaining them with tales of her recent adventures on location in Kathmandu.

"Child welfare agencies across the country lose hundreds of kids every year," Finn said. "Florida's DFC is the poster child for what's wrong with the system. If these kids had anyone watching out for them, they wouldn't have ended up in residential care in the first place. Once they do, it's real easy for a kid to fall through the cracks."

"Especially when they want to disappear," Regan said. She'd seen it too many times to count. When she'd been on patrol, she'd done her best to coax as many street children as possible into nonprofit agencies who knew best how to help them, and she'd always carried phone cards paid for out of her own pocket so the kids could call home.

"We can't let him go back," fretted Shannon, who'd not only filed charges against her husband but also made an appointment with an attorney to begin divorce proceedings.

"The boy won't be going back to Florida," the judge said, speaking with such authority not a single person in the kitchen doubted him.

"Are you sure you should have left Josh at Beau Soleil?" Regan asked later that evening, as Nate drove away from the house.

"He wanted to spend the night. He seems okay, and after all he's been through, it's probably good to be with kids his own age."

"I suppose so." She reached over and put a hand on his thigh.

He covered it with his own and squeezed her fingers. "You want to go to the inn? Or my place?"

"The inn," she decided. "It's closer."

What was it about this woman that kept putting him at a loss for words? As they entered the suite, just the idea of taking her to bed again had him burning from the inside out. It was as intense a feeling as when he'd been wracked by chills at the idea of Mike Chauvet deciding to play shooting gallery. If it wasn't love, it had to be one helluva case of flu.

"You're awfully quiet," she murmured.

"Just enjoying the company." He forced a smile he still wasn't quite feeling. "And thinking how funny life can be."

"Yeah, today was a real barrel of laughs."

"Not that kind of funny. If I hadn't been remodeling the office, I never would have been cleaning out those old files. And if I hadn't been cleaning them out, I never would've found that journal."

"And if you'd never found that journal, you wouldn't have come to L.A., I wouldn't have come here, and we wouldn't be about to spend the rest of the night making each other crazy."

"I'm already crazy, *mon ange*." His hands settled on her waist. "Crazy about you."

She looked up at him from beneath her lashes, the way belles seemed to know how to do from the cradle. It seemed a little out of character, but he couldn't see a bit of guile in her warm gaze. "I'm almost beginning to believe you, Callahan."

"You should." He pulled her closer. " 'Cause it's the truth."

He pressed her against him and kissed her. When her tongue stroked his, it was all he could do not to throw her over his shoulder and carry her to bed.

"I think I made a mistake," he groaned.

"What mistake is that?" She dipped her tongue into the space between his lip and his chin he'd never realized was directly connected to his groin.

"I shouldn't have upgraded you to this suite."

"Why not?" She brushed her mouth against his, retreated, then came back for seconds. "Aren't I worth a suite?"

"Sugar, you are worth the entire inn." He skimmed a hand through her hair and splayed his fingers on the back of her head as he kissed her again. Harder, deeper, longer. "It's just that there's somethin' to be said for a room where the bed's closer to the door."

"Well, then, I guess we'll just have to start here." She tugged the T-shirt from his jeans. "And work our way across the room." Her fingers played with the hair on his chest, skimmed beneath the waist of his jeans. "Anyone ever tell you that five buttons might be considered overkill?"

"They're classic. Traditional."

"Granted." She flicked open the first metal button with a skill he'd admire later. Much, much later, when his skin didn't feel as if she'd just set a match to it. A second button opened. "They also make it harder to seduce you."

"Is that what you're plannin' to do?"

"Absolutely." The blood that had been pounding in his head surged straight down to his cock as she moved on to the third. And fourth. He sucked in a quick, painful breath when she skimmed those short fingernails over his belly. "And you are going to love it."

The final button gave way, allowing his erection to jut out of his jeans. When she curled her fingers around it, lust tightened into a painful knot.

"It must be hard," she murmured, moving her hand up and down in a long stroking motion.

"I'd say that's self-evident," he managed.

Her laugh was rich and throaty and sexy as hell. "That's what I meant." She continued to torment him with her fingers and her nails, tracing the shape, the length, breadth, and heft of him. "There's nothing subtle about you men." She followed a throbbing vein from root to tip, causing his penis to jerk in her hand when she flicked a thumb over the hood. "There's no way to hide the fact that you want a woman."

"Women get wet."

"Well, there is that." She smiled, a slow, breathstealing smile. "In fact, my panties are drenched right now."

He groaned at the idea of sliding his fingers into that hot moist flesh.

"Not yet," she murmured, backing away as he moved to do precisely that. She undressed him as he had her, driving him to the brink again and again, teasing, tasting, tormenting. Every time he tried to caress her, she'd slip deftly away and find new regions to explore.

Somehow they made it to the bedroom, and as he lay on the antique bed, watching her undress in the silvery moonlight streaming in through the window, it crossed Nate's mind that this was the first time that he wasn't expected to do anything but to take.

She returned to the bed, wearing nothing but a wicked smile. "I love the way you feel." She ran her palms down his chest. "And taste." Her tongue swirled around his nipple, dampening the puckered flesh, nipping at it gently before moving on to plant a lingering kiss against his navel.

Even knowing what was coming, Nate was not prepared for the slap of lust when she took him into her mouth, her tongue and teeth following the same scorching trail her devastatingly clever fingers had blazed earlier. He was about to warn her that she'd pushed him to the very brink when she went up on her knees and reached over his aching supine body.

"I have a surprise for you."

"You went shopping this morning," he guessed as she took out the foil package.

"I did." She tore it open. "But that's not the surprise." Took out the condom. "Watch."

How could he not, Nate thought as he watched her put it between her luscious lips. Surely she wasn't going to . . . No, he told himself—his detective was sexy as hell, but she was not the kind of woman who'd—*mon Dieu*. She lowered her mouth to him again and without touching him with her silky lady's hands, smoothed the thin latex all the way down.

The last thin thread of Nate's control snapped.

"That's it." He dug his fingers into her waist, lifted her up, and thrust his hips off the mattress as he lowered her onto him. They both froze for a moment, body and eyes locked together, Nate buried deep inside her, looking up at her as she stared down at him.

Then they began to move. She pressed her knees against his legs, riding him hard and fast as they both raced over that dark edge together.

"How the hell did you learn to do that?" he asked when he could speak again.

She was curled up against him like a kitten, but her smile was that of a sleek, satisfied cat who'd just polished off a bowl of rich cream. "Back when I was working vice, we raided this place that had hookers working upstairs while the owner had a thriving porno studio on the first floor. Part of the evidence was this so-called instruction video with an obviously phony nurse showing women how to get men to use a condom."

"If I didn't already practice safe sex, that little trick would certainly change my mind." He skimmed a hand down her slick body. "I'll bet it took a lot of practice." He wasn't all that fond of the idea of his detective tangling the sheets with a string of California males, but since he couldn't claim to be a monk, he decided the stab of jealousy was unfair.

"Not that much." Her quick grin pulled a thousand unnamed chords. "Though the room service waiter did look at me a little funny this morning, after my third fruit bowl."

"Are you saying—"

"I don't think I'll ever be able to eat another banana again."

He chuckled and kissed her, enjoying her taste, the feel of her in his arms. "That's quite a sacrifice. Perhaps we can come up with some way to make it up to you."

"Well, now that you mention it." She flicked a finger down the center of his chest. "I've always fantasized about making love in one of those old-fashioned lion-footed tubs."

Amazed by the surge of renewed energy that shot through him at the prospect, he scooped her from the cooling sheets. Regan laughed with throaty pleasure as he flung her over his shoulder and carried her into the adjoining bathroom.

27

$\approx \approx \approx$

*B*lue *Bayou's* *Fat* *Tuesday* festivities demonstrated yet again that this part of southern Louisiana was a world apart. Beginning with the fact that they left the inn just as sunlight had begun to spread gilt-tipped fingers of lavender and shimmering pink over the bayou.

"What kind of party begins before dawn?" Regan doubted she'd gotten more than two hours sleep. Not that she was complaining about the way they'd spent the nonsleeping hours.

"A good party," he assured her. "I promise you'll pass the best time you've ever had."

"I'm not sure that's possible. If I'd passed a better time last night, I wouldn't be able to move this morning."

He laughed, leaned over, and with his eyes still on the narrow causeway, gave her a quick hard kiss. "The *courir* is somethin' special," he explained. "No one's real sure when exactly it started, but we do know our Acadian ancestors were doing it before the War between the States. It's fashioned after a French medieval holiday called the *fête de quémande*. It was the one time a year peasants were allowed to mock royalty without fear of the consequences.

"They'd dress up in outlandish costumes and roam the countryside, singing and begging for alms. Our *coureurs* do the same sort of thing, but these days we dance and sing for *une 'tite poule grasse*, which is a little fat hen, and the ingredients for tonight's gumbo pot."

"Like singing for your supper," she said.

"That's pretty much it. These days it's just part of the tradition, but I suspect that in medieval times the people really did need help from the farmers to get enough food together for the feast."

A crowd had already begun to gather when they arrived at Beau Soleil. There were a great many men and women on horseback and others in the back of pickups. Two tractors had been hooked up to flatbed trailers outfitted with benches and festooned in traditional Mardi Gras colors of green, purple, and gold, as well as bright yellow and red.

The mood was already festive; more than half the people were in costumes reminiscent of the colorful scraps of cloth the long-ago peasants might have sewn together. Many wore tall conical hats, much the same as medieval women once favored, and several had donned animal masks adorned with hair or feathers. Neighbors were milling around, catching up on any gossip they might have missed, including, Regan guessed, stories of yesterday's adventure at the courthouse. There was already singing and dancing, and more than a few celebrants had begun drinking their breakfast.

"It's part of cuttin' loose," Nate said when he saw Regan's slightly furrowed brow. "But it's the *capitaine*'s job to maintain control so things don't get out of hand."

Her gaze moved from Josh, dressed in a Harlequin costume and laughing with Holly and Ben and some other kids she hadn't met, to Judge Dupree, who was seated astride a gray stallion, wearing a bishop's miter and looking very much in control of things.

"I doubt the town could have chosen better."

"He's been *capitaine* since before I was born, 'cept for those years he spent in Angola Prison after bein' framed by a bunch of wise guys who were trying to get their hands on Beau Soleil to turn it into a casino. It's good to have him back again." He waved to the judge, who gave a regal nod in return.

"He doesn't look as if he's having that good a time." His expression was stern as his gaze swept the crowd.

"Since it's his first *courir* in seven years, I'll bet he's having a dandy time. He's just sorta like Finn." Nate waved to his older brother, who, while not in costume, at least had arrived wearing not his old standby FBI suit but a pair of neatly pressed jeans and a black T-shirt. "Dancin' on the inside."

Given the choice between riding a horse and riding on the flatbed, Regan opted for the flatbed. Although she suspected that Nate would have preferred being out front with the others, he stayed with her, explaining events as they unfolded.

"*Capitaine, Capitaine, voyage ton flag,*" the throng sang out in unison. "*Allons se mettre dessus le chemin.*"

"Captain, Captain, wave your flag," Nate translated. "Let's take to the road."

They continued to sing as they traveled through the countryside. A great many of the songs were in French, and a few sounded as if they might actually date back to the Middle Ages. When they broke into "The Battle of New Orleans," Regan was able to sing along.

They reached a small wooden house set in a grove of oak trees. "Everyone has to stay here," Nate explained as the judge rode toward the house, carrying a white flag that symbolized the chase. "While the *capitaine* asks the folks if they'll accept us."

A man and woman came out, and there was a brief discussion, after which the judge turned back to the group and waved his flag.

"Now we have to go start earnin' the feast."

The tractor rumbled into the front yard and everyone piled off. Musicians with fiddles and accordions began playing, while the others danced and sang and begged for a contribution to the gumbo pot. After receiving a bag of onions and several links of sausage, they were off again.

"*Capitaine, Capitaine, voyage ton flag. Allons aller chez l'autre voisin.*"

"Captain, Captain, wave your flag," Nate translated again. "Let's go to the neighbors."

And so it continued for the next four hours, each stop an opportunity for a party that managed to be spontaneous without losing any of its tradition. Every so often someone would throw a live chicken into the air for the Mardi Gras celebrants to chase, like football players trying to recover a fumble. Often when they'd stop, several young men would climb trees.

"I don't know why," Nate said, when she asked him about it. "I read a book once that said it's some ancient fertility ritual, like symbolically associating with the tree of life. Or maybe they're just fooling around. The one thing that professor never mentioned is that Mardi Gras's supposed to be the last blowout before Lent, and it's hard to have a bad time when you're climbing a tree."

That explanation, Regan thought as she watched Josh and Ben scramble up an ancient oak, was as good as any. Swept up in the timeless event, as the brightly costumed *courir* advanced across the drab late-winter countryside, Regan knew if she lived to be a hundred, she'd never forget this day.

When they finally arrived back at Beau Soleil, they were welcomed back by those who'd chosen to get up at a more sensible time. The food they'd gathered was dumped into huge gumbo pots cooking on open fires. Outdoor tables groaned with more food brought by neighbors.

The sun that had been rising when Regan had dragged herself out of bed eventually sank with a brilliant flare of red-and-purple light into the water. Campfires had been lit to ward off the night chill; sparks danced upward like orange fireflies; smoke billowed from the many barbecues; dust rose from dancing feet. The mood was joyous, the food lavish, seasoned with enough Tabasco to clear Regan's sinuses for the rest of her life.

"I am never going to eat again," she groaned as she swayed in Nate's arms to the slow ballads that were beginning to replace the jauntier dance tunes. Although she'd never considered herself much of a dancer, she was able to follow him smoothly as he twirled her with fluid ease.

"That's the trouble with Cajun food." He pressed his lips against the top of her head. "Four days after you eat it, you're hungry again."

She laughed lightly, nuzzling against him. She'd tried to put away thoughts of Linda Dale for this one special day, wanting it free of any unpleasant memories. But now, as the celebration began winding down toward its midnight conclusion, Regan couldn't help wondering how her life might have been different if her mother hadn't been killed.

She knew from the journal that Dale and her lover were planning to leave Blue Bayou. But would they have stayed in Louisiana?

"A *dix* for your thoughts," he murmured as he nibbled on her earlobe.

"What's a *dix*? And if it's anything more to eat or drink—"

"*Non.*" She could feel his chuckle rumbling in his chest. "A *dix* was the French currency. It's where the word *Dixie* comes from."

Regan truly doubted that there was any other place in America, with the possible exception of New England, that clung to its past the way Blue Bayou did.

"I was just wondering, if things had turned out differently, if we would have met earlier."

"Probably not."

Having expected him to spin a long, colorfully creative scenario, Regan was surprised by his uncharacteristic bluntness.

"If there's one thing watchin' Jack and Finn, and bein' with you, has taught me, it's that people can't fool around with destiny. We were fated to meet this way, *chère*. In this time." He skimmed his lips along her cheekbone. "If I'd met you earlier, me, I might not have appreciated you." He tilted his head back a bit. His eyes gleamed a deep, warm blue in the glow from the camp-fires as he smiled down at her. "It's been suggested that I might have been a bit shallow."

"Never." She twined her arms tighter around his neck and fit her body closer to his. "That's just what you wanted people to think, so it wouldn't screw up your role in your family."

"Which was?"

"The jester."

"Jester?" Hell, Nate figured, that was even worse than Peter Pan. "You mean one of those guys with the funny hat and bells on his curly toed shoes?"

"No. I mean the wise man of the court who was clever enough to tell the absolute truth, no matter how unap-pealing, in a way that left people smiling. When anyone else who tried to be that frank might have had his head cut off."

He thought about that for a moment. "How do you see Jack and Finn?"

"Oh, they're a lot easier, because what you see is pre-cisely what you get. Jack's the half-reformed bad boy with the heart of gold. Finn's the rock." Her fingers were stroking his neck in a way that made him want to make love to her. Then again, listening to her read a suspect his Miranda rights would probably having him wanting to jump her lovely bones.

"No foolin' a woman with a psych degree," he said easily, deciding he'd best shift his train of thought before giving the town something else to talk about. He scanned the crowd. "Sure was a good turnout. Even more than last year."

Although Nate obviously hadn't been real happy

about sharing her, he'd stayed typically good-natured as she'd danced with seemingly every male in Blue Bayou, including Cal, whose moves had been surprisingly fast for a man of his years.

"I suppose getting to see what you've done inside Beau Soleil was a draw for everyone," she suggested.

"I imagine so. Toni cornered me while you were inside frosting the King cake with Dani. Seems the old lady has most of the family money in company stock, but Toni's planning ahead for the day she's no longer with us, and wants to talk about me givin' St. Elmo's a facelift."

"That house doesn't need a facelift. It needs a heart transplant." Regan glanced over at the *gallerie*, where a stone-faced Caledonia stood guard over her frail charge. "I'm surprised Mrs. Melancon's here tonight."

"She's never missed a Mardi Gras that I know of. And she seems more lucid this evening."

"I thought so, too, when I saw her singing along to some French song a while ago. Music has a way of making connections with people when other things can't get through." Up on the bandstand, the Swamp Dogs had broken into a rousing rendition of "You Are My Sunshine," which made Regan think of her mother.

"I 'spose so." He cupped her butt in his hands, pressing her closer. "What would you say to sneakin' off for a while? I just remembered that I need to measure for the crown molding in one of the guest bedrooms."

The molding had actually been installed last week, but it was the best excuse Nate could come up with, while his body was bombarded with sexual needs like he hadn't even experienced when he'd been thirteen and learning all about sex by reading Finn's *Playboy* magazines out at the camp.

Regan laughed. "I love a man who takes his work seriously."

He led her through the throng of people, and just before they reached the *gallerie*, Charles Melancon stepped in front of them.

"May I have the honor of a dance, Ms. Hart?"

Regan instinctively glanced up at Nate and read the resignation in his eyes as he shrugged. Stifling a sigh, she returned the older man's friendly smile. It was, after all, only one dance. She and Nate still had the rest of the night.

"So," he asked as he moved her through a complex series of steps, "are you enjoying yourself?"

"I'm having a wonderful time. Sorry," she murmured as she stepped on his toes. He was clearly a better dancer; then again, he'd probably had a lot more practice.

"My fault. It's too crowded here to try to impress you with fancy moves." He slowed the pace. "A lot of people think of Mardi Gras and they tend to think of Rio, or N'Awlins. But I've always felt that Blue Bayou's is special."

"You won't get any argument from me about that."

She'd just returned his smile when Bethany Melancon popped up from her wheelchair like some wild-eyed jack-in-the box, wispy hair flying around her face.

"*Putain!*" she screeched, pointing her scrawny finger at Regan. She spat, then reeled down the steps, leaping on Regan, fists in her hair. "You have no business here. I won't allow you to ruin my family!"

"It's okay, Miz Bethany. Nate grabbed hold of her from

behind, lifted her off the ground, and pulled her away. "You're just a little confused right now."

Finn and Jack cut through the crowd, putting themselves between Regan and the old woman, who was screaming incoherently in French. Ragged nails clawed impotently in the air. If she hadn't been concerned about breaking her in half, Regan would have just taken her down.

"It's okay," Nate repeated soothingly.

"I'm not letting you take my son away from Blue Bayou, Linda Dale!" Mrs. Melancon screamed, switching to English.

It took a moment for Nate to realize what he'd just heard. He knew he wasn't alone when the quiet began to slowly extend outward from the *gallerie*. A spooky hush came over the crowd as everyone turned toward a stricken, white-faced Charles Melancon.

By unspoken consent, Mardi Gras came to an abrupt halt. People began to leave, the low level of excited conversation echoing over the swamp.

Eve Ancelet appeared from somewhere in the crowd. "My bag's in my car," she said. "Try to calm her while I get a sedative."

"Take her upstairs," Dani suggested. "You can put her to bed in the guest room."

"I'll go with my mother," Charles said. He did not look all that eager.

A typically stoic Caledonia took the woman from Nate's arms. "Mo' better you stay down here, Mr. Charles," she instructed. "You caused enough trouble as it is."

She lifted the frail woman into her arms as if she

weighed no more than a rag doll, walked into the house, and followed Dani up the stairs.

Regan's heart was still pounding in her ears as the rest of them gathered in the library.

"You want to explain what just happened?" Nate asked Charles, who'd gone from ghost white to a sickly shade of gray.

"The past caught up with me." He looked a thousand years old.

"The past, meaning me," Regan suggested.

He sighed heavily. Wearily. "You probably won't believe this, but in a way I'm relieved the truth has finally come out."

Regan still didn't know what, exactly, the truth was. "Perhaps if you began at the beginning," she suggested.

"I fell in love," he said slowly, painfully. The fifty-something man was far from the congenial Rotarian she'd met at Cajun Cal's; he looked drained and grim. He also had not looked once at his wife, whom, Regan noted, didn't appear that surprised by the revelation. "For the first time in my life, I was truly, deeply, in love."

"With Linda Dale," Regan said.

"Yes." He dragged both his hands down his haggard face. "I fell in love with her the first time I ever met her at a nightclub in New Orleans. I was entertaining clients. She wasn't a star yet, but every man in the place wanted to be the one to take her home at the end of her set."

"But you were the lucky one who did," Nate said.

"Yes."

"Even though you were married," Regan, who usually was able to keep her mouth shut during questioning, said.

"The marriage was a business arrangement I entered

into at my mother's insistence. Love had nothing to do with my arrangement with my wife." He finally glanced over at Toni. "It still doesn't."

"The deal was that you wouldn't embarrass me, Charles. I believe you're doing a very good job of that tonight." Toni Melancon rose from her chair with a lithe grace learned in finishing school. "I'll be calling my attorney first thing in the morning."

A little silence settled over the library as she left the room. Regan took a deep breath and dove back into the dangerous conversational waters. "The man Linda Dale wrote about had a name beginning with the initial *J*."

"My father was Charles Melancon, senior. I was called Junior while I was growing up, and it wasn't until he'd been dead for two decades that I began to finally put that name behind me."

Regan thought about what Nate had told her about the elder Melancon being so influential. It must have been hard growing up in his shadow, especially at a time when the family had begun to lose their power and influence.

"What happened after you took Linda Dale home from the club that night?"

"We made love. All night long." Both his expression and his eyes softened at that long-ago memory.

Regan had figured that part out for herself. "And afterward?"

"I explained to her about my situation. My responsibilities to my mother and the stockholders. There was no way I'd ever be free to marry her."

"I can't imagine she was thrilled with the idea of being your mistress."

"To be honest, I believe the idea of not being able to make a life with her bothered me more than it did Linda. She was an amazingly generous person and understood responsibility, more than most. She was willing to accept whatever life we could manage to carve out for each other."

"Which is why she moved to Blue Bayou from New Orleans."

"Yes. I thought it would be easier, having her here close by, where I could see her more often. But it proved harder. Because the more time we spent together, the more I wanted to be with her. It became frustrating, and after a time, my regret and bitterness at my marital situation threatened to ruin what we had together. That's when I knew I had to do something drastic."

"So you killed her?" Nate asked, slipping a protective arm around Regan's shoulders.

"Of course I didn't!" Charles leaped to his feet. "I loved her, dammit. I wanted to spend the rest of my life with her. I decided to leave Blue Bayou and start a new life with Linda. Mother did not take to the idea."

"Because if you ran off with your mistress, your wife would file for divorce and take her money with her."

"Yes. We argued. She told me I was no better than my father. I'd promised Linda I'd come over after my talk with Mother, but I was so angry, I drove to New Orleans and drank my way through the Quarter."

Regan found it hard to feel sorry for him. He was, after all, still alive.

"What happened to Linda?" she asked. The fury that had twisted Bethany Melancon's face flashed in her head. "Did your mother kill her?"

"Yes." He raked his fingers through his pewter hair. Shook his head. "No."

"Which is it?" Regan asked, reining in her impatience.

"Both." He huffed out a deep breath. "My mother never drove. Never needed to. There was always a chauffeur to take her wherever she wanted to go. But of course servants talk, and that night she didn't want the staff to know where she'd been, so—"

"She had Caledonia drive her," Nate guessed.

"Yes. She hadn't believed me when I'd told her that Linda loved me as much, if not more, than I loved her. She was so sure this 'white-trash golddigger,' as she'd called her, was only after my money. So she took along twenty-five thousand dollars in stock certificates to buy her off."

"But Linda didn't want the money." Regan had learned enough about her mother to know this. She'd also dealt with enough homicides to envision the scene. The old woman, who would have been about the age her son was now, would have started out cold. Regal. Like a duchess talking down to a peasant. But she was about to discover she'd met the one individual Melancon money couldn't buy.

Frustrated, she would have argued. Probably even started screaming, as she did tonight. Screaming, Regan thought, like the *cauchemar* in her nightmare.

Her mother would have stayed calmer. After all, she had a child asleep in the bedroom. She might have even tried to get past her to open the door, perhaps to call Caledonia for help. There would have been pushing. Shoving. The room was small; although Regan couldn't recall the furnishings, there must have been tables in it.

"It was an accident," she decided.

"That's what Mother said," Charles confirmed flatly. "Apparently Linda fell and hit her head on the corner of the coffee table. Caledonia would lie through her teeth to protect my mother, but I believed her story then." He sighed heavily. "I still do. Mother was apparently distraught, and together they decided to make it look like a suicide. Caledonia helped her carry Linda's body out to the garage. They put her in her car, turned on the engine, then left."

"Did it occur to either one of them that they left a two-year-old child alone in the house to fend for herself?" Nate asked, furious on Regan's behalf.

"That was"—Charles paused, as if searching for the right word—"one of the worst parts of the tragedy."

Nate felt guilty he'd even brought this mess into Regan's life. If it hadn't been for him, she'd have gone on thinking that her father was a war hero, rather than this man who'd chosen to remain quiet and allow his daughter to be taken from him.

Regan thrust her hand through her hair. "Let's get one thing straight, Melancon. You don't have to worry about suddenly having to turn paternal. I've gotten along thirty-three years without a father, and—"

"What?" His surprise was too genuine to be faked. "I'm not your father, Ms. Hart. You were an infant when I met Linda."

Nate could tell Regan was as surprised as he was by this revelation, but she managed to hang onto that inner strength he admired.

"Then she obviously had another relationship," Regan said.

"I'm sure she had several before she met me. I never held that against her."

"That was goddamn big of you," Nate muttered.

Charles shot Nate a look. "I loved her," he repeated. "I was willing to give up everything for her." He turned back to Regan. "And you." Despite the seriousness of the conversation, his lips curved slightly. "I'd never thought I'd have children—Toni made it very clear from the start that she wasn't the maternal type—but I came to care for you as if you were my own daughter."

"Do you happen to have any idea who she'd been with before you?"

"No. But even if I did, it wouldn't tell you who your father was."

"Why not?"

His eyes gentled, revealing a caring side of the businessman Nate had never seen. "Because, detective, Linda Dale wasn't your birth mother."

28

I don't understand." Regan felt the blood drain from her face, and she was distantly aware of Nate tightening his hold on her.

While she had learned to expect the unexpected during investigations, she felt as if she'd landed in one of those Halloween haunted houses, where goblins and ghouls kept leaping out at you as you wandered through twisting hallways in the dark.

"It's obvious that I'm the toddler the police discovered in the house after Mr. Boyce found her body." The image of Linda Dale lying in the front seat of that car would stay in her mind for a very long time, and she hated that it wasn't softened with happier memories. "I have the elephant."

"Gabriel." He closed his eyes and exhaled a long breath. When he opened them again, he smiled faintly. "It was from a little store in the Quarter. You dragged it around with you everywhere. It was the first—and last—child's toy I ever bought.

"When I first returned home from my weekend binge and heard Linda was dead, my first thought was that Toni had killed her. She might not have any love for me, but she definitely enjoyed being Mrs. Charles Melancon. Her people had made their fortune in the slave trade, which even down here was considered unseemly. Marrying into my family bought the respectability she craved."

"And made her queen of the parish, once your mother couldn't hold the crown," Regan guessed.

"Exactly." His look was one of respect. "That's a very good analysis, considering you haven't been in Blue Bayou very long."

"I'm a quick study." It helped in the murder business. "When did you realize your mother killed Linda?"

"Decades later. She and Caledonia kept their secret well; it was only when her mind began to go and she'd have these flashbacks to the past that I discovered the truth."

"That must have been rough," Nate said. "Realizing that your mother was responsible for the death of the woman you loved."

"Yes. But it wasn't as difficult as believing Linda had committed suicide because she thought I'd betrayed her."

"How do you know she wasn't my mother?" Regan asked.

"Because she told me, of course. We shared everything."

Regan's mind spun as she tried to think why on earth an unmarried woman with a career not conducive to motherhood would take on the responsibility of an infant. The answer, when it hit, was staggering.

"She was my aunt, wasn't she?"

He nodded. "Karen Hart was your birth mother. She'd married your father while they were both in law school, and they had plans to go into practice together. He drew a bad lottery number, so since it was obvious he was going to get drafted, he enlisted in the marines. While he was in Vietnam, he discovered he liked being military police and decided he'd go into law enforcement when he got out, which wasn't what he and Karen had agreed upon.

"Shortly after she'd filed for divorce, she discovered she was pregnant. She was going to get an abortion when Linda talked her into going through with the pregnancy and giving the baby—you—to her." This time his faint, reminiscent smile touched his eyes. "Karen wasn't the only tough-minded sister. In her own way, Linda could be very persuasive. And she knew what she wanted—which was you. She was also a natural-born mother. I don't think she was ever happier than during those years with you."

That was something, at least, Regan thought, trying to find some silver lining.

"I called Karen to tell her what had happened," he continued, answering a question that had been niggling at Regan: how Karen Hart could have known about her sister's death when Nate's father hadn't been able to locate her. "She came to get you. I asked if I could stay in touch, since we'd gotten close and I knew you'd miss the woman who'd been the only mother you knew. I never knew if Karen didn't believe the story of Linda's suicide and perhaps didn't trust me, but she said she didn't want to confuse you about who you were. She also warned me that if I ever tried to contact you, she'd do everything she could legally to ruin not just my reputation and my business, but my life as well. I believed her."

As did Regan.

"But the real reason I allowed her to have her way was because I thought perhaps she was right about it being better if you never knew about the circumstances surrounding the first two years of your life."

He heaved out a long breath, as if relieved to finally get the secret out in the open. "I realize this has all come as a shock," he said, proving himself the master of the understatement. "But I'm going to say the same thing to you I did to Karen. I'd like to stay in touch. If you think that might be possible."

"I don't know." Regan was not going to lie. "I have to sort things out in my own mind."

He nodded gravely. "I can understand that." He stood up. "I'd better go retrieve Mother and take her home."

There was no statute of limitation on murder, and while it might have been an accident, the woman lying upstairs had taken a life. Even knowing that, Regan didn't make a move to stop him as he left the room.

Regan was extremely grateful when Nate didn't talk on the drive back to the inn. She felt too drained for conversation.

A little more than an hour after Bethany Melancon's attack, they were back in the suite.

"Well," she said on a long sigh. "I was thinking earlier that I'd never forget this day. Charles Melancon and his mother certainly made sure of that."

"Helluva story," he said.

"No kidding."

"What are you going to do next?"

"I can't see that there is much to do. There's no point in trying to open an investigation. Mrs. Melancon's obviously not capable of presenting a defense, and Caledonia's an old woman who doesn't need to be hit with an accessory murder charge."

"Linda must've been a really special person," Nate offered. "Taking on her sister's baby that way."

"Yes." Regan sighed again, weary from the strange emotional roller coaster. "She must have been. I suppose I have to give my mother credit for having carried me, when she certainly didn't have to."

"I am certainly grateful for that." Regan seemed to be doing remarkably well with all this. Then again, his detective was a remarkable woman. "I feel guilty about having opened this can of worms," he said carefully, trying to find a way to say the words he'd never thought he'd want to say to any woman.

"I'm fine."

He doubted that was precisely the case yet, but she would be. He knew that.

"It occurred to me," he said with as much casualness as he could muster, "sometime between when you were being held hostage and tonight's party, that the thing to do would be to spend the rest of my life making it up to you."

He felt her stiffen in his arms. Not a good sign.

"Oh, Nate." She dragged a hand through her hair.

Damn. Definitely not a good sign.

"I love you, Regan."

"You can't."

That was certainly definitive. "Of course I can. I was going to tell you earlier this evening, but then things got a little crazy."

"That's certainly an understatement." She shook her head and looked out over the moon-gilded bayou. "There's a full moon."

"It's real pretty."

"It is. But everyone knows people behave differently during full moons. I've learned never to schedule weekends off then, because homicides always increase, and heaven knows, when I was a patrol cop—"

"What I'm feeling isn't related to any full moon." Wishing she seemed a little happier about his declaration, he took her distressed face between his hands. "I love you, Regan. And I want to marry you." There. He'd said the M word and survived. In fact, hearing it out loud sounded amazingly cool.

"It's too soon."

"Okay." He could live with that. "I understand that women like long engagements so they have enough time to plan a big blowout wedding, and while I'm really looking forward to our honeymoon—Jack recommends Kauai, by the way, since he and Dani had such a good time there—I'm open to anything your little heart desires—"

"Nate." It was her turn to interrupt him. "I'm not talking about needing time to make wedding plans. It's too soon to fall in love."

"Well, now, I would have thought the same thing myself, once upon a time. But since meeting you, I've decided that love sort of makes its own time. When it's right, it's right." He brushed his knuckles up her cheek. Threaded his fingers through her hair. "And this is right."

"It's lust."

"That, too," he allowed. "But I think that's a plus, don't you? That I know I'll still want you when we're old and gray, and we're watching our grandbabies—"

"Grandbabies?"

"I sorta like the idea. But if you don't want kids, Regan, I'm okay with that." The idea of a houseful of little girls who looked just like Regan and who'd dress up their Barbie dolls in police blues and have them arrest Ken was surprisingly appealing, but Nate figured he'd have plenty of time to convince her.

"It's too soon to be talking about this," she insisted. "We haven't known each other long enough to even be thinking about marriage. We both have our own lives, our own work—"

"They don't need contractors in California?"

"What?"

"Relocating for the woman you love is kind of a family tradition." He was winging it here, but surprisingly, he figured he could handle Los Angeles if he had to. For Regan. "My dad moved here from Chicago for *Maman*. Finn moved to California for Julia. And I'm willing to relocate if you want to keep detectin' in L.A."

She was staring at him as if he'd just suggested they become a modern-day Bonnie and Clyde and start robbing banks for a living.

"Besides," he said, realizing that he ought to let her know what other changes he was planning to make to his life, "Josh might get a kick out of surfing in the Pacific Ocean."

"You're going to adopt him?"

"Yeah, I thought I would. But I'm not askin' you to marry me to find him a mother, if that's what you're thinking."

"No." She waved away his suggestion. "Of course I

wouldn't think that." Things were definitely on a down-hill slide here. "I think you're making a good decision, where Josh is concerned."

"Thank you," he said dryly.

"Even if it is a bit impetuous."

"That's me. Mr. Impetuosity."

He figured it sounded better than Peter Pan, and while there were a lot of things he was willing to try to change for Regan, Nate knew it'd be useless to attempt to change his nature. Which had him belatedly realizing that he never should have expected her to fall into his arms and tearfully accept his out-of-the-blue proposal. She'd already told him she wasn't a go-with-the-flow type of person. The gods, who obviously had one helluva sense of humor, must be laughing their heads off at hav-ing fixed things so he'd fall in love with a female version of Finn Callahan.

"I don't even know who I am," she murmured, looking away again.

"Of course you do. You're the same person you've always been. Your family situation might have been a lit-tle screwed up, but if you want an old-fashioned kind of family, you've got one waiting for you." He held out his arms. "The Callahan clan might seem big to someone who grew up pretty much all alone, but we've always got room for one more.

"Look, *chère*." When he saw a sheen of moisture that hadn't been in her eyes the entire time she'd been learning the truth about her past, Nate was sorely tempted to pull her into his arms and kiss her doubts away. "I'm glad to give you some time to make up your mind, but there's something you need to know. When I found out you were in that courthouse with Mike, and realized I could lose you, it dawned on me that part of the reason I've spent my entire life dodging serious relationships is because I lost two of the people I loved most, and I didn't want to take the risk of getting emotionally hammered again.

"Now, I'm not going to beat myself up about that, since I've never—ever—met a woman I wanted to spend all that much time with, anyway. Until you. I love you, Regan. Enough to risk someday goin' through the pain of losing you, because the alternative is not having you in my life at all. And that flat-out isn't acceptable."

"Dammit, Callahan." A tear escaped to trail down her cheek. He brushed it away with the pad of his thumb. "When you said I was an Acorn kind of silverware woman, you said I was like your mother. But that's wishful thinking. To hear Dani tell it, she was a cross between Donna Reed and Mother Teresa. I'm nothing like either one of them."

"I think you may be a bit off the mark about that, but I don't want Donna Reed or Mother Teresa. I want you. What you have in common with *Maman* is that you're willing to take risks, that you're brave enough to trust your instincts, even when they might go against the norm. I can't imagine it was easy for her to go to college, back in a time when folks around here tended to think people who went to college were lazy and just didn't want to work, since an education wasn't going to help you on the farm or in the sugar refinery. Or help you raise up your babies, which is pretty much what women were expected to do.

"But she did go to college. Not only that, she broke family tradition and ventured north across the Mason-Dixon line. Then to top it all off, she up and married herself a Yankee, which certainly set tongues a-buzzin'. But you know what?"

"What?"

"She didn't care. Because she trusted herself. And she trusted my dad. And never, not once, tried to change him."

"That's just as well. Since it's impossible to really change a person."

"True. Which is another reason why I know we belong together. You've never once mentioned changin' me."

"Why would I?"

"I have no idea. Bein' how I'm pretty damn close to perfect." He grinned to lighten the mood a bit. "But every woman I've ever met starts gettin' the urge to change me."

"Which isn't going to happen." She'd never met a man more comfortable in his own skin. "And I'd never want to change you."

"See? We're perfect for each other. You're smart, and strong, and brave, and honest—"

"Now you're making me sound like a Boy Scout."

"You interrupted me before I got to the good parts." He laced his fingers through her hair, pushing it back from her face. "You're also gorgeous, sexy as all get-out, and I can't get within twenty feet of you without wanting to do this."

Partly because he couldn't resist those tempting, sweet lips another moment, partly because he wanted to leave her with something to remember, Nate bent his head and gave her a long, deep kiss that left them both breathless.

"I don't supposed you'd be willing to run off and marry me right now?"

"Of course not."

He hadn't thought so, but it'd been worth a shot. "Okay. See you around, sugar." If he didn't leave now, he never would, and Nate knew it'd be a huge mistake to risk her someday feeling that he'd pressured her into spending the next sixty years with him. "Give me a call when you make a decision."

Ignoring the shock on her lovely face was the second hardest thing he'd ever done. Getting up and walking out of the suite was the hardest.

"Nate?"

He paused in the doorway. Closed his eyes. Braced himself. Then slowly turned around. "Change your mind already?" he asked pleasantly.

"I want to donate the proceeds from the petroleum stock to charity. I thought you might be able to suggest some local ones."

Stifling a sigh, Nate reminded himself that he shouldn't have expected an instantaneous one-hundred-and-eighty-degree turnaround. "I'll send you a list. In L.A."

"Thank you." She did not, he noted, reject the notion of returning to California.

"C'est rien. Speaking as the mayor, I can assure you that the town'll be real grateful."

He left without looking back. And reluctantly prepared himself for a long, lonely wait.

Nothing was the same. Her job, which she'd already begun to find frustrating, grew more so every day. There was nothing wrong with her new partner, who'd transferred in from Narcotics, but he wasn't Van.

She'd always liked California, but the view of the

swimming pool from her apartment window couldn't live up to herons nesting on the bayou, and the constant sun, which was such a part of the Los Angeles lifestyle, now seemed too predictable.

She'd received a letter from Charles Melancon, and on impulse called him back. She wasn't certain that she'd ever think of him as a surrogate father, but she thought they might be able to be become friends one day.

Other than a polite official letter written on Office of the Mayor stationery, thanking her for her generous contribution to various local charities, she hadn't heard from Nate. She might have thought he'd written her off and moved on had she not received a pager message from Dani a week after her return to L.A., suggesting she might want to call Nate.

The cop in her instantly feared for the worst, and she immediately called, only to get his answering machine.

"Hi. Josh and I are at baseball practice. If you're calling about a booth at the Cajun Days festival, call Jewel Breaux at 504-555-1112, and she'll be glad to take your reservation. If you're calling about the upcoming parish council meeting, it's Monday night at seven-thirty. Give or take a few minutes. We'll be voting on what color to repaint the bleachers at the Buccaneer baseball park. If you want some construction work done, leave a message and I'll get back to you as soon as possible. And if this is Regan calling . . . I still love you, chère."

Regan's heart was thrumming a thousand miles an hour with anticipation as the pirogue wove through mist-draped black waters.

"I really appreciate this," she told Jack. It was a month

since Mardi Gras. After having discovered a recent tropical storm had temporarily turned the road to Nate's house back to water, she'd been afraid she wouldn't be able to pull off her surprise.

Jack's grin flashed white in the moon-spangled darkness. "It's easy enough for someone who's lived their entire life in this bayou to get lost at night. If you got lost, it could take the search-and-rescue squad until morning to find you. Which would give you the chance to change your mind 'bout marrying my little brother."

"I'm not going to change my mind."

"I'm real pleased to here that, *chère*. Since Nate isn't, either."

"I know." She'd been calling him every day, choosing times she guessed he'd be working. While the answering machine message changed every day, the closing line had remained the same. The idea still amazed her—delighted her. She finally realized that he'd been right. She'd been falling in love with him from the beginning—if not when he'd shown up at the station, at least from that night they'd rescued Josh together.

Time didn't really matter at all. Except for the fact she'd already wasted thirty long days and nights they could have been together. It was past time to put her heart before her head.

"It's also very nice of you and Dani to take Josh for the weekend."

"The three of you have a real good start on a nice little family." The house came into view as they came around a corner. Jack cut the electric engine and drifted toward the dock. "But sometimes a man and woman just gotta have themselves some privacy."

A welcoming yellow light shone from the windows. For the first time in her life, Regan understood the concept of coming home.

"I don't 'magine you've ever been to a Cajun wedding?" Jack asked as he tied up the boat.

"No, I haven't." The idea of any wedding was still more terrifying than facing down an urban riot. "I was thinking of something quiet. Maybe just for family and a few close friends."

His rich, bold laugh startled a trio of herons nesting in the reeds. They took to the night sky, wings silhouetted against the full white moon. "There's no such thing as a quiet Cajun wedding. The womenfolk have been planning the festivities for weeks."

"They were that sure I'd cave in?"

"We were all that sure the two of you belonged together." He retrieved her spruce green canvas carry-on from the bottom of the pirogue. "You sure you don't need me to carry that for you?"

"It's not that heavy." She smiled up at him. "Thank you. For everything."

"It is truly my pleasure." He bent his head and brushed a kiss against her cheek. "Welcome to the Callahan family, *chère*."

She waited until he'd climbed back into the boat and disappeared around the corner. She was definitely on her own now. There'd be no turning back.

She took the cell phone from her purse and dialed the number she knew by heart.

"Hi," she said when Nate's familiar deep voice answered on the first ring. "I'm calling about the sheriff's job. If it's still open, I've just arrived in town—well, actually, I'm here at the dock—and I'd like to schedule a personal interview."

The door flew open. Regan thought her heart was going to sprout wings and fly when she saw Nate standing there, illuminated in the moonlight.

"I'm also looking for a place to live," she continued into the phone, "so I'd appreciate any suggestions Blue Bayou's mayor and best contractor might have."

He was coming toward her on long, purposeful strides as she walked toward him. "Of course, since I've given away all my inheritance and the parish budget can't afford to pay me nearly what I was making back in L.A., I'm willing to take a signing bonus. I was thinking along the lines of season tickets to the Buccaneers' home games—I hear the team has a new sophomore player this year who's a phenom."

They were only a few feet apart.

"This is Regan calling."

She flipped the phone closed and wondered how on earth she could she have stayed away from this man for so long. A wealth of love was gleaming in his eyes as she went up on her toes, twined her arms around his neck, and lifted her lips to his.

"And I'll always love you."

POCKET BOOKS
PROUDLY PRESENTS

FIREFLY FALLS

JoAnn Ross

Available in paperback September 2003
from Pocket Books

Turn the page for a preview of
Firefly Falls. . . .

It was dusk—too late for sunset, too early for stars. Ian MacKenzie had expected at least another hour of daylight, but night was coming fast to the Smoky Mountains. Making matters worse was the storm blowing in from the west. Slate gray clouds rolled across the ancient rounded mountaintops; thunder rumbled ominously in the distance.

Before being talked into this damn fool scheme, he'd been on his way to Monte Carlo, where he'd planned to spend the next month sailing and romancing supermodels and princesses.

Instead, he'd come to this remote mountain borderland between North Carolina and Tennessee to catch a thief. The plan was to reclaim his family's property by stealing it back, if necessary. Then, his duty done, his conscience cleansed, he was heading to Monaco to begin making up for six long months of enforced celibacy.

The sky darkened like a black shawl settling over the mountains. The dashboard thermometer revealed that the temperature outside the rental car was plummeting. Ominous drops of rain began spattering against the windshield.

"This is insane." He'd been telling himself that ever since he'd landed in New York from Edinburgh. From there he'd switched flights to Reagan National in D.C., after which he'd climbed aboard a commuter jet to Asheville, North Carolina, where he'd rented a car for the final leg of his journey.

The Hertz agent had told him Highland Falls was approximately sixty miles from Asheville. "As the crow flies," he belatedly remembered her saying as he'd handed over his credit card. "It's a bit longer by road." That was proving to be a vast understatement, and unfortunately he was no crow.

The wind picked up and the rain began to slant. He hadn't passed another car for at least an hour and it had been nearly that long since he'd seen the last of the small cemeteries, with their worn gravestones grown over with rambling honeysuckle and blackberry briars, or the weathered cabins which, rather than take advantage of hilltop views, tended to be tucked into the more protective, fog-shrouded hollows.

Beginning to suspect that he'd taken the wrong fork ten miles back, Ian considered turning around. The problem with that idea was that he'd undoubtedly end up getting mired in the mud.

"You didn't come all this way to give up because of a little squall." He was a Scot, after all, accustomed to miserable weather.

Thunder, once faint, now threatening, shook the tree-covered mountain and rumbled from ridge to ridge; soup-thick fog reflected the yellow beam of his headlights. Which was why Ian didn't see, until it was too late, the creek that had overflowed its banks. Clenching his jaw, he plowed ahead.

His relief on getting through the torrent rushing across the narrow road was short-lived, as he heard the engine cough, then shudder to a stop.

"Damn." He slammed his fist against the steering wheel. "Damn Duncan MacDougall's black heart." Ian twisted the key in the ignition. Nothing. "And damn the bloody Stewart clan, every bloody last one of them."

Forcing himself to wait a full thirty seconds—during which time he also damned the ridiculous rock-hard Highland mindset that had allowed the feud between the Stewarts and his mother's branch of the MacDougalls to continue across continents for seven hundred years—he tried again.

Still nothing.

Rain streamed down the windshield in blinding sheets as he turned on the dome light and studied the map. If it was at all accurate, he was approximately a mile from his destination. "Not even a decent jog."

Giving the car one last chance to redeem itself, he tried the ignition one more time. When the attempt proved futile, he jammed the keys into his jacket pocket, grabbed his duffel bag from the backseat, and began marching up the road, cursing into the wind.

"Well, what do you think?"

Lily Stewart glanced up from the uncooperative computer, which had already crashed three times tonight, and took in the redhead twirling in a blaze of glitter. "I don't believe I've seen so many sequins since you dragged me to that Elvis impersonator convention in Memphis." The scarlet sweater was studded with red sequins and crystal beads, and the short red leather skirt displayed firm, stocking-clad thighs. "You're certainly showing a lot of leg tonight."

"If you've got it, flaunt it." Ruby rings blazed, diamonds flashed as the fifty-something former chorus girl fluffed her cloud of firecracker-bright hair that was several shades brighter than Lily's own strawberry blond. "I'm not tryin' to be subtle, baby doll. Ian MacKenzie is showing up tonight with his video cameras, and you know what I always say: Too much—"

"Is never enough," Lily completed the motto she'd heard innumerable times while growing up. Zelda Stewart was part Auntie Mame, part Dolly Parton. She was also the closest thing to a mother Lily, who adored her aunt, had ever known. "I never have understood how you manage to walk in those ice-pick heels."

Lily had been seven years old when she'd broken her ankle by falling off a skyscraper-high pair of her aunt's gold platform sandals while playing dress-up with her sisters. That was when she'd realized she'd probably never be the glamorous type.

"Practice, my darling niece, practice." Zelda performed another spin Lily suspected even Cindy Crawford wouldn't have been able to pull off on the end of a runway. "So, when is this Scotsman who's going to save our collective butts due to arrive?"

"I don't know. He's already late." Since confirming that his plane had landed at the Asheville airport more than three hours ago, Lily had begun to worry he'd been delayed by the storm.

Even worse, was the possibility he'd taken a wrong turn and gotten lost. She'd grown up on tales of people who'd disappeared in these mountains, never to be seen again. Wouldn't that start the annual Highland games off on a good note?

She could just see the tabloid headlines now: Oscar-winning documentary director disappears deep in *Deliverance* country. "And I don't think he's coming here to save anyone's butt."

Actually, Lily hadn't been able to figure out why the filmmaker was gracing Highland Falls with his famous presence. Unlike everyone else in her family, she wasn't certain Ian MacKenzie's out-of-the-blue announcement that he was considering documenting the town's Highland games was a good thing. His work, while admittedly technically brilliant, showed a dark and pessimistic view of the world that always left her feeling depressed.

"It's just as the cards predicted," Zelda claimed. "We desperately needed a savior. So the gods sent us MacKenzie."

Lily, who didn't share her aunt's faith in the well-worn deck of Tarot cards, didn't respond as she rebooted the computer.

"Did you see the piece *Biography* did on him last week?"

"I caught a bit of it."

Liar. She'd been riveted to the screen for the entire hour. Of course, her only interest had been in discovering whatever scraps of information she could about the notoriously reclusive director. She'd barely noticed, and then only in passing, how sexy his butt had looked in those faded jeans with the ripped-out knees, which she doubted had been meant as a fashion statement.

Zelda sighed. "Such a tragic past the poor man's suffered. No wonder he's chosen to document the dark side of life. My first thought, when I saw that clip of him walking in the fog on the moors, was that if he hadn't made a name for himself with his documentaries, he'd be a natural to play the role of Heathcliff in a remake of *Wuthering Heights.* Not only is he gorgeous, in a dangerous, 'gone to the dark side of hell and lived to tell about it' way, he's going to put us on the map."

"Highland Falls is already on the map."

"You'd need a magnifying glass to find us. But this Highland hunk is going to change that."

Lily opened her mouth to warn Zelda, yet again, that Ian MacKenzie might not be the miracle man everyone was touting him to be, when the thick, towering front door burst open. One look at the very wet male silhouetted by a bright flash of lightning revealed that Zelda had at least nailed the dangerous part.

His lean, rangy body, shock of black hair glistening with raindrops, strong, firm jaw, broad shoulders, and long legs made her think more of an ancient warrior wielding a claymore in the midst of battle than an emotionally wounded Heathcliff pining after a lost love. Or perhaps, Lily considered as her imagination took flight, he might be better cast as the Christopher Lee character in a *Dracula* reprise.

Dressed head to toe in black, with the storm raging behind him and the wind howling like a banshee, Ian MacKenzie could easily have been a creature of the night.

All those photographs and video clips on *Biography* hadn't done him justice. His lived-in face was all planes and hollows, decidedly masculine, but starkly beautiful in a way Lily, who'd spent twenty-nine years plagued by the description of being the "perky" one of the three Stewart sisters, found eminently unfair.

Her assessing gaze locked with eyes that were swirling shades of gray as stormy as a winter sea. As she was unwillingly pulled into those fathomless depths, Lily dearly hoped that the violence depicted in his films wasn't echoed in this scowling Scotsman—who certainly didn't look like anyone's savior.